To Roger
with very best wishes

Clare Nida .

Nov 2016

The
Titan Kiss

by

Clark Nida

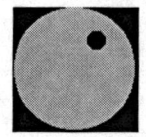

Published by Earthspot Books, 2016
9 Normanby Terrace, Whitby, YO21 3ES, England.

First published 2008 as "Interspex" by Undead Tree Publications.
Republished 2014 by Earthspot Books as "The Titan Kiss".

ISBN 978-1-898728-37-5

1 2 3 4 5 6 7 8 9

Contents

1   The canny lass from Mars

When did it all start to unfold—this flower, this sickly bloom, this *fleur-du-mal?*

Six weeks ago, to the day, Jack and Hilda had heard the news from Harry. He was on the Moon with his fiancée and they were just about to board the spaceplane to Teesside.

Three days later they arrived, in time for tea, which for Jack and Hilda was the main meal of the day. A car drew up outside—an H_2-hybrid. It wasn't the sort of car you saw much in Esh Winning. It came to a halt like a tiger on Vaseline and a young man got out. And with him came the strangest girl that Durham had ever seen.

·····★ ● ★·····

After the initial shock of meeting her, Jack and Hilda quickly recovered their sense of hospitality. They took Tvoul's jacket and sat her down at table. Hilda spent the meal prattling at the girl, hardly letting her get a word in.

With huge relief they discovered she could talk—as if that was actually something to be established. And she seemed to understand every word of theirs—no small achievement in County Durham. For all they knew she spoke English as well as anyone did on Mars. As Harry himself did, no doubt. They guessed of course that here on Earth he was pulling on his Durham accent like a well-worn jumper, to go back in mothballs as soon as he got back home. Home... as Mars was now for him.

Tvoul's speech was precise and clear. But it took a moment for Jack to register whatever it was she said. Was it due to the unusual stress she laid on ordinary syllables? Was it her bookish insertion of every adverb in its proper place? Perhaps she wasn't speaking English at all, but what passed for it on Mars—where it was called M2: Martian-Two.

Or was it because Jack, listening to her, had the sensation of being plunged deep underwater, watching a sea-creature never seen by human eyes as it drifted in the searchlight beam of his bathyscaph?

What colour was the girl? As they'd waited anxiously all afternoon for the young couple to turn up, Jack had told himself to pay no attention to the colour of her skin. Her name was so strange that it was no use expecting her to look English. But now, as he stared at this girl, her skin it was that clawed kitten-like for his attention.

What colour was it? It wasn't the same from one moment to the next. Was it blue with red-brown patches that blossomed out of points under her eyes and spread over her hairless head and down her neck? Was it brown with blue veins? Yellow veins? Veins that flashed silver? Green patches, green with red stripes, red with green stripes... veins again...?

Now, for one brief instant, she'd gone putty-coloured, just as an English girl might hesitate and blush. Then the vivid palette welled up once more in spots and striations, which coalesced and waltzed and span in time to her song... was she singing? No, she was talking in her normal voice. Speaking to Hilda, ordinary English words.

Harry held back, letting her speak for herself. But all the while he'd glance up sideways from his plate, eyes careful not to meet his father's.

"Was it a good journey?" asked Hilda, like a child offering a bun to an elephant.

Tvoul appeared to give serious thought to Hilda's artless question. "Neither good, nor bad," she said in her precise way. "It was a *long* journey..."

Harry, swallowing an over-large mouthful, choked as he tried to speak. "Six long months. When you arrive, you wonder why you set out in the first place ...Ooh, not us of course." he added with a hasty grin. "What I meant was: six months is a big chunk out of my young life. I can't recall my frame of mind on setting out."

Tvoul smiled for the first time. Jack thought of the Mona Lisa— withdrawn—inscrutable—eyebrowless. The Mona Lisa in carnival colours, as Picasso might have done her.

"I think what Harry is trying to say," she cautiously attempted, "is that it is not so much a journey as a tour of duty. If you leave Mars and come to Gaia—I mean Earth—then there has to be some continuity of intention..."

She stopped speaking, sensing the silence. "Yet there is a gap to bridge, because the interval spent on *Oberon* does not reinforce such continuity..."

Cumbersome but correct English. Perfectly logical, once you unravelled it.

Harry glanced at her mischievously. "No," he said, "but that's not to say you can't pass the time most agreeably." Everyone laughed.

Jack said unguardedly, "So, you've had your honeymoon already?"

Hilda shot him a glance. But Tvoul undertook to give a serious answer, as though to take offence would never cross her mind.

"Yes, and we are hoping for another honeymoon too, while we're here on… Earth. We are planning to go to Brazil." Her face made a puffy golden cloud as she glanced aside at Harry. "I've always wanted to see a rainforest."

Was it his imagination? A moment later an image had flashed across Tvoul's face: an evocation of leaves and lianas, tall trunks and gaudy butterflies flitting in a sun-drenched canopy. And then… dark shadows.

"Lucky things," said Jack. "I've never seen a rainforest. And I live here."

"I'd offer to take you along with us…" Harry shrugged in mock resignation, "But you know how it is…"

· · · · ✱ ● ✱ · · · · ·

That Sunday the women were doing the washing-up together. There was nothing secret they wanted to chat about, so they left the door open. Jack, feet-up in the armchair for his after-dinner doze, heard everything that came to pass.

Hilda put the last of the pans on the draining board and flopped down on the kitchen chair, panting heavily. "Phew! That was a big do. We don't often get guests—it's nice to put on a show once in a while. Can't promise it every Sunday though."

Beneath his eyelids, Jack saw Tvoul leaning back on the sink, regarding Hilda with concern. He knew what Hilda's face would be looking like by now: puffy—an unhealthy puce. He watched in wonderment as Tvoul's skin began to go the self-same colour.

"Be a love and pass my pills, dear."

Following Hilda's gaze, Tvoul located the tube of pills on the window ledge. Without being asked, she filled a glass with water and placed it by Hilda's elbow.

"Thank you, dear. You're a treasure. I see I'm going to get used to having you around. A pity when you have to go away again."

"Hilda… I don't want to pry into what you'd say was none of my business…" She hesitated, uncertain of how that had been received. "But are you going to get that heart condition seen-to?"

"I'm under Dr Peart for it. He's put uz on these nitro-glycerine tablets."

"Nitro-glycerine…" Tvoul didn't actually shudder, but Jack saw the patterns on her face do just that. Groubians cannot hide what they are thinking.

"A bit over-the-top, I thought. But Dr Peart reckons it's for the best. I asked when I'd be able to come off them, but he said I'd be on them for the rest of my days."

"There are doctors in Nix City," said Tvoul quietly, "who could cure you completely. Why, there is even a first-class surgical team in the Galen Clinic under Mr Sullivan, who can do just about anything with hearts and lungs. With time to spare before *Oberon* departs, it's an excellent opportunity to get things fixed and convalesce en-route. You could even enjoy Mars when you got there."

Hilda held Tvoul's gaze and started laughing. "What, at my age? I'd never manage the journey." She shook her head, as a horse might whisk its tail at a fly. "No. When I come to depart from Planet Earth, I'll be leaving my body right here—in Newhouse churchyard."

Tvoul said gently "You ought to give it serious thought."

Hilda shook their head again as if the whole idea was a joke. "Think of the expense. I doubt Dr Peart could get it for uz on the National Health, like."

"I have friends…"

"Now listen here, young lady…" Hilda tapped the table with her forefinger. "You youngsters have your own lives to lead. You've got to stop bothering about us old fogies. You—your generation—you'll have the whole skies to play in. As for me—I'm a thing of the past. And I've got to stay here on the ground, in the past."

She softened her voice. She'd been letting it get a little too strident. "Don't go wasting your young lives fretting about things as can't be mended. You'll have your own troubles—and things to save up for, I haven't the slightest doubt."

Tvoul cast her eyes downwards. "I hate to see you suffering like this. It's so unnecessary."

"Who's to say what's necessary and what isn't? I put myself in Our Lady's hands. She's been good to me in my life. Whenever I've asked her for anything, she's never let me down." Hilda took a deep breath. "That's better. Now let's have a cup of tea."

Tvoul made the tea. She needed to be told where to find things, but not what to do. Jack caught himself thinking: what a lovely wife this girl will make our Harry. But he checked himself. Isn't she all out to make us think just that?

Hilda's antennae had been twitching too. "Do you know something about medical matters, dear?" she inquired sweetly: a shade too sweetly to conceal the challenge.

Groubians are bad at reading faces which don't colour-change, but they pick up well on tones of voice. "I occupy the Chair of Human Reproductive Biology at *Pérvii Universitèt.*"

"Beg your pardon dear—I didn't catch that?"

"Oh I'm sorry…" Tvoul's face erupted in a little firework display of confusion. "I'm so used to calling it that. Its proper name is *Pérvii Universitèt imeni Gagárina.* In M2 it's called Gagarin First University. But that all sounds so clumsy that, whether speaking M1 or M2, people just call it *Pérvii Universitèt.*"

"So you're a *professor?*" Hilda's voice soared aloft in wonderment.

"Yes. That's how Harry and I first met. His firm sent him on a course which I happened to be teaching." Tvoul smiled coyly, but even if she hadn't, the pink bubbles bursting all over her face said it all. "It is considered bad for lecturers, especially principal professors, to make advances towards their students." She giggled. "So I let Harry finish the course before we started going together."

Both women laughed. "And how long ago was that?" asked Hilda.

Tvoul thought for a moment. "Two years ago last January."

Hilda thought in her turn. "The beginning of 1972… Yes—that's just about the time your name started turning up in Harry's letters home…"

•••••✳●✳••••

"Are you growing leeks this summer?"

Jack turned away towards the leek bed. "Oh—aye. I can't get by without entering something for the Leek Show. Though I doubt I'll take first prize this year. Frank's been stealing my secrets for years, bless his little horns, and he's been creeping up on uz steady-like. The fellas at the club are kidding uz to take out a contract on his leeks. 'Course two can play at that game, like, y'know."

Harry sniggered. That was one thing he did know about horticulture in the North-East of England—the rivalries and animosities, sometimes bitter, which surrounded the growing of prize leeks. Every prize-winner had his cherished secret recipe for fertiliser. Not a few of them involved going out at night and urinating on the crop in the weeks leading up to the Big Show. Of course nobody ever wanted to cook and eat the things afterwards.

"Your mam says that if my leeks aren't in the prize-winning league, she will use one of them to take the prize off Maud for the Best Dressed Leek Of The Show."

Harry doubled up with laughter. "What a comedown! Well I suppose a prize is a prize."

Jack opened the door of the potting shed. He produced a couple of cans of beer from a decrepit old chest of drawers.

"Aye… that's a canny lass you've got there."

Harry took a sip of his beer before he answered. "Do you really think so, dad?"

"Why-aye!" Jack turned to face his son, bristling. "And she's a Catholic. That's canny. What more could we ask, yer mam and me? Though we wouldn't have held you to it—in this day and age."

"Well," said Harry, "that's a load off my mind." His voice was flat, as was the silence that followed.

"Was she a Catholic before you met her?"

Harry took a deep breath. "She started taking instruction as soon as we were going steady. I didn't push her. But she considered it important. She was baptised and made her First Communion not long before we left Mars to come here."

Jack shrugged. "Nothin' wrong with that. It's the chief way people enter the Church I'm told. Because they're marrying Catholics…"

"I hope you realise Tvoul is a bit more committed than that. It's going to be very important to have the backing of the family for what we're doing. On Mars they just don't understand."

Jack's eyebrows met in a furrow. "Why's that? I'd have thought they'd be very broad-minded. Far more so than down here on Earth. New World—new ideas. Why bring the clutter of the past with you, I say?"

"True enough, as far as it goes. But the present can make enough clutter of its own. The fact of the matter is: we couldn't have got married in church on Mars because there are laws against it."

"What sort of laws?" Jack growled. "Racial laws? Religious laws?"

"Nobody talks about 'race' these days," said Harry. "There is total religious freedom—and there's no prohibition against blacks marrying whites, or anything like that. If you're both *gaian*—what you've been calling 'human'—you can marry freely. Or not marry, as the case may be. You can bring up a child quite well in Nix City without getting married. Many women do. It's having children by a groubian that's the sticking-point."

"Pardon me—I don't follow you."

"Gaians and groubians are free to form whatever liaison they want— and in any plurality they want—whether you call it a marriage, a triada, a coven or whatever. But if a gaian and a groubian dare to contemplate having *children*—that violates the transgenic laws. These laws are very strict—and very strictly applied. Rightly so, in my opinion. What price human rights if we have to argue over every single individual: is he, she or *it* human?"

Jack stared at his son for a long time. Eventually he said "There's something I'm missing in all this. To start with, what precisely do you mean by *gaian*?"

"Oh… okay—right. I see we are going to get into deep sh… confusion if we are not careful." Harry put his beer down on the chest of drawers, freeing both hands to gesticulate.

"Originally *gaian* meant someone from planet Gaia—that is: Earth. But it's come to mean the species: *Homo sapiens*. Individuals from Earth, whatever their species, are called Terrestrials, just as people from Mars are called Martians. The word *human* on the other hand—as in *human rights*—means any individual which the Goubernator says is human. Such as a groubian. Now Tvoul is groubian. On Mars that makes her officially human."

"That's all Humpty-Dumpty. You can't make a word just mean whatever you want."

"No, of course you can't—and that's why it's so important. What a word legally means is something defined by your *mir:* the world you live on. On Mars the definition of *human* is carefully chosen to rule out robots, no matter how intelligent. It also rules out *chimorgs*—chimaeric organisms—which unscrupulous scientists slung together in the early days of bio-engineering. But it doesn't rule out people—and I'll call them people—who are going to be bio-engineered to prolong their lives in order to colonise the galaxy. That's why the granting of human rights is so tightly controlled. And, I regret to say, absolutely riddled with politics."

Whilst Harry was talking, Jack took nervous sips of his beer. Finally he stuck the can on the chest of drawers, none too gently, which freed up his own hands to gesticulate.

"I can't pretend I'm following you, lad," he said. "But one thing I am getting out of all this. You said Tvoul is human—but she's not our species: not *Homo sapiens*. Did I hear you right?"

"Yes, dad, you did."

"Then she's not human at all…"

"She is on Mars… Oh shit!"

"Look: if she isn't human—gaian—*homo-sap*—how's this going to be a marriage in any sense Hilda and I would understand?"

"What do you think it's going to be? *Bestiality?*"

"I didn't say that. Don't put words into my mouth." Jack let the air rush out of his nostrils. "Look son—I'm out of my depth in all this…"

Harry reached across and put his hand on his father's forearm. "Dad… I know the laws of the Church as well as you do. A marriage is null and void if there is no intention of having children. Or rather if there is the intention *not* to have children. But two people can contract a valid marriage even if they can't have children. Like they're too old… for companionship…"

"So, she's just going to be a companion? Because that's all that's possible?"

"No, dad, no. In our case—Tvoul and I—we actually want children. You're going to have *grandchildren*, dad. You'll be a *granddad*…"

Jack scrunched his empty beer can in his hand.

"And how's that gonna come about, for heaven's sake? No—don't babble on at me about God and Abraham. What with you being a bio-engineer I suppose it'll be a test-tube baby…"

"No, dad." Harry patted his father's arm gently. "There will be children—and they will be conceived purely by natural means. *Trust* me!"

Jack was almost in tears. "I can trust you all you like, but you can't fly in the face of Nature!"

"Now listen, dad. I may be only a bio-engineer, but Tvoul is *Principal Professor of Human Reproductive Biology* at PUG: the all-time centre of excellence for the bio-sciences. Dad, we *do* know what we're doing! There's no two people in the whole world—the whole universe—who are better equipped to tackle it than we are."

2   All the time in the universe

"Your father doesn't like me."

Jack, in the next room, gripped the glass of scotch he'd just poured himself. He drew back into the dark behind the serving-hatch. Eavesdropping on your own kids—what a weird thing to do. It was none of his business these days what they did on the sofa together. He would have moved away quickly and silently had he not heard mention of himself.

Harry didn't answer immediately. "Oh, he'll come round."

"I don't think he will. I think he'll just drop into endurance mode and stick there."

"You've got to understand. He's an old man—a sick man. He's not easily disabused of his prejudices."

"Well—you're the one to know."

Having raised the matter in the first place, Tvoul was now for changing the subject. "I half-expected we'd run into Shval Meteor in Lunaborg," she murmured.

Harry's head jerked up. *"Shval?* What the hell is *she* doing on the Moon?"

"Lunar Survey. She's their Hon Sec. She's taken out Selenean denizenship." A bitter laugh. "She's a reformed character now, is my sister Shval."

"So—she thinks the Moon's a softer touch than Mars, does she? I guess she's right. Selene won't know what's hit it."

"Oh, don't you worry about Selene. Commissioner Vermat won't pay her out much slack."

"What can she do to us?" Harry's voice came low and grim.

"Nothing—just yet. She's waiting for us to get spliced and back on board *Oberon*. But of course, we've got the answer to *that*…"

There was a pause, as if Tvoul had said something both close to the heart and painful. Harry sighed, though whether in relief or dread Jack didn't know. "Tell me again what the bairns'll be like."

"They will look like gaians…" Tvoul's voice grew trance-like, "with hair on their heads and circular eyes. But they will have colourful groubian skins… and a groubian lifespan, which makes them ideal galactonauts. But—and this is the important bit—their insides will be gaian. They will come in two sexes, male and female, able to conceive and have babies exactly like gaians."

"A-ahh!" came Harry's voice in another long drawn-out sigh.

"*We* never flew to the stars: we couldn't have increased our numbers when we got there. But our children will. And how they will!"

A silence ensued, broken only by the creaking of the sofa. Jack wondered what expressions they were wearing. Blissful and sensuous? He risked a glance. They were lying there hugging each other, but he could see their features anxious and withdrawn, like two babes lost in the deep dark woods.

"Your mother, now—she's an absolute love," said Tvoul, returning to the first topic. "Maybe she just covers up well, but she seems so genuine."

"Mam—oh Mam! A lovely woman. I was once the apple of her eye."

"And you still are," soothed Tvoul. "Even a groubian can see that. And you are of your father, too, though it manifests itself differently. He's very jealous of you, you know."

Harry hesitated before replying. "Are you sure you've got the right word there?"

"*Jealous*? Yes, I'm sure I have. The dictionary definition is 'vigilant in guarding'... or do I mean *zealous*? Zealous for your best interests?"

"Oh, I see what you're driving at. Just the sort of mistake an M1-speaker would make. Either will do here, as it happens. I suppose I am the only egg in his little basket."

Tvoul laughed. "That is such a lovely way of putting it. But you're hatched now. You've spread your wings and flown the nest."

"Last week I'd have agreed with you. But now I'm back, I'm not so sure. Squid—how far have I really come?"

Tvoul murmured in a dreamy voice "To the world's end—and back again."

"How many miles to Babylon?"

"Three score and ten." She'd followed him implicitly.

"Shall I get there by candlelight?"

"Aye—and back again..." Her voice was rich with lover's reassurance.

> *Though you travel half the night...*
> *You shall get there by candlelight!*

They finished the nonsense-rhyme in unison, giggling like children.

"See, Monkey?" said Tvoul in a silky tone of voice, her skin swirling with pastel colours like oil on a sunlit pool. "You *are* back again." Her voice and skin lost some of their lustre: "But you've come back betrothed to a fairy. Or a mermaid… or perhaps it's an undine?"

Jack wondered at the word. Later that week he looked it up. *Undine:* an elemental spirit, a being of water. Some seek to acquire a human soul through the love of a mortal man. So HC Andersen's Little Mermaid was really an *undine?*

Harry's chin jerked up. He had been nibble-kissing her, chasing a rose-pink eddy round her shapely breast. Now his voice was truculent. "Look, we're here now. Dad'll have to come round in the end."

"He may do with a little help."

"What do you mean?" Suspicion curdled Harry's voice. His fingertips, like a raptor's talons, clutched deepening dimples in her waist. "What squiddy little thoughts are there crawling all over your creepy skin?"

"*Interspex…*"

Harry sat bolt upright.

····· ✶ ● ★ ·· ···

"You really ought to do it more often, if you've going to do it at all," chided Hilda.

"Give over worriting, pet." Jack tucked his vest into his running shorts. "What time has there been, what with guests?"

"Don't overdo it, love. That's all I ask."

Jack opened the kitchen door. It was left unlocked during the day— you never knew who might be round for a cup of tea and a chat. Outside—*whee-yow!* It was chilly for June! Emerging from the access passage he turned right, making for the River Deerness and its long- distance footpath, which followed the track of the old railway line.

"Jack!"

He stopped and turned his head at the sound of his name. It was Tvoul. She must have been all ready and waiting inside the house in her running shorts, to spring a surprise on him when he set out.

"May I join you?"

She was wearing a radiant smile and her face and limbs were the colour of the bright blue sky. She was even getting a fluffy white cloud to drift across her forehead.

"Why—of course, pet!" He couldn't very well send her back to the house. As it was, he was glad to have someone with him. It had been a while since his last jog and he was fearful of being racked by a coughing fit, far from the house.

"Do you do this sort of thing a lot?" she asked.

"Do *you?* Tell me that! I can't picture you jogging round the Martian craters."

She laughed. "Right you are! Nix Olympica, the crater Nix City is built within, is more than seventy miles across. I do my jogging round the Areopagus, that's quite far enough for me. Most people get their exercise in the gym."

"If there was a gym in this bit village I'd use it. Particularly when it's as chilly as this. And it looked so lovely out of the window when I got up."

It wasn't far to the start of the Deerness Valley Footpath. "Are we going all the way?"

"Why—man, no! Far too far for me! It leads past Durham City to Penshaw. It's the old railway line, if you hadn't noticed."

"How marvellously retro! To have a railway line and then to dig it up and replace it with a *footpath,* of all things! It's just what Martians imagine Terrestrials doing all the time. Wiping out the Hand of Man—restoring the Wilderness."

"Huh, bonny lass! We've still got to live here."

Tvoul's laugh tinkled like a mountain stream. "It's only what Martians think. Few enough of them have been on Earth. They haven't had the privilege, like I have."

They ran side-by-side in silence to begin with. For Jack it wasn't so much a run as a hobble. Tvoul could have easily kept up with him by walking at a stroll.

"Forgive me for being personal," said Jack, "but tell me something."

"M-mm?"

"Why does Harry call you 'Squid'?"

Tvoul's freshet laugh bubbled again. "Because I call him 'Monkey'!"

Jack chuckled. "Why do you do that?"

She weighed her answer, setting her mouth as an English girl would. "He isn't a monkey, of course. And I'm not a squid. We're just alluding to each other's relatives."

"Squid?" Jack stopped in his tracks.

"Why, yes! Don't say you hadn't noticed? Perhaps 'cuttlefish' is more accurate? Have you never seen a live cuttlefish?"

"No-oo," said Jack, exaggerating his dialect, "I can't say I have! Ye divn't often see 'em waakin' down the street, like…"

"Well, I'm one-up on you there," replied Tvoul. "The other day Harry and I drove across-country to Chester Zoo, as you'll recall.

They've got monkeys in cages there, not to mention an aquarium. Harry had quite a conversation with the monkeys."

"I didn't know they could talk!"

"They don't talk—that's a purely human faculty. But you gaians share a lot of gestures with monkeys. Body language—monkeys don't need to verbalise in their uncomplicated lives. But if you spit, or put your tongue out, they'll do it back at you. If you turn your bottom…"

"Well, I didn't know that!" said Jack in exaggerated awe. "But it strikes me we can only say rude things to each other."

"Mostly, I'm afraid. You must get to know another species very well indeed before you can say nice things with any degree of confidence."

"What about the cuttlefish? Did you have a good chat with them?"

"I tried to. They have cuttles there that live on coral reefs. They might almost have been my ancestors. They can change colour instantaneously—all cuttles can. But the ones I saw used their ability for communication. And their mentality was sunny enough for it to be mostly in primary colours, like me."

Jack stopped again in amazement. "You're not kidding, now?"

"No. I'm serious."

"So they really did have something to say?"

Tvoul shrugged. "Not a lot. Terrestrial cuttles only live for a year or two. They were like tiny children."

By now Jack was running out of energy and his panting breath came in rasps. Gently but firmly Tvoul took his arm. "Let's take a rest, Jack."

She led him off the path to a grassy bank. Jack bent down and patted the grass. It was dry: the sun had even warmed it up a little. He flopped down gratefully. Almost immediately he commenced one of his coughing fits.

Tvoul put her hand on his back. It felt like a proper hand. It was comforting, even if it was boneless—but that just made its touch all the more tender. "Why—you are in a bad way." She said it like a nurse would, only a fraction more kindly.

"Don't fret yourself, lass," said Jack. "I've got the new spray in my pocket here." He took it out and used it. The coughing fit subsided.

"I'm glad I came along with you."

"Aye—the missus would agree. Did she send you?"

"Hilda? No—I came of my own accord."

She lay back on the grass with a sigh. The sun's heat was beginning to bite. "Will you think me rude," she said, "if I slip out of my things? I'm dreadfully vain about my appearance. The sun's bright enough to bleach my chromatophores. It'll leave lines around the tops of my limbs."

Without embarrassment she slipped off her vest and shorts and lay back naked, her body shimmering sky-blue in the grass like a pool of water.

"Hey, wait a minute! —what're you doing? You can't do that here, in public!"

But Tvoul was undeterred. She chaffed Jack like a child. "Well there's no need to go looking at me like that. See the cows in the field over there? They're naked too. They don't shock you, do they? They're closer related to you than I am."

Jack flushed in confusion—bright red—giving a demonstration that gaians too could colour-change. What was she trying to do—seduce him? He recalled that word he'd overheard the night before: *interspex...*

"We don't exactly have this footpath all to ourselves..."

Unwillingly his eyes took it all in. Breasts, hips and narrow waist— some girls would kill for a figure like that. He looked at her hands, cast up loosely above her head. Tiny round suckers speckled the fingertips in place of normal fingerprints, with their loops and whorls. But apart from that—that and the poorly-defined knuckles—they could have been the hands of an ordinary girl.

"It's all right, I won't embarrass you. If anyone comes I'll hide."

It dawned on him then that this wasn't the act of a scatterbrained little goose. She was taking the opportunity to lay her kit out for inspection. To reassure him that his son wasn't marrying a monster? Or to appeal to him somewhat more directly?

"Grass!" she murmured, caressing the blades which slipped through her fingers. "There isn't a native of Mars who wouldn't sit here in absolute wonderment. Grass—growing wild all over the place—under the open sky! It's simply... too fantastic for words!"

She turned on her side to smile at him, eyes all but closed. "There's a patch of grass around the Areopagus, near the University. They don't let you lie on it of course. There are three glorious trees—at least I think they're glorious. Each day I inspect them carefully to see they're all right. If anything were to happen to them, I think it would break my heart."

"I don't imagine there are many trees on Mars," muttered Jack thickly, cheeks still burning. Suddenly he looked up. Someone was coming! A junior class, with their schoolmistress, out on a nature-walk! Well— they'd see some nature alright!

"Get yourself covered up, hinny," he growled. "There's someone coming!"

"Grass…" she murmured again, as if she hadn't heard. "It's growing up all around me… creeping across my skin… flooding into my mind…" Her voice drifted off.

"I'm serious," said Jack, urgent and low. "They're not as broad-minded around here as you Martians are!" He dropped his forehead into his hand with a sigh, hoping that none of the kids would recognise him. A baseless hope in a small village.

The party of children trooped on past, ignoring him. The sound of their schoolmistress lecturing them on birds and bees, flowers and seeds, dwindled as they disappeared in the distance.

"Calm down, Jack. They've gone."

Jack looked up with a start. Where Tvoul had been lying, there was nothing to see but grass.

"There—I didn't disgrace you, did I?"

Jack's head swivelled wildly at the disembodied voice. He looked again at the spot where she had been lying. Gingerly he put out a hand and his fingertips met warm flesh. The moment they did so, Tvoul's body flashed into view, bursting out in swirling flames from his point of touch. Then her skin settled down to shimmering once more with the blue of the sky. At intervals, tiger-stripes rippled from head to toe, circling her eyes and nipples before plunging in.

"That was a nifty bit of camouflage!"

"It comes naturally to a groubian."

"What do you mean? You can't have been lying on much grass before you came here. You said as much. You must have been practising since you've arrived."

"Oh no—it's the first time I've ever done it. On grass, that is. All I had to do was to gaze at it close-up and it simply spilled over from my eyes onto my skin. You can tell just what a groubian is thinking from her skin."

"*Geddaway!* So why are you going all stripy now?"

Tvoul grinned, showing teeth of pearls. "It means I'm laughing at you."

••••• ✱ ● ✱ •••••

They'd gone about as far as Jack had wanted to. To his immense relief Tvoul put on her things when it was time to go.

As they jogged back home together, Jack asked as casually as he could "What does the word *interspex* mean?"

Tvoul stopped running in surprise. The question had hit her like a hammer blow. With a pang of dismay Jack realised she was at a loss as to how to answer him. Head down in silence, she began jogging again. After a moment she said "That's not a very nice word, Jack. Where did you come across it?"

"I read it somewhere," Jack lied—a little too glibly, he thought. But he could hardly say "I overheard you using it to Harry as he was kissing you on the sofa last night".

Tvoul shrugged her shoulders, like a parent reluctantly deciding her child should have an accurate answer to a touchy question. "It's an M1 word. Actually its the same word in M1 or M2: a contraction of 'interspecies sex'. Between gaians and groubians in particular."

Jack was sorry he'd opened his mouth. Tvoul however, in token of their new-found confidence together, was going to treat him to the full explanation. "I guess it's called *bestiality* in England—and it's against the law. But they're now accepting the Martian definition of *human*. Harry and I were careful to check up on that before we came."

"I see. Is it against the law on Mars?"

"Not between gaians and groubians—not sex as such. Reproduction is a different matter. We have these things called *transgenic laws*…"

"Harry was telling me you'd get wrong on Mars for marrying."

"Not for marrying—for having children *by natural means*. As good Catholics are supposed to do. Of course, artificial hybridisation—by cytosurgery, say—would legally result in *chimorgs*. That's a status we don't want for our children."

Jack swallowed. Since that difficult chat with his son about it, he'd dwelt a lot on the matter. "I suppose on Mars they don't know what the hell you're pl… planning to do…" He had nearly said "playing at."

"There is a lot of prejudice. I suppose it's understandable, given the history of Olympia. But the very word *interspex* is an inflammatory one. It is hurled at groubians by gaians deliberately meaning to be offensive. The implication is all too clear: groubians, according to popular wisdom, are dirty creatures. The only motive they have in befriending a gaian is to have sex with him—it's always 'him' of course. The ample evidence to the contrary is never admitted. Groubians form relationships across the board, with gaians of either sex, including pure friendship, lesbian love, politics, business partnership, even conspiracy to defraud. But to the bigoted: it's all just *interspex*."

"I'm sorry…" He had learnt rather more than he'd wanted to.

"Why be sorry, Jack? It's nothing to do with you. At least—I hope it never will be. Harry and I will overcome our difficulties with Martian society. But if we'd known what it was all going to entail, we'd never have got together."

She shrugged again. "There's a word for that, isn't there?"

"Love?"

"Yes."

·····**✶ ● ✶**·····

The ice well and truly broken, they spent the day together. Now they were sitting in the kitchen over a pot of tea. "It's Friday night!" announced Tvoul, her face going into a flurry of colours.

"Yes it is." Jack's mouth was grinning but his forehead rose in puzzled wrinkles. "So what about it?"

"*Erev shabbat*—the Sabbath Eve—begins when there are three stars in the sky."

"I didn't know that—and I live here. How come you know?"

"I study religion as a hobby. It's really part of my job—at least that's how I defend it to my academic colleagues. My inaugural lecture was 'Organised religion as a sexual display modality in *H sapiens*'. A principal professor at PUG must at least look disinterested in her topic, even if she isn't."

Harry strolled in, glanced at them both and promptly absented himself again. Tvoul stayed sitting motionless, but her habitual *gioconda* smile grew even more enigmatic.

"It's a canny evening," Jack said. "I wonder how many stars we can count?"

They wandered out into the garden. Tvoul shivered. Jack put his arm around her shoulder. She in turn slipped a sleek wrist around his waist.

"The Sabbath must have kicked-off proper-like by now," he said. "Just look at all them stars."

They stared upwards in silence for a while. "I had a teacher once," said Jack. "I recall him saying 'Ours is the last generation that's bound to the planet. Instead of poppin' our clogs, all we have to do is shed our shoes and we'll be out there, all over the place'. And it's all happening!"

"What did God say to Abraham?"

Jack was taken aback at Tvoul's question. He turned his head to gape at her. She turned hers too and cheeks and noses brushed. Then she lifted her face to the sky—and starlight seemed to fall upon her graceful throat.

"Look up to heaven and count the stars, if you can. Such will be your children." She was quoting accurately from the Bible.

Jack looked up—and straightaway looked back at her face. For a moment her eldritch eyes, like two black holes engorged with swallowed galaxies, dared him to tumble in—to his everlasting ruin.

"*Your* children, Jack," she whispered, "are going to *walk among* the stars. They'll need more living space than just one planet can provide. More than one solar system—one Milky Way. And if it takes a billion years to reach the furthest star... ten billion... why, they will have all the time in the world. All the time in the Universe!"

Letting her gaze drop to earth, she snuggled up to him, her cheek pressed against his shoulder. "Like an ageing parent, Gaia will dwindle. It will become a holy planet. Then a legendary planet—and in time people will forget which planet it actually was. But *Gaia*, as a legend, will never die. The Earth itself may disappear. But, once at liberty out there, your children never will."

"My brain can't take it in."

She gently took his fingertips in hers and kissed them. "No asteroid will wipe them out, as once it wiped out the dinosaurs. Incidentally giving rise to my species on Titan through coral debris, flash-frozen on ejection into space. A supernova, sterilizing everything within a hundred light-years all around—even that won't snuff them out. Humanity will expand with the universe: a never-ending quest. A new humanity... all of them descended from you."

She turned to face Jack squarely, running fingers round his collar in trembling determination. "It's a stupendous adventure. And I'm telling you, Jack, I want a part in that adventure. And with your son Harry—I'm going to have it!"

3   A groubian wedding

Jack dug a shovelful of earth and cast it into the hole. It hit the coffin with a hollow sound, something between a fist-thump and a kiss. Others took their turn. Then the gravedigger set about filling the hole like a miner shovelling coal.

In ones and twos they nodded to Jack, the chief mourner, exchanging a word, shaking his hand and turning to go. Two of his best friends waited outside the gate to intercept Jack, who was clearly meaning to walk home alone.

Jack declined the invitation back to their house. "I'll just go home," he said. "There's times you want to be all by yourself." Aware he was being boorish, he patted the arm of his friend's wife and said "I'm grateful for your offer, Maud, really I am. But right now I wouldn't make good company." And with that he walked away.

They called after him but he didn't look back.

"Remind me," said Jack's friend to his wife, "not to let a Martian get her hooks into one o' *my* bairns."

••••✷●✷••••

Back home, Jack walked slowly up the garden path. In his head he was still following the coffin.

The box with Hilda in it. The idea revolted against common sense. It was like saying "the shoe-box with Hilda in it" or "the pill-box with Hilda in it". Now the box in question was buried deep in the ground— and Hilda wasn't coming home tonight.

He touched a rough unplaned strip of two-by-one which held a sign: *For Sale*, shaking it moodily. "Isn't it a bit early to be selling-up and moving away?" his friends had pleaded with him. "Give it a week or two before you make any hard-and-fast plans."

But Jack hadn't made any plans, hard or fast. He just wanted to get out of the village. Out of Durham. Out of England. He thought of going back to Brazil, living off the money he expected to make from selling the house. He'd begin a patient search, a proper one this time, before the trail went altogether cold. He might even find something of Harry. A garment discarded at the hotel. A button dropped in the rainforest. Something—anything—to remember him by. All too late to save Hilda. But he owed it to her, as well as to their son Harry. It shouted defiance in the face of grief, the silent grief of feeling so powerless, which had drained Hilda's poor life and left her only fit for throwing away.

Once indoors, casting around for something purposeful to do, he steered his body like a fork-lift truck into the kitchen and put the kettle on. Brewing two mugs of tea, he put them on the table and sat down. Then he stared at them… and his skin rose up in gooseflesh. Cursing himself for going mad without putting up a fight against it, he snatched up the furthest mug and poured it away down the sink. Then sitting down he lifted the remaining mug to his lips. But he did not drink.

Eleven o'clock. Getting dark at last. Two days to go before Midsummer's Eve. It didn't go completely dark these nights, even at midnight, though stars were already appearing in the livid sky. Seen through the window, the garden called to him in silence. He put the mug down and crept outside through the back door.

It was chilly for June, but he didn't feel cold. He just felt empty. A deep mauve emptiness, studded with mineral stars, disintegrating slowly into light.

····* ✱ ● ✱ *····

Less than three weeks ago, on Saturday, 1 June 1974 to be precise, Newhouse Church had witnessed an altogether jollier occasion. After the ceremony the congregation had repaired to the Catholic Club. Hilda, her health delicate at best, had stayed to see the couple wed, but she'd then gone back home to lie down. It had all been an enormous strain, but she'd been determined to play her part. Jack had stayed at the Club. Out from under Hilda's eye, he'd had a *canny sup,* as the saying goes, everyone buying him drinks. If you can't get skimmished at the wedding of your only son—to such a remarkable girl too, as everyone agreed—then when can you?

But standing in the open, without coat or scarf, to wave off Harry and Tvoul, the evening damp had touched his emphysemic lungs, triggering a coughing fit. Handkerchief to his distended mouth, he'd had to stagger indoors to the gents.

A man patted him on the back as he coughed and retched into the washbasin. "Are you all right, old chap?"

Growling with phlegm, Jack raised his face, gave it a quick wipe on the roller-towel and forced a brittle smile. He saw a spidery individual dressed in DJ, bow-tie and starched shirt-front, with jet black hair slicked back with brilliantine. A bit overdressed for Esh Winning, he thought to himself, even for a wedding.

"Couldn't be better," Jack lied with easy confidence.

"A bad business," said the other, face suddenly grave. He hadn't been referring to Jack's state of health, however. For all his finery he was not one of those who'd been invited to the reception. And he had evidently not recognised the groom's father.

Jack rounded on the man. "What d'you mean by that remark?"

"All these people, having a good time. But they tell me the bride is groubian."

"So?"

"A groubian wedding. Where I come from, that would hardly be a cause for celebration."

Jack eyed the other in glazed amazement. "Where *you* come from," he said eventually, breathing hoarsely in his face, "is where *you* ought to be gettin' back to." Lifting his nose he glared down it at the man. "Where's that anyway?"

"Nix City. Heard of it?"

Jack began to bristle at the nape of his neck. Nix City was on the planet Mars. It was where Harry lived these days. "Who are you, exactly?"

"Here, on Gaia, I'm nobody at all. Just think of me as a friend."

"The devil you are!" Jack's voice took an angry rasp. "Well, Mr Nobody-At-All, do you know who *I* am? *I'm* the father of the *bridegroom!*"

"I'm… er… sorry to hear that," said the other.

Jack squared up to hit him. But something stayed his hand, at least for the moment. It was the man's tone of regret. It had been sincere. In saying sorry, he hadn't been apologising, but expressing sympathy.

Lowering his fists, Jack straightened up. "What d'you mean you're sorry? You ought to be delighted! My son's gone and found himself a canny lass…"

"No, she isn't a 'lass'. She's a groubian."

"What's wrong with that? Let me tell you: in the time I've got to know her, I've found her to be the most wonderful person you can imagine. And d'you know what it does to me when some slithery stranger comes up and offers me *sympathy?*"

The man was unabashed. "You don't know much about groubians, do you?"

"A fuckin' sight more than you do!"

Jack rarely gave way to bad language—Hilda saw to that. It was a measure of how angry the man had got him.

"What I know about *fucking* groubians," the stranger carefully enunciated, "would make your hair stand on end..."

No doubt his repetition of the swearword had been to emphasise its literal meaning. But Jack didn't hear it that way. He thought he was being scoffed at. He clenched his fists again.

Insouciantly the man added "And I bet you've never even heard the word *interspex*."

At that, Jack's visual field exploded in a pash of red sparks. He seized the other by his silk lapels and butted him, thrilled to see blood flow. He did it again—another Glasgow Kiss. Blood trickled down Jack's forehead, but it wasn't his.

Now right-left-right went Jack's fists into the other's chest and shoulders, but his stance wasn't up to the onslaught. Both men overbalanced, Jack clawing at the other for support. Down they went, Jack on top, coughing and spluttering.

"*Whey*, lads—what's going on?"

Firm hands hauled Jack to his feet. Several more brushed him down and straightened his clothes. The stranger was left to stagger to his feet unaided.

"Jack—man! What the devil's goin' on?"

"Frank, canny lad..." Jack's voice choked off. "I'm knackered..."

"What's this geezer been doing t'yer?" Frank and his friends turned angry faces towards the stranger, who was busy staunching blood from his swelling nose with his silk handkerchief. Rinsing it out under a running tap, he said in a muffled voice "Believe me, gentlemen, I didn't lay a finger..."

Jack interrupted him, driving each word home like a hellfire preacher. "He *insulted me daughter-in-law!*"

The stranger's twangy voice was heard again. "I was trying to tell your friend something he really ought to know..."

••••✷●✷••••

Standing in his own back garden, facing north in the deepening dark, Jack stared up at Polaris, the tip of the Little Bear's tail. Now facing due west he saw Leo the Lion poised above the still glowing horizon. He didn't know astrophysics, but nowadays he knew the planets and constellations. He knew the zodiac, the ecliptic and the Milky Way. He knew exactly where to look that night for the planet Mars.

When you've got a boy on Mars, you soon learn where to look for it, on any night of the year. And when your boy sinks out of sight below the horizon—and your wife goes and follows him—your firmament is derelict and cold.

······ ✶ ● ✶ ······

It had been two days before Jack was back on his feet. He'd suffered a reaction to his fight at the club. Hilda had put him to bed in a sort of anxious fury, fussing over him, winding him up still further in anxiety over her heart condition.

"Jack. What a thing to do—and at your age. You're too old for that sort of thing."

"What can a man do when someone insults his family like that?"

Having told-off Jack like a scrapping schoolboy, Hilda let it be known that she too would have flown in a rage. And most likely slapped the man about a bit.

It was then that the beautiful dream pupated—and from that grotesque chrysalis emerged a nightmare from which Jack was never to awaken. He was at liberty to reject the stranger's warning, but he couldn't pretend it hadn't been given. He got acquainted with *Areopedia*—and a whole lot more besides. Frank passed him an offprint of the article on groubians and he learned things he'd rather not have known.

His son was in mortal danger. Transatlantic phone-calls, expensive nail-breaking minutes of pressing a sweaty telephone receiver to a throbbing ear, had failed to reach Harry. The manager of his hotel in Manaus, state of Amazonas, said the honeymooners had gone off into the rainforest all by themselves. A phone-call to *Interverden*, the spaceplane line, established that only one of the two return tickets had been used—by someone calling themselves "Tvoul Williams".

Like an eggshell lying cracked on the ground, hope drained out of Jack. But he knew where his duty lay. He must find out what had become of Harry. Hilda and Jack talked it over—and over—but eventually they planked their holiday money on a ticket to Brazil for Jack to go alone. Even if they could have afforded it, Hilda, with her cardiac condition, was in no fit state to travel. Matter-of-fact neither was Jack, with his emphysema. But equipped with pills from the doctor, plus a fancy new spray, he had set out with some semblance of being hale, if not hearty. Ten days later and ten half-bottles of scotch, he had discovered nothing they hadn't already known. By then his money had run out, not to say his stamina, and he came crawling home.

He got back late on Sunday night to a house in darkness. To avoid giving Hilda a jolt he called out through the letter-box, but no one came.

A note was tied to the front door handle. But Jack, jet-lagged and
fuddled, overlooked it in his haste to find out what was amiss.

He came upon Hilda laid-out in the front room, as was the custom in
a Durham pit-village. There were no flowers: they would arrive on
Monday in profusion. The coffin stood on trestles before the bow-
window, curtains still open, and the lid was standing propped against it.
Yellow street-light glowed on Hilda's face. Surely it must be a marble
statue of her there: the real Hilda was in bed upstairs, warm and soft-
breasted, ready to embrace him as he slid in beside her.

Hardly breathing, he stood beside the coffin—for how long he
couldn't say. Then he went back to the front door and read the note. It
said: *Don't go in the house, come straight round to us however late it is. Frank &*
Maud.

•••••★●★•••••

They had found Hilda lying dead on the kitchen floor. A heart-attack,
the doctor said, brought on by grief and anxiety. Unable to contact Jack,
Frank and Maud had put the necessary arrangements in hand. Like a
speak-your-weight machine, Jack had thanked them both over a cup of
hot sugary tea, then risen to go.

They had implored him to stay the night with them. Maud had a bed
all ready and aired. But he replied "I wasn't there when Hilda needed
me. I can't go off again like that and leave her all alone."

•••••★●★•••••

In his darkened backyard, Jack's neck strained as he stared up at the stars.
Count the stars, Tvoul had challenged him. Count the stars for your
descendants. What a cynical betrayal that had been!

His gaze dropped to earth. A little to the right of Leo's brow, the
Twins—Castor and Pollux—shone out, ready to plunge together below
the horizon in hopeless pursuit of the setting sun. And there it was: the
planet Mars. It stood between Leo and Gemini, having forsaken the
company of the happy Couple for the crouching Lion. Above a band of
twilight stretched out on the horizon like a sleeping anaconda, the tawny
eye stared back at him. A coloured gem, a polished pebble, a scale on the
serpent's back—an isolated orange scale among the blue.

"You old bastard," he cried aloud. "Grinning away at me. Aren't
you satisfied? What more d'you want?"

He raised his voice still higher. "You've taken me bairn—you've
taken me wife—you've taken *everything!*" Enraged and emboldened by the

echo of his voice he shouted "What more've I got to give you? Shall I turn out me pockets, like?"

In furious absurdity he did so there and then, onto the garden path. Coins rang in the darkness as they rolled around in little orbits before flopping flat.

"And d'you think you can just bugger-off back to Mars now? Scot-free—to carry on living your useless life? Leaving a trail of wreckage behind you? Leaving me face-down in the mud with arrows in me back, like?"

Heavy silence swept in like a black tide to swamp his voice. But once more he broke the peace, bellowing over garden walls and across the sooty landscape.

"It won't do you any good. I know all about you now. You're nothing but a living fossil. All of youse—you're fossils. You're extinct. You're doomed. Doomed. *Doomed!*"

Somewhere near at hand a window was pointedly banged shut. But Jack chose not to notice. Let the neighbours listen—or not, as they preferred. He wasn't going to be living around here for much longer. He raised his fists, shaking them at the planet as it loured in the sky.

"I hate you. *I hate you.* Do you hear me? I HATE YOUUUUU…!"

With each word "hate" he crouched down to thump the crazy paving with his fists. Reaching out with grazed and gritty hands, he screamed "Thanks to you I've lost everyone I love. Everyone! And d'ye think I can't get back at you?"

Silence.

Once more he howled "I tell yuz, flower—I'll find a way. *I'll find a way.* If I have to accept help from the *devil himself!*"

In the house a floorboard creaked, snapping his attention back to earth. He must have left the front door open. Briskly he stepped back into the kitchen… and stopped dead.

There was someone standing there. Someone he'd met already.

"I'm… so sorry," said the intruder after a shocked pause. He was no longer dressed in DJ and bow-tie and his face now showed no sign of damage. But still he contrived to look like an undertaker: someone who'd use embalming fluid for hair-oil.

When it became clear Jack wasn't going to reply, he carried on "There's a notice outside saying *For Sale.* I'm in the area looking for a second home to buy. The door was open—no one answered when I called—so in I came."

With Jack still emitting not a sound, the man shrugged and turned to go. "Don't let me disturb you now: I know it's late. I'll call back in the morning, if that's all right."

"No, wait a minute, sunshine. Now you're here, you might as well stay."

The man turned round. Again he shrugged, pulling an apologetic face. "No really—it was inconsiderate of me. I'll go away and come back at a proper time…"

"I've got all evening," said Jack, although there was very little of the evening left. He opened the fridge. "Can I offer you a glass of something?" He lifted out a bottle of Criolla which he'd brought back from Brazil for Hilda, got two glasses out of the sideboard and stood them on the table. "I don't like it when I drink alone."

The newcomer visibly relaxed. He sat down with a grateful sigh. "Well, thank you. Most hospitable. I'm not known around here…"

"Why, man, I recognised you straightaway." Jack smiled—bleakly—but at least it was a smile.

The other winced. "A dreadful misunderstanding. I should have held my peace."

"If you had a-done," said Jack, pouring out two full glasses, "I'd be sitting here now, with me bonny wife on me lap—and we'd both be thinking everything's all right with the world."

"Oh, I say. You're—you're not the man…?"

"…Who's buried his wife today? Sure I am: Jack Williams is the name." He held out his hand. Seemingly out of his depth, the swart stranger took loose hold of it.

"I'm Markus," he said. "Markus Efimovitch Potapenko."

"Well, Markus," Jack raised his glass and took a sip, "you were right. That 'canny lass' went off into the jungle with me son—and *ate* him."

Markus cringed like a bedraggled cat. "I really am… most dreadfully sorry."

"Don't be sorry, man. I'm grateful." Jack took a gulp of wine as if to flush away any hint of sarcasm. "I could be sitting here thinking I've got a son… and no—I haven't." He gave a silly giggle. "And I haven't got a wife either. The panic killed her while I was away in Brazil, searching for me son Harry. Dicky heart, y'know, like."

"So you checked up on what I had to say?"

"Why-aye. I've been all the way to the Jungle and back. And the biggest thing I'm sorry about is not checking up before. Before I let my son go off with that—that…"

"…Invertebrate?"

Jack stared at the man. He pointed his finger. "Invertebrate. The very word."

Markus, jaw sagging, shook his head. "I really don't know what to say."

"Don't say anything. Have another drink." Jack topped up both glasses. "The house, now: d'you know the price, like?"

"I'll buy it."

Jack scowled. This was absurd. "But I haven't told you the price yet."

"It doesn't matter: I'm from Mars. Whatever it is, I'll pay."

"Well… huh! That's quicker than I anticipated. We'll drink to that." Jack picked up the bottle again to top up, but both glasses were still brim-full. He put the bottle down as if he'd been rebuffed. The insolence—to still be full.

"What happens next?"

"Well," said Jack, trying to look businesslike and think straight at the same time, "you get yourself a solicitor…"

"What's that? You can't mean somebody who hands out leaflets?"

"*Na-aw*, man, a *lawyer*. Your lawyer gets in touch with mine and makes an offer. If the offer comes near the asking price—which I can't recall offhand—then that's the job done."

Jack stopped and thought about that. "Well, it's done as far as I'm concerned. But lawyers have to make a living, like. So they'll to-and-fro a bit, checking up on title deeds and all. They can really spin it out, like."

"I don't know about you," said Markus, "but I love cutting through red tape." He leaned across the table and put down a piece of plastic.

Jack blinked. It looked like a credit card, but when the man let go of it Jack was sure it changed from green to blue.

He picked it up: it turned green again. He put it down on the table: it went back to blue.

"Groubian technology," said Markus. "Cannot be defeated. It goes green when the rightful owner touches it."

"It goes green when *I* touch it."

"That's right—it's yours now."

Jack stared at the card, but didn't make a move to pick it up.

"Look," said Markus, leaning across again. He took the card and held it, glowing blue, under Jack's nose. "I've just given it to you. Now you, in your turn, can give it to anyone you like. Not that you'd want to, mind. But if you did, you'd just hand it to them with the intention of doing so—it can tell if you're being coerced—and it will register its new owner. I can't take it back now, unless you voluntarily give it me."

"What is it?"

"It's a booner card. On Mars it's called an *econinst*—an economic instrument. A monetary instrument, you'd call it here on Gaia. It makes you a *booner*: a Martian envoy in effect—a civil servant of the Strana of Olympia. I've just given it to you. In return for your house."

"Not my soul...?"

"The house will do for now."

"What's it good for?"

"What do you want?"

Jack guffawed. "But surely this is no earthly use to me? I mean not here on Earth—Gaia—whatever it is you call it?"

Markus leaned back and fixed his eye. *"It will get you to Mars."*

Jack boggled as if Markus's head had turned into the planet itself. The two men stared each other out for some five seconds. Then Jack began to chuckle once more, wobbling silently.

But Markus wasn't laughing. "I mean it," he said. "It will get you to Mars."

A playful note crept into Jack's voice. "Shall I get there by candlelight?"

Markus blinked. Then gradually his face creased in a knowing grin. "Aye—and back again...

> *Though you travel half the night—*
> *You shall get there by candlelight!"*

Abruptly Jack got to his feet. "I'm afraid I'm going to leave you the washing-up."

He sauntered into the hall and put on his overcoat.

"Why the rush? I'm not throwing you out."

Jack came back and clapped the stranger on the shoulder. "Once you've made a decision, there's no point in hanging about, like."

He began to button up. "I'd best be off: I've a long journey ahead o' me." Leaning across the table he picked up the booner card and slipped it beneath his lapel into the top pocket of his Sunday best suit: the suit he wore to funerals. Scorning to pack a single thing he strode down the passage to the front door. It was open—as he'd guessed he'd left it.

He went on through the doorway without breaking his stride, without so much as a backward glance. A sense of liberty enveloped him: a cloud of incense in a cathedral. He drew breath in preparation for a long, long sigh. As he did so, emphysema stabbed a warning from within.

Gazing once more at the western sky, he found himself eye-to-eye with the planet Mars. It hovered in the summer midnight glow above an inky horizon pierced with streetlight pinpricks.

Screwing one eye shut he muttered "Watch out, flower, Jack's coming f'yer."

4   Unbound from the planet

A bleak morning. A slate grey sky: as grey as Jack's face. He staggered aimlessly down Fawcett Street, crossed the road and found himself on Wearmouth Bridge. A cruel breeze was hissing through the gigantic girders.

He hadn't slept all night, apart from half-an-hour's doze on the bus from Durham. He had walked the six miles into Durham City, setting out with a light step and a song on his lips—but very soon the song had passed into coughing and spitting. Before long his spray had run out. At Durham they had sent him on to Sunderland and he'd caught the last bus and waited out the night in a Park Lane bus-shelter, coughing and spitting until he felt like a crushed slug.

When the ticket office opened, he was first-in. But they hadn't wanted to accept his card. The young fellow behind the window had looked blankly at it and asked him whether he had some other source of funds.

"I'll think about it, bonny lad," Jack had said—and strolled back out.

So Markus had bamboozled him. He'd got his own back for his shaming at the club. In his washed-out state Jack couldn't find it in his heart to be angry with the man. More fool him—it had all seemed too good to be true. A few inconsequential thoughts chased each other through the cracks of his brain: it wouldn't be hard to go back to Esh Winning, get Frank and a few of the lads together and send the fellow packing.

But he couldn't be bothered.

As he wandered to the centre of the bridge, high over the river Wear, its two massive arches soared above his head, letting down long struts to hold the roadway. Struts ending in big joints where they plunged into the kerb. Struts you could scarcely close your fingers round. Barely a stone's throw away, another bridge, black and squat and nowhere near as beautiful, carried the railway line. Like man and wife they spanned the river Wear, linking the hundred or so yards between their towering buttresses which sprouted from the banks.

Down below, the river swept along in microscopic ripples.

It was a popular spot. Plenty of people had sampled a drop of something there—a 150 ft plunge into the dun waters. None had come back for more.

At the centre of the bridge, the coat-of-arms of the Borough of Sunderland, cut from a thick steel plate, was let into a frame above the railings. Jack read the motto:

NIL DESPERANDUM

There is nothing to despair about.

"Nothing," echoed Jack aloud. Life is a succession of days—and one day they simply stop. During each day that comes, things nice and not-so-nice occur. They bear little relation to the things you do yourself. And on the final day, who knew what it was they'd done that deserved death? It was a lucky man who could stand erect under the sky and know that this was the last day he needed to endure. He, Jack Williams, was about to take supreme charge of his life: to perform an act of immediate and everlasting consequence.

Should he? Or should he cast himself instead back into the muddy waters of fate? To endure once more a stream of days which ran out in the end, like sand-grains in an opaque hourglass.

Jack took the useless card out of his top pocket. He inspected it. He couldn't understand the writing on it—but so what? Putting both hands on the handrail, card between his fingers, he took a slow, deep breath. His chest twinged.

One day—today—it wouldn't do that any more.

Unnoticed, the card turned blue as it slipped from his fingers. Jack felt a sense of freedom, like a shroud of slate-grey gossamer descending on him from the sky.

When you died you'd meet up with your loved ones—or so they used to tell him. But not if you took your own life. Hilda had died and gone straight to heaven. But if you killed yourself, you went to the other place.

No. Hilda had died—period. She was no more. When he too was no more, they would meet again only in the sense of sharing the same lack of being. He would never see her again. Never again lie in bed beside her. Never feel the comfort of a warm smelly body in the night and know for sure the roots of his existence.

Now she lay beneath a heap of earth in a damp graveyard, with nobody to cuddle up to and get warm. Soon he himself would lie beneath cold waters, sunk in mud. Maybe in time to be washed up on Roker Beach, to the disgust of whatever wretch might stumble on his crab-clawed body.

Away to his left there came a noise that drilled through his skull into his private grief. Somebody was striding up to him, calling out in a frantic voice "Excuse me, sir… Excuse me, sir…"

Slowly, like a turret on a battleship, he turned his head.

"Excuse me, sir. Are you the gentleman who came in earlier with an econinst?"

"What of it?"

The man was abashed at the rebuff. But he went ahead anyway and said what he had to. "I must apologise for the incident…"

"It doesn't matter now."

"My student helper didn't know the ropes. He was unaware there was a number to contact. All you had to do was say you'd got an econinst and get him to ring the Olympian Consulate, just to alert them to a transaction on its way. They don't need details…"

"Nice to know," said Jack, nodding curtly to dismiss the man. The other held his ground, clasping his hands as if to comfort himself.

"If… if you'd like to accompany me back to the ticket office, sir, I'll be able to complete your transaction."

"Okay, sunshine. I'll be along in a minute."

The man turned and walked away. He glanced back once over his shoulder before quickening his step. Soon he was lost to view.

Jack slowly turned his head again, to gaze across at the dull black railway bridge. It rumbled like a dyspeptic dragon as a local train crept between its girders to crawl into Sunderland Central Station. He focused on the steelwork: it was crisp and clear. Clearer than he'd ever seen before. But he couldn't judge the intervening distance. It felt close enough to reach out and touch. He knew though it was far away in space and time. Between them lay a dizzy gap above unending waters. He felt himself become detached and start to float across.

No regret. No pain. Nothing… but vertigo, winding down to the core of his life.

Nothing to despair about.

It was just another day, in a series of days like it, during which both nice and nasty things happen to you. The day on which the series stops will start no differently from all the others. His eyes sank slowly down, to come to rest upon unheeding waters.

And it struck him like a fist in the face. *There was his card!*

Groubian technology: cannot be defeated. Glowing sky-blue, it lay at the foot of the coat-of-arms, cantilevered over the void, on a ledge which ran beneath the handrail struts. Its colour reminded him of a body which sunbathed next to him once.

There are moments in one's life, maybe at the very end of it, when one has no choice over what to do. The whole scenario is played out like a film script. Clutching the coat-of-arms through its cut-out holes, he hauled himself up to sit astride the handrail and swing his leg over. Now he was straddling the rail like a naughty boy contemplating sliding down the banisters. Feeling the ledge with his right foot, he tried to get a purchase with his toe. There came the *clack-clack* of several pairs of approaching feet.

At last he achieved a foothold: none too solid, but firm enough for now, and he moved his hands from coat-of-arms to handrail. Leaning back, holding on to the rail with both hands (the palms of which were sweating now), he dragged the other leg over until it flopped down and dangled.

The action swung him round, face outwards, tearing loose one hand. The bridge seemed to break away from its piers and float loose in space. Scrabbling backwards with his free hand, he grasped a strut. He felt corpse-numb. But every muscle in his frame was wooden, as if he was completing an electric circuit..

Then his shoe fell off.

Jack looked down at his left foot swinging free, now clad only in a sock which sagged below the ankle. He watched his shoe speeding away from him, turning over and over, getting smaller and smaller until it vanished. A powerless feeling took charge of him. His fate was no longer his to sway. He was a pawn uplifted in some mighty hand—a gambit for sacrifice?

The other side of the handrail, people were thudding to a halt. Their distant shouts chimed like fairy voices calling through the mists of a thundering waterfall.

Crushing the strut to his left shoulder, he was able now to let go of the rail. His right arm now swung free as he stared down at a grey-green wall of water. The far-off voices rose in pitch and stridency. His muscles trembled with the strain. Teeth grinding, his face snapped into rictus. Ignoring hands which felt around the coat-of-arms, gripping his overcoat, pinching him, pawing him, trying to fetch him back, he eased himself down gradually, reaching out with his right hand... reaching out... reaching out... until the card tipped out of sight—then came back level.

It had turned back to green. It wasn't going to leave him now.

Snatching it, he slipped it in his suit top pocket. Already several pairs
of hands, clawing his arms and flanks, had got a purchase on his clothes.
Fists were gripping him by the scruff of his neck. Were his buttons sewn
on tight enough?—only Hilda would have known if not. If they weren't,
he knew, he'd drop clean through his overcoat.

They were. His wife's industrious hand was posthumously saving
him.

He tried to haul himself over the handrail, but all the muscles in his
thighs had cramped. He couldn't budge. He hollered out in pain. A
grating sound, like a match being struck—and his foot slipped off the
ledge. At once he banged his knee and forehead. Blood began to trickle
into his eyes. Both feet now dangled over the river Wear as he saw the
other shoe falling away, joining its partner in oblivion.

His ears filled with the sounds of grunts and shouts. "Easy lad!
Come on old fella." Hands were reaching past the struts, around the
coat-of-arms, clutching him, raising him an inch or two before being
nipped against the ironwork and snatched back. Gradually they hauled
him up to safety, a morsel snatched from the all-devouring jaws of death.
The fabric of his coat stretched as the buttons snagged, then slipped one-
by-one, grudgingly permitting him to slither off the rail head-first onto
the walkway in a heap of shame.

His rescuers were shouting at him, reassuring him, abusing him,
remonstrating with him…

"Are you all right, man?"

"What d'ye think yer doing, yer daft git?"

"D'ye need the police?"—"*Naw-w! Geddaway!*"—there wasn't much
support for that idea.

"D'ye need an ambulance…?"

"D'ye need the little white van?"

In response to all this fuss, Jack smiled and shut his eyes, shaking his
head hugely from side to side. A man thrust his face into his. "What
d'you want to go and do a thing like that for? Is life all that bad?"

Jack's face lit up. Reaching into his top pocket he took out the
rescued card and waved it. "I dropped me econinst over the rail. Ye
canna lose a thing like that."

The expletives which came flooding in reply were ones which Jack
chose to forget. Muttering crossly, perplexedly, concernedly, relievedly,
the crowd dispersed like woodlice from the cover of a lifted stone. They
hadn't even taken the trouble to pick him up and stand him on his feet.

Were they afraid of him clambering back over the handrail before they'd made their getaway?

Jack, sitting in his rumpled clothes, back to the railings, silently began to laugh. Soon his laughter was not so silent and was heard by the last of the woodlice scurrying away. A few glanced back over their shoulders. If any of them had been superstitious, thought Jack, they'd have crossed themselves.

Looking upwards with a start, Jack saw a shadow looming over him. Just one person had remained behind. Clasping himself across the chest, the man stood frowning down at him. "Are you sure you're all right now? Are you *quite* sure?"

"Why-aye!" Jack's face was beatific. Having let the man assist him to his feet, he bent to brush the bridge grime from his best clothes. "Never felt better."

It was true. He'd all but died... and come to life again. Nothing could touch him now.

······★ ● ★······

Jack was just about to step into the ticket office when he remembered he had no shoes on. He laughed to himself—it didn't embarrass him: it merely accentuated the dreamlike quality of his experience. A lucid dream: once you know you're dreaming, you discover you are all-powerful. Casually he padded in his socks out of the railway station and across the precinct to a shoe shop, where he tried on a pair of smart shoes.

The young assistant regarded him with something close to panic. It's not every day a man comes in with a sober suit, a black tie, no shoes and a thumping great bruise on his forehead—and asks to try-on the most expensive shoes in stock. "I've got a Martian econinst," he said. He extracted it from his top pocket and waved it.

The look of fear drained from the girl's eyes. After he had said the word "Martian", she was up for anything. "That'll do nicely, sir," she said, dialling the number Jack showed her to phone.

That had been easy. His first-ever purchase with extra-terrestrial funds: a new pair of shoes.

······★ ● ★······

Jack asked what he could afford and the sales clerk told him: first-class—no problem. Carrying an econinst, he didn't have to ask things like that. He was royalty. Someone else was paying.

"As you'll know, sir, we have this thing called money on Earth, which your consulate converts into Martian info credit—however that works. Someone tried to explain it to me once…"

"What do you think they use on Mars?" Jack replied with a laugh. "Barter?"

The sales clerk laughed too. "I suppose, sir, you think you're joking."

Then it dawned on Jack. Nobody was asking to see his passport, as they had done frequently on his trip to Brazil. The econinst positively-identified him. It told them his name, plus all it was good for them to know. It was then taken for granted he was a Martian envoy returning home. He wondered how he was going to explain away his complete ignorance of his home planet.

Jack expected to be directed onto the station platform. But no—first-class travel meant you got a courier as far as Lunaborg. After that, he was the responsibility of *SV Oberon*— *SV* standing for "space vessel"—which could be relied upon to roll out the red carpet. And since he was the only first-class passenger from Sunderland that day, he'd have the courier all to himself.

"And I think I know who it's going to be," the clerk said. "Lucky you!"

Jack hadn't long to wait. A flaxen-haired girl in a smart crimson tailored suit came up and stood smartly before him. "Hello," she said crisply, "I'm Gabrielle."

A sudden smile brought her fashion-plate face to life, showing her up as less of an archangel and more of an earth-child.

"Would you like to come with me, Mr Williams?"

He got to his feet. "Call me Jack, pet."

•••••★●★•••••

The flight to Lunaborg departed from Teesside Airport, not Newcastle as Jack had expected. The spaceplane sat snuggling up to the terminal, connected by the fat umbilicus of a covered walkway no different from a Terrestrial aircraft. But unlike the other planes in their bright liveries, it was brownish grey, scorched by frequent atmospheric re-entry. The others showed it up—an ugly duckling among its colourful bretheren.

Once aboard, Gabrielle straightaway disappeared and he was shown to his seat by a smiling stewardess. The seat stood all alone like a dentist's chair—adjustable, reclining, with swivel-trays, screens and side tables within easy reach. He'd had visions of the trip being like the economy flight via Miami to Brazil: cramped seats, no legroom, elbows all scrunched up. But now, as the stewardess reminded him, he was travelling first-class.

The take-off differed little from the Miami flight, but the pressure of the seat on his back was much, much greater. They climbed for a lot longer. Gabrielle reappeared when the spaceplane had made it through the stratosphere and had set course for the Moon. All at once the sense of climbing vanished and they were flying straight and level—or so it felt. Out of the window Jack saw stars in a black sky.

"Where did you get to? I thought they'd give you a seat next to mine."

"No, once aboard I have to work. Mainly it's bar-duty—plus looking after you." She flashed a smile of orthodontic perfection. "Speaking of which, I'd better fix that bruise on your forehead."

"It's all right lass, there's nothing you can do."

"There's a lot I can do: I'm a nurse. Hold still…"

Opening her shoulder-bag she worked briskly, cleaning the abrasion and brushing on masking salve. Jack half-expected her to kiss it better. She brought the mirror up on its bendy stalk and showed him the result. There was scarcely anything to see.

"What a lot of things you couriers can do." said Jack.

"Have to, in my job. I just float from one thing to the other."

"I thought we'd all be floating around in zero-gravity. Why aren't we?"

"That's all old-hat nowadays. This isn't *2001: A Space Odyssey.*"

Jack laughed. He visualised the stewardess clumping sideways from floor to ceiling in magnetic boots to get through the cabin door. "You wouldn't have liked zero-gravity," said Gabrielle. "It resembles falling off a bridge."

Jack looked up at her piercingly. Her face betrayed no sign that she knew what had happened to him that morning. Anyway, how could she?

Unaware of Jack's keen glance—or maybe mistaking it for something else—she continued "We're going straight up, roof-first. There's a rocket underneath providing a continual $g/6$ acceleration in the direction of our flight-path. It doesn't hasten us on our journey much but it simulates lunar gravity and gives us the chance to get used to it. So you can get up and walk around whenever you feel like it."

"The Wonders of Science!"

"It would be a grim flight if you had to spend it strapped-in for the whole three days." She flashed her brilliant teeth again. "Just don't try skipping up the aisle."

Jack was disappointed he wasn't going to have Gabrielle sitting beside him for the entire trip. He wondered if he couldn't have arranged things differently by paying more, if you could call it payment. Why—with Martian "barter" he could have bought a ticket for her as well. A ticket to the Moon—and beyond.

"Tell me when you're doing the bar and I'll come and prop it up for you." He wasn't for letting the other passengers ogle her all by themselves. She was meant to be *his* courier.

Gabrielle laughed. "I can do my bar-duty now," she said. "Why don't you come along when you're ready?" With that she disappeared up the aisle.

Jack thought of Hilda. She was never out of mind—just out of sight. But Hilda was past caring now, wasn't she. Past being. He only held onto her in his mind. Did she still have any hold over him?

The way he felt as he watched Gabrielle's black calf-boots flash along the aisle would have smitten him with guilt were Hilda still alive. Now there was no back-hander, only gratitude. It was a covenant: a meteorite from the hand of God—a shiny black stone to kiss—assuring him that he still existed. It's meaningless to talk of keeping faith with someone who's no longer there. But keeping faith with your own grief: wasn't that essential to ensure that you were still there?

5   First-class to Lunaborg

It was dinner time and Jack was starting to feel hungry. But when
the meal came, though it was superbly cooked, it took an effort
to swallow and gave him an oppressed feeling. To take his mind
off his qualm he picked out the *Interverden* house journal from his
private magazine rack.

> *Velkommen til Selene!*
> *Vi onsker dig god rejse!...*

That must be Selensk. He glanced on down the page. Sure
enough, there was a translation:

> *Welcome to Selene!*
> *We hope you have a good flight!*
> *If you are new to Selene you may appreciate a few facts...*

He didn't. Not yet awhile. He glanced idly down the page.

> *...Many Seleneans are of Inuit (Greenlander) descent, which they*
> *proudly claim suits them to a cold hostile environment having long*
> *spells of darkness.*

Bully for them. ...Hey—what was this place he was going
to?...

> *But the fabled harshness of the Moon is a thing of the past.*
> *Lunaborg and Jordvik are cities with every modern amenity*
> *and know how to cater for visitors.*

So there'll be somewhere to get a drink. Champion. He
returned the journal to the rack, leaned back in his seat and shut
his eyes.

His thoughts turned to the *Areopedia* offprint, which he'd
brought along with him. A bitter treasure: he hadn't once
consulted it since coming back from Brazil. But now he took it
out and settled down to read...

> *By the terms of the Treaty of Nix, which concluded the Second*
> *Olympian War, all groubians were extended full human rights*
> *by the victorious coalition...*

You mean—they didn't have them before? When he'd first
read that passage he'd thought: poor downtrodden groubians.
Wicked imperialist settlers, doing what they've always done. But

now he wondered if the victorious coalition hadn't been over-generous to these man-eating monsters.

The next section had a mythic quality...

> *In the nurturing environment which Titan then afforded, the Chicxulub detritus quickly gave rise to an extensive biosphere, ranging from the most primitive life-forms to the most advanced. This is not to assert that conditions on Titan remotely resembled those on Gaia, then or now...*

He wandered off along strange tunnels just below the surface of consciousness. The offprint dropped from his grasp and he realised he must have dozed. Picking it up, he once more focussed on the page...

> *Approximately 50,000 years ago, a cataclysm known as the Fall of Titan (which may or may not have been natural) sterilised that world, giving rise to the hostile environment in evidence today...*

Let's remember not to go to Titan.

> *Some groubians question that Titan was altogether sterilised, arguing for the persistence to this day of a massive and dangerous life form: the Titan Kraken (another cephalopod) able to endure the low surface temperatures, at which methane liquefies.*

Jack put down the sheets and shut his eyes, swampy shapes like vapours rising behind his eyelids. Once more he fell into a dream, in which he was assailed by vast tentacled creatures rising out of the methane ocean. Fury and destruction all around him, he struck them down, one after another, with a weapon of blinding flame.

But no matter how many times he shot the kraken, for he knew that's what they were, they re-materialised at random on the periphery of vision...

••••✦●✦•••••

The lights had come on in the cabin, signalling it was morning, although there was no daylight to confirm it. The kraken evaporated like breath on a mirror, but they left behind a pain in his chest.

"Don't rush," said Gabrielle. "Tell me when you're okay and I'll draw the curtains for you." She put a cup of tea on his swivel table.

Jack reached for it, hands trembling. His ribs burned like an iron basket filled with coals. He'd been able to get a fresh spray at Teesside Airport before boarding the spaceplane, but it wasn't a type he'd had before. It had suppressed the urge to cough, as it was meant to, and with it the embarrassment of having to use a spittoon. But it hadn't eased the discomfort.

He had his own tiny bar, in a sort of *prie-dieu* which stood before his seat. His eye fell on a miniature scotch whiskey, one of a small collection. Seizing it he tore off the top and downed it in one hot corrosive gulp.

Scotch—what a way to start the day! Sometimes though it was the only thing that worked. A fierce warmth in his food-pipe began to supply an altogether purer, more chemical pain of its own. The two kinds of pain mixed and became numbness.

As soon as the shower came free, Jack slipped gratefully into it. A shower on a plane. Wherever did they find all the water? It was no doubt being endlessly recycled, but he didn't like to think of that. It was a piddling shower, even by British standards, but a good buffeting with warm air loaded with light drying spheres made up for that.

Jack marvelled at the things they'd been able to fit into such a small space. Everything was miniaturised, everything dual-use. But this Lilliput existence was getting on his nerves. In spite of his combat with the exercise machine, his limbs were growing stiffer by the hour.

He groaned inwardly. A whole day and a night to go before making landfall.

······ ✦ ● ✦ ······

The morning ritual over and breakfast things cleared away, Jack returned to the offprint. What bad dreams it had given him. Though aggravation of his emphysema was more likely to have been responsible for those. He read on...

> *Those mental functions which are thought to be the provenance of the cerebral cortex in gaians are taken over by the skin, an organ rich in nervous tissue; and one responsible for the groubians' most spectacular faculty: the ability to change colour instantaneously at will.*

This was less scary. Just weird...

Groubians maintain that all aspects of their mental life, including superior activity analogous to poetry or music, are displayed openly on their skins.

He had known from Tvoul how her colour-changing skin displayed her emotional state. But this went further: it implied that groubians' skins endowed them with a complex non-verbal language as expressive as English: a language capable of such things as poetry and music. And mathematics, science, history— and legend.

His eyes were beginning to smart. It felt so nice when he closed them…

······ ✶ ● ✶ ·······

He awoke to a meal, brought to him by Gabrielle. He discovered he had some appetite at last. He sniffed in pleasure. Not too deeply, though, or too hard, because of the warning pain.

"Don't sleep now. There's the night to go yet." Gabrielle was not for letting him forget she was a nurse.

"What you mean is they'll simply dim the lights. Will it be dark everywhere?"

"No, not at the bar."

"What a hardened clientele you've got!"

"What else is there to do here? You can't go out to the club."

After lunch Jack decided to prop up the bar and pass the time in Gabrielle's presence.

"Can you give me another of those drinks you made me yesterday, flower?"

"Another Midsummer Madness?" She raised her eyebrows in mock disapproval. "It's not midsummer anymore."

"Never mind that, pet. It's not what you make so much as the way you make it."

She got out a tall glass and began filling it with fruit.

Jack said "No harm in making midsummer last three days. After that it's downhill all the way to Christmas." He barked a laugh distinctly short on mirth. "I suppose they don't have summer and winter where we're going?"

"No, it's the same all year round. Though it varies a lot in the space of a month. The sun disappears for half that time and the temperature plummets. The Seleneans hate it: they call it the Fort Night."

Jack loved the way she smiled. And he also admired her professionalism. A pretty girl like that, he thought to himself— she must get a lot of her clients flirting with her. Bothering her, if she was the type to be bothered. But she looked as if she'd take it all in her stride. None of this you're-at-play-but-I'm-at-work business.

"Two weeks of darkness! I'm not looking forward to that."

"No. The Seleneans don't. They have a big party at sundown, the Terminator you'll hear it called, and they all go around the next day with long faces, not to say hangovers. There you go…" She finished making the drink and set it in front of him with a flourish.

"Here's to the Terminator," said Jack.

"You don't notice it so much in Jordvik," Gabrielle continued, "because the whole city's underground and they keep it brightly lit. But Lunaborg is mostly on the surface. It gets *freezing* there. Particularly as you go along plastic tubes from one heated building to the next."

Another customer made a bid for her attention, so propping himself firmly on one forearm Jack got the offprint out and carried on reading…

> *Courtship between two individuals took place over a period of days, a process known as edulation. During this deeply invasive method of intercourse, the edulator would consume the internal organs of the edulee, who died in the act of coitus.*

At that point Jack stopped reading—he couldn't stomach any more. Anyway, he'd read that section already: very, very carefully. And that was when his life collapsed and the nightmare began.

He put the offprint on the counter under one elbow and rubbed his eyes. The man next to him said "Do this trip often?"

"No, first time. You too?"

"No, I commute regularly between Teesside and Lunaborg. I'm an importer. Of bottled fruit, would you believe?"

Jack felt his interest awakened. "Is there a big demand for bottled fruit in Lunaborg?"

"I can't keep up with it."

"I'd no idea there was a whole city on the Moon."

"Two whole cities…"

"Yes, there's Jordvik too. Why didn't anyone tell us?"

"Come on, you've heard of Lunaborg, surely?"

"Yes, but I thought it was in Greenland. Or Iceland... away up there."

The man laughed. "Like County Durham being in Northern Ireland?"

Jack laughed too. It was a standing joke in Durham: the rest of England had no idea where it was.

"So... Yuri Gagarin: first man in space—it's all a load of baloney?"

"First man in space *by purely Gaian efforts!* That's the important thing. They're very proud of him on Mars—re-named a university after him. They're proud of him in Lunaborg too."

"How long's Lunaborg been in existence?"

"It's an old Hansa port. Way back then the only space-going vessels were groubian. The Basques monopolised the oceans and the groubians monopolised space—they were far more numerous then. Then as now, Lunaborg controlled the trade with Mars."

"Trade with *Mars?* Do you mean Nix City? How long has *that* been going on?"

"There are more settlements on Mars than just Nix City. It is certainly the largest, but there are far older cities. Valles. Cydonia..."

"Groubian ones, of course."

"No—Gaian ones. Going back to Egyptian times. People think they know where Punt was, but Meluhhah's always been a guess. The groubians never built a city as we'd recognise it. Think of a coral reef, not a blocks of flats."

"So Nix City is fairly new?"

"What? New? It's been going longer than Philadelphia. Founded 1601—that's eighty years before Philly. Around the time Shakespeare was writing plays about that other famous boom-town: Elsinore."

"Never did know where that was," said Jack.

"We English should be ashamed of ourselves. People did back then. There were English pubs in Elsinore in Shakespeare's day. All ships passing down the Kattegat and up the Skagerrak had to stop there and pay their dues."

"So why didn't Shakespeare write about Nix City too?"

"He did. And Lunaborg. *A Midsummer Night's Dream. A Winter's Tale. The Tempest.* But Bowdler went and changed all the names." The man took a sip of his drink. "Politics. Everything's politics when you get down to it."

"How did people get to Mars? They didn't have spaceplanes in those days, did they?"

"Got to thank the groubians for that."

"A sort of slave-trade?"

The man screwed up his nose. "Yes—and no. *They* claim they were just after companionship." He nudged Jack's arm in complicity and took his drink back to his seat.

Just at that moment Gabrielle came back and picked up the conversation exactly where she'd left off. What a girl, thought Jack. How her employers must prize her.

"You're not planning to stay in Lunaborg, are you?"

"I've not thought where I'll stay. I'll take a look around and see where I fancy. I'm just killing time until the *Oberon* leaves for Mars."

"Well, let me recommend Jordvik. Lunaborg gives me the creeps. I wouldn't live there for a million crowns."

"But Jordvik's all underground, you said. Doesn't it get a bit claustrophobic?"

"It doesn't seem to. The streets have walls and ceilings like big flat TV screens. It's like living in a huge arcade game all the time. And the Gaiascope is gorgeous. I could spend all my time-off there."

"The Gaiascope? What's that?"

"It's a fixed observatory pointing towards the Earth, which as you know stays put in the sky. In Jordvik, sited at map-ref 0-0, it's directly overhead. So they've built this huge *camera obscura* just to go and gaze at it. Part concert hall, part pleasure pool, part winter garden… Oh I can't do it justice. You'll have to see it for yourself."

•••••✶●✶••••

Jack pushed his nose in the fruit and drank deeply. "Ay, that's canny. I can see this stuff getting a grip on me." He took a deep breath without thinking—and as he did so a jolt of pain went through his core like ten thousand volts.

"Are you okay, Jack?" Gabrielle's face showed she had noticed.

"Just a bit of lung trouble, pet. A bit of 'doost'…"

"I saw it on your health disclosure. I'm meant to be keeping an eye on it."

"It's not too bad," lied Jack. "But I'd be wise to see a doctor soon after we land. Can you fix me one?"

"Sure, Jack, no problem."

"I've done so much travelling recently. Far more than I've ever done before. And I'm not so young as I was."

"As soon as we are off the plane I'll take you along to one. There's a medical practice at the spaceport, but it's mainly for emergencies. The Galen Clinic is not far away however, so why don't we go straight there?"

"The Galen Clinic. I've heard of that. Never knew where it was, though."

"It's where I mostly take my clients."

"That's champion. It strikes me I've got all the time in the world to get it properly seen to. Instead of simply kicking me heels in Jordvik, crawling from bar to bar, I ought to take the opportunity."

He drained his glass and put it down. "Another of those would go down just fine. I'll tell you this for free, hinny: behind that bar you've got some of the best medicine there is. Doin' me a power of good."

Gabrielle took his glass away and put out a clean one. As someone medically-trained she wasn't going to go meekly along with *that* assertion. "You're not about to smash the joint up, are you? I'll throw you off the plane…"

"Why-aye—can you just see me? The geriatric ape-man." He leaned across the bar and murmured, "Between you and me, this hooch is working better than me lung-spray."

"Take care now, Jack…"

"Just walk me back to my seat before I make a proper fool of meself." He looked down at his legs. "But I seem to be pretty steady on me pins at the moment. So long as we don't hit any turbulence…"

"Turbulence!" Gabrielle laughed. "No, that's one thing you don't get up here." She presented Jack with a fresh drink. "X-flares, meteorites—you take what comes. But *turbulence? Na-aw!*"

* * * * ✸ ⬤ ✸ * * * *

Jack had nearly reached the end of the *Areopedia* article. But he was determined to read and re-read it, to see if he could drain its bitter poison and spit it out unharmed.

> *Almost all groubians alive today were conceived during the Last (or Titanic) Zygogeny... No male groubians survived; this being intentional. However the failure, due possibly to a sex-linked retrovirus, of any male progeny to come to term was unintended and unforeseen...*

Jack stretched back in his seat and sighed. The Fall of Titan was some 50,000 years ago. The Last Zygogeny took place on Mars shortly afterwards, hatching tens of thousands of groubians: all female. No groubian had since been born, nor ever would again.

The consequence was staggering, but inescapable. Tvoul, a child of the Last Zygogeny... *was fifty thousand years old!*

What was the oldest animal on Earth? A giant tortoise: 150 years? Trees could live longer—redwoods, yews: a thousand years or two? But we're talking about *fifty* thousand years!

Immortality—but sterile immortality. What a truly horrible fate.

But instead of his forehead bleeding with sorrow for the woes of the groubian species, black crystals of hatred precipitated in his breast. "They're vampires," he muttered to himself. "They're the Undead. They've eaten all their own damned menfolk—and now they want to start on *ours!*"

This wasn't Tragedy—this was Evil. Ancestral, monumental Evil!

Jack now began to understand the Olympian Wars. Wrong though it was to fall upon a people who were meant to be at peace with them—a dreadful wrong—why hadn't the gaian settlers finished the bloody job? Then we gaians could all have shed tears of guilt over our crime of genocide, as the Romans used to over Carthage. A luxury to enjoy in total peace, with no risk of our children ever again being edulated. And in all honesty we could have reclaimed the word "human" exclusively for ourselves. Not to mention the word "humane"...

54

The irony of it wasn't lost on Jack. But he felt no guilt. It was sheer black humour. But when you've lost a son in appalling circumstances, humour loses its capacity to amuse.

•••••✳●✳••••

"So groubians first made contact in Egyptian times?" Jack was once more propping up the bar and Gabrielle was making him another of her specials.

"Long before that," she said. "There's always been stories of shepherds meeting goddesses in lonely places."

"So they were careful not to contact anyone who mattered? Anyone who'd be believed?"

"So it seems. Leaving aside Sodom and Gomorrah."

"Go on—you'll be telling me it was groubians who visited Abraham and Sarah next!"

A sudden thought struck Jack: a reminiscence of that starry Friday evening in his back garden at Esh Winning. God's promise to Abraham... Tvoul might even have been speaking from direct knowledge. She was certainly old enough.

"Maybe Abraham, maybe not. But always solitary males in primitive surroundings. Childless ones, you'll notice. The groubians had grave misgivings about contact with civilization."

Jack snorted. "Amply borne out by events, I guess." The Olympian Wars sprang to mind.

Gabrielle rested her pretty chin on her folded fingers. "At school they told us about this papyrus snippet. A fisherman down by the river Nile meets a woman who shines in the mist like a rainbow."

"What does she want with him?"

"The usual thing: a good time. She tells him it gets lonely in the sky. There's nothing to do up there."

"You mean they only came to Earth for a dirty weekend?"

"Well," said Gabrielle with a chuckle, her shrewd eyes running round the cabin, "you could say that about half the people on this plane."

Jack winced and stutted. "I can't believe that's all they've ever wanted from us. What do the groubians themselves say?"

"Well, you're going to Mars—why don't you ask one?"

"Yes, but they're not going to tell me the truth, are they?"

"Whyever not? Groubians don't lie: they can't. They'll tell you that we gaians are The Way To The Stars for them."

The irony of it tickled Jack. Before Yuri Gagarin was fired into space—or rather, before Selenean spaceplanes came to earth—groubians had provided the only way off the planet. And now *we* were the vehicle for *them* to the stars?

Symbiosis? Synergy? Jack scowled to himself and shook his head. Something far more predatory.

6   Murder on the Moon

In the end, getting to see a doctor turned into an emergency after all. They had to bring a stretcher to take Jack off the plane. The morning of the day they were due to land, Jack had commenced a coughing fit. This time the spray hadn't helped. Streaks of blood appeared in the sputum— and then it was all blood.

Gabrielle drew the curtains round his seat and stayed by his side. She was a tower of strength. She didn't cluck round him, as Hilda used to do, like a fussing hen. But she was there for him. It hadn't sunk in with Jack that one of her principal functions was to escort sick patients from Gaia to the Galen Clinic.

As the stretcher-bearers carried him off the plane in slow dreamy bounces, Jack could see the lunar landscape through the glassy walls of inflated tubular corridors. It came to him in a series of static impressions: *tableaux vivantes* of impossible crags and craters.

The horizon, viewed from the prone position, was vertical. He was a fly on an Artexed wall. He was a maggot in a vat of green cheese: a maggot with a fish-hook stuck in him. Shutting his eyes, he watched as his shoes tumbled away, first one, then the other, into the river Wear, a wrinkled wall of grey-green, like the moonscape.

Why hadn't he followed them?

Gabrielle had to trot to keep level with the stretcher. She was carrying a drip-feed which snaked into his arm. Her angel face was serenity in an iron mask. He drew strength from the very sight of her.

••••• ✶ ● ✶ •••••

A middle-aged surgeon was sitting beside his bed, watching him with an amiable if neutral smile.

"That was a nasty turn you took back there, young man."

"A stethoscope!" exclaimed Jack, spotting it around the surgeon's neck. He cleared his throat and found that he could speak. The pain had gone. But that wasn't to say it felt all right in there. Far from it.

"A real old-fashioned stethoscope. Back home me doctor has one of those microphone things which goes bumpity-bump."

"We're pretty traditional here," said the surgeon. "All this advanced technology gets out of hand. People cure themselves, you know."

"Well, tell me how to cure myself of this."

"Between you and me, there isn't much we can't do in here," The surgeon projected an air of quiet confidence, not boastfulness. You didn't have to go impressing patients when you were the Galen Clinic. "What do you want? New lungs? New heart?"

"Now there's an idea. New heart. A really brave one would be champion."

"We could grow you a nice pair of lungs from your stem cells. There's plenty of time to do it too, before *Oberon* leaves for Mars. Off back home, are we?"

"I wouldn't say 'back'…" replied Jack cautiously.

"You're a Martian denizen, aren't you? You're carrying an econinst."

Jack saw no point in prevaricating. "That was given to me on Earth," he said. "This is the first time I've been off the planet."

"Well, you're a Martian so far as we're concerned. All we care about is who's paying. Martians generally go for the best that money can buy. Only they aren't shelling out for it themselves, are they?"

"Then who does pay?" said Jack, his interest piqued.

"The economic slack. Just so long as you don't go home with the whole Moon in your pocket."

"Could I do that?"

"Oh, people try it all the time. You're a bit unusual, though. We don't get a lot of Martians coming to us here. They've got the University Hospital in Nix City, attached to PUG. Most of our patients are from Gaia."

"Well I suppose that counts me too, econinst or no econinst. What are you really planning to do with me?"

The surgeon stretched his legs. "That's entirely up to you. But don't spend too long mulling over it, or our options start to dwindle. If it gets bad like that again, there will be no time to grow you lungs and we'll be forced to fit you with an SP unit."

He got to his feet. "Then you'd be walking around feeling as if you'd got a water cooler inside your chest."

"Anything's better than what I've got now."

"Don't speak too soon: the gratitude comes out with the stitches. Notably so with SP units." The surgeon held out his hand. "I'm Mr Sullivan. I'll be back to see you tomorrow. Meanwhile, rest well—and keep your chin up."

······ ✳ ● ✳ ······

The Selenean underground railway, the *Orm,* disgorged Jack at the headquarters of Selstyrke. Going up the steps he found himself in a marble-panelled vestibule. How there came to be marble on the Moon was one of those frequent surprises that nature springs on us. In the wall on the right was a window.

Jack spoke to the girl behind the window. Without a word she handed him an electronic slate and pointed down the corridor to a waiting room. Jack took the slate and stepped on the piste to glide into the room. It was bare and whitewashed like the corridor and there was a continuous bench around the walls. The only other people in the room were a young couple, dressed in gaudy but shabby clothes. The girl was clutching the man's arm and both were looking strained.

Jack sat down and began to puzzle out how to use the slate. There was no stylus and it didn't respond to his finger. An idea occurred to him. Touching his booner card against it he was rewarded with a message thanking him in English and asking him to describe the incident in a series of menu choices. It proved to be a point-of-gaze device. Not a thing he'd had much experience with, but he soon caught on.

Jack had been in police stations before. Not often, but he knew what to expect. They were much the same the world over. Off-world too, it seemed. You didn't go there unless you had to—and you had to resign yourself to spending the morning just sitting around. There was always the stink of fear in these places: stale pheromones emitted by a stream of anxious people.

Jack had spent a restless night in the Galen Clinic, but that morning he had felt much better. What was he doing incarcerated in there, with Tvoul at liberty so close at hand? He got a nurse to fetch his clothes. The senior nursing officer had come and tried to persuade Jack to remain in bed for the sake of his lungs, but Jack had loudly demanded to know whose lungs they were, anyway. So they had pointedly brought him a form to sign, said something about pneumonia and complications, given him some tablets as an afterthought—and he'd discharged himself.

Now here he was, sitting on an uncomfortable bench in a police station, having traded his nice warm bed for this. Well... he wasn't on this jaunt for his health—or pleasure.

After what seemed an age, during which nothing at all happened, a helmeted officer approached Jack and took the slate, beckoning him to follow. It was his first sight of a Martian helmet, but he didn't know that. He assumed it was simply a piece of regulation Selstyrke uniform. He hadn't exchanged a word with the young couple, but as he rose to his feet they both glanced up at him fearfully, expectantly, as if he had somehow become the decider of their fate. As the Egyptians used to say: He Who Is Called Is Given A Wide Passage.

The interrogation room into which Jack was led was like the waiting room—bare and white-walled, with a desk and three chairs: one behind and two in front. There was no way he could confirm his impression, but he imagined his interviewer to be an elderly woman, who moved like a dancer in chronic pain. She didn't raise the visor of her helmet, opaque to someone looking in, but her voice came clear and unmuffled.

"What can I do for you, Mr Williams?"

"I want to report a crime."

"Surely nothing criminal has happened to you in the short time you've been here?"

"No—the crime took place a few weeks ago. On 3 June, to be precise."

"Why wasn't it reported at the time?"

"Because I'm chasing the person who murdered my son, trying to get her arrested. But of course I can't begin to think of that until I've caught up with her."

The interrogating officer shifted in her seat, painfully, Jack thought. It was only while he was speaking that he realised how bald and hollow his story must sound.

"Are you certain the person you are seeking is here on the Moon?"

"Aye and I'm pretty certain she's on her way back to Mars, where she comes from."

"And are you quite sure that a crime has actually been committed?"

Jack gasped in exasperation. But it did occur to him that from the point of view of the Man in the Moon this was not an unreasonable question.

"She's killed my son! Isn't that a crime in this fabulous world?"

He belatedly reminded himself it wasn't clever to say anything which might be interpreted as sarcasm to a police officer. Especially a foreign police officer, indeed one on another planet. But the officer replied in reasoned tones.

"Mr Williams. Murdering someone on the Moon is indeed a crime, as it is anywhere, and it lies within my authority to investigate it. But if the murder did not take place here, but on Gaia—in Brazil, as you've declared in your statement—then there is little scope for me to take action on your behalf. That would be the responsibility of the Brazilian authorities."

She looked down at the screen in front of her. "The police in Brazil—in Manaus, State of Amazonas, to be precise—confirm that you reported the incident on 7 June, UT. But they haven't found a body. All things considered, this is not to be wondered at: but it does mean they cannot confirm that a crime has actually taken place. They do agree however that it looks suspicious."

She raised her head from the screen. Although Jack couldn't see her face behind the visor, he felt she was looking him straight in the eye. "Two people arrive, one leaves. It poses an obvious question."

She leaned back in her chair. "Has the possibility occurred to you that the person you are seeking may not actually have left Brazil? Or if she did, it was at a later date than you imagine? Might she still be on Gaia?"

"I'm pretty certain she's here."

"What percentage likelihood is 'pretty certain'?"

Jack was finding it hard to keep his temper. The drugs they had given him to kill the pain were making him feel unreal. "I checked up in Miami. It was there in the spaceline records—plain as you like. Tvoul *Williams!* She was actually travelling under my son's surname, as his wife. Travelling alone, having cancelled the other ticket—as if she was his widow."

The officer leaned her elbows on the desk, folding her fingers. "Let's be quite clear about what we *know* to have happened. A person called Tvoul Rainbow—a groubian—has gone through a form of marriage with your son on Gaia. That in itself is not a crime..."

"I know all about groubian weddings. I've read it up since. So-help-me I should have read it up long before. *Fifth-rank murder!*"

"And you're convinced that a *groubian* wedding, as such, has taken place?"

Jack blustered. "Just what other conclusion is possible?"

The officer lowered her head. She paused as if discarding options before she replied. "Mr Williams, I'm not trying to provoke you by disputing your assumptions. But what perplexes me is this. Right at this moment there are no visiting groubians on the Moon. None, that is, who are not themselves Selenean denizens. And I know the whereabouts of all of them—all two. And neither of them is the Tvoul you seek."

She paused. Jack felt her hidden eyes peering at his incredulous face.

"I ought to know. No groubian travels through Lipsky Rumhavn without my knowledge. Nor is there any record, on Gaia or Selene, of a groubian disembarking from the spaceplane from Miami on the day in question."

"What?"

"I can only go by the information I have to hand. I repeat: according to the record—there was no groubian on that spaceplane."

Jack leaned back and slapped his knee. "I can't believe it. I just can't believe it!"

The officer sat still and silent, as if doing so would in the end compel him to believe it. He said "Are you trying to tell me I'm making it all up? That I never had a son? That no groubian called Tvoul ever came to Earth and married him—in my church, in front of half the village?"

"Not at all." She glanced down. "Indeed I have in front of me evidence to the contrary. In the passenger list for the spaceplane from Lipsky to Teesside on 8 May, UT, I see quite clearly a groubian calling herself *Tvoul Rádouga* (which becomes Tvoul Rainbow in Standard English) travelling in the company of a gaian called Harry Williams. Your son—no?"

"Yes. That's them. Well, how about it then? It's the same Tvoul we're talking about. Hasn't she been back through Lipsky?"

"I'm well acquainted with the groubian in question. One could hardly call Professor Tvoul Radouga an obscure individual. On Mars she's famous."

The officer leaned back and folder the screen back into her desk. "No—according to our knowledge she has not been back. Not under her own name at least—and not as Tvoul Williams either."

Jack sat staring at the Selstyrke officer. Still no face was showing behind the visor. Was he being fobbed-off? Whether he was or no, it was clear he wasn't going to get much help here. Right now there was little he could do about it. He wasn't sure enough of his ground to lodge a complaint, nor how to go about it.

With an effort he said quietly "So what do you suggest I do?"

"The proper thing would be to go back to Gaia and pick up the trail again, this time more carefully, starting in Brazil. As someone with the privileges of a Martian envoy, thanks to your booner card, you have control of ample resources to do this. More than I do in fact—my authority stops at Lipsky. You also have plenty of time on your hands before the *SV Oberon* leaves for Mars—just over a year in fact, while Mars approaches us again from the other side of the sun. You would have to seek assistance of course. Selnet will give you a list of suitable investigators."

Jack stood up. "Thank you for listening to me," he said. His voice was hollow.

The Selstyrke officer stood up too.

"But don't do anything in a hurry. I propose to make some enquiries in the next few circadians. I cannot rule out the possibility that the person in question has been travelling under an assumed identity."

"You said no groubian could pass through Lipsky without your knowledge."

"I did—and none has."

"They did tell me at Miami that Tvoul boarded the spaceplane to Lipsky on Thursday 6 June."

"No. They would only have told you she was on the passenger list. Did they tell you that the spaceplane was delayed until the following day?"

"No!"

"There you are, you see. All is not as it seems. The passenger list does not tell us who was *actually on board*." She smiled. The vaguest of faces had appeared behind the visor—a hologram, Jack guessed. "As I said, I propose to make a few enquiries. There are aspects of this matter I find… unsettling."

She held out her hand. "I am Commissioner Vermat. I'm the officer in charge here at Lunaborg. When something turns up I shall get in touch with you. Meanwhile if anything occurs to you which sheds light on the matter, come back here and ask for me by name. Unless I'm otherwise occupied, I will see you straightaway."

•••••★●★★•••

Jack came away from Selstyrke feeling less than satisfied. Commissioner Vermat had had a few encouraging words to say at the end, but he'd got the impression she was finding it hard to take his problem seriously.

Or was she hiding something?

In his present condition he risked becoming paranoid—he was well aware of that. Of course she was "hiding something". Police everywhere kept their own counsel and didn't go telling laymen everything they knew. But he would be well-advised, he told himself, not to rely on Selstyrke for much in the way of information.

That morning, after discharging himself from the clinic against medical advice, he had booked-in for a month at the Jordvik Artemis, planning to extend his stay month by month as necessary. He got back to his room, meaning to use the telephone. He was used to hotels in big cities going up and up. But since Jordvik was entirely underground, this one kept going down and down. His room was on the 35th floor and, getting into the elevator (levitators weren't dignified enough for the Artemis), he experienced a moment of disorientation when it dropped away under his feet. It felt like going down to the 35th level of dungeon.

There were no windows in his room of course, but there was a TV screen resembling a window with curtains drawn across it. Peering behind them he saw that the screen was blank. He thought he'd leave it that way, not daring to think what a load of junk might be delivered if he switched it on.

There was no sign of a telephone as he knew it, but there was a v-unit, which gave him a list of ten private detectives. Having a brainwave, he queried which spoke both English and M1. That whittled it down to three. He tried the first one but got no answer.

The next man on the list was a man called Jens Andersen and he replied in person. To start with, Jack thought he was a native English speaker, but was struck by the way he pronounced his A's and slurred his consonants, especially dropping D off the ends of words and syllables. His own name he pronounced 'Ennerson'. Jack couldn't as yet recognise a Selensk accent.

Andersen had his office in Lunaborg, some three thousand miles away on *Mørkside*: the "dark side"—a misnomer because it got as much sunlight as the rest of the Moon. But instead of making an appointment for Jack to see him there, he suggested coming to Jack's hotel and speaking with him in the bar. Jack began to warm to the fellow.

"That's if you're not too worried about our conversation being overheard," said Andersen.

"I suppose I should be," reflected Jack, "but the hotel bar's probably safe enough, particularly over lunch time."

"Lunch time!" snorted Andersen. "You Terrestrials kill me."

••••• ✳ ● ✳ ••••••

Andersen turned out to be a stocky Dane with sandy hair and the sort of bony face not at all uncommon in Wear Valley. No surprise there, since the Valley had been opened up by Viking settlers. He made a point of paying for his own lunch, although Jack was sure it would eventually appear on the bill.

"Forgive me but I've never hired a detective before. You'll have to make allowances for my ignorance."

"No problem," replied Andersen cheerfully. "Very few people employ a private investigator more than once in their lives. Making a habit of it suggests a suspicious sort of mind." He gave a short laugh. "Of course I'm talking about my bread and butter…"

"Where shall I begin, then?"

"Right from the beginning. Go back to the day you met your son's fiancée for the first time."

Andersen took a dictaphone out of his top pocket, clicked it on and placed it on the table between them. Jack felt a grey emptiness when he talked about Hilda, he was surprised at how objective his voice sounded in his own ears. But when he described how Tvoul had made a special effort to win him over, he felt the anger bubbling up from deep within his chest and staining his voice. He couldn't bring himself to pronounce the word *interspex* and he didn't say a thing about his adventure on Sunderland Bridge. But he did describe Markus—and how he'd given him the booner card that had, for all practical purposes, turned him into a Martian envoy.

Andersen listened impassively for the most part, occasionally clarifying his understanding with a question. He gave no sign of considering Jack's behaviour bizarre in the extreme, walking out of his house and leaving it to a total stranger. Presumably he was familiar with what grief can do to you. But as soon as Jack mentioned Markus by name, Andersen's eyes came alive and he questioned him closely about his two meetings with the man.

"Who is this Markus?" Jack asked.

"Don't know for certain. But I'll sure as hell find out. What he did was illegal, giving you—a Terrestrial—a booner card. Explicitly forbidden by the Treaty of Moscow. I'll need to make inquiries about that, but I'll tread carefully. If Markus gets arrested for it, it could make your position precarious. Particularly once you get to Mars, as I understand that's where you're heading?"

"Not if we can track down Tvoul here on the Moon."

"I can't promise that. It may seem as if we've got all the time in the world before the *Oberon* departs, but if Commissioner Vermat herself doesn't know Tvoul is here, then she's not going to be easy to find." He clicked off the dictaphone and slid it in his pocket.

"Even so," he added hastily, in case he was talking himself out of a job, "there are plenty of things I'd want investigating, if I were in your position. And, sitting here as you are on the Moon, you are best-placed to do it. It's the fulcrum of travel, communications, trade… everything between Earth and Mars. It really bugs me that Vermat doesn't know where Tvoul Rainbow is."

"Might she be hiding something—Vermat I mean?"

Andersen narrowed his eyes and shook his head in little twitches. "It's unlikely. I have much respect for Vermat. I don't think we should pursue this investigation on the assumption she knows something vital we don't. On the other hand we *should* pursue it on the assumption she's going to move heaven and earth to find out whatever it is she doesn't know. Which means there's a real risk of treading on her toes. Not a smart thing to do with Commissioner Vermat."

"So where will you start?"

"With the boring stuff. Check the passenger lists of all flights that 'Tvoul Williams' might possibly have come on. Find out what happened to every one of the people who came off Flight Zero-Nine from Miami. And I'll check the movements of this Markus too while I'm at it." He coughed dryly. "Do you want regular reports? Or just one big one at the end?"

"Regular of course. Verbal reports—don't bother with written ones. And get straight back to me the moment you turn up something."

"I'll do a final written report anyway. You'll need it for the investigator who takes over when you get to Nix City." Andersen sighed and smiled in a twisted way. "Because I've a feeling that's where you'll be going in the end."

•••••✱●✱•••••

After Andersen had left him, Jack went to his room for a lie-down. The drugs were making him sleepy and it felt far from all right in his chest.

He awoke with a start. Looking at his watch he discovered he must have slept for four hours. He got off the bed, staggering in the unfamiliar gravity, and put his shoes back on. As he began to move around he realised how much better he was feeling. He thought he'd go in search of food. But first a drink would be nice. He went back to the bar off the lobby where he'd had his meeting with Andersen.

A winking sign beside the entrance proclaimed it was Happy Hour. Because he'd actually bothered to read the welcome pack in his room, he knew that there was meant to be complimentary food put out on the counter at this time. Frugally brought up, Jack never missed the chance of free food. Not even in the most expensive hotels. Not that Jack had ever stayed in many of those.

Now it so happens that even in the most expensive hotels, if nobody's eating the freebies, they don't get put out. Sitting up at the bar, Jack asked the barman: where was the advertised food?

A woman on the stool beside him was just starting on a large pizza cut into eight slices. She tugged discreetly at Jack's sleeve and, shaking her head because her mouth was full, pointed to the pizza, with every sign that he should help himself.

"Oh there it is." said Jack. "Right under me blinking nose. Sorry barman—all is forgiven."

The barman snorted and walked off round the corner. The woman swallowed her mouthful and held out her hand.

"How're you doing? I'm Kitty." She had a Californian accent.

Jack took her hand and replied with his name. "Thanks for pointing out the free food to me," he said.

"There isn't any. It doesn't look like they're bothering with it tonight."

"Well, what's this then?"

"I ordered the pizza. I didn't want a sit-down meal so I thought I'd eat something simple at the bar here before I go off and prepare my talk."

Jack was overcome with confusion. "Forgive me," he said. "It didn't occur to me this was yours…"

"That's all right. There's plenty here. Far too much for me. They always bring huge portions."

The barman returned with Jack's pint of beer. "How are you set up for drinks yourself?" Jack asked. "Can I get you one?"

She shook her head. Her mouth was full again. "No I daren't drink anything just yet," she said after swallowing. "I have to stand up and talk in a minute in front of twenty strangers. I'll need all my wits about me."

"Is there some sort of conference going on in this hotel?"

"There's always a conference of one kind or another, but that's not me. I've simply been invited by the local Lions to give a talk."

"Really?" said Jack. "What's the topic?"

"Groubian history."

Jack's eyes widened. "Can anyone come along and listen to you?"

"Sorry—closed meeting. Members-only. You could come and listen as far as I'm concerned, but they probably wouldn't let you past the door. They are signing-in attendees. You could try having a word with the chairman. If you come with me I'll point him out to you."

Jack didn't feel he wanted to sit through a meeting alongside twenty strangers, much less risk disrupting it with a fit of coughing. The Lions sounded far too forbidding. But Kitty's topic had grabbed his attention.

"Are you leaving Jordvik straight after the meeting? I'm very interested in groubians myself and I daresay I could book you to address my own little club. What do you charge in the way of fees?"

"Really now? What's your club?"

"Oh—it's just a manner of speaking. The club consists of one person—me. And I was wondering whether you'd consider having dinner with me tonight as a sort of fee?"

Kitty looked at him and laughed. "You're as bad as me—still running to Earth time. 'Dinner'", she added, "is a moveable feast up here on the Moon."

"Well, whatever meal it is that comes after Happy Hour."

"I think the meeting is likely to drag on a bit—they often do. People are full of questions about groubians—you've no idea the things that interest them."

"Tomorrow night then?"

"I was going to suggest that myself," she said. "And I was going to offer to buy the dinner—I could probably wheedle it into my expenses."

An independent woman! Refused his offer to buy her dinner—but was making it clear it wasn't because he didn't appeal to her. At least that's how it looked to Jack—the drugs were starting to make him feel good. Or perhaps it was the pizza working through his system—the first meal he had enjoyed since setting foot in Jordvik.

"Let's meet up here again," he said. "Then we're handy for the Flammarion Restaurant just behind us. I take it Happy Hour is going to be the same time again tomorrow?"

"Which is…?" She grinned. "Up here the hours may be the same as on Earth, but the days aren't. Happy Hour is one in every 25, I think it said in my hotel room. They call that the circadian. Have you noticed the clock above the bar?"

Jack hadn't.

"Have you ever seen a 25-hour clock before? They have a twenty-fifth hour on Mars too. *Marsvrem*—Mars-time—they call that, as distinct from *zemvrem*: Universal Time."

"So that's what the 'Z' stands for?"

She didn't answer—she thought it was a comment, not a question. They ate on in silence for a while.

"Where're you from?" she asked.

"You've never heard of it. Esh Winning, County Durham. A little pit-village in the North-East of England."

"No I don't know it, I've only been to England once. London—and from there straight on to Stratford-upon-Avon. Do you know it?"

"Stratford? I've heard of it, of course, but I've never been there."

"I'm from Oakland, California. I guess you've never heard of that either. It's not far from San Francisco, just over Bay Bridge."

"That must be nice there. The nearest I've been to California is Brazil."

I'm just making chat, thought Jack. Brazil is a long way from California. She'll think I'm a clod.

"Never been to Brazil…" her voice tailed off. She took another bite of pizza and glanced anxiously at the clock. Jack was conscious of losing her interest.

"How did you get to be an expert on groubians?" he asked.

"I'm writing a dissertation for my PhD. I managed to get some money from the Historical Research Society to study groubian history—and they were generous enough to stand me a trip to Mars to go and get it from the horse's mouth, so to speak."

"So you're going to Mars?"

"Well, it sounds obvious in hindsight, but you've no idea how many people in California go around claiming to be groubian experts—never having once met a groubian."

"I can see that's kind of limiting…"

"Well—it doesn't seem to limit them in the least. But I reckon I've achieved a breakthrough. My USP: groubian history—as the groubians tell it. Not just somebody poring over the Book of Titan with a spatial Fourier analyser."

They both laughed. "In fact, that's why I'm here. People want to know about groubians, everything they can. I'm dining out on it. Maybe one day the dinner I get will be an improvement on pizza."

"Maybe tomorrow…" reminded Jack.

She turned in her seat to face him squarely. "What makes you so interested in groubians? Just curiosity?"

"I've got a groubian daughter-in-law," said Jack quietly.

Kitty's eyes lit up and she inhaled, as if she was going to say "How wonderful!". But then she hesitated. A complex series of expressions passed over her face. At last she said in a sober voice "However did that happen?"

"My son is a Martian denizen." Jack didn't want to say "was". "He met a groubian girl in Nix City and brought her back home and they've recently got married and gone back."

Groubian girl. How silly that sounded. But he'd wanted to give the impression it was the most ordinary thing in the world. "Marrying a groubian" sounded as stark as saying "eaten by a tiger".

Kitty's face lapsed gratefully back into its original choice of expression. "How wonderful!"

"M-mm," said Jack, smiling and looking away.

"I know the name of every groubian alive. You wouldn't mind telling me who it is, would you now?"

"Tvoul Rainbow."

She gasped. "Tvoul Radouga! *The* Tvoul Radouga? Heroine of the Siege of the Nix? Thrice-serving Forty-Seventh Goubernator of the Strana of Olympia? Incumbent of the Chair of Human Reproductive Biology at PUG?"

Jack was about to say "I didn't know all that..." but he bit it back. "I guess so," he said weakly.

"So you're on your way out there to spend a vacation with her... and your son?"

It saddened Jack that he'd had to commence his relationship with this attractive woman by telling her white lies. But he was determined he wasn't going to bleed over somebody who, after all, was an acquaintance of just twenty minutes' standing. Far too many professional people had seen him in abject distress over the last few days. It was a relief to be able to talk to someone ordinary as an equal.

"Well—kind of. I don't have a home on Earth any more. I'm going out to join them." He was getting bolder with his lies. "For good."

"You must be very proud of your son—and daughter-in-law. They must love you very much. It's a welcome change from all the tales one hears... Goodness!" Kitty, glancing up at the clock, suddenly slipped herself off the bar-stool. "Jack—I'm going to have to run."

She squeezed his arm. "I need to make sure my equipment works with the hotel's wall display before my audience starts cruising in. How do I get in touch with you?"

"I was going to ask you that."

"The name's Kitty Martin. I'm staying here at the hotel. Ask for me at the front desk." With that she was gone.

Sitting in the empty bar, Jack felt like a migratory bird, storm-blown into solitude on a strange continent.

7　Consummation of an unlawful union

It was a quiet and lonely dinner that Jack had in the hotel restaurant. He couldn't stop thinking of Kitty. He didn't know if it was a good sign or a bad one that he was beginning to hunger after female company.

Was that a singles' bar he'd been in? He had no way of telling—he and Kitty having been the only customers. Perhaps it was too early in the evening for people to arrive. Or what passed for evening on this great ball of ash. He glanced around. He seemed to have the restaurant to himself, too.

He got back to his room. He'd had a good sleep before dinner, but he felt in need of another one. A 25 hour circadian, eh? Perhaps he'd catch up on his rest. Or perhaps he'd had too much wine with his meal—he'd sunk half a bottle.

He awoke six hours later, fighting for breath. His chest felt stabbed with scissors. He started coughing and brought up blood on the counterpane. He was still in his clothes—he must have crashed out on the bed. He struggled into a sitting position but collapsed back with a groan. Making an enormous effort he reached for the v-unit.

"Reception. How can I help you?"

"Get me a doctor…!"

$$\cdots\cdots * \bullet * \cdots\cdots$$

"If you did this sort of thing on Gaia," said Mr Sullivan, "discharging yourself against medical advice and then having to be readmitted in an emergency, they'd very soon lose interest in you."

"Sorry…" whispered Jack.

"But here at the Galen we're very tolerant." The surgeon smiled, though there wasn't a lot of humour in it. "Forget what I said about growing lungs from your stem cells. There's no time for that now—we're going to have to make the best of a bad job. How are you feeling?"

"Lousy."

"Not surprising. But don't worry, we have it all under control. Superox perfusers are old technology—*very* old technology—but at least the operation has a 99.9% success rate."

"Whatever you can do for me, Doctor," moaned Jack.

"If you're still going to Mars, you might even thank me—in time. Superox is a lot cheaper there than bottled air. And you don't have to lug it home in your hot little hands."

He gathered together his notes, preparing to get up and go. "In case you don't know, *superox* is the trade name for neat stabilised hydrogen peroxide, H_2O_2, 47% available oxygen by weight. The residue is water, sufficient for your daily needs." He sniffed. "Groubian technology— you can't beat it. Here on Selene you can tank up on it for free in all the rest-rooms. Same on Mars."

He rose to his feet. "But of course the cost won't matter... to a booner."

••••✶●✶•••••

Kitty took the elevator up to the lobby. If that was Jack asking after her, she'd give him a piece of her mind. Standing her up like that! Brits had a reputation for politeness, but that all seemed to have evaporated in recent years.

As it happened she was profoundly disappointed. Long business trips had always had the effect of making her heart slip its moorings. She'd been too engrossed in her career to marry, but not too busy to get a life and a full address book. With her good looks she was never short of admirers. But one thing was lacking on trips to the Moon: male company of a congenial sort. The strange Englishman on his long lonely journey had touched her heart.

But the real prize Jack held out—and she was shy of admitting it to herself—was a first-names introduction to Professor Tvoul Radouga. The celebrated Forty-Seventh Goubernator of the Strana of Olympia. The heroine of the Nix. The great reconciler. What stories *that* groubian woman would have to tell! For Kitty it would be the coup of her career.

However it wasn't Jack in the lobby. A short stocky man she'd never seen before was leaning against the desk. The receptionist, catching her eye, nodded towards him and he introduced himself.

"Jens Andersen." He presented his card.

"Well, Mr Andersen, what can I do for you?"

Glancing at a pair of empty armchairs facing each other, he murmured "Can we talk?"

Once they were sitting down he said "I think you've met my client, Jack Williams..."

"Well, you can just tell him I don't think much of his British manners!"

Jens sighed. "Mr Williams was rushed to hospital thirty hours ago. They tell me at Reception he tried to leave a message for you, postponing an engagement..."

Kitty gasped. "They simply told me he'd checked out! Where is he now?"

"He was taken to the Galen Clinic in Lunaborg."

Kitty, still unacclimatised to lunar gravity, leaned forward so sharply she had to clutch at the arms of the chair to stop herself toppling head-first into the man's lap.

"What happened? Is it bad?"

"Yes." Jens looked downwards. "He's in Intensive Care. They didn't let me in to see him. What's happened to him I don't know. The specialist he's under is called Mr Sullivan. I haven't managed to track that worthy down, but I will."

Kitty felt a gush of pity. Her fury evaporated at having been stood up. If that had been the reason, things were altogether different.

"Please Mr Andersen, will you do something for me…?"

A smile. "Call me Jens."

"As soon as you find out anything, would you be so kind as to inform me?"

"I'm going back there now. I was hoping maybe you'd accompany me."

Kitty put her hand to her mouth as if to stifle a ready lie. Jens pressed the suggestion. "I'll tell them you're a close friend. With the two of us, perhaps they'll let us in to see him. It so happens you're the last person he spoke to before he was taken ill." Jens paused. "If it was 'taken ill'… and not something else."

"Give me a break, Mr Andersen. I had nothing to do with that."

"No, Miss Martin, I'm sure you hadn't. But he's unable to speak. Unable to breathe. He's on life-support. So he can't tell us yet what happened. I was hoping you might remember something he said—anything—which could cast some light on his present condition."

"We chatted in the bar. It was a superficial conversation. I doubt I can add anything useful to that."

"Did he mention groubians?"

"Why, yes. His son has married one. He even told me her name."

"Which was…?"

Kitty took a short breath. "Look, Mr Andersen, I don't know you from Adam. How can I be sure you're really who you say you are?"

"You can't. And I applaud your caution. But give me the chance and I'll try to reassure you over the next couple of hours."

"It's more like five hours to get to Lunaborg."

"Not in my hopper. I go a lot faster than the *Orm*."

"If you imagine I'm going to get into a hopper with a complete stranger…!"

"It's a ride I'm offering you…" Jens got to his feet. "If you've no interest in helping Mr Williams, then I'm sorry you've been bothered. But just now I could have sworn you were concerned about him."

"I am—desperately! Look…"

"You're at perfect liberty to take the *Orm*. We can meet up at the Galen."

"No…" Kitty made her decision. "I'll come with you."

•••••✱●✱•••••

"May I call you Kitty?"

"Please yourself, Mr Andersen." Her voice was cool.

Crags and craters flashed beneath them. Jens's moon-hopper was hurtling eastwards at sixteen hundred miles an hour, taking the sunny way round to get to Lunaborg. Kitty was glad of that. Hoppers are poorly insulated and she wasn't suited-up against the Fort Night.

"I've been debating with myself how much to tell you. But since you've paid me the compliment of trusting me so far as to accompany me, I'm going to trust you, with a little of my client's business. In normal circumstances that would be highly unprofessional. But Jack Williams is in no condition to instruct me."

"In the course of my research people tell me a lot of things. I make a habit of keeping confidences."

Jens seemed to take that as sufficient reassurance. "Since you won't tell me the name of Jack Williams's daughter-in-law—quite rightly of course—why don't I tell you instead? Tvoul Radouga."

"Yes, that's right."

"What do you know about groubians?"

"I study them. I'm a groubist."

Jens took his eyes off the controls long enough to turn and gape at her. "Are you now? That could really come in useful."

He returned his attention to the driving. After a pause—a longish pause thought Kitty—he said "Then you'll be aware of the term *groubian wedding*?"

Kitty drew in breath sharply. "No," she hissed. *"No!"*

"Yes—*yes*. I'm afraid so."

"Tvoul Radouga! I just cannot believe it. Not *her*…"

"It's true."

She turned sharply in her seat to face him. "How can you be so sure?"

Kitty wondered if he had decided to ignore that question. Like the police, private investigators prefer to mop up information, not let it all ooze out. But he was simply taking his time to reply.

"They went camping in Brazil. In the Amazonian rainforest. In the last 25 hours the Brazilian police have discovered their abandoned tent."

Kitty caught her breath, dreading to hear the words that followed.

"Empty. Except for a little blood… and a quantity of sepia."

"No!"

"Only one of the couple used their return tickets to Voronka via Lipsky: Tvoul Williams. Somehow she slipped past Commissioner Vermat's eagle eyes. Assuming she's on her way back to Mars, she's most likely to be somewhere on the Moon. Doing what both you and Jack Williams are doing: killing time, waiting for the *Oberon* to depart."

Kitty muttered "So he's not going out to Mars to join her for a vacation like he said. He's trying to track her down. Here—on the Moon."

"Exactly."

"And you're assisting him. You're his private dick."

Jens didn't bother to answer. Why else was he meddling in the affairs of a groubian heavyweight?

"Tvoul Radouga is a pretty big fish to land."

"Don't I know it!"

"What's he trying to do? Have her arrested and tried for murder?"

"Why shouldn't he?"

"I don't have any views about that. But he's going to have his hands full, pinning it on *her*, of all people."

"This is Selene, not Mars. It will be easier here."

"Oh yes? What about Vermat?"

"So you've met Commissioner Vermat?"

"Yes. She called me in to see her as soon as I got here. We share a common interest… in groubians."

"Look, I have every respect for the professional integrity of Commissioner Vermat…"

"Oh don't get me wrong—so have I. But Vermat will simply refuse to believe it. She will demand to see cast-iron evidence. Have you got it?"

"It's coming through, in dribs and drabs."

Kitty looked him up and down. "Hmm. There are limits to what *you* can tell *me*."

Again Jens appeared to concentrate on the driving. Of course there were.

After a long pause Kitty said "Groubians ejaculate sepia only in exceptionally heightened states of arousal. Extreme fury… extreme fright… in their death-throes…"

"*Interspex?*"

Kitty thought about it. "I doubt a groubian achieves that level of passion when humping a gaian, otherwise it would never have caught on. They're pretty cold fish you know—no pun intended. In spite of their sex-appeal for gaian men."

"And gaians don't normally emit blood during sex. Not males. Not straight sex." He sighed. "It was the Titan Kiss."

"No!" Kitty banged the armrest with her fist. "I can't believe it! Not Tvoul Radouga! Why, her reputation…"

"…Is in tatters anyway—for marrying a gaian."

"I thought they were pretty free about that on Mars. You can shack up with whoever you like. Just so long as you don't do anything so awful as having *children*…"

"That's exactly what they were planning to do."

"*What?*"

"Conceived by purely natural means—as befits a good Catholic couple. Trouble is, Canon Law wasn't formulated to take into account what's natural for a groubian."

•••••✱●✱••••••

It was a week since Markus had come into possession of the house. He smiled a slow, happy smile. He wouldn't have been so happy to know that his call to Lunaborg the week before had been intercepted—and by whom. Again he picked up the phone and dialled a number never given out to the general public.

"Which world?"

"Selene."

It did annoy him. For compliance with the Treaty of Moscow, inter-world calls were supposed to be operator-connected. But when you made a call it was invariably a synthesised voice you got.

"Number?"

"*Mørkside* 580 63 94 02." The same as he'd made a week ago.

"Calls to Lunaborg are subject to a 2.54 second response delay. Do you want duplex transmission?"

"Yes."

The Moon was nearly 250,000 miles away. Nearly 500,000 miles there and back. Radio waves travel at the speed of light: 186,000 miles per second. It takes the signal almost three seconds to make the round trip. Duplex conversation over the Gaia/Selene link was an art acquired only by practice. "How are you?"—"Fine, and you?" suffers a certain loss of spontaneity when the person you're calling takes three seconds to think about it.

"Please hold whilst you are being connected."

Markus watched the pendulum on the hall clock slice away the seconds. He was just going to put the phone down when Duke's voice came on the line.

"Missed him. Twice. He's in the Galen Clinic—with a guard on his bedside."

"*Shto ti!* What have they done to him?"

"Don't know. But he won't elude me a third time."

The next call was further afield. To "Which world?" he replied "Mars."

"Locale?"

"Nix City."

"Name?"

"Sviatoslav Iliich Krov', TMG."

"Calls to Mars are subject to a 39 minute 34.81 second response delay. Do you want duplex transmission?"

"Course not, you bloody fool."

"Please answer yes or no," said the synthesised voice. "Do you want duplex transmission?"

Markus sighed. "No."

Terrestrials! Performing clowns, the lot of them. Why did they suppose anyone wanted to hang on the phone for nearly half an hour between "How are you?" and "Fine, thanks"?

"Please record your message after the tone."

Markus spoke crisply without a pause. He was well-practised in launching coded messages into the far distance. "Svi—breakfast for two, I think."

Once again he dialled the inter-world operator. "Which world?"

"Titan."

"Name?"

"Tvoul Williams, to await arrival."

"Communication with Titan is currently indirect due to solar occultation. Your call will be relayed via Mars. Duplex transmission is unavailable. Please record your message after the tone."

This time Markus hesitated before dictating.

"Tvoul...? Hallo darling. My congratulations—or should that be condolences? We know what you've been doing. Gaia's pre-empted: we're sitting on your bolt-hole. Come back to Mars to have your babies. We understand these things in Nix City."

By now he was smiling broadly. "And don't imagine you can just stay put...

> The Kraken sleep, perchance to dream;
> On Titan, no one hears you scream."

Still smiling, he put the phone down.

His smile sagged as the front doorbell rang. Who can that be—and at this time of night? One of Jack's friends? The insufferable Frank perhaps, dropping by to see if there's any news of Jack?

If it was one of Jack's friends, though, why weren't they knocking on the back door instead of ringing the bell at the front?

Attaching the safety chain, he opened the door a crack.

"No!"

Slamming the heavy door shut, he hurled his shoulder against it. The door collapsed on him in a shower of glittering sparks. As his glowing ribs crumbled to embers, titanium sandals sang like undine bells on the crazy paving. A shadowy figure, veiled in black lace from top to toe, was speeding down the front path. It dived into an H_2-hybrid in darkness pointing the wrong way.

Lights came on one-by-one behind the neighbours' windows, revealing sooty smoke billowing from the doorway of Jack and Hilda's old home. As they did so the strange car slipped quietly away.

8   The Moon-Dog drags its chains

Gently the nurse opened the door of the dimly lit ward.

"I'm sure it'll do him good to see you, Miss Martin. When he was admitted in a delirious state he was desperate to get a message to you. Strictly he's not allowed visitors, so don't stay too long. He underwent an emergency pneumocardiectomy yesterday and he's presently under heavy sedation. He's been having a few flickers of consciousness, but don't expect too much."

Kitty gasped. "You mean you've taken his heart and lungs out?" The nurse nodded. "So he'll have to remain hooked up to that machine for the rest of his life... unless you can find a donor?"

"We've ordered an SP unit for him. It will be here in a day or so. We manufacture them here in Lunaborg."

Kitty glanced uncertainly at Jens and they both followed the nurse in.

Jack was lying on his back, very still. His eyes were almost closed, but Kitty could see them glisten beneath the eyelids. As they stood beside his bed, a painful smile gradually drew back his cheeks. Then he closed his eyes completely and they got nothing further out of him.

As they stepped out of the Galen Clinic into the concourse, Jens said "Let me run you back to Jordvik."

"Is that where you're going anyway?"

"Well, no: my office is here in Lunaborg..."

He's just whisked me halfway round the Moon, thought Kitty—and now he's offering to go out of his way to run me back!

"No, don't trouble yourself. I'll just take the *Orm*."

"Can I see you again?"

"On the case?"

"Yes of course... but I was thinking..."

"I'm extremely busy at the moment. If I can render any assistance over Jack Williams, I'll gladly make time. I'm sure you won't go just finding excuses..."

She saw the sting of rebuff lash across his face, but it was gone in an instant, to be replaced by his normal expression. Alert. Bleak. Emotionless.

"I'll walk you to the *Orm*. There are still a few things I'd like to ask you. On the case—of course."

She turned to face down the concourse in the direction of the *Orm*
station, watching him do the same. Together they stepped on to the
piste.

"Tell me about Shval Meteor."

Kitty smiled and looked down at her feet.

"I do have a need to know."

She jerked her head up to look him in the eye, still smiling. "You
know what Thumper's mom drilled him to repeat...? 'If you can't say
anything good about somebody—don't say anything at all.'"

"If everyone kept to that rule I'd be out of business."

Kitty's smile vanished in a flick of irritation. "What do you want to
know?"

"Is she any relation of Tvoul's?"

"They're sisters. But that doesn't mean a great deal. The Last
Zygogeny produced several hundred thousand individuals. They are just
two out of fifty-odd."

"No: they are a little closer than that."

"Well, okay—they're twin sisters. Not just the same mother but
sprung from the same zygocyst. I still don't think it makes them that
close."

"Are there any other sisters still alive?"

Kitty pondered. "I don't think so. I'll have to check my Rolodex.
But I guess they're all dead."

"In the Second Olympian War?"

"If I recall. An awful lot of groubians died then."

"Tell me... do you think both Tvoul and Shval nurse a grudge against
gaians?"

"Well..." replied Kitty, "that's the winning question, isn't it?"

She pondered it nonetheless. "Tvoul—I very much doubt.
Everything she's done since the war has been totally above board, and it's
well documented. As Forty-Seventh Goubernator she was instrumental
in instituting *Nedélia Slëz*, the Week of Tears. It's played a major role in
enabling both sides come to terms with what's happened. In many ways
Tvoul's been the leading champion of reconciliation. That's gotta say
something about her feelings towards gaians."

"What about Shval?"

"Well: there's the Meteor Gang... some of her best friends are
gaians, you could say. But I don't think Shval needs any excuse to be the
way she is."

"And what's that?"

"Bad."

* * * * ✱ ● ✱ * * * * *

"I asked to see you," said Vermat, "because your enquiries have been making you conspicuous of late. Exactly whom are you working for?"

Jens shifted in his seat. "That is privileged information, Commissioner."

"So, you're daring me to confront you with every person, Selenean or Terrestrial, you've been in contact with over the last month? To show you the movies?"

Jens sighed. "My client is Mr Jack Williams, a Martian denizen."

Vermat's visor was totally blank. "No," she said, "a Martian denizen he is not. But let's not go into that. Tell me: whom are you *really* working for?"

"There is nobody else, at present."

Vermat sat in silence for a while before replying. "Selene is a small world. Rattling around it, as you have been doing, is apt to cause *reverberations*."

"Mr Williams has grave family problems, which I'm not at liberty to divulge. Our relationship is entirely professional, but I feel he has had a raw deal. I'm determined to see he gets the redress he deserves."

Vermat inclined her helmet slightly, tapping her thumbs together. "If that is the case, Mr Andersen, then how are you receiving instructions from your client? You know—and I know—that he is lying incommunicado in the Galen Clinic. And has been doing so from the day on which he first contacted you."

"My client briefed me well and gave me *carte blanche* to pursue my investigations in whatever way I saw fit."

"So it appears, Mr Andersen, so it appears. But has it occurred to you that you have been duplicating my investigations? Into matters of far deeper import than your client's narrow family problems?"

Here it comes, thought Jens. I've been treading on her toes again.

"My brief is a limited one," he replied carefully. "And I don't enjoy access to your superb resources."

"So your brief is a limited one, is it? Then let us widen it a little. It matters less to me that you're wasting your efforts pursuing questions to which I already have the answers, than that you've not been taking the care that I have to avoid alerting your target."

"Commissioner Vermat, I try to take normal reasonable care in my investigations. But I'm always open to suggestions as to how I can do better."

"Normal reasonable care isn't good enough in the present case," snapped Vermat. "Do you imagine that you can go around asking questions about someone of the calibre of Shval Meteor without her presently becoming aware of it?"

Jens swallowed. "I knew that Shval Meteor was here on the Moon…"

"Not only her—the whole triada. They've made no secret of it. They've taken out Selenean denizenship, would you believe."

"If Shval has been making me her business, then I'm puzzled why. And I am also puzzled how you come to know of it. My case has nothing to do with her, so far as I'm aware."

"Oh, but it has, Mr Andersen, it has. It's not so much that *she's* been making *you* her business as the other way around. Like as not, she has made the not-implausible assumption that if someone like *you* is prying into her affairs, then *I'm* simply bound to be. Anyway something has panicked her and she's made herself scarce."

Vermat leaned back in her chair. "I freely admit it to you: right at this moment I have no idea where she is."

"If I hear of anything I'll let you know."

"Thank you. You anticipate me."

"I do believe in maintaining good relations with Selstyrke."

There was no way of telling whether Vermat was smiling behind her opaque visor, but Jens got the distinct impression she was. Not a pleasant smile.

"So let me do something for you in return. If I were to say to you: Markus Efimovitch Potapenko…?"

"…*The Master's Genes.*"

"Good, Mr Andersen. That's good. So you concern yourself with off-world affairs?"

"All the time, Commissioner."

"Out-system as well as in-system?"

"I can't avoid it, where the former impinges on the latter."

Vermat said "impinges" and made a dismissive noise. "Well, what's your impression of Markus and his congregation?"

"An odious little group. But so far as I know it stays within the law."

"Oh yes—it stays within the law. Olympian law, we are talking about. The law is putty in its hands. It wields it as a weapon. Though no doubt you are aware of all that."

Jens nodded slowly.

"And what is your attitude towards Markus himself?"

"I believe he headed up the organisation until recently. Whenever I think of one, I think of the other. My client feels some gratitude towards him for buying his house—but I wouldn't trust Markus further than I could throw him."

"Or *blast* him?"

Jens's eyebrows went up. "I didn't say that."

To his surprise, Vermat's visor went completely transparent. He knew her appallingly disfigured face, so it wasn't such a shock to him as it would have been to most people. She was grinning broadly, as far as her features allowed. "But you wouldn't be unduly distressed to learn that he's dead?"

Jens made a sharp movement. "When did this happen?"

"The evening of Tuesday 25 June, UT, according to the police on Gaia. Somebody paid him a late-night call. And when he tried to slam the door on them—they let rip with a triton pistol. Which, as you can imagine, tore out the whole interior of the house."

"A triton pistol! They are banned on the inner planets."

"Quite right. Nothing but trouble. I'm getting asked some very hard questions. Why did we let a banned weapon through our security systems?" She shook her head in frustration. "I have enough on my hands to relish being diverted by that sort of thing."

"Have you any idea who did it?"

"If you mean: do I *know*?—the answer is no. But there are some interesting leads. Have you had a chance to talk to Gabrielle Starr?"

"No... who is she? And why would I want to talk to her?"

"She is a trained nurse—and a courier for 'Destination Lunaborg', the travel subsidiary of the Galen Clinic. For obvious reasons they make a point of recruiting nurses for the job. And she is extremely pretty."

"I'm too busy to go chasing pretty faces..."

"Oh I don't know..." Vermat smiled maliciously. "If you can find time for Kitty Martin, why can't you find time for her?"

She saw Jens bridle and decided maybe he deserved an explanation—just this once. "When Jack Williams arrived on the spaceplane from Teesside, Gabrielle Starr was his escort. She will have some interesting things to say about Jack. Which of course he would be perfectly willing to tell you himself, were he able to speak. Which he isn't—and won't be for a long while."

Jens's face relaxed. "Where can I find her? She's not Selenean, is she?"

"No. But she speaks good Selensk. She'll be back at Lipsky on torsdag 12 here, which is Monday 1 July, UT, escorting a first-class passenger from Teesside. Another Martian, travelling in style, or so they say. I recommend you meet Miss Starr off the spaceplane."

"Thank you for the information, Commissioner."

Jens supposed the interview was at an end. But Vermat had something more to say. "I am impressed with your knowledge of *The Master's Genes*—or TMG, as I think it's generally known?"

Jens nodded. Vermat continued "So you might even know the name of their resident agent in Lunaborg?"

"A man called Duke Treikle."

"We found him dead eight hours ago. We suspect Shval Meteor's *triada*. It was their *modus operandi*. Shval will have the perfect alibi—as usual. *When* I eventually locate her."

Jens whistled. "TMG has been having a bit of a run-in lately."

"Hasn't it just. And here's something else you ought to know. Treikle was looking for Jack Williams with a gun in his pocket. On two earlier occasions he only narrowly missed him. Once when Mr Williams precipitately discharged himself from the Galen Clinic—and once again when he was equally precipitately readmitted."

Jens was shocked. "It didn't occur to me that my client was in personal danger. That is, apart from his poor state of health."

"We don't know if Treikle meant him harm. He may simply have been trying to make contact with him. We don't know if the gun wasn't for Treikle's own protection—amply vindicated in the light of events. But we don't know what precipitated your client's collapse either. And he won't be able to tell us for a while. Mr Sullivan, his surgeon, says it was aggravated acute emphysema—he sees no evidence of foul play. But I for my part would like to be sure of the exact semantics of 'aggravated'. So, as a precaution, I've put an armed guard on his bedside."

Jens raised his eyebrows. "Isn't that rather extreme?"

"Not if you know what I do."

Jens was under no illusion that Vermat was going to tell him any more than she wanted him to know. So he was surprised at what she said next.

"There are at least three distinct parties with a consuming interest in Jack Williams. All of them are concerned to stop him falling into the hands of the others—in fact you could say that it is their *overriding* concern. Mr Williams's present incapacity suits them all—to an astonishing degree."

"I see."

It was hard for Jens to say precisely what he saw. The need for an armed guard certainly. Vermat had yet more to say.

"Duke Treikle was acting under orders from Markus Potapenko. We intercepted Markus's inter-world call to Treikle the night that Jack Williams walked away from his house in Esh Winning. Unfortunately for Markus, so did someone else."

"Shval Meteor? There can't be many people capable of that."

"Three, by my reckoning." Vermat held up fingers one-by-one, "Shval Meteor... myself, of course—and Tvoul Radouga."

"*Tvoul?* A massively gifted person, but I never thought of her as an information expert..."

"Tvoul—or whoever *or whatever* it was that married Harry Williams—was in a position to do so with the simplest equipment. A bugging aid purchasable over-the-counter..."

"Commissioner—are you suggesting that Tvoul is still on Gaia? That all this time she has been hiding close by, spying on Markus?"

"Let us not beg the question by prematurely supplying a name to the person *or thing* that shot Markus Potapenko. Sherlock Holmes said 'When the impossible has been eliminated...'"

Jens crumpled. He looked like a man for whom the roof had been torn off his mind, letting galaxies shine in from the beginning of time. "Then what is the impossibility that we have to eliminate?"

Vermat folded her fingers. "It is this. At the present time, Tvoul Radouga is not on the Moon—and she is not on Gaia. And quite possibly she never has been on either."

······✱●✱······

In her hotel room, Kitty was preparing her visuals.

> *Old men reminisce on their campaigns and wars,*
> *But no one remembers the Battle of Mars.*
>
> *Of crucial importance in ruling the sky;*
> *Mankind went to live there, and men went to die...*

There's so little surviving footage of the Second Olympian War, she considered. Not surprising: nobody was proud of it. Except the few valiant defenders of the Nix—and they were dead.

Mostly dead.

They died in their thousands, so we sent thousands more,
To stain Rugged Red ever redder with gore.

Let them sing their vain songs about victories in wars…
There are no tunes of glory from…

How did it go? Opening the desk drawer, she got out her anthology of M2 verse. It contained the full text of the often-misquoted poem by Kostoglotov.

Formidable castle commanding the plain;
The Nix was assaulted again and again.
Through dust and through craters the mars-rovers roamed,
Spilling blood on the soil which bubbled and foamed.

Historically suspect, but it did at least capture the mood of the war.

From their campaigns and wars, old men show their scars…
But no one trades wounds from the Battle of Mars.

The First Olympian War was all about conquest of the planet—the *casus belli* of *interspex* was just an excuse. But the second war broke out when the two species of humanity were supposed to be living in peace together. It wasn't so much a war as a massacre. And this time it was whipped-up gaian disgust at *interspex* that had been the cause.

We pick up the pieces to this very day.
The war's not been fought that blows problems away.
But, with every fresh battle, new issues unfold;
To stand alongside and tower over the old.

She searched the archive for groubian commentary on the poem. Two highly significant critiques: both in spatio-color. She would have to translate.

History is so much a question of what you call things. At least, it is to gaians. But you can't cover up meaning in spatio-color. Whether you called it a war or a massacre, the symbolism was all death and sepia. And tears. A lot of people don't know this: groubians can cry.

While on Earth, loved ones prayed as they gazed out in space:
Oh! Bring the boys home from that terrible place!
But for all that she wept and implored for his life;
Not a soldier came back to the arms of his wife.

Would she have occasion to use the poem in full, or should she just quote snatches in her talk? The essential message to get across was this:

Let us never forget, as we sail for the stars,
That the voyage began with the battle for Mars.

Kitty threw down the headset and got to her feet. A little too briskly because she had to ward off the ceiling. She took the elevator up to the lobby and wandered out into the concourse.

Side-alleys were cut at intervals into the solid basalt. On a previous visit they had caught her attention. Now, with time on her hands, she decided she'd go and explore them.

People didn't use them much. They were relics from the early days of Jordvik. No moving handrail here, not even a levitator to float you up like a bubble in a glass of soda. Just steps. Absurdly huge steps, almost her height. Gravity on the Moon is one-sixth that on Earth, so when you jump down a step it's like jumping down a mere sixth of the height on Earth. It works for jumping up steps too.

What superb exercise these steps were. That's one thing you're apt to miss on the Moon, with buggies and pistes to take you everywhere. Moon-trim: a euphemism for obesity.

Soon she was at the top, looking out onto the surface through the self-darkening glass of a small dome. Overhead the Sun blazed down. Near it, at the zenith, a thin crescent pointed at its heart like a drawn bow: Earth. They were now two circadians away from Transit, which happened every *månad*—every lunar month. Normally the Sun missed the Earth by quite some way. But one month in six the path of the Sun passed through the Earth. Occasionally the Sun itself passed right behind the planet in an eclipse. Seen from Earth it was an eclipse of the Moon, usually partial. But every few decades the eclipse was total.

In two circadians the Sun would just graze the Earth: not an event particularly worth celebrating, though people were going to. But the next time it happened, the following 25 May to be precise, the eclipse of the Sun would be total.

Kitty knew they were planning an enormous celebration to mark the event. On Earth it would be a full-moon and eclipse. But on the Moon, the Earth would cover the Sun completely, with plenty to spare.

But it wouldn't go completely dark. Seen from the Gaiascope, the Earth would become a perfect ring of fire, the combined sunrises and sunsets from all around the planet. It would be bright enough to light up the Moon's cheese-green landscape with a reddish glow.

Sometimes the eclipse dipped the mountains in saffron, sometimes it made the Moon look smeared with blood. It depended how healthy the

Earth's atmosphere was. Volcanoes sullied it and caused the blood. So did forest-fires, sandstorms in the Sahara—and wars.

A flash to the north-west drew her eye. A meteorite had landed near Schröter. She put her hand to the glass of the dome and started counting seconds until she felt the impact coming through the ground like a hammer-tap.

Only seven miles away. That was close.

The Moon swept through space at an average speed of 66,000 miles an hour relative to the solar system. With no atmosphere to speak of, space debris reached the surface intact. A lump of rock a yard across, hanging motionless in space, would hit the ground at 66,000 mi/h, exploding with the energy of one ton of TNT. It was one of the reasons why Jordvik folk didn't venture much on the surface—except for those rugged souls who owned moon-hoppers. The danger was no greater than being struck by lightning on Earth, but the manner of departure was significantly more impressive.

Radiation was a far more present danger on the exposed surface. The X-flare forecast for the next 25 hours had been bad. Kitty knew she shouldn't stay long in this tiny dome. It was nowhere near as well-shielded as Jordvik in general. Swinging her arms like windmills she descended the steps in great voluptuous jumps. She felt she was a little girl again.

At the bottom of the steps her foot turned under her. Laughing helplessly she tumbled head-over-heels, coming to rest in the arms of a passer-by.

"Oh, Jens, er… hi!"

"Kitty! How nice to bump into you like this."

He tried to brush her down, but she gently pushed his hand away. She was much more taken up with what was going on around them. A crowd had gathered, lining the sides of the concourse. She asked Jens what it was all about.

"There's a parade coming along in a minute. Didn't you see the announcement on TV?"

Kitty never watched Selenean TV. It was the worst mind-rot imaginable. Even by US standards.

"No," she replied, "I've been too busy. What's the occasion?"

"*Oberon*," said Jens, peering down the concourse in anticipation.

"*Oberon* has been orbiting the Moon since the end of April, UT."

"Yes, but today's the first day they're letting people aboard. They always mount a parade to announce it."

"But it doesn't leave till next July."

"No," said Jens, "but people like to take a break. A cruise round the Moon during the Fort Night—just the thing to shift the Lunar Blues. And Terrestrials can't wait to get up there because it's Earth gravity on board. At least it is in the *Zemgrav* pod."

He stopped and smiled suddenly. "Why don't you give it a try? I'll come with you…"

"I'm booked for the journey to Mars. Once aboard, they won't let me back down to Selene again—you know that." She turned and treated Jens to a frown. "And then who'll visit Jack in the Galen Clinic?"

It struck her then that he was just as worried about Jack as she was. Jens irritated her. But they did share a mutual concern over the fate of the lonely Englishman. She resolved to be nicer to the detective.

They had been ambling along in gentle hops, nudged by the crowd which flowed at its ease out of Avenue Five and into Moon-Dog Square. A minute's stroll up the Avenue, the Square was a popular rendezvous for couples and parties going to the Gaiascope.

Situated in the centre of the Square to which it gave its name, *Månehundtorvet*, the *Månehund* or Moon-Dog was mega-bizarre, even by Selenean standards. Public seating surrounded a smooth silica dome which housed the prize-winning sculpture: a nightmare in scorched bronze, an eyeless smeary churning mass draped in chains with oblong-links, its jaws stretched skywards in an endless howl.

"What *is* that god-awful thing?" Kitty couldn't take her eyes off it. "It's enough to give you bad dreams."

"That is the *Fenris*," said Jens, "the son of Loki the Trickster, chained down by the gods. When the Fenris snaps its chains, on that day the world will end."

"Oh gawd—so that's what it's meant to be." She knew her Edda, so she'd heard about *Ragnarok*: the day the gods themselves are fated to perish. "Why do they have it here?"

"For the same reason they used to have a skull in the centre of the table at feasts. Even though there's laughter and merriment all around, we're meant to bear in mind that frightful forces are being held in check, just to give us the peace to enjoy ourselves."

Kitty winced but made no reply.

The parade came down the Avenue and debouched into the Square. Tumblers led the way, bounding and gambolling in impossible leaps and rolls, as a kid might fling his toys about. Streamers floated like seaweed, wafting in the air with the coloured smoke, through which laser-beams stabbed elaborate patterns. A marching band played a rousing Sousa number on trombones and tubas, two beats to the step.

"What a pity Jack can't see this," she murmured, more to herself than to Jens. "He'd enjoy it."

"Would he?" Jens sounded moody.

No—perhaps he wouldn't. Maybe his wound went too deep for that. For she knew now that having his heart and lungs out was nothing compared to the real hurt Jack had suffered.

9 The Black Widow speaks

Three thousand miles away from Jordvik, as the hopper flies, Lunaborg glittered in the darkness of the Fort Night.

Lunaborg: biggest, ugliest city in System Sol. Hidden away on the far side of the Moon, permanently out of sight of people on Earth, it was big not so much in population as in extent. Lunaborg was a port for the new age—a spaceport. Its passenger facility, *Lipsky Rumhavn*, or simply Rumhavnen as it was called in both Selensk and English, dwarfed even Voronka Cosmodrome on Mars.

But Lunaborg didn't just provide a haven for the biggest vessels ever built: it built them. Compared to a Terrestrial shipyard, the scale of things was enormous. There were cranes here which could hoist a loaded oil tanker, albeit in the pygmy gravity of the Moon. Great lathes that could rotate a body the size of a mighty space-liner, building it up layer-by-layer with sprayed-on water plus reinforcing rayon fibres to make *Pykrete*: the most resilient, versatile and abundant material in the universe for building large space structures.

This was where the giant space platforms had been built—and even bigger ones were under construction. This was the home port of *Oberon*, currently drifting overhead once every 109 minutes, and of its sister vessel, *Titania*. It was also the home port of *Prometheus II*, the thermonuclear ferry not long launched to ply the infamous Titan run. All of them were synthetic comets: their shells being over 99% water-ice.

Prometheus II was the prototype for a proposed fleet of eight ferries to replace the *Oberon*, cutting the trip to Mars from six-to-nine months to as many days. Travellers would be able to depart in any year, at any time of year, not being subject to *Oberon's* constraint to set sail only when Mars and Earth approached conjunction in a two-year cycle. The proposed ferries would draw Beautiful Blue and Rugged Red into a far closer embrace than hitherto—for good or ill. For how long then could Gaia go on ignoring the other settled worlds: acting as if they didn't exist?

But *Oberon*, obsolescent though it was, for sheer size and opulence would ever be the jewel in Lunaborg's crown. Its memory would long endure—along with that of the ill-fated *Titania*.

As he parked his hopper and secured it, Jens meditated on the topic. Funny how everything with "Titan" in its name seemed to attract bad luck.

The piste which carried him to the spaceport was scarlet. Not a restful colour, he mused. It wasn't supposed to be restful. It was supposed to be full of aggressive energy: what Lunaborg was all about.

He went straight to the arrival gate. He hadn't left himself much time. He knew he could rely on the spaceplane being punctual. Sure enough, there was the crimson uniform of a "Destination Lunaborg" courier, coming his way.

Jens got to his feet. God—she *was* pretty!

And then his eyes widened and his heart started pounding. Not so much on Gabrielle's account, but at the passenger she was escorting.

At first he took her for a Muslim woman in purdah. A svelte, sinuous figure, completely shrouded in black lace, presenting the stock image of a widow in mourning. Completely shrouded, that is, except for her feet, which sported a striking pair of iridescent sandals. Scorched titanium, as Jens recognised.

Beneath the paper-thin straps of the sandals, the black widow's bare ankles flickered blue and green as she stood on the piste coming towards him. The reflection of lights at floor-level? No: the lights were dim yellow. She was a groubian!

Ignoring her passenger, Jens bowed politely to the courier and presented his card. *"Goddag! Frøken Starr, synes jeg?"*

Gabrielle halted in surprise. *"Ja, det er det."* As an inter-world courier she was not at all fazed by being addressed in Selensk. But she had never been accosted while actually escorting a passenger.

"Mit navn er Jens Andersen. Jeg er sikkerhedsofficer." Security officer sounded better than private dick.

"Arbejde du for Rumhavnen—eller Selstyrke?" Gabrielle certainly had her head screwed on tight.

"Neither Rumhavnen nor Selstyrke." Jens switched to English. It wouldn't do to persist in cutting-out the passenger by talking Selensk—and quite possibly it wasn't working anyway. Groubians generally spoke only one gaian language, M1. But some, like Shval, were polyglots. "I work for Mr Jack Williams, a passenger of yours on your last trip. When you have time to spare, I'd like a chat with you, please."

This flustered Gabrielle. Glancing nervously at her passenger she said "When? Now?" The black widow straightaway inclined her head, as if she were perfectly agreeable to that.

This wasn't at all to Jens's liking. He'd hoped to make arrangements to talk to Gabrielle in private. Now he wondered how he could possibly convey that hint without appearing rude to her passenger. He quickly decided he couldn't. He'd have to make his story up as he went along.

Addressing the woman in black, he said "I really am sorry—I hadn't meant to interrupt your journey like this. I'd be perfectly happy to arrange a later time with the young lady and allow you to proceed to wherever you're going..."

"Please, Mr Andersen," replied the black widow, "Feel free. I have time on my hands."

Jens shrugged in embarrassment. "Well... won't you two ladies be my guests?"

• • • • • ✶ ● ✶ • • • • •

They sat in the nearest bar—there was a liberal sprinkling of bars in all the public places in Lipsky Rumhavn—and Jens ordered drinks, which the waitress brought with a perfunctory *"Værsgo."*

"Tell me, how is Mr Williams doing?" said Gabrielle with concern in her voice.

"Not at all well, I'm afraid. Since his arrival on the Moon he has been taken ill and rushed to hospital."

"I know," said Gabrielle. "It was me that got him admitted."

Jens hesitated. Gabrielle could only know about the first occasion. "This was actually the second time it happened. He discharged himself, you know—and then had to be readmitted in a hurry."

Gabrielle put her hand to her mouth. "Oh—how dreadful! His condition was frail enough when he arrived."

"It's even frailer now. His lungs collapsed and haemorrhaged. But happily the Galen has matters in hand. They are going to fit him with an SP unit."

"That's a bit drastic."

"I'm sure you know more about these things than I do," said Jens with a dry laugh, recalling that Gabrielle was a trained nurse. "But the specialist, a certain Mr Sullivan, recommended it."

Gabrielle frowned. "I'm surprised at Mr Sullivan," she said. "He isn't a great fan of SP units. Things must have come to a pretty pass."

Jens nodded with a strained smile. "But I think it's all going to turn out for the best." Without meaning to, he glanced at the black widow, who had been sitting there in silence. She took it as an invitation to join-in the conversation.

"It will turn out for the best—if Mr Williams is going on to Mars. It won't if he plans to return to Gaia. On Gaia, being reliant on superox is nothing but an encumbrance. And it's such a pity… the only planet with a breathable atmosphere."

Jens hesitated before speaking. He didn't like giving gratuitous information to strangers. Moreover he got the impression that this woman was subtly prompting him to reveal whether or not Jack Williams was travelling on to Mars. But how could she, a groubian, possibly be acquainted with Jack: a little-travelled man from a forgotten corner of England?

"My client is in fact on his way to Mars," he said. On reflection it was something the stranger would be able to find out anyway, with very little effort.

"And is he planning to stay there?"

"Yes," said Jens. He felt it was safe enough to air Jack's cover story. "He has a son out there. He is going out to live with him and his newlywed wife."

Gabrielle flapped her hand momentarily in front of her mouth. "Oh I'm sorry, I should have introduced you both. Mr Andersen, er—this is Miss Tvoul Radouga."

Jens felt something rather like an electric shock go through him. Had he managed to keep an impassive face?—he doubted it. Could groubians read gaian faces? With luck, no.

He decided to play it cool. "Not *the* Tvoul Radouga?"

"I try to travel incognito."

"So it isn't really you? You're not really here?"

"You've got the general idea, Mr Andersen."

That was it. Vermat, mistress of the most sophisticated surveillance technology in the known universe, had opined that Tvoul was neither on Gaia nor Selene. Of course not—she had been on the spaceplane.

Jens re-crossed his legs. "Forgive my curiosity, but why the veil? Are you in *mourning*, by any chance?"

"We groubians always travel inter-world like this, don't you know? You feel safer, as a woman, wearing a veil. All those masculine eyes upon you…"

Jens laughed nervously. "I thought it was only during *Nedélia Slëz* that groubians went about veiled. But to tell the honest truth I've hardly ever seen a groubian on the Moon. They rarely leave Mars, do they?"

"They rarely leave Mars *conspicuously*."

······ ✳ ● ✳ ······

"It was Tvoul Radouga, I tell you!"

"Let me counsel you against an over-ready acceptance of the apparent," replied Vermat. "Did you see her face?"

"Well, no. She was wearing an all-over black veil. But surely Gabrielle…"

Vermat interrupted him. "Come straight to SHQ and ask for me. I have something interesting to show you."

Jens knew as well as she did that wristlink was not secure—particularly with the Meteor Gang on the loose. He climbed into his hopper and made the short trip to Selstyrke headquarters in downtown Lunaborg. Presently he was sitting with Vermat in her office. Unlike the bare interview room where they'd conversed before, the whole of one wall was taken up with what resembled a picture window with the curtains drawn.

"Gabrielle Starr's mystery passenger gave me the slip in Godunov."

"No doubt. Groubians are an order of creature enjoying a billion years of evolutionary experience in evading predators. And this was no ordinary groubian."

Jens heartily agreed.

"Well—she didn't give me the slip. Thanks to my superb resources, as you've had occasion to call them, I was able to follow her via the security cameras."

Intensive deployment of security cameras in Godunov Condominium was something the freedom-loving Seleneans were forever complaining about in *Rådhuset*, the governing assembly. Every time the matter came up Vermat would justify her policy to the minister by alluding to the mischief that Godunov residents were capable of.

She shrugged. "So you'll be pleased to know that at last I've relocated Shval Meteor."

Jens gasped. "That wasn't *Shval*… was it?"

"Yes—and no." Vermat lightened her visor, letting Jens see her smile. "Oh, by the way: thank you for being my catspaw at Rumhavnen. There was nobody else I could trust to send at such short notice."

"I'm flattered at your confidence in me." Jens was taken aback by Vermat's admission. Did she mean she was surrounded by untrustworthy colleagues? Or was it the nature of the matter in hand?

Seeing Jens's reaction, Vermat's smile broadened. "It was hardly an appointment I could have kept in person now, was it?"

"Where did the Black Widow go after I lost track of her?"

Vermat rose to her feet and drew back the curtains from the picture window. "I'll show you." Four distinct images appeared on the screen, tiled four-square. "Here's your quarry—and here are you."

Jens watched intently, then gave a long sigh. "So *that's* how she did it. Okay, then what happened?"

"Let's omit the sequence of you wending your weary way back to your hopper," (one of the images faded to grey) "and focus on your quarry."

"Well," said Jens, after watching in silence, "she certainly knew where she was going."

"Of course. It's where she came from. Or, following the Martian idiom, where *it* came from."

The black widow had reached the front door of an altogether unexceptional apartment: one of several thousand in Godunov Condominium with little of distinction about it. In the greyed-out quadrant an image appeared of the scene behind the door. Vermat pressed a button on her desk enlarging it to fill the screen. Three people were sitting in full view of the hidden camera, watching the door.

"The Meteor Gang!" exclaimed Jens.

"Ten-out-of-ten. But I wonder if you'd have recognised Shval without her triada? *I* can recognise her as my own daughter. But lacking acquaintance with her spatio-color signature, can you?"

"Don't let me pretend I can tell groubians apart. The events of the day have convinced me of that—if I needed convincing."

"Yet back in Godunov you were so certain it was Tvoul you'd been trailing."

"Gabrielle Starr said it was."

"Gabrielle Starr wouldn't have known her passenger from Eve—supposing Eve to have been a groubian. She would have had to go by the passenger list like everyone else. So take my word for it: that is Shval. As for the other two—why don't you tell me."

In marked contrast to the groubian figure, the people to whom Vermat was alluding were unmistakable. They certainly were a remarkable pair. One was a heavily-built borderer who must have been all of seven foot tall. You could imagine his reiver ancestors riding out of the mist in steel bonnets, demolishing anyone and anything in their path. He lounged on the sofa next to Shval, his hand trailing idly over her tight-fitting suit of green velvet.

A little to the right of them, in a mobility trolley equipped like a battle tank, sat the ugliest individual Jens had ever seen. Beneath two veiny eyeballs resembling fertilised eggs, rolls of fat descended past a mouth like a gash in his face. A wax garden gnome melting in the sun might have described him, were garden gnomes never so hideous.

"The big brute on the left is Hamish McDougall," said Jens, "and the wight in the trolley is Peter Zwillinge."

"Have you ever met them?"

"No—but I've seen pictures of the Gang."

"Now watch what happens."

Still seated, Shval was seen to operate a remote control to unlock the door. The black widow made her entry as if walking in a funeral cortège. Shval, rising to her feet, extended her arms with every appearance of meaning to embrace the newcomer. But the man in the trolley urgently waved his hands, possibly crying out too—although there was no soundtrack to the camera footage. Instantly Shval dropped to the floor, the big Scotsman leaping to his feet. Cautiously he approached the black widow, who seemed to have been petrified where she stood. With a swipe of his burly fist he tore off the lacy veil.

Jens lurched forward in his seat. "It's an ectoplast!"

"So much for your impression that it was Tvoul Radouga." Vermat halted the movie and single-stepped to the next clear frame.

"What's that it's holding?"

"Have you never seen a triton pistol?"

"No, I can't say I have. They're not exactly on sale in the shops."

Vermat let the movie roll. Jens watched as Hamish threw himself on the ectoplast, dashing it to the floor where he pummelled it to pulp. The triton pistol went skidding away and Peter Zwillinge trundled off out of the frame to retrieve it.

An ectoplast is little more than a pixel-covered membrane enclosing a paste of electrically configurable nanoparticles: ectoplasm. Very soon the membrane ruptured, spraying Hamish with grey goo. Once again Vermat froze the scene at a suitable frame.

"What saved Shval from being cremated?"

"Peter Zwillinge. A technical wizard: as accomplished as Shval herself."

"A quick thinker, too."

"I'd guess he'd scanned the ectoplast before it came through the door—and had already spotted the drawn pistol under the veil." Vermat shrugged. "One thermonuclear weapon slipping through my systems I can just about swallow. Two I can't conceive of happening. That's got to be the triton pistol that killed Markus."

"And the ectoplast… is that what went to Gaia and pulled the trigger?"

"Have you an alternative scenario?"

Jens shook his head. "And then it came back to Selene, ready to do the same to Shval. I don't understand."

"What you've just witnessed is Agent Zero in action. It's how Shval contrives to be in two places at once. But I think we've seen its swansong on the Moon."

"Agent Zero, did you call it? So Shval sends it off on errands, having configured it to look like her?"

"Like her—or anyone else she chooses. An ectoplast doesn't bear close scrutiny from somebody who knows the individual concerned. But it'll generally fool other people."

"And on the spaceplane to and from Gaia, Shval had it impersonate Tvoul Radouga?"

"Yes. It fooled Gabrielle Starr—not to mention you. But it didn't fool me."

"Why did Shval choose *Tvoul*, of all people, for Agent Zero to impersonate?"

"For several reasons I can think of. One: an ectoplast needs to assume *some* persona or other, else it's just a bag of slime. Two: to flush the real Tvoul from cover. There's no denying the Markus business has made things hot for her. Three: to mess us all around."

Jens rubbed his eyes. "Well, she's certainly made *me* look a fool."

"Don't be too hard on yourself. Shval is a past-mistress of disinformation. But it was a bold thing to do, even by her standards. And it's turned out to be a bad mistake."

"Why?"

"Why? Because she's lost her precious *doppelgänger*. She cannot resurrect Agent Zero until she goes back to Mars. And even there she won't be able to."

"Why not?"

"Because we'll resurrect it first. I've been in touch with *Komissár* Miro, my opposite number in *Zastavlénie*…"

"What—already?"

"No time to waste."

Zastavlénie, Jens knew, was the Olympian Information-Police, charged with guarding the integrity of the Nix intensor. It took him only a moment to realise it was the obvious way to exploit the situation.

"Even though the entire Meteor Gang is here on Selene, Shval might retain some info-capacity on Mars," said Vermat. "Miro is understandably keen to express Agent Zero in the context of the Nix intensor. Once he's done that, he's going to enlist it as a law-enforcement agent: a *zastavlénnik*. Shval will lose control of Agent Zero once and for all. Her precious creation will be turned around to employ against her."

"Well…" conceded Jens, "It's nice to win the odd trick against the Meteor Gang."

"The odd trick? Miro is convinced this wins the rubber!"

·····★·●·★·····

The smile that Jack gave Kitty showed his obvious pleasure at seeing her again. She kissed his forehead as if they were already intimates. And he let her, as if he knew that too.

"I took the day off. It's the Fourth of July, UT. A big day in the USA. Stuck out here on the Moon, I thought I'd have a celebration of my own."

She sat down on the edge of the bed. There were a couple of chairs provided, but they were occupied by two men sitting either side of the doorway, with tasers in their laps. They didn't speak—and Kitty didn't try to speak to them either, because she could see they were Selstyrke.

"So I bought you a little present." She unwrapped it and placed it in Jack's hands. It was a writing slate, just like the one Jack had used at SHQ the day he met Commissioner Vermat.

His eyes lit up. He motioned to have another kiss. This time their lips met.

It quickly came back to him how to use this sort of slate. Rapidly he wrote something with his eyes and showed it to Kitty. *How did the party go yesterday?*

"Well… it wasn't up to much. Very disappointing from what I'd been led to expect. Perhaps they are saving it all up for the Big One next May."

Jack took back the slate. *Saw it on TV. Earth just grazed the Sun. Nothing to write home about.*

"But you've simply gotta see the Gaiascope," gushed Kitty. "They've got everything there. Ballroom, pool, water park, three or four pocket review theatres, endless restaurants—that's vital for a Californian… And of course—the Camera itself."

Only seen pictures, Jack wrote. *Must go there. Will you come with me?*

"It's a date!" said Kitty enthusiastically. "Just as soon as you're out of here. Me, I've never seen anything like it outside Vegas. The locals call it a 'tivoli', but I don't know what that means."

Tivoli Gardens, Jack wrote. *Pleasure park in Copenhagen.* He'd passed his time absorbing all things Selenean, including its parent Danish culture.

Kitty sat and watched him, eyes sparkling, as he played with the device, trying to make it do different things. Still smiling, she chanced to catch the eye of one of the men with the stun-guns. But the man just stared through her.

Jack showed her the slate, surprise in his face. Kitty grew excited like a child. "Well, just look what it's doing! That's spatio-color. How did you make it do that?"

Jack raised his eyebrows in bewilderment. The screen was pulsating in coloured patterns as he held the slate. But it wasn't under his conscious control.

"It's responding to what you're thinking!" said Kitty. She grabbed the slate from him and stared at it for a few moments, checking her assertion. Then she pushed it back into his hands.

"Go on. Think of something."

Jack looked down at the slate. She put her chin on his shoulder to see what he was able to see. *Can you really speak groubian?* he wrote.

"No, silly. You have to be born groubian to speak a groubian language. But I know a little spatio-color. You have to—to make any sense of the Book of Titan. The patch of yellow there means pure pleasure. The mottled purple border is pain—displaced for now, thank God. And that rose-pink blotch…" her voice faked disapproval, "stands for sexuality."

She nuzzled the point of her chin into his shoulder. "Go on—try some more."

Jack turned his face to hers, eyes questioning. Their cheeks brushed. "Think of something. Anything. Moon-and-stars…"

Jack returned his gaze to the slate. Kitty whooped in delight.

"That's cool. You're outside counting the stars… in a tiny back-yard… and you're standing up close to *somebody wonderful!*" She flung her arms round his neck and gave him a smacking kiss.

Jack stared at the slate in horror, as if the top had been taken off his head. "That's what it said," chirped Kitty. "You can't tell lies in spatio-color."

10   Footsteps in a lunar valley

"So that's it! You're finished at the Galen Clinic?"

Jack was striding out, covering the ground in giant paces. Kitty had trouble keeping up with him.

"Yes. End of the 'Day Light'—end of the billing period." He could talk now, too. "It seemed a good occasion to kiss them goodbye. But really I could have gone at any time during this last month."

"It sounds like they were in no hurry to kick you out."

"Heavens no. I was making buckets for them. It's not often they have a 'Martian' to play with."

They ascended to the hopper pad. Jack unlocked a shiny brand-new hopper.

"Have you hired this?"

"No. Bought it. It was easier than clarting around signing here, there and everywhere."

"Wow!" said Kitty, scrambling in beside Jack. "The things you can do on a booner card."

The hopper leapt aloft. Kitty clutched at the side-straps. "Do you know how to fly these things?"

"There was a simulation on the slate you gave me. Anyway the man said they fly themselves."

"Well they do… up to a point. Where are we going?"

"Crater Flammarion. The physio said there was some good climbing there. And there's a bar in the lookout point."

"I guess that's the main attraction, huh?"

"Well what do you expect us to do? Sit at the top and eat butties?"

Jack brought the nose of the hopper round as it hovered high above the ground.

"How far is Flammarion?" Kitty asked.

"About seventy miles south of here. It takes three minutes."

As the hopper shot over the lunar terrain, Kitty complimented Jack on how well he was talking. "You've really come on a treat with that voice-chip over the past month. And you're actually getting it to sound like your old voice."

"Can you remember that?"

"How can I forget? Feeding you pizza in the hotel bar…"

"It's harder to control than they tell you at first," said Jack. "It still says things I don't mean. The therapist spent a lot of time playing poker with me."

"Is that all they have to do in there? What a swell life."

"No, he said it was important. He said I had to learn to tell lies all over again."

Kitty bent double in her seat with laughter. "Well—just don't go practising on me!"

•••••✷●✷••••

There was a hopper pad outside the crater rim. They left the hopper there and started bounding up the outcrops and crags like children playing on a rocky beach. Jack kept up an incessant monologue. He was showing off in front of Kitty: showing his rejuvenation—his new-found health. Showing that he wasn't too old for her—that she didn't have to treat him like her dad.

"Hey Jack! Stand still a moment and let me catch up."

Jack adopted a casual pose, leaning against a spike of rock. Kitty drew level with him, panting. "And it's no good talking at me the whole time because I won't answer. I can't talk and climb at the same time. *I* have to *breathe*."

"Look, we're nearly at the top. We can have a good long rest there. Just keep going for a short while."

Suddenly the rock face vanished. The rim of the crater ended like a jagged blade of flint. Jack was swept up in a sense of vertigo. He gazed down into the crater, trying to focus his eyes. Nothing on Earth, not even the Hole of Horcum, had prepared him for this sight.

Kitty stood beside him and all she could say was "Wow!" She clutched his arm tightly, though whether to steady herself or keep a tight hold on him he didn't know. "It just feels like I could take a running leap and go floating down like a feather."

"That's six hundred feet to the bottom, if it's an inch," exclaimed Jack. That's as bad as jumping off a hundred foot cliff on Earth. You wouldn't live."

Kitty drew him round to gaze into his eyes. "You're getting pretty hot on your technical detail these days."

"It's all I've had to do this last ten months. Lie on me back and think—think—think. Now look over there, in the middle of the crater, and tell me what you think that is. It looks too artificial to be a volcano."

"It sure does."

Kitty shielded her eyes. The Sun was low in the sky, hovering over the crater rim. Another hour and it would be sunset—the start of the Fort Night. It would get seriously cold.

But it wasn't just the Sun that was shining straight ahead of them. There in the middle of the crater was a vast hemispherical cloud, lit-up from below by a blood-orange glare. Vapour billowed up, glowing white in the sunlight.

"That's an Adin beam."

"Yer—what?"

"Adin beam. It's the main source of water on the Moon. You're looking at a waterworks."

"Geddaway!" Jack turned to face her. "Where's the reservoir—the filter-tanks?"

"There aren't any. That's a pure beam of protons coming down there. When they hit the bottom of the Adin crucible they turn into hydrogen to make water."

"So where are the protons coming from?" Jack gazed searchingly into the sky. "I can't see a great big flashlight up there beaming down."

"Oh you can see the Adin satellites with the naked eye, if you know what you're looking for," said Kitty. "Way out there at the L4/L5 Lagrange points there are huge Fresnel lenses hundreds of miles across which focus the solar wind."

"What do you mean, 'focus the solar wind'? It's incredibly tenuous. We're talking about three or four protons per cubic centimetre of space. I remember that from my schooldays."

"Yeah, but they zip along. So in one second a lot fly past."

"The lenses are not made of glass, surely?"

"No. Very thin superconducting wire in a double spiral. It sets up a magnetic field that focuses the protons inwards and deflects the electrons the other way."

"So there's these great big cobweb things up there, focusing hot-spots on the surface?"

"Not quite. The focus of the Fresnel lens is moved by varying the currents in the wires, but it's not precise enough for the surface. Besides, the geometry's all wrong. Instead there's a number of so-called Adin satellites in orbit. As each comes past it grabs a primary beam, collimates it and focusses it down here. Don't worry, it's fail-safe. If the primary beam misses the collimator it defocuses again before it reaches the surface so it can't do any damage."

"That's still a pretty energetic beam over there, flower."

"Sure. Enough energy to melt moon rock and release oxygen from the silicates. By-products: magnesium, silicon and aluminum in the metallic state. When the protons have given up their energy and come to rest they marry the local electrons to make hydrogen—which combines with the oxygen they've just released to give us H_2O. Water. That's Adin's Process."

Jack was impressed—and not a little humbled. "You went to a better school than I did," he muttered. "Tell me, hinny—that beam isn't likely to drift off-target and toast us, is it? Or do you reckon it would steam us?"

"It would blast us to atoms," replied Kitty. Seeing the expression on his face, she nudged his ribs. "Don't get scared now. Each collimator has the crucible co-ordinates firmly lodged in its memory. They sure take care nothing goes wrong. Why—a beam that powerful could burn the heart out of Jordvik."

•••••✶●✶•••••

When they reached the lookout-point, they were the only two people there. The bar was shuttered. It wasn't clear when it had last been opened. But the heating was on, so they took the opportunity to slip out of their pressure suits in the dry air. Holding hands, they watched the Sun sink down below the far rim. It took 20 minutes from the first notch in the Sun's disc to the disappearance of the last blip of sunlight among the crags.

Jack was surprised at how soon the afterglow faded. It died away visibly. Living in the Galen, or below ground in Jordvik, he hadn't yet watched a sunset. Soon the only light was from the Adin crucible, which lit-up the bowl of the crater like an enormous firework being let off in the middle of an amphitheatre. Somewhere there'd be a switch for the room light, but they didn't bother to go looking for it.

There were padded seats below the chamber's great curved window. So, turning their backs on the view outside, they sat and watched the orangey-red light flickering on the inside walls. Without thinking about it, Jack put his arm around Kitty's bare shoulder. Kitty put her head on his chest.

"You're fizzing."

"I've got half a gallon of superox in there."

"Can't hear a heartbeat. Didn't they give you a heart?"

"Don't need one now. The SP unit does the job."

"Don't you miss it—not having a heart?"

"No. If you don't have a heart you can't have a heart-attack. You can't get it broken. A heart is just so much baggage in life."

He had said it so matter-of-factly. Kitty raised her head to look into his eyes. "Jack," she said softly, "you don't really mean that?"

••••• ★ ● ★ •••••

Once again Jens Andersen offered to come to the Jordvik Artemis, where Jack had re-installed himself. But Jack said he'd come over to his office in Lunaborg. He had a hopper too now and was keen to try it out on a serious journey. There was the added appeal that the Sun had risen over Lunaborg, having just gone down at Jordvik. Like the Seleneans, Jack had acquired a hearty distaste for the Fort Night.

"Fly west—catch up with the Sun and come round the sunlit way." Jens had said. "Be careful not to fly far in the Fort Night. You'll use up power heating the cabin and you may go short of fuel."

Clearly there was a knack to running one of these things, thought Jack, as sunlight began to singe the crags. It all looked so easy from the vendor's blurb.

Jens had suggested joining the next Selstyrke convoy, which was already forming up in the sky over Jordvik. But it was no fun going at their pace. What was the point of owning a hopper if you always trailed along with other timid souls in a kindergarten crocodile? You might as well take the *Orm*.

An hour or so into the journey, the map alerted him that there was a hopper on a parallel course to his. For a moment he couldn't think why—the hopper was hardly on a collision course. Then he remembered the warning about *ilbuder*—the so-called "messenger boys" of the lunar wilderness. His course was unique to him, randomised by the autonavigator. If someone was flying in parallel then they must be tracking him.

"Who are you?" commanded Jack. The hopper took the message, coded it and sent it to the suspicious craft. No reply.

He dropped down into a sinus. Never enter a crater, warned the safety drill—you'll be trapped. A sinus twists and turns, however, and a pursuer has no unbroken view of you. Sure enough, the other hopper changed direction, though not provocatively towards him. Then it too dropped out of radar visibility. The navigation map—the latest model, Jack hadn't stinted himself—computed a triplet of predictive "ghosts", which warned Jack that the stranger might have entered the very sinus he was hurtling through, aiming to meet him coming the other way.

What was it planning to do? Something brutal and straightforward, Jack guessed. *Ilbuder* didn't mess around. They simply scavenged hopper wreckage for anything saleable.

Jack broke the covers off the buttons on his left and right joysticks, which armed his emergency moonrakers. "Are you sure you want to do this?" flashed the map. Gritting his teeth in fury, he confirmed his intention. What a silly bloody thing to ask! Was that something you could do by accident?

Actually the warning served a purpose: it was the weaker of two possible responses to Jack's action. The other was "It is illegal to do this"—though it wouldn't have stood in his way.

It wasn't illegal. It was illegal to alter course towards another hopper without mutual identification. His hopper was recording and analysing the encounter and had simply confirmed that Jack would be acting within the law.

An overhang loomed ahead. Jack lurched to a halt and hid, hovering between natural jaws of rock. He had taken his emergency drills seriously. You don't lie in hospital for months on end with an armed guard at your bedside without it beginning to sink in that there may be some point in all this security. A few seconds earlier he had jettisoned a radar repeater, flipping it over the rim of the sinus onto open ground. He could now see without being seen.

The strange hopper sped past. Detecting him, it halted after rounding a bend, undecided what to do next. Then it turned and crept back. *Ilbuder* didn't usually sustain an attack if they missed first go—they simply flew off and waited for another sucker. But this one was either desperate—or exceedingly determined.

Nor as a rule did lawful citizens stick around to slug it out with hostile strangers. But Jack's temper was up. He hadn't come all this way, enduring everything he'd had to, just to be picked-off by some lunar savage like an unwary rabbit. He forsook the cover of the jaws of rock and took up a position round the next bend.

When the *ilbud* reached the point he'd just left, it paused once more. Then it hopped up out of the sinus to get a radar fix on its quarry, dropping back quickly. But not quickly enough: the jettisoned repeater spotted it. Meanwhile Jack's thumbs were already pressing hard on the firing buttons, knuckle whitening. As soon as the moonrakers identified a target they detached themselves, cocooning the hopper in a fluff of smoke. Instantly Jack turned tail and made a dash for it. A brief double-flicker lit up the rubble on the hillside ahead, but he didn't look back.

As Jack approached his journey's end, he was still trembling, though it felt less like terror and more like sated fury. He had never seen Lunaborg at a distance from above-ground, always coming and going by the *Orm*. The sight of it made him wish he hadn't offered to make the journey, quite apart from his deadly encounter in the wastes. He was reminded of Middlesbrough, with its docks and chemical works, but Lunaborg was far, far worse.

Three quarters of it looked abandoned. Long low sheds, many without roofs, lay strewn about like discarded logs in a wilderness of shattered stone. Firms needing factory and office space found it cheaper to throw up something new than re-use existing structures. The Moon's natural assets didn't improve the view either. *Mørkside* was less cratered than *Klarside*, the side visible from Earth. The scenery was far less interesting in consequence, looking like the skin of a badly-cooked crumpet. The only notable crater he could see, just south of the city, was labelled Lipsky on the radar. Maybe that's where they got the name for the spaceport.

Following Jens's directions, he brought the hopper down on one of the public pads—one numbered 223 in big digits clearly visible from a thousand feet up. Before he got out he extracted the journey log—he was determined to show it to Jens. Then he locked the hopper and gave the key to the attendant. It amazed him that this sort of thing wasn't handled by an automat: that hoppers had such things as keys at all. But the prevalence of petty crime in Lunaborg, home to many poor people, made it not only economically feasible but vital to have live attendants.

A rickshaw-buggy took Jack to Jens's unit, in what must once have been an industrial complex. A gigantic derelict linear-motor track, of the sort used for propelling satellites into orbit, towered over a long shed looking like one of hundreds he'd flown over on his way there. Beyond the airlock Jens was waiting to meet him.

"Welcome to Lunaborg," he said, extending both hands, one in front, one behind in Moon style to keep his balance. "Journey okay?"

Jack told him about his adventure. "Let's see the log," said Jens. "You know for every moonraker you fire off, you have to turn the movie over to Moonforce."

"Moonforce should try doing its job. Then all this palaver wouldn't be necessary."

"They can't secure thirteen million square miles of moonscape," Jens replied. "It's not like Gaia, where vehicles keep mainly to roads which can be policed. You should have joined the convoy like I said..."

"Hell to that." Both men grinned.

"Well, it's good to see you're getting out and about. How's the SP unit faring?"

"It's canny. I hardly notice it now. At first it was weird—no breathing, no heartbeat. I felt like the living dead."

Jens smiled. "Well I must say you're looking very much alive and well. How long does a charge of superox last you?"

"That depends how active I am. Ten hours nominally, but I recharge it every eight. Before going to bed, on getting up, in the middle of the circadian. It's quite convenient really. There's a free nose hook-up in every restroom."

"Just like gasoline eh?" Jens laughed. "What happens if you run out?"

"I get an audible warning—and so does everyone else. In the end it puts me into a protective coma. Hasn't happened yet, touch-wood."

"Sounds like you've got on top of your SP unit remarkably quickly, from all the tales I hear about them."

Jens turned and led the way to his office.

"The voice-chip's going to take longer,' Jack said. I'm still conscious of it when I try to talk. And I have to listen carefully, to hear what I've just said."

"They tell me that goes away," said Jens, getting out coffee and cakes. "You're earlier than I expected, so let's waste precious time before we start the briefing." He reached in his desk for a couple of shot glasses and a bottle of *Gammeldansk* in a makeshift attempt at Selenean *hygge*. "Let's take a look at those movies…"

•••••✳●✳•••••

"You've hit the jackpot. There's a bounty payable for him." Jens single-framed once more over the instant when the first moonraker struck. In the final two frames the *ilbud* was clearly to be seen through the hopper canopy. It was such a silly expression on the fellow's face as he gawped into the moonraker's nose-camera that both men sniggered, temporarily heedless of watching a man die.

"I don't need *selkroner*. Have you got a charity box…?"

"Donate the money to Moonforce widows. You'll have Vermat eating out of your hand." Jens made a gesture to mime a crocodile eating his other hand.

He brought up the movie from the second moonraker. In the last three frames the *ilbud's* body was clearly to be seen breaking through the canopy of his hopper. It was beginning to dissolve in a spray of flesh, like a branch of pink hawthorn in blossom.

"That's the first person I've ever killed," muttered Jack. As the voice chip manufactured the words for him, he knew it wouldn't be the last.

"It was him or you."

"It doesn't help that sense of fellow-feeling." Jack turned away. "Have we seen all we need to?"

Jens switched off smartly. "Anyway, I guess it was an accident."

"What do you mean? That I didn't mean to kill the guy?"

"What I meant was: you were just another sucker. I doubt he had a contract to take you out."

"Might he have?"

"Vermat didn't put an armed guard on your bedside for a joke."

Jack drew his shoulders back. "Then I guess it wasn't very clever of me treating myself to a hopper and gallivanting about all over the countryside."

"Oh, I'm all for that. I've got one myself. I can't stand it sitting on the *Orm* for hours."

"Are you really saying that's what I should have done?"

Jens's eyes grew round in boyish reassurance. "No. You're very wise not to go using public transport. You'd be too easy to follow. Keep them guessing what you'll do next—that's what I say."

"Who's 'them'?" Jack picked up on the word with alacrity. "Do you mean Tvoul? Does she know I'm here, looking for her?"

"No, not Tvoul—at least not just Tvoul. She's drawn unwelcome attention to herself throughout the Four Worlds. She's in as much danger as you are. More, probably. She seems to have vanished right off the face of the Moon. I often wonder if she's back on Gaia."

He stretched. "I've got a small army of investigators looking for her there. All on your account, by the way. But you needn't worry—Mars is paying."

"Any leads?"

"Ten damn' months and not a dicky bird. Except some entertaining false trails…"

"Laid by Tvoul?"

"No, laid by Shval Meteor, Tvoul's sister: the black sheep of the family. It's clear she's looking for Tvoul herself—and she's determined to stop us finding her before she does. On the other hand she's not averse to using me as a truffle hound, if she can."

"And Vermat?"

"Is being most helpful. In a resentful sort of way. Frankly I don't know what we'd do without her. Thanks to her, we have the massive resources of Moonforce at our disposal. I'm not up to dealing with someone like Shval all by myself—who is? But sometimes I feel Vermat is moving us about like pieces on a board."

"Playing chess—with a missing piece. The White Queen?"

"Spot-on. Another possibility is that Tvoul may have dodged us all and slipped aboard the *Oberon*. I was going to ask you to authorise me to check it out."

"Consider yourself authorised, bonny lad. Why did you wait to ask?"

"It's not that straightforward. *Oberon* is a world of its own. Two separate worlds, in fact—and they're both enormous. Each has its own population of permanent denizens. Wealthy recluses, fugitives from God-knows-what, or people who just fancy going on a cruise for the rest of their lives. Fancy it myself, sometimes."

"At least we ought to try looking on board."

"Well, here's the problem. *Oberon* doesn't want any trafficking, so right or wrong they think that anyone going to-and-fro must be up to no good. So for me, a Selenean, they allow me on board—once—per round-trip of two years. For you, a non-Selenean travelling to Mars, they let you board any time from now on. But there you have to stay, incommunicado, until departure."

"That's awkward. I can see your point now. I'd better not go just yet or I'll burn my boats. There's a case for you going, though. But not too soon. I need you down here."

"Oh, and another thing. *Oberon* has two pods, called *Marsgrav* and *Zemgrav*. M1 for 'Mars gravity' and 'Earth gravity'. You can choose whichever you like, but once you're there the other pod is out-of-bounds."

"Why do they do that?"

"Containment. Of contagious disease nominally, but really to combat piracy. Anyone wanting to hi-jack the *Oberon* has to capture both pods with separate teams unable to communicate. Such a measure would have saved *Titania*."

"Dammit! What are we going to do? Each of us board a different pod? Then how do we communicate?"

"I've already commissioned a couple of investigators, one in each pod. Both know who Tvoul Radouga is: they've met her. They can get simple messages through to me, courtesy of Vermat. However we won't really know what they've found out until the *Oberon* departs. But Tvoul won't be able to evade them—not if she's going about as herself."

"What if she isn't?"

"Well, it's hard to think what she can disguise herself as. Only another groubian, unless she wants to lead a hermetically sealed life. Eight months of misery, if you ask me. For a start, groubians like lots of sex."

"*Sex...* with each other?"

"Well, don't look at me like that. It's a wild world out there."

"But I mean... *interspex* is bad enough, but *that!*"

"Groubians don't share our standards. It's normal behaviour between sisters. Though the more distantly related they are the more it's frowned upon. It's not as if they have any menfolk of their own. What would *you* do?"

Jack declined to answer that.

"So they'll happily have incestuous lesbian sex," continued Jens, ignoring Jack's embarrassment. "Whether they'll go all the way—to edulation—is a different matter. The institution of *triada* is a defence against it, so even sisters take care to keep it casual. And have someone else around as a chaperone. You can't imagine what the Groubian Alliance gets up to at its regular soirées."

"Is this just prurient hearsay? Or do you know?"

"Sorry, I don't intend this as a titillating diversion. It's germane to the matter in hand. Look—Vermat has a theory that Shval is here precisely to edulate Tvoul. She may already have done so, which would explain why we can't find Tvoul. After all, they *are* sisters."

"Sisters? In the literal sense?"

"Absolutely. They're sprung from the same mother at the Last Zygogeny. Along with forty-nine others—all perished in the war. Tvoul is a war-leader among groubians: a heroine. The sole survivor of the gallant defenders of the Nix. Your friend Kitty Martin told me that—and, as a groubist, she ought to know."

"What of Shval?"

"Was nowhere around when things got hot. Fraternising with the settlers, it is said. The Groubian Alliance has a pretty low opinion of her. She's the only groubian who has never been a member. Although no doubt they'd have slung her out anyway for her subsequent activities. They've publicly branded her a disgrace to humanity."

"You mean 'groubianity'... whatever?"

"No, 'humanity'. Just about the only people who use the word these days are groubians."

Jack rubbed his eyes. "This Shval is a gargoyle. She's incomprehensible."

"Oh no. All too comprehensible, I'm afraid. By Mars standards that is—not earthly ones."

"What's the difference?"

"Let me answer that with a question." Jens poured more coffee before he continued. "What has replaced corporate greed as the prime mover on Mars? By corporate greed I mean the rush for first place, to be the market leader, to monopolise non-renewable resources. It's something quite different. Something not there before."

"The urge to colonise new worlds?" said Jack, thinking back over all the stuff he'd read about Mars when Harry had considered emigrating.

Andersen nodded emphatically. "The stars," he said. "Galactic colonisation needs world co-operation—to a level unprecedented in history. The Roman Empire, Hadrian's Wall, the Great Wall of China: games in the sand by comparison. Among the Four Worlds, Selene happens to lead this particular race, but only in the sense of building the hardware. Vehicles like *Oberon*, *Titania* and *Prometheus*, each the size of a major city—or a small sovereign state at the beginning of the twentieth century. These are the blueprints for what will be sent out to colonise the stars."

"Whole cities in the sky," mused Jack.

"Whole countries. Whole worlds. But notice it's Mars—not Selene or Gaia—that's commissioning this world-building. Gaia is preoccupied with itself. Selene is supplying the hardware, coping with the filth and pocketing the dosh. It's on Mars they really understand what it's all about. You need a world to found a world. Worlds must become living beings. Sexual beings."

Jack scratched his ear. Worlds as sexual beings? What a crazy idea. However would they meet up for a night out?

"By itself, Selene is sterile," continued Jens. "It doesn't have the resources to give birth on its own to new worlds like *Oberon*. For that it needs Mars. On Mars there's no more talk of who is to monopolise resources. But talk of monopolisation has not gone away—far from it. Now it's all about..."

"...Whose children!" cried Jack. "Whose children are going to populate these new worlds? Isn't that it?"

"Precisely. For instance there's an organisation called TMG—The Master's Genes. Your friend Markus was one of its top men. They're dedicated to a vision of the galaxy being colonised by the offspring of one single man."

"Who's that?"

"Oh, they keep *that* a big secret. He's been dead a long time—that's all they'll tell you."

"Crazy!"

"Yes, crazy, to you and me. You'd think there'd be enough worlds to go round. But humanity doesn't think like that. And I mean 'humanity', not just TMG—not just gaians. Here, for once, groubian and gaian aspirations run parallel. And always have done."

Jack grimaced. "But the groubians are out of the race."

The two men gazed at each other silently for several seconds. It was Jens who spoke first.

"No, they're not. Thanks to Tvoul Radouga—Tvoul Williams as she nowadays styles herself—the groubians are back in the race... with a vengeance."

Jack put his elbows on the desk and tugged at his hair.

"Now," said Jens, "you understand why Shval wants to edulate Tvoul. To adopt the offspring that Tvoul is gestating. To give birth to them herself. To become the All-Mother of the fabled Star-Children. What a smack in the eye that would be for the Groubian Alliance. For TMG—and for everyone else on Mars."

Jack goggled. "Adopting Tvoul's offspring: is that really possible?"

"Oh yes. Groubians are simpler creatures than gaians. They're not as cellularly differentiated. It's the secret of their immortality." Jens looked aside, his face was sad. "Two savage wars have been fought over that particular dream. Its very feasibility has been hotly debated. By the whole of humanity—and I mean *humanity*. But Tvoul, by edulating your son, has established it beyond all doubt. Now what can be conceived by edulation can be transmitted by edulation... between Shval and Tvoul, that is."

"Why Shval and Tvoul?"

"Identical twins. Sprung not just from the same mother, but from the same zygocyst. By genotype they're one and the same organism, split over two separate bodies."

Jens got to his feet and paced around in slow gliding hops. "Morally and emotionally however they are two distinct individuals. Shval is Tvoul's very antithesis, her Jungian shadow—her *Mørkside*. But in the

final analysis their goals don't differ one jot. Nor do they differ from the
rest of 'groubianity', as you called them...

> *The true mother it is who suffers the loss of her offspring.*
> *Let it fall to thy lover to deliver the fatal blow.*
> *You may ask: what is the valuta of life itself?*
> *And the answer I give: naught, lest it be found*
> *In children's footsteps in an empty valley."*

"Is that some quotation or other?"
"It is the last verse of the Book of Titan."

11   Revelations in the Week of Tears

Jack picked up the handset of the v-unit and said "Kitty". A sleepy voice answered him. "Do you know what time it is, Jack?"

Jack looked at his wristwatch. "12.52pm on Saturday 10 May. Are you free now?"

"Jack, really! It's about time you went over to *seltid.* It's ten minutes past midnight on søndag 1 taurus. I was in bed asleep when you rang."

"Sorry," said Jack. "I was hoping you'd come with me to the Gaiascope. I haven't seen it yet."

"Why, what's on there?"

"It's the New Moon. Which means the Full Earth. Best time to see it, they say."

Kitty yawned audibly. "I'm sorry Jack," she said, trying to sound a little less irritable, "I'm going to have to let you go on your own. I've been dreadfully busy and I'm trying to catch up on some sleep. *Nedélia Slëz* started yesterday, lørdag 28."

"That's a groubian thing. You don't celebrate it yourself do you?"

"No, but it's the time that the people who are paying me want a whole series of lectures on the groubian resistance. I've been working all day and I'm bog-eyed." She sweetened her voice. "Another time maybe?"

"I'll have to go by meself then," said Jack. "Talk to you later, pet. Night-night." He put down the handset. Women!

······ ✳ ● ✳ ······

One of the things Jack found hard about being a widower was going for a day-out on his own. For most of his life he'd never done that. In fact he was hard put to think of the last time he'd done anything by himself purely for pleasure. In his new wandering way of life he'd have to start learning. "All work and no play makes Jack a dull boy," he told himself.

The Gaiascope was crowded. Obviously Jack wasn't the only one to have heard that the New Moon was the best time to see the Earth. Crowds streamed from the *Orm* station towards the entry booths. Once inside they milled around in the cavernous lobbies which surrounded the Camera, the vast auditorium—stadium more like it—which lay at the heart of the Gaiascope complex. Children scrambled underfoot. Or, evading the snatching hands of their elders, went tumbling head-over-heels into the faces of bystanders. Or they ran up the walls as far as they could manage, to collapse back in a giggling heap—as children are apt to do on the Moon unless kept under strict control.

Dodging a girl of about nine who was whirling her kid brother around her on his reins, Jack took a peek inside the Camera. There was no queue to get in. People were coming and going as they pleased.

But once inside, all was silence. Jack, on tiptoes, thought for a moment he'd strayed into a church service. Wondering faces, their cheeks and eyes shining with reflected blue light, rose in file after file around the central arena. A brilliant azure column shone down from the zenith of the vault. Set in the roof was a colossal lens, beneath which shining particles of ever-present moon dust drifted like plankton.

A handrail surrounded the central recess, over which people were leaning, leaving no space between. Some of those behind, rude youngsters mostly, were putting their hands on the backs of the people by the rails and jumping up to catch a glimpse of what they were missing. If only they'd taken the trouble to file quietly up the gangways between the seventy tiers of seats, they'd have seen all they wanted.

Jack did the proper thing and joined a line of people processing up the aisle. A lady with a tray of binoculars handed Jack a pair, conspicuously coloured in the blue-and-gold livery of the Gaiascope. Squeezing in front of motionless people, some standing, some sitting, he forged his way through to a solitary empty seat. Then he turned... and marvelled.

At the bottom of the central recess, wider than any circus ring Jack had yet seen, was a type of cinema screen, but a circular one, not intended for any pictures of human contrivance. For the great lens high overhead continuously projected onto it an image of the Earth itself. The Camera was literally that—an enormous darkened chamber that served as theatre, observatory and temple to the planet Earth. Because the Earth scarcely moved from its position in the lunar heavens, it was possible to build a permanent fixed telescope to watch it—and this the Seleneans had done as a magnificent act of homage to Gaia, the mother of mankind. They had built it at the precise natural origin of the lunar map-reference scheme: 0-0, located in the Sinus Medii, next to Crater Priscilla. Here the Earth hung permanently at the celestial zenith like a sapphire chandelier. This, together with its situation in a lunar sinus, gave the city its name: Jordvik. "Earth Creek".

Like the city itself, the entire Gaiascope complex was built underground. As a Site Of Universal Heritage, nothing must mar the surface of *Klarside*, the "bright side" of the Moon. Certainly nothing sited at the exact centre of the iconic lunar disk as seen from Earth. All that broke surface was the head of the telescope shaft, plus the occasional hopper pad and observation dome. It was of course impossible to hide the Adin crucible in Flammarion. Viewed from space it appeared as a brilliant dot. But the huge industrial installation attached to it was built far underground, essential anyway for safety reasons.

Such structures were merely functional. The Gaiascope however was recreational, indeed ritual. As one of the Seven Man-made Wonders of the Universe it was a supreme act of hubris to have built it. As a famous monument it had the rare distinction of being invisible from everywhere except inside it. But viewed from within—it was spectacular.

For fully five minutes Jack stood still, forgetting to blink, so that when he did so his eyes stung. Then, lifting his binoculars, he scanned the Earth's surface this way and that, in no particular order.

He recognised the Americas, plastered in an arc on the rightmost edge of the globe. Instinctively he looked for Brazil, but that was just over the horizon and wouldn't come into view for another hour. A spiral of cloud covered Florida and the Yucatán peninsula, site of the ancient Chicxulub Event, which had extinguished the dinosaurs and spawned the groubians. It looked like a static bloom of fungus. No matter how hard he strained, he could not see it move. But to those on the ground it was a hurricane, in the act of devastating hundreds of miles of Caribbean coastline.

He saw wide swathes of cloud like foam upon the sea. He saw sunlight glinting off the Pacific Ocean in a grainy patch at the centre of the sky-blue disk. He was astonished to see that the oceans were covered with minute rippling waves, some even with caps of spray, making wrinkles like a drying-out tomato. But each wrinkle, he knew, was a cluster of Pacific breakers, each of stupendous size.

As above, so below.

Wasn't it funny how water still looked like water, especially with the sunlight on it, even when a whole ocean was shrunk to the size of a circus ring. He thought back to the days as a young man when he used to wander out in the dead of night with bad thoughts in his head. He'd go and soothe himself by taking a walk along the Deerness Valley footpath and gaze at the moon reflected in the stream at the ford. How dry and parched the white spot had looked, even with water streaming over it.

Now he was standing on the Moon, gazing at the Earth, brought down out of the sky to the arid lunar ground. How liquid and succulent it looked, a droplet in free fall, even as it lay spread out on the dry screen.

Which looked the more appealing? Which was the more desirable place to be?

He knew that paradoxically many would choose the Moon. Selene— the world of opportunity, a playground for the well-to-do, where it was possible for a son of a poor labourer to become as rich as Croesus. And for a man from Mars, even a nominal denizen like himself, to strut around like royalty, as if it were beneath him to handle money.

There's no such thing as a free lunch, Jack reminded himself. Who was really paying? Were they all just sucking the life-fluid from the juicy blue ball that lay squashed out before his eyes?

Putting such thoughts aside he raised the binoculars once more and scanned the globe for cities. He was amazed to see them, or what he took for cities. He fancied he could see haze over them. If the continents were like big jungle leaves, fawn and green, the cities were dingy cankers growing in their clefts and tips.

He made a resolution to come back in fourteen days' time, when the Earth would be in darkness. Then he would be sure they were cities, because, as he knew from the brochure, he would be able to see the cankers glowing with light.

Phosphorescent spots of rot.

He slipped out of the row of seats back into the aisle. It was possible to get out by going up as well as down. Up into a winter-garden of tropical plants, pools in which people could paddle and play, fountains which cascaded in big gluey blobs, as only a moon-fountain can do. Fountains lit from above and below with lights which changed colour to music, as the jets danced in time and span the water into living shapes. And there too people played, virile boys and nubile girls in the prime of their health and beauty, intertwining with the globules and each other in slow motion, parting and twining again, dancing without shame as the warm foamy water caressed their skins.

And then came the hurly-burly of the fairground rides, flaring lights and sudden darkness, tough plastic wheels clattering on tracks twisted into fantasy shapes to yield rides of violent rapture, to an extent possible only in Moon gravity. Rides to make grown men scream, to send the mind splattering into struts, flung to the floor, flattened against the ceiling—rides where sound and light writhed in inextricable fury and the body learned motions too bizarre even to be dreamed.

And then you'd pass through more greenery, quiet pools and pagodas, with fancy Japanese carp, grown to monstrous size, lurking in rocky depths lit with mauves and blues and grotto green. Cafe after cafe, where people lounged in dreamy abandon over heavenly wines and earthy foods, *osteanretninger:* platters of cheeses redolent of the body washed down with aromatic beers. Dishes of truffles and chanterelles fried slowly in butter as if kissed all over in bed. Watery foods, lobsters and langoustines, oysters and abalone, swallowed with a lick of lemon and a pinch of crunchy pepper and salt and chased by sips of chilled white wine, shudderingly dry.

The austere half of Jack's soul surveyed the scene with puritanical resentment. The other half yearned to be in there among it all, with Kitty on his arm.

What did she mean by it: "do you miss not having a heart?" He'd show her. He'd make her pay for that remark. As soon as she'd got her ruddy lectures out of the way, he'd wine and dine her and get her between the sheets and show her he still had some organs left—the ones that mattered.

Was that being disloyal to Hilda's shade? Was Kitty married? He didn't think so. Divorced maybe. And, guilty though he felt, Hilda no longer had any legal claim to him. "Till death do us part", he had promised. And death had done just that.

And yet... and yet. Given the choice between Kitty, and Hilda at Kitty's age—or even Hilda in their last few fragile weeks together— whom would he choose? Put like that, he saw through himself like a pane of glass. Were he to apply his mind to seducing Kitty, he would be using her, not loving her. Using her as a surrogate for Hilda because she was no longer there when he needed her.

Kitty was right. He was missing a heart.

And someone was going to be made to pay for that. Oh yes, he was hunting for a woman all right, if "woman" it could be called—and it wasn't Kitty. That was the one thing he mustn't let out of his mind.

Longfellow's demon-driven hero coursed across the landscape of his mind on a foam-flecked charger, brandishing the banner with the strange device: *Excelsior!* White flames of purifying anger licking around his empty glowing ribs, he stepped briskly from the Gaiascope.

•••••✶●✶•••••

A leaden moodiness drove Jack back to the Gaiascope once more, where he discovered the spa. They'd had a therapeutic spa at the Clinic. He'd spent days with his physiotherapist—weeks—floating in tepid moon water, getting used to its gloopy dynamics. Coming to terms with what they'd done to his chest, learning to carry himself and his new steely burden and control the pain. Moon gravity was highly beneficial to a gradual introduction to the vertical state after a long spell in bed. The Galen Clinic had been established at Lunaborg precisely to take advantage of it. It specialised in rehabilitation after major accidents and extensive surgery.

Jack hadn't been back to the Galen spa, although he was entitled to. The trip round the Moon to Lunaborg was a chore, whatever the object. Besides, he'd spent months there and he wanted to get the stink of the place out of his nostrils. Discovering a magnificent spa so near at hand was an unexpected blessing. He had wondered why the hotel hadn't possessed one, but clearly there had been no point.

He hadn't realised how badly he'd been missing the soothing caress of warm water, the languid manatee-like swimming in one-sixth gravity, the thrill of alternate hot and cold on his skin. The spa at the Gaiascope was going to be a regular fixture with him, he could see. He took out a one-month membership, judging that it would tide him over nicely until it was time to board the *Oberon*.

It was five days into *Nedélia Slëz* (which had started this year at 3am on 10th May 1975, UT, being scheduled of course according to *marsvrem*, MV). Kitty, still busy with her lectures, hadn't been able to spare the time to join him and he was getting lonely. He yearned for company— any sort of company. He was ready for anything, he told himself.

He wasn't ready for the form it took when it came.

As he lay resting on a lounger, eyes closed, he felt a hand touch his forearm. He looked down at it. Violet stripes were running up it from the fingertips to the wrist, disappearing under a veil of black lace.

His SP unit gave an audible click. It emulated the startle response which would have set his heart racing, had he got one. He jerked up into a sitting position. Apart from the hands and feet, the figure that stood before him was completely shrouded in a black veil like a burkah, except that no eyes were showing.

"Mr Williams, could I ask you please to accompany me?"

Jack got to his feet. Sheer surprise numbing his mind to the risk he was taking, he put his terry-towelling dressing-gown back on and followed the black widow past more loungers, past the Jacuzzi, into one of the treatment rooms. Inside, a masseur in a white jacket sat reading a magazine. He put it down with a snap and hurriedly got to his feet.

"Vermat," he said, with quiet reverence.

"Arne! Thank you so much for waiting." She turned and indicated Jack with her hand. "I wonder if you'd mind? Mr Williams is an old friend. I would like him to talk to me while I have my massage."

The masseur nodded with ready assent, though Jack caught a glint of puzzlement in his eyes. He brought up a chair to the head of the massage table and bade Jack sit down.

Catching up her veil, Vermat lifted it over her head. Underneath she was naked. Jack's SP unit clicked again... in sheer horror.

"Yes, Mr Williams. The scars of parturition are not lovely. But I wanted you to see them for yourself—in case you are inclined to doubt what I am going to tell you."

Her body was pitted with egg-sized craters—a lunar surface in miniature. Where the skin of her arms reached her shoulders, it no longer glowed with ever-changing colours, but became bone white. Her face was hideously disfigured—no other reason need be sought for why she habitually kept her visor opaque or projected a holoface. A single eye with its horseshoe pupil was fixed on Jack. Zygocysts had taken out the other eye, together with half the face. Gingerly, as if in intractable pain (which she was) she lowered herself onto the couch. She gave a grateful sigh of relief and relaxed—deflated would be a better word—into the upholstery.

"I always come to Arne," she said. "He picks his way so deftly round the scars. It might seem to you that there is scarcely enough skin to massage, but in the little unbroken skin that is left—that's where the pain is."

Gently caressing the pitted back with both hands, Arne smoothed in some ointment.

"Pain is my life, Jack... may I call you Jack? Each day I take enough heroin to fell a horse. It has to be heroin. I can intercept the illegal traffic from Gaia. Anything more up-to-date would draw attention to myself."

"I marvel that you manage to do your job at all, Commissioner," said Jack, with awe in his voice.

"Please call me Vermat," she said. "I don't stand on ceremony. Certainly not out of uniform."

Jack's voice held surprise. "Human drugs—I mean gaian drugs—work on groubians too?"

"You and I share the same cocktail of hormones and neurotransmitters with nematodes, our common ancestors. Feelings... emotions... pleasure... pain... it's all paid-for in the same currency.

Heroin forges that currency." She added ruefully "It's just the dose that's different."

"But you manage?"

"Yes I manage. Though maybe not for much longer. This has been going on for a very long time now."

Jack gasped inwardly when he thought how long that might be.

She seemed to tremble as she lay on the couch. It had nothing to do with the motion of Arne's hands. "I owe this, at the very least, to my contact with gaian civilization: heroin is better than what I once had to use."

It intrigued Jack to think that a humble nematode could feel the same things that he could. Anger maybe—and fear too? And in a fiercer, more primitive way. Nematodes had no civilization to filter and re-badge feelings and their responses to them. "Culture" to them was a Petri dish. But groubians now... they'd had culture. They'd had civilization— though maybe nothing at all like his.

"I didn't expect to find a groubian living and working on the Moon," said Jack. "I thought you groubians were only to be found in Olympia."

"I'm too well-known in Olympia," she said. "Mars has too many bitter memories. It has become emotionally stale for me. I find it better for my mental stability to live as far away from my fellow groubians as possible. It's not that I detest their company. But being the only one alive of my generation, I do rather stand out."

"How come that you are alive and the others of your generation are not?" said Jack. "You must be extraordinary resilient to endure the pain."

"No Jack, it was just chance. Pure chance. I won't call it a lucky chance, because it is not a blessing."

She shifted her body uncomfortably. Arne's hands went to her waist to help her into a better position. "It is not childbirth, as such, that kills a groubian. It is vital organs getting ruptured. That doesn't always happen. In fact several of the mothers of the Last Zygogeny survived parturition. But they have all since died. All except me."

"How did they die? Did the pain get on top of them?"

"No. You cannot kill a groubian just by inflicting pain. You have to bomb them. Crush them. Hack them to pieces. Incinerate them with napalm."

She shifted her body painfully again and immediately Arne's hands positioned themselves once more to help her. "They died in the last war. It was living on the Moon, as I was then, that saved my life."

"I'm… sorry."

"What for, Jack? I can't imagine you had anything to do with it."

"I'm sorry for what my people—my race—I mean my species—did to you. Your species."

"It's the story of humanity, is it not? And who's to say they were not doing the right thing? Groubians have long outlived their time. We are an extinct species. We have no future. Not as a separate people."

"I'm amazed that you can find it in your heart to say that. To forgive and forget as you do."

"We forgive… or rather we reconcile ourselves to the fact that our only purpose in carrying on living is to contribute our very best to the forging of a new world: one which *does* have a future. But oh no, we don't forget. Every year, in the first week of March, the month of Mars—MV of course, not UT—the 5,000 or so remaining groubians, including myself, celebrate seven days of mourning for the dead of the two wars. During this time we go about covered entirely in black veils. Today is the fifth day of *Nedélia Slëz*, which means in M1: "The Week of Tears". Did you know that, Jack?"

"Yes I did, as it happens."

"And you knew we went about veiled?"

"Yes. Kitty Martin told me." Jack rightly guessed that Vermat would know all about Kitty. He wondered, though, whether Kitty knew that Vermat was a groubian. If so, why hadn't she mentioned it?

"Then why did you startle when I touched your arm? Oh, don't pretend you didn't. I know the sound of an SP unit changing gear."

"I thought you were someone else."

"Someone like… Tvoul Rainbow? Or Shval Meteor?"

"Yes. Someone like that."

Vermat saw no reason to go discussing Agent Zero with Jack. The same will was at work in any case. "I take it that Jens Andersen has told you about Shval's little escapade a few months back? How she impersonated Tvoul on her journey back from Gaia?"

"Yes he did. Are you quite sure it was Shval—and not Tvoul?"

"Utterly sure. I know my own daughters."

"Your *daughters?*"

"Why, yes. The only two still alive. I am glad Jens Andersen is investigating this case for you. I am up against a severe conflict of interest. Severe enough to make me consider my position."

"You're not thinking of resigning, are you, Vermat? On my behalf?"

"Rest assured, my friend. You are nowhere near as important as you think. If I resign, it will be a combination of the pain I am in, the sorrow, and the inability of people to accept that loyalty to my offspring hasn't been getting in the way of my duty to *Rådhuset*, my employer. To Selstyrke—to Selene."

"Where is Tvoul now?"

"I don't know, Jack. And that is the honest truth. I'm trying to find her just as hard as you are."

"And Shval… is she hiding her? Does she approve of what she's done? For that matter—do you?"

"No, on all three counts. Shval is searching for Tvoul just as diligently as we are. And I dread to think what will happen if she finds her first."

"No more than she deserves?"

"Jack, you have no idea of the enmity between these two—and of what hangs on it. Nor of what Shval is capable of doing. The likelihood of her destroying Tvoul happens to be the least of my worries. May I ask you something in my turn?"

"Go ahead—I can't stop you."

"Why are *you* hunting Tvoul?"

"Isn't it obvious?"

"Not at all. Yes, it is obvious why you may want to *seek* her. What is not obvious is what you propose to do when you catch her up."

"I want to see justice done."

"Selenean justice? Terrestrial justice? Or some idea of your own?"

"Natural justice," snapped Jack. "She can't be allowed to do this sort of thing and get away scot-free."

"If I find her," said Vermat, "I shall send her back under heavy guard to Brazil, there to stand trial for murder. That I solemnly promise you. Legally speaking, it is the best I can do. Will it satisfy you?"

"It'll be a start. Whether it satisfies me depends on whether they convict her. And what they do to her as a result."

"They will imprison her for life."

"For her lifetime? Or for the lifetime of her captors?"

"Or just your lifetime, Jack? Isn't that what you're afraid of?"

Jack spoke slowly, as if pronouncing sentence of death. His voice-chip detected his emotional state and generated a growl. "I want her to get the heaviest sentence it is possible for her to get—anywhere in the solar system."

"She would get a heavier sentence on Mars. Since she is a Martian denizen, the Brazilian authorities might decide to send her back there to stand trial. They certainly will if you petition them. On Mars, the law— so rarely administered—is severe. Fifth-rank murder. Do you know what that means?"

"I have no idea."

"Third-rank murder as you may know is deliberate and premeditated termination of someone's life. Fourth-rank requires proof of the termination of the lives of all progeny as well, so as to invalidate the attempts of the victim during his or her lifetime to reproduce. Fifth-rank requires proof of hostile intervention in the victim's very genome. Edulation is defined as falling under that heading. There is no defence."

"And what is the punishment?"

"She will be dispersed."

"What does *that* mean?"

"She will acquire the status of a disperson. Her persona will be downgraded to class zero. Her living body then becomes the property of the Martian *mir*. She will have no redress against whatever they care to do to her. Like as not she will be sectioned… and the pieces employed in scientific experiments."

Jack nodded thoughtfully. That sounded gratifyingly severe. But he would have to check with Jens what it really meant. "Then it looks to me," he said, "as if I'd be better off letting Tvoul get back to Mars—and have her arrested there. Sending her back to Brazil would be a complete waste of time."

"That's your choice, Jack. I won't say whether it's a good or a bad one. But the fact of the matter is, I'm not able to locate her whereabouts on Selene and I'm afraid she's going to elude me."

Vermat seemed to melt still further under Arne's ministrations. Any more, Jack thought, and she'd liquefy altogether. "There are two places Tvoul can go from here," she said. "Back to Gaia—but we already know that TMG is hell-bent on denying her a bolt-hole there to have her children and raise them. They've tried once—and they'll keep on trying. And your man Andersen has stirred things up no end by commissioning an army of investigators, all on your payroll. He's made it far too hot for her even to contemplate going back to Gaia."

Continuing in a muffled groan, she said "So she can only go on from here to Mars. And she has got to go via the *Oberon*."

This of course was everything Jack had been hoping for.

"So which pod do I pick?"

"Whichever one you like. If she's not in that pod, she will be in the other. Simply negotiate with the Mars authorities before you make landfall in Voronka Cosmodrome to arrest *any* groubians disembarking from *Oberon*. I can tell you how many groubians there are currently booked on that voyage. None."

"What about Shval Meteor? Won't she try to go back to Mars too?"

"She's a Selenean denizen now. She lives here."

"Yes, but if Tvoul is trying to get back to Mars..."

"I've made arrangements to detain Shval the moment she tries to board. I'd be grateful if you'd told nobody about that—I don't want the slightest chance of her being forewarned. But I can't risk her travelling back with Tvoul in the same pod."

"Vermat, I'm enormously grateful. This will hurry things up a lot."

"Save your gratitude for when I've caught her. But as I said, I fear she's going to elude me. How—I don't know. I feel it... in my scars."

Now it really did seem as if Vermat was on the point of dissolving. Jack watched her suffer in horror, fighting down disgust.

"Suppose she does elude me," she continued feebly. "What will you do then?"

"Follow her. To the end of the universe."

"And when you catch her up? What then?"

"Well... we'll be a long way from Selene."

"In other words it's none of my business." Jack saw Vermat's mutilated face sink into a twisted smile as she lay on the couch. "Jack... can I give you a piece of advice?"

"Fire away."

"Let her have her babies."

"What?"

"Let her have them. Whether she lives or dies, the agony will be far, far worse than anything you, or Mars, can do to her."

······ ✶ ● ✶ ······

Eventually Jack did get the chance to wine and dine Kitty. They spent an evening, or rather the tail-end of a circadian, onsdag 4 taurus to be precise, at a candlelit table on the top deck of a fake galleon built over the lily pool in the Gaiascope.

The gardens were currently simulating a balmy summer evening on a tropical island. In the fast-waning dusk Jack and Kitty watched as concealed lighting came-on in the depths of the pool, behind clustered rocks and streamers of water weed. Iridescent fish and snake-like creatures played around the lamps, biting something unseen from their glass covers. Above them, mooning couples drifted in pedal boats shaped like giant swans.

Kitty was excited when Jack told her Vermat was a groubian. She'd never suspected it, she said. Since it appeared Jack now knew Vermat socially, Kitty begged him for an introduction. She wanted to interview Vermat for her research.

Jack said "I thought you knew the names of all living groubians since the Last Zygogeny."

"I do—I'm sure I do. But Vermat pre-dates them all. She's one of the Mothers. I thought they were all dead."

"Vermat said that groubians don't necessarily die from childbirth."

"They don't. But in the Second Olympian War it was the Mothers in particular who were hunted down and exterminated. They were the natural leaders. The settlers claimed they'd got them all. I guess it is still a secret that they missed Vermat."

Kitty turned to gaze out of the window. "She does well to keep her head down. And holding the position she does will go a long way towards protecting her."

"Surely she doesn't need protection—not nowadays?"

"The war's over… but not everybody's come to terms with that. But if only I'd thought! Her very name gives her away."

"Her *name*? Why so?"

"Vermat: *The true mother it is who suffers the loss of her offspring.* That's how it's usually translated. But what the spatio-color really means is: *True motherhood entails the loss of childhood.*"

"That sends a rather different message."

"Yeah, doesn't it. Every groubian is named for a quotation from the Book of Titan. Of course it's really a spatio-color pattern, but there's a standard M1 translation of the Book." She smiled. "Not a very good one, I have to say. I'm working on a better one. In English. And I don't mean M2."

"What's the difference?"

"Trust a limey to ask that. If they want it in M2 on Mars, they'll have to translate it themselves. And they'll have to buy my dictionary, because I'm the author of the only English-to-M2 dictionary there is."

"American English, of course…"

"Of course."

"So how do you get 'Vermat' from—what did you say?—*the true mother…*?"

"It's a contraction of the M1: *vérnaia mat'*—'true mother'. 'True' in the sense of being real, not 'telling the truth', which is *právda*. The phrase appears in Dolpou Zvezda's translation."

"I see." Jack took that piece of intelligence with a sip of wine.

"Now Dolpou is a groubian. Groubians don't speak M1 as their mother tongue. They don't naturally speak any verbal language, of course: it's spatio-color with them. But some of them are avid students of gaian languages, which they've been learning on and off for the last two thousand years. They simply love Russian literature, perhaps because it's so like M1. Dolpou Zvezda took a shine to Lermontov's poem 'Angel'...do you know it?"

Jack, wide-eyed, shook his head.

"It runs like this, in M1:

> *Po nébou polóunotchi ángel letél,*
> *I tíxouiu pésniu on pel, ...*

"...and she copied the metre—though with five-line verses, not four."

"What's the poem about? Is it anything like the Book of Titan?"

"In an eerie sense, yes. It's about the angel Gabriel bringing a young soul from Heaven to Earth, to be born into the world of sorrow and tears. And as they pass the Moon and the stars and the fluffy clouds he sings to it. And the child never forgets that blessed song, for all the *scóutchnie pésni Zemlí*—the boring songs of Earth."

"Gabriel, eh? Why should an archangel be bothered with one tiny soul?"

"He's the Angel of the Moon, in ancient tradition. The special custodian of childbirth. That's why Luke the Evangelist simply had to have the angel Gabriel bring God's message to Mary, the chosen mother of the Messiah."

Jack stared at her without blinking. Kitty had certainly opened his eyes to what being a groubist was all about.

"Anyway," she went on, "that's the pattern for a groubian name. It kinda mirrors its appearance in spatio-color. First name: shrunken quotation in M1. Second name: some beautiful natural phenomenon. Thus you get Dolpou from *dolína poustáia*—the 'empty valley' of the Last Verse. And *zvezdá* means 'star'."

"Give me another example."

"Vermat is *Vérmat Avróra* in M1. In English we say 'Aurora'. Meaning the goddess of the evening sky, not the electrical discharge."

"And what's 'Tvoul'? I can see the Rainbow bit now—I guess *Rádouga* is M1 for Rainbow?"

Kitty replied "It sure is. *Let it fall to thy lover to deliver the fatal blow.* In M1, *Thy lover* (in the feminine) is *tvoiá liubóvka*. This gets shortened to Tvoul."

"And how about 'Shval'?"

"*Shto est' valiúta ou zhízni samói?* What is the valuta—the inherent exchange-value—of life itself."

"Jens quoted the Last Verse of the Book of Titan at me. At the time it went right over my head. But he mentioned an 'empty valley'—and you've just said it again."

Kitty blinked. She'd lost her easy air of conviction. "I'm not at all sure what that is. I wonder if the 'empty valley' isn't a metaphor for new unpeopled worlds beyond Titan. Groubians say that the whole of life is ultimately in vain, unless one day your descendants get to walk among the stars. In their imagination, the stars go on and on for ever. Thanks to Einstein, we Terrestrials say the universe is finite, but in practice the stars are impossible to count."

Jack crinkled his nose. "Finite—infinite—it *does* make a big difference, you know, like."

But Kitty, not being a mathematician, didn't see why. "I think it's just a question of attitude. Groubians have kept themselves going for fifty thousand years on the hope implied in the Last Verse. They still do—when everyone knows it's a total, total lost cause."

•••••✦ ● ★•••••

They didn't get to the second part of Jack's agenda: Kitty was too tired after a week's lectures on the meaning of the Week of Tears. But she did prevail on Jack to come with her to the Gaiascope for the Ring of Fire. Jack had been planning on giving it a miss.

"You simply must come. It will be the most spectacular thing you've ever seen! If it's anything like the pictures of the last one."

"Well… just to please you."

"And you've got to go in fancy dress."

"Aw, pet, come off it."

"You've got to! Everyone else will. I'm going as Pierette. It will be a chance to prance around in a skin-tight costume. Now I've got my figure down, I want to show it off. Why don't you come as Pierrot?"

"A right couple of clowns we'll look!" Jack's scowl broke and he laughed. "I'll think about it."

"No. Say yes. Say it now. Keep me company."

"Can you just see me in a pierrot outfit? The Dancing Dustbin…"

"Jack—I think you'll look very nice. It doesn't show. Really it doesn't."

"It's just… it's just that I'm self-conscious of my shape now, with this ruddy SP unit."

"Well—this will give you the chance to get out of yourself. Let your hair down for once. Everybody else is going to." Hardening her attitude, she planted her knuckles on her hips. "Do you really imagine anyone's going to take any notice of *you?*"

12   The Ring of Fire

It was now less than three hours before the total eclipse of the Sun by the Earth. People began to congregate in the lobby of the Gaiascope, many in extravagant costumes far grander than anything seen in a Terrestrial *mardi gras* parade. Gravity, of course, was on their side.

A procession had formed and had marched down Avenue Five in the direction of the fingerboards saying *til Gaiaskopet*, collecting revellers on the way. It was just arriving as Kitty and Jack, arm-in-arm, in matching Pierrot and Pierette costumes, came down the levitator from the hopper pad. They had not long returned from Crater Flammarion, Jack's favourite spot on the Moon, where they had been watching Mars together with Jupiter sinking low in the West. Hardly a spectacular event, but to Jack it seemed symbolic. Besides which it had given him the chance to be alone with Kitty.

The main event was to be held in the Camera—and there Jack had booked a box. Seventy tiers of seating rose from the ringside, but additionally five circles of boxes descended from the dome. Their box was in the outermost circle—the best—letting them look down on the arena at a 45° angle.

Jack had also invited Jens. And, to make up the foursome and give Kitty the chance to meet her socially, he had extended an invitation to Vermat. To his surprise she had accepted, with evident delight.

Jens and Vermat were already there in the box when Jack and Kitty arrived. They were deep in conversation. Both were in fancy dress as the occasion demanded, Jens having chosen to come as a Viking raider. In the erstwhile Danish dependency of Selene, he was far from being the only one in a horned hat. Vermat came as Madame de Montespan, which allowed her to wear a voluminous dress and a high wig and domino mask to conceal her disfigurement. Caterers were in attendance—Jack could afford not to stint the hospitality—and champagne was served, with strawberries and canapés.

Jens murmured in Jack's ear "Vermat and I have been comparing notes before you came. We have some important news for you—we think we've tracked down Tvoul. You'll be totally amazed..."

Jack's eyes lit up. "Champion! Let's drink to that. Tell me all about it over dinner after the show. We're booked in at the Pagoda, the four of us."

"That's really celebrating!"

"I've got news too." It was Jack's turn to murmur in Jens's ear. "Whilst we were in Crater Flammarion, I asked Kitty to be my wife. She's said yes…"

"Jack, that's—that's wonderful! I'm very happy for you both. But what if you have to go to Mars…?"

"We'll be going together. Kitty's already got her ticket."

••••★●★•••••

At precisely 24:59 on lørdag 14 taurus (which was 4.42am on Sunday 25 May, UT), when the discs of the Earth and Sun were just in contact, the pageant began. Or rather the Rite of the Ring of Fire, for that was how it was billed.

At the end of that final minute, when 24:59 tipped over into 00:00, the clocks stopped. It was the commencement of the two-hour intercalary, which always takes place in *seltid* as lørdag gives way to søndag. Almost two hours were to pass before the moment of maximum eclipse, but such a full programme had been arranged, of dancers, singers, comedians and circus acts, that the time just slipped by. It was time-out-of-time anyway: *forlorn tid*. It is a singular fact that the cataclysm of the Ring of Fire took place in non-existent time.

Jack, peering down at the arena, turned to Vermat. "Do you know what's going on?" he asked her.

"This is the crowning of the Sun King, who will rule over the proceedings. The man dressed in Roman armour represents Mars. He has just presented the Sun with a sword, to arm him against the dark."

"Why Mars?"

"You won't have noticed, but Mars has conjoined with Jupiter in the West. And four days ago, Mars was at its closest to the Sun."

"I know." Jack's voice was smug. "Kitty and I went to Crater Flammarion to watch it."

"Did you now? You really keep your eye on that planet, don't you, Jack?"

"And shall I tell you what else we did while we were there…?"

"I know," said Vermat smugly in her turn.

"What do you mean?"

She grinned. "You can't hide a thing like that from Selstyrke."

The action onstage proceeded by a succession of *tableaux vivantes* connected by scenes of flamboyant ritual. Jack hadn't bothered to read the program and was unfamiliar with much of the symbolism. Vermat put him wise.

"Now the Moon-Hare comes onstage for her dance. The Hare is traditionally associated with the Moon, though in recent times it has become the Easter Bunny. Viewed from Earth, they tell me, the Moon's disk appears to have a hare emblazoned on it. Early peoples must have gazed at that and wondered."

The dancer who took the part of the Moon-Hare performed spectacularly, taking advantage of the low lunar gravity to engage in extravagant leaps over and among the assembled performers. Finally she came to rest prostrated before the Sun King in an attitude of homage, her huge ears flopped forward so as almost to touch his toes.

No sooner had she done so than a princess, clad in white and blue, was borne in procession on a litter smothered in flowers. Jack was reminded of the traditional garb of the Madonna—but this was a black Madonna. Vermat explained it by the Earth currently being in darkness, as seen from the Moon.

"See now, the goddess Gaia has entered in state. She is about to be married to the Sun."

An elaborate wedding ceremony was now performed between the goddess and the god—a *hieros gamos* symbolising the conjunction in the sky of the Earth and the Sun. At its climax the audience raised their voices in a shout of acclaim which reverberated in the vastness of the *camera*. The great lens in the roof was momentarily opened a fraction to show the celestial event unfolding overhead, and the audience felt a blast of solar heat on their faces. Already the sun's disk, seen flaring on the floor of the arena, was largely devoured by the unseen orb of the Earth, but the tiny fraction of sunlight trickling through was enough to simulate a bright fire in the centre of things. Dancers in flesh-coloured cat-suits periodically jumped the fire as they whirled around it, their bodies flashing briefly in the shaft of sunlight and their protective fabric smoking copiously.

An enormous egg was now brought onstage on a litter borne by seven boys and seven girls. "The World Egg," explained Vermat, "from which all Earth's living creatures are supposed to have been hatched."

As the company broke into a chant, the Sun King descended from his throne and touched the egg with his sword. Instantly it flew to pieces and dozens of dancers leapt out, clad in an assortment of scaly, furry and feathered outfits. These made mischief onstage and then they climbed the tiers of seats and mingled with the audience, to cat-calls and shrieks of delight from the children.

Now came the climax of the show. The performers withdrew from the circus ring to stand under spotlights in the aisles like a brilliant many-rayed star. In the ring itself the floor was revealed as an iris-lens: this gradually opened up to expose the delicate circular screen onto which the image of Gaia was normally projected. But now the diffracted light from the hidden sun shone red through the atmosphere of Gaia, turning it into a fiery circle comprising the combined sunsets and sunrises from all around the globe.

Outside the Gaiascope the lunar landscape lit up blood-red with earthlight. And seventy miles away, in Crater Flammarion, the Adin crucible burned thousands of times brighter than usual as the solar wind was lensed by the Earth's magnetic field.

It was just then that Jack's wristlink vibrated.

"Whoops! Somebody wants to see me urgently."

"What a time to choose!" said Jens. "Where? Here?"

"No. By the Moon-Dog. It says to come alone."

"I think I'd better come with you," said Jens, a note of alarm in his voice. "You'll be on your own out there."

"No, you stay here with the ladies. If whoever's out there has got something to tell me, it might scare them off to see the pair of us."

"Okay, but keep talking to me over the wristlink as you walk out there."

Hurriedly nodding to the others, Jack left the box and made a discreet departure from the Gaiascope. Getting to the Moon-Dog, he walked briskly round the fearful monument. There was nobody there—indeed there was nobody to be seen in the whole of the *Månehundtorv*. Everyone was at the Gaiascope. He waited in growing puzzlement.

"Not a soul," he said over the wristlink.

"It's a ruse, Jack!" came Jens's reply. "Vermat has alerted the patrol. Selstyrke will have the *Månehundtorv* sealed off in less than twenty seconds. Stay right there, but keep your eyes skinned..."

Abruptly Jens's voice ceased in a crackle. Jack stared in puzzlement at the wristlink. Moments later a blast of heat sent him reeling back against the transparent dome. He saw fingers of burning hydrogen groping towards him along the ceiling of Avenue Five. They were coming from the direction of the Gaiascope. Hurriedly he slipped inside the dome through the nearest port as flames, like hunting dogs, sped up and licked around the monument.

A hatch caught his attention. It was marked with the intermondial fire-escape symbol. He leapt at it, plunging through, and found himself slithering down a chute, coming to rest in an empty chamber. Stairwells led off in various directions, but a single levitator went straight up. White-hot lava started trickling down every stairway. He couldn't stay there—and there was only one way out.

Rising through the rings of the levitator, Jack came to a small domed chamber on the surface of the Moon. He stared through the glass of the dome.

The Earth still glared in the sky like a single angry eye. Round about him the lunar landscape glowed blood-red in the earthlight. But something else besides the Ring of Fire was tingeing the nearby cliffs with blood. Close at hand a brilliant red light flickered and flared like a welder's torch. The spectral red of hydrogen atoms newly-formed from naked protons.

Jack turned and clawed at the glass of the dome, pressing the nose and forehead of his pierrot-mask hard against the surface. Less than two hundred yards away, the Adin beam which should have been directed down into Crater Flammarion was blazing down from the black sky, flinging up molten rock like a glowing spray of gingery mucus. A vast dome of condensing vapour bore down upon it, lit-up from below with flickering red—a turtle in the sand giving birth to a clutch of glittering horror. A rain of ash hissed down on the dome.

"Kitty! *No... o... oh!*"

Crater Flammarion was no longer the site of the Adin crucible. It had relocated itself here... to the Gaiascope.

····* ✷ ● ✷ *····

Jack was lying on an unslept-in bed in his hotel room, in the grip of post-traumatic stress for which he had scorned treatment. Real men don't seek counselling. He froze as the v-unit announced a call. Grappling for the receiver, he received a summons to Selstyrke HQ, though the sender took good care not to call it that. On Earth it was Tuesday 27 May, 1975. On Selene it was gaidag 16 taurus: the circadian after the disaster.

A deep sense of gloom pervaded SHQ. In the vestibule Jack was confronted by the crossed flags, at half-mast, of Selene and Selstyrke. The Moon-Hare emblazoned on the full disc—and the Viking Hat, its horns a gleaming crescent. Flowers were strewn between the flagstaffs and all around there shone a forest of candles, jujubes of flame wobbling atop each one, as happens with candles on the Moon.

At the receptionist's window he announced who he was and asked to see the officer who had called him in. The receptionist stared at him.

Looking down, Jack realised with dismay that he was still in his pierrot costume. He suddenly lost faith in his grip on reality.

The receptionist tried to keep a level voice. "Acting Commissioner Nilsson is expecting you. I'll tell her you're here."

A slight woman in uniform appeared and held out her hand. Her face was comely but severe, her blond hair worn in a crisp page-boy cut. Unlike the receptionist, she gave no sign of noticing Jack's inappropriate attire. She knew the capacity of an overloaded brain.

"Thank you so much for coming—and so promptly. I hope you are feeling better now?" It was mere politeness. She knew how he felt. "May I say how sorry I am about your friends, particularly your fiancée, Miss Martin. We have all been deeply affected by the tragedy…"

"I don't call it a tragedy. I call it an *atrocity!*"

Nilsson hesitated, not sure how to respond to that outburst. She continued in the same tone of voice "We have lost several colleagues. Notably Commissioner Vermat. That is a blow to the entire Selenean *mir*, not just Selstyrke. It has left me in charge of the policing of Lunaborg—a job I don't much care for."

"It's a blow to me too. Recently I'd come to consider Vermat as a friend."

"She had a high regard for you, Mr Williams. She was very concerned for your… family problem. Which she viewed as hers too. Her family problem. But I gather she explained all that to you?"

"Yes. I guess you'd say we were… in-laws, like?"

Nilsson led the way to a vacant interview room and ordered coffee and pralines over the v-unit. Jack knew for sure that interviewees didn't usually get those.

"You used the word 'atrocity'."

"I meant it. That was no accident. I'll make a statement if you like."

"I can take your statement later, Mr Williams. But first let us talk off-the-record. Vermat was one of your party at the Ring of Fire, wasn't she?"

"Yes, together with Jens Andersen and Kitty Martin. I miss them all terribly—especially Kitty…" His voice caught, like a sleeve in a splinter. "I'm sorry—I'm nowhere near over it yet. That was nearly me in there, too."

"Yes. If someone hadn't called you away…" Nilsson's voice tailed off. "We've analysed the wristlink traffic over the period in question. It is a puzzle."

"How, like?"

"The message to you, unsigned as you know, came from a dating agency—the sort of thing youngsters tease each other with. But some hostile process had pounced upon it prior to delivery—and had then let it go forward. But not before it had trawled through the agency's files looking for anything that might tell it the sender's identity and whereabouts. It looks very much like Shval Meteor's handiwork—the interception, I mean. But at this stage we can't be certain."

"But it found out who the message came from? And you know that, too?"

"Yes. From someone calling themselves *Tvoul Williams.*"

A look of incredulity froze on Jack's face. Nilsson waited for him to say something. When he didn't she continued. "There is no reason to believe it *wasn't* her. She has been in hiding ever since arriving on the Moon, as I hardly need to tell you. But she may have been trying to make contact with you personally, to arrange a meeting of just the two of you."

"That's what the message seemed to want to say."

"Yes. I have the text of it here. I also have Vermat's alert to the patrol in Sector D, which covers *Månehundtorvet* and the Gaiascope. She orders them *not* to assume that they are only looking for a groubian. Did you tell her what your wristlink said?"

"No. I simply said somebody wanted to see me outside. Alone."

"So… Vermat must have known something anyway."

"Yes, she did." Jack stroked his chin. "When Kitty and I arrived, Jens told me that he and Vermat *knew where Tvoul was.* We were going to talk about it over dinner after the show."

Nilsson sat and digested that, as if it was news to her. "Did Vermat ever utter the words *Agent Zero* in your hearing?"

"No. I can't think she ever did. Who—or what—is Agent Zero?"

Nilsson shook her head vaguely. "It doesn't matter."

She thought some more. "Why are you so sure it was an *atrocity* and not just an accident?"

Jack's eyes widened in astonishment. "Well, it stands to reason, doesn't it? Somebody knew it was going to happen. And they called me up on the wristlink just to get me out of the Gaiascope."

"I see." She obviously didn't. Something didn't add up for her. "Suppose I could prove to you it hadn't been Tvoul Williams, née Radouga. Then who do you think it might have been? And why do you suppose they might have wanted to do that?"

"Well…" Jack screwed up his mouth. "Until you said the message came from Tvoul, I straightaway thought of Shval Meteor."

"Yes…" said Nilsson. Again that note of uncertainty in her voice. "That is the theory we commenced with. That the incident was an act of terrorism occasioned by *Nedélia Slëz* to intermondialise the Groubian Question. And that the Meteor Gang was under contract to carry it out."

"Well, what's wrong with that for a theory?"

"The facts do not support it."

"What do you mean? Kitty was telling me it's just the sort of thing Shval's good at."

"It's certainly her *modus operandi*. But you see… it so happens that when the Ring of Fire celebrations began, Shval and her triada were being held in custody. An hour before the show, Vermat put out an order for their arrest."

Jack was about to ask why, when he realised he knew. Hadn't Vermat assured him she was determined not to let Shval board the *Oberon*?

"They weren't hard to find," said Nilsson. "Shval had booked a box right next to yours and was actually detained in the act of occupying it."

"So, if you hadn't arrested her, she'd have been *there*—right beside us—when the Gaiascope went up?"

"So it seems. Unless she was planning to slip out just before it happened. But it's a pretty good alibi, don't you think? Except it's the exact opposite of an alibi—an un-alibi, would you say?"

"I'm sorry, I don't follow you…"

"An alibi is a claim to have been elsewhere when the crime was committed. Shval claims that she would actually have been *there*—and we can't dispute that. Shval and her triada are not given to suicide-attacks."

Nilsson shook her head as she continued "We had to let them go. With Vermat gone, we had no authority to hold them—and their lawyers were well aware of that."

"But that's amazing! You mean Shval had no idea what was being planned?"

"So it seems. But it's not clear that anything *was* being planned."

"*What?*" Jack's features crossed the line between a grimace and a grin. "Are you trying to tell me the whole thing was an accident?"

"Strange as it sounds in the circumstances: yes. We had the Adin satellite brought down for examination. We expected to find that it had been hacked. But it seems to have been a simple hardware error. An altogether random event."

"*Geddaway!* The Adin beam—redirected to wipe out the Gaiascope when it was crammed full of people? How could that possibly have been a random event?"

"Well, I'm not an expert on the fine detail of Adin collimation, but the position/time chip certainly has a fault in it. An intermittent fault. One that only shows up when the start of circadian 15—always a søndag as you'll know—coincides with an Earth transit of the Sun."

Jack thought fast. "You mean—bearing in mind that søndag 15 always begins at the very moment of the *Sun's* transit of the zenith?" He had made a point of studying "times and seasons" ever since setting out for the Moon. He wasn't at all fazed by astro-chronological detail. But his grasp of electronics wasn't up to much.

"Yes. You'd think the time-of-day clock in an Adin satellite would run on Universal Time, but it doesn't. It runs on *seltid*—geared to the *månad*—the solar cycle. That makes perfect sense when you realise that the Adin satellite has to know where the Sun is in the sky at any given moment. Universal Time of course pays no regard to the Sun's whereabouts."

"Why does it matter what time-standard it runs on?"

"Well, whenever there's a total eclipse—which hasn't occurred before in the lifetime of this particular Adin satellite—there's a stray cross-potential on the chip, high enough to pull up the co-ordinate register's RESET line."

"I'm sorry, I've lost you. What does that do?"

"Look." Nilsson picked up a pencil and drew on her blotter as if explaining to a child. "That's the co-ordinate register, which aims the beam. Let's write a number in it: so. Those are the lunar co-ordinates of the Adin crucible in Crater Flammarion. Now that's the Gaiascope, built precisely at lunar co-ordinates: 0-0. Zero degrees North, zero degrees East. Now reset the whole register to zero, and—*pouf!...*" she scribbled hard with her pencil, ripping the blotter. "Bye-bye Gaiascope."

"A time-bomb!"

"Sort-of... a date-bomb. A calendar-bomb. A disaster waiting to happen. Waiting for some cosmic event to trigger it."

Jack rubbed his chin. "Waiting for the very moment of the *Ring of Fire!*"

• • • • • ✶ ● ✶ • • • • •

Jack sat in his hotel room. His mind was numb—so numb he couldn't bear the silence. He turned on the TV. For him to do that was an act of desperation.

It was some sort of comedy show. The comedian made a joke about going to the spa and getting an eyeful of protons. Jack was disgusted. He threw his shoe at the window-screen which gave out a crackling sigh and shut down.

Sitting still in the darkness, Jack's wristlink told him it was the magic time of sundown, when the clocks stopped. The start of the Fort Night, when lørdag 21 turned into søndag 22.

The v-unit whined. Jack answered. "Sundowners in the main bar, sir. Start of the Fort Night."

"You won't be celebrating *forlorn tid*, surely?"

"Yes, sir. We think of it as an act of defiance."

Seltid was geared to the major solar events as seen from Jordvik—midnight, sunrise, transit and sunset. Thanks to Jordvik's zero-zero position these events coincided with the moon-phases as seen from Earth: new moon, first quarter, full-moon and third quarter respectively. They always fell on søndag, 'sun-day', the 1st, 8th, 15th and 22nd of the *månad*, the lunar month. It merely needed an intercalary period of two hours tacked onto the end of each lørdag to pad the *månad* out to fit the sun-cycle: the Creator having rashly overlooked the benefit of making the Moon's orbital period a whole number of 25-hour units.

The intercalary: *forloren tid* in Selensk—lost time. "Lost" in the sense that sinners were lost, or the Prodigal Son. A time outside Time, between lørdag and søndag, when clocks stopped for a couple of hours—work stopped too (if you worked weekends) and bottles were uncorked. A time for lovers to lie in bed in each others' arms. A time for *hygge*, for remembrance of absent friends... and for grief.

In sudden decision Jack leapt to his feet and took the elevator—not to the bar, but to the hopper pad. He wasn't the only one with that idea. Standing shoulder-to-shoulder in the small silent crowd, he looked south over the site of the Gaiascope.

It was a grey gruel of molten rock and girders, harshly strewn with long shadows. A half-Earth glowed blue in the sky, indifferent to having lost a glittering temple of worshippers on its faithful satellite.

Jack tried to pray, to reach out in spirit to the souls of the thousands who had perished, leaving not a rag behind. But the *De Profundis* died on his lips. He couldn't summon the perseverance—or was it the gall?—to mutter them an obscure formula all the way through to its final *Amen*.

A woman next to him got out a camera and held it up to her eye to take a picture. It clicked beside the ear of the man in front, who span round with an oath and struck it out of her hand. She turned to face the others in indignant appeal, but she must have seen in people's eyes nothing but sympathy with her assailant. With a petulant flourish she scooped up her camera and stalked off. Jack too, his chain-of-thought broken, slipped away not long after.

Sundown had begun—the Terminator was approaching—but there was still an hour and a half to go before the sun sank completely beneath the horizon. That put the notion into his head. He got in his hopper and flew to Crater Flammarion, where the Adin beam shone down as ever. And, as ever, he had the look-out chamber to himself and his darkly flickering thoughts.

The last of the sunlight died away and the crater cliff-face quickly dimmed. The only illumination now was the ruddy glow of the Adin crucible, trembling on the walls of the chamber. He sensed Kitty sitting by his side. But it was only his imagination.

In the space of a single year he had lost five people close to him—*five people!* How much grief could a man endure? And yet he himself was still alive. Why?

The Will of God? Or a random event, like the fall of a die? Or worse, a diabolically inverted Russian Roulette: five perish, one lives? Was he supposed to see some meaning in that? Back home he'd have asked the priest. But to whom could he turn now, to tell him what it all meant?

Then it struck him that he'd spent his whole life looking to other people to invest that selfsame life with meaning. Church, family, employer, village… to tell him the meaning of life: *his* life.

Some would have it that "meaning" was nothing but a personal construct, a pattern one projects on the sheer contingency all around, like seeing faces in the fire. If it *was* a purely personal construct, then wasn't it his personal duty to construct it? No one else's. He couldn't expect it to be handed down ready-made, oblivious to the experience of his own lifetime.

He was back in spirit on Wearmouth Bridge. Life, he had concluded then, was nothing but a series of accidents—why see any meaning in it?

But the Gaiascope had been no accident.

You don't get deliberately rescued from an accident. Someone had known it was going to happen—someone lower down the scale than God. Someone… who could use a wristlink.

13　The Mirror Of Understanding

A fragment of light outshining the stars hung over the shallow arc of the lunar horizon. It formed itself into a tiny revolving dumb-bell. The second-hand of an invisible clock, it was taking exactly one minute to turn full-circle.

The dumb-bell grew until it nearly filled Jack's field of vision. With a shock he saw the instruments telling him it was still a mile off. The shaft bulged with an eccentric hub which swelled to a round face with a big-O mouth. Hovering before that gaping mouth, he was a fruit-fly to be sucked-in and swallowed

The snout of the monstrous face became a name inscribed in huge black letters:

OBERON
LUNABORG

As he drifted towards the mouth, mandibles of steel reached out to taste him and suck him in. Now, as far as Selene was concerned, he was dead. He was being reborn into a new world.

•••••★●★••••••

The mechanical arms that had seized his hopper now stacked it away in something like a double-door wardrobe, one of many spaced around the hub's rim. But there were not sufficient wardrobes for everyone who wanted to take a hopper along. On arrival at Lipsky, Jack (enjoying booner privileges) had been granted permission to ascend to the *Oberon* in his own hopper. But once aboard he knew it would have to go back empty to the surface. In a little under two hours, when *Oberon* was once more over Lunaborg, the hopper would be plucked out like an unloved doll from its cot and flung back down to the surface.

At Nilsson's suggestion, Jack had donated the hopper to a good cause: the charity for Selstyrke bereaved. For a moment he wondered if Vermat had any next-of-kin. What a fool he was—of course she did: twin daughters! But which of them would have the nerve to claim?

There was ample time for Jack to float himself and his meagre luggage out into the brightly-lit chamber where his hopper lay clamped to the floor—or was it the wall? An asiatic steward, all smiles, made his appearance and ushered him through a round yellow hatchway. Oh, my ears and whiskers, Jack thought. Wonderland—or was it a hobbit hole?

They sank in echelon through parallel levitators down the thousand-foot boom to the *Marsgrav* pod. As they went, Jack felt the quasi-gravity of centripetal force begin to pull on his cheeks. One full turn a minute: that's all it took to simulate Mars gravity at a thousand feet out from the hub.

Jack had elected to "go *Marsgrav*" to acclimatise to his destination. After a year spent on the Moon, the Earth-gravity in *Zemgrav* would have crumpled him to the floor like a handful of paper-clips dropped on a magnet. As it was, he felt obese and oppressed, like a force-fed goose, in the doubling of gravity from Moon to Mars.

Stepping from the levitator, its rings lifting to reveal him like a conjuror's rabbit, Jack met a sight which would have set his brain on fire, were he not drained of feeling by what he had been through.

A cavernous stairwell traversed all fourteen decks of *Marsgrav*. A Fritz Lang fantasy—a *Metropolis* in the sky. Thousands of tivoli-lights glinted like sparks in a bonfire. Velvet-sleeved chrome rails lined the balconies on every deck. Gigantic chandeliers, each a waterfall of frozen fire, hung from a gothic vaulted roof.

Seven beacons on alternate landings, fairy castles swathed in iridescent mists, reached up like giant stalagmites to the tip of each chandelier. Monuments on black marble plinths, through which escalators ran, each beacon was a sheaf of bubble-columns and clusters of coloured globes crawling inside with electric fire.

Altars to the classic Seven Planets, the beacons were ordered as the Days of the Week. Starting with the Sun, which had a chandelier of golden bulbs, the largest of all, they ascended the Stairs through Moon (pale white), Mars (flame-red), Mercury (mixed), Jupiter (purple) and Venus (sea-green)—the chandeliers diminishing in drop—to Saturn (ultra-violet) louring beneath the vault in fierce dark majesty. In this Oranieborg, this Castle-of-the-Heavens, *art-deco* had embarked upon its all-time voyage to the stars.

On every deck, glinting in the beacons' light like gems in the galleries of King Solomon's Mines, stood countless bars and chic boutiques. Matchstick figures in colourful costumes—no two alike—struck attitudes of nymphs and satyrs lounging gracefully against pillars or propping legs on spidery stools. A rustle of voices like gold leaves descended as, twined in soaring counterpoint, strains of strings seeped down from crystal spheres.

To glide down steps in one-third *g*, even the hundred-and-sixty-nine steps needed to span fourteen lofty storeys, makes few demands on stamina. But, for the weary, escalators of progressively advancing speeds ran down the centre of the stairway, past lovers lounging on the sable carpet and children capering with echoed calls.

Onto these moving stairs the steward conducted Jack. They could have gone by levitator straight to any deck, but that was to contravene instructions from the owners, *Interverden*. Every new-arrival from the Moon had to be shown *Oberon* in all its gothic magnificence.

They glided along corridors which opened every three yards onto views at once expansive and crowded. Jack felt like a diver wading among wispy weed and rainbow coral ever out-of-focus.

Somewhere in all this lurked Tvoul.

The steward showed Jack to his cabin. After the roominess of his private ward in the Galen Clinic, to say nothing of his stay at the Jordvik Artemis, a single-bed cabin seemed stuffy and cramped. Casting a practised eye around the cabin to check that all was in order, the steward stood back to let Jack creep in.

The bed was made up. Towels stood neatly folded in their rack. Complimentary scents and lotions clung by magnetic bottoms to a gleaming tray. Silently, without a word, not even to invite a tip, the steward closed the door.

Jack found himself alone, standing in what felt just then like a prison cell. Six months to go before landfall on Mars. The prospect of the journey stretched ahead of him like a custodial sentence—or a lifelong vow, taken in a fit of disregard. But he didn't want to roam outside. The terrifying vastness he'd encountered on the Stairs, and glimpsed again through corridors, had shrunk his stomach to a knot.

Agoraphobia: the dread of open space. Had he become a chronic sufferer now? Was he reduced to skulking in his cabin for the next eight months, having all his meals sent in?

He ran his fingers through his hair. What was the matter with him? He used to think of himself as a confident, outgoing person. But now he was a hedgehog, wanting to curl up and present to the world a seamless coat of prickles. Post-traumatic stress disorder, PTSD, but he had no way of knowing he'd succumbed.

Kicking off his shoes, he flopped on the bed and slid with loathing underneath the duvet. There he lay in silence, tensed-up, fingers laced painfully behind his neck. There was no comfortable position. Like someone crucified, he could only shift his weight from one wounding nail to another.

He tried to think of Earth, of the Durham countryside, of the big grubby ports along the North-East coastline. But life, as he was striving to recall it, had ended long ago. To grope for one single wisp of memory was to try to think back to a time before birth.

Reborn as a galactonaut, a novel breed of planetless humanity, was he doomed to spend his life in bright-lit coffins, serviced by impersonal stewards with disinterested smiles? Outside the walls, was there never to be anything but empty space, stretching to infinity on every side? Was this the fate of anybody fool enough to shed his shoes and flee the mother-planet?

•••••✳●✳•••••

An upside-down seashore: a negative photograph. A flaming, foaming flood-tide smearing the sands in glares of red and orange. Tumbling waves of blazing hydrogen sweeping across the ceiling of Avenue Five to engulf him. The *Fenris*-wolf, a-howl amid the wreck of *Ragnarok*, lashing its broken chains. Fire licking through his spattered, spitting, spitted lungs, barbecuing them, filling them with greasy fumes. There was no pain: just stifling panic. He tried to scream, but his cry was turned to rubbish in a steel dustbin stitched behind his ribs.

Now all was darkness.

He found he could still move his hands. Clawing and groping, he encountered bedclothes up to his chin. Is that how they put you in your coffin? He reached out sideways, expecting to feel cushioned fabric, or the mahogany veneer of an all-enclosing chipboard casket, but the back of his hand knocked over a bowl of fruit onto the floor. A bunch of grapes went flop and apples rolled about.

"Everything all right, sir?" A voice, needle-sharp but reassuring, came out of the dark behind his ear. Familiar context crystallised around him and the nightmare dispersed.

He hadn't been buried alive. He was embarked on board the *Oberon!*

"Just a bad dream. Sorry for the fuss..." He groped upwards for the bunk light, found it and switched it on.

"No trouble, sir. Sleep well."

Jack struggled up into a sitting position. "Oh, don't go yet. Tell me something."

"Yes sir?"

"Is there a bar still open?"

"Whichever one you like, sir. We never sleep."

•••••✳●✳•••••

Thrusting aside the bedclothes, Jack staggered to his feet. If this was hell, then let's be getting on with it. Soon he was back on the Stairs-to-the-Stars, stepping across the ebony treads to one of several escalators drifting down past columns of mist and flashing coloured fire to the ballroom on the bottom deck. At the end of the Stairs he stepped off onto a darkened landing and pushed his way through cinema doors which took him one deck further.

Then he halted in lip-sagging awe.

He was in an endless open space, seemingly without walls. Pillars hung down from the dark ceiling like twisted icicles, or the trunks of spectral trees blotched with glowing colours like magic lichen. Each descending pillar fanned out in an inverted canopy to retain the floor... if floor there was, for it was quite transparent. Indeed it was mostly ice—as was the major part of *Oberon*.

Jack felt the experiences of a lifetime up-ended. For beneath his feet the heavens lay spread-out, as if reflected in an unruffled pool.

The stars were real though, not reflections. *He* was the pool, the insubstantial image, standing as it were on empty space. He and the forest of icicles in which he hung suspended. As *Oberon* rotated, familiar constellations crept between his toes, to sink in everlasting night. He gazed down at the Milky Way. It was a shining path beneath his feet, leading through the dark of an empty valley.

He was standing in *Forstandens Speil*, as it was rendered in HC Andersen's archaic Danish—the Mirror of Understanding. It was a stunning conception of the Castle of the *Sneedronning*: the terrible Snow Queen. Along with the ill-starred Gaiascope it ranked as one of the Seven Man-made Wonders of the Universe. Here and there, carved into the floor, were runes of icy shards, repeating over and over the same word in Selensk, M1 and M2:

Evigheden
Vétchnost'
Eternity

...the very word which Little Kay was told he must spell, in order to become his own man and win the whole world—plus a new pair of skates into the bargain.

Kay, his heart warmed back to life by his faithful Gerda, didn't stay to collect the promised skates, but in the Snow Queen's absence fled her realm. Yet hordes of people in dazzling white, slipping and weaving like the formidable snow-bees, which had all but overpowered Gerda, skated on the *Speil* to the echoes of a cathedral organ, evolving melodies at once familiar and strange.

As he watched them slither and spin, the inverted lunar horizon peered beneath the rim of the icicle ceiling, causing it to glister in a rainbow rope. The greeny-white Moon goggled in, cat-like and greedy, ogling the prancing pixies in their frosted glade. It spread across the glassy floor until the whole ensemble stood on nothingness a hundred miles above the pitted lunar surface.

Then, at the rim where the Moon-Cat had first peered in, the dark horizon reappeared, now the right way up, and the lunar surface tilted away. Once more, night spread across the icy floor.

Presently Jack saw the Earth beneath his feet, just as though he had undergone a heavenly ascension to a height absurd. The pearly globe crept between his ankles, rolling like a glass marble he might pick up and put in his pocket. But it wasn't his for keepers.

The planet Earth had come adrift from the soles of his feet. Now it would sink like a pebble in the depths of memory. Inconceivable that his shoes had ever rested on that rolling ball!

As if sleep-walking, he sat down at a vacant table. It was carved from clear ice, as were the chairs. Ample furs gave comfort, whatever people chose to wear. The *Speil* was by no means cold. Ice conducts heat badly. So does space—or thermos flasks wouldn't work. The icy floor, chilled just sufficiently by empty space, took little harm from the room-temperature above. Builders of igloos have known it for millennia.

Presently, seeing no waitresses, Jack got up and wandered across the starry deck towards the lights of the nearest bar.

And there Little Kay met his Gerda.

·····✳●✳·····

"Gabrielle!"

Her lovely face froze in amazement as she turned to take his order. "Jack, it's you!"

"What a surprise to see you here. Is bar-work your life now, like?"

Her pencilled eyebrows, raised in surprise, now lowered in an easy smile. "*Naaw*—but it breaks the tedium. It gets me out to meet people. People like you." Her smile broadened. "So... what'll it be, bonny lad?"

"The mixture as before." Jack caught the sound of a laugh escaping him. A laugh of pure glee. It must have been the first time that had happened since the Gaiascope.

"Midsummer Madness, if memory serves." Gabrielle's voice sounded just as lively, as he couldn't fail to spot. "Endless summer days: is that what you've achieved, Jack?"

"A minute ago I wouldn't have said so. But all of a sudden, coming across you like this…"

Gabrielle, still smiling, dropped her gaze. He hadn't meant to flirt with her, Jack told himself. Nor she with him, no doubt. Just boon-companions in a chance reunion, sharing a private joke.

"When do you come off-duty?"

"Any time you like," she said. "That's if Fritz doesn't mind." She glanced aside to indicate the barman. "I'm only doing an hour or two, now and again."

"Well, tell you what: make yourself one of those things too and bring 'em both to where I'm sitting. Over there: the nest of green icicles with the seat inside."

······★ ● ★······

Jack had scarcely settled back in his nook than Gabrielle was there. Two tall glasses of Midsummer Madness were set down on the crystalline table. Sitting down beside him, she raised her glass.

"To Health, Jack—and I must say you're looking well. Better than I saw you last."

"That wouldn't be difficult." Jack twisted his mouth. "If I recall, I had to be carried off the spaceplane like a sack o'potatoes, straight to the Galen. *You* were a tower of strength."

"Just doing what I'm paid for," she replied, smiling modestly before sipping her drink. "You've no idea the state some folks are in when they come off the spaceplane."

"Why-aye!" Jack tried a laugh, but it came out like a puppy yelp. "A three-day space-flight is a wee bit gruelling for an ambulance run."

"But people do it all the time."

"What a lot of clowns there are." Smiling, Jack shook his head, dismissing himself along with everyone else who undertook the journey for their health.

Her eyes smiled blandly over the rim of her glass as she put it to her lips for a miniscule sip. He guessed what she was thinking: come on Jack, talk about something else besides your operation.

"Holiday of a lifetime for you?"

Her eyes flashed. "You bet."

"Have you got a place to go when you get to Mars? That's if you're not staying on board." Jack toyed with the notion, altogether premature, of inviting her to come and stay with him. He was being absurd: this girl knew what she wanted out of life. Would she be travelling to Mars without everything fixed up?

The hesitancy of her reply came as a surprise. "There's five days while *Oberon* orbits Mars, shipping its passengers and taking on supplies for the journey back. I won't stay on board. If my first sight of Nix City doesn't put me off completely, I'm simply going to jump ship."

"Can you do that?"

"Just let them try to stop me. The worst the Galen can do is fire me. But as a nurse I'll get a job anywhere. The Vratch will take me on, if no one else. It's for the Mars authorities to decide whether or not to let me stay. If they don't want you, they let you know pretty quick."

"It sounds a bit daring."

She took a breath and her face went solemn. "Oh, Jack, you can get heartily sick of shuttling to and fro between Middlesbrough and Lipsky, carting off an endless stream of old crocks to the Galen... Sorry— present company excepted."

Jack laughed and put down his glass. "Don't worry lass, I sympathise. I wasn't exactly a bundle of laughs when you carted me off to the Galen."

Her chuckle was an absolution. "I must say you're looking fit now, though. Does it give you any trouble?"

"The SP unit? You heard about it?"

"Jens told me. I can't imagine what Mr Sullivan was thinking of. He's not exactly popular with the superox firms. 'The SP-killer', they call him on the ward."

"It wasn't his first suggestion. He offered to grow me a new pair of lungs."

"That's more like the Mr Sullivan I know..."

"I didn't give him a chance. My own fault. But I'm happy with my SP unit. It's a lot better than what I had before: a pair of clapped-out lungs from years of quarry dust."

"No trouble getting superox?"

"*Naah.* There's a nose hook-up in my cabin. I don't even have to go along to the gents, like I did on the Moon."

"Then you're..."

Gabrielle stopped trance-like in mid-sentence. Jack was no longer taken aback by such a thing. He did it himself—everyone did. It was the natural response to your wristlink vibrating. She glanced down at her lap.

"I'm sorry, Jack, I'm going to have to leave you. My passenger wants to see me back at the cabin." Rising to her feet, she said "Remember me to Jens, when you're next in touch."

"I won't be seeing Jens again," said Jack quietly, staring at his fingers.

"No, I suppose you won't. Not if you're planning on staying in Nix City." She raised her hand in muted farewell and turned to walk away.

"Jens is dead," Jack muttered at her back.

She froze and rotated like a shop-window dummy on a motorised plinth. "What did you say?"

"Jens is dead. A lot of people died in the Gaiascope. Jens… Vermat… Kitty Martin…"

"Jack!" She bent down and clutched briefly at his forearm. "We've got to talk!"

Then she was gone.

••••★●★••••

Other people might like to hang-out in the galleries overlooking the Stairs-to-the-Stars, but Jack foresaw spending much of his time in the *Speil*. Sitting in the crystal gloom beside the winding skaters, watching the Milky Way drift beneath his feet, he had other words to spell besides Eternity.

Words like Love and Hate. Yearning and Desire. Satisfaction and Redress.

The next day, after the best night's sleep he'd had for ages, he wandered down to the *Speil* and saw Gabrielle there in her crimson uniform. So she was here as a courier, after all. Escorting another first-class passenger—to Mars.

She was sitting at an ice-table in the company of a big man with hair cropped like a wallpaper brush. Two heavy tumblers made of ice and holding bluish drinks stood on the table. They looked untouched. She glanced briefly up at Jack but didn't let-on. That caused him fleeting pain, but he realised he ought to be grateful. He had no wish to meet her companion, hulking great brute that he looked, though Jack only had a rear-view of the man. So he took himself off to one of the bars overlooking the Stairs.

Around 10am, stewards rounded up the passengers from the bar and strapped them into pull-down seats along the walls. It was time for the

Big Jump. In a little under an hour the public address announced that the *Oberon* had detached from lunar orbit and was now in free-flight. They were underway for Mars—and the voyage would take thirty-three weeks.

When Jack got back to his cabin he found a note pushed under his door, scrawled in pencil on a folded page torn from a shorthand-pad: "C U Sp 1400 G".

"Sp" clearly meant the *Speil.* "1400" had to mean 2pm. He was just about to send a text reply by wristlink when he thought better of it.

Gabrielle could have used wristlink, but she hadn't. Why not? Risk of interception? By whom?

Shval, of course. Nilsson had warned him she'd be on board.

······ ★ ● ★ ······

"Another rich client? Another Martian?"

"The same passenger: the last one I brought from Teesside. Since then I haven't been home."

"Who is it?" It was only when he'd blurted it out that Jack remembered what Jens had reported to him about Gabrielle and her strange passenger at Lipsky.

"I'm forbidden to tell. It's meant to be super-confidential. But I wonder if you don't know her name already. When you were in hospital I bumped into your man Jens at Lipsky Rumhavn as I was escorting her. I couldn't avoid having to introduce her…"

"Tvoul …Radouga," muttered Jack. He'd had to think hard to remember which name she'd been travelling under. To start with he'd nearly said "Shval Meteor"—but Gabrielle was not supposed to know that. Then he'd almost come out with "Tvoul Williams"—which would have triggered all sorts of awkward questions. Starting off with: how was it that a groubian, of all people, had the same surname as him?

Gabrielle nodded. Her face showed not a flicker of surprise. It was almost as if she knew as much as he did. But she couldn't possibly know about Shval and the Meteor Gang being let out of custody to board the *Oberon.* Nor could she know that the "Tvoul Radouga" she had escorted back to Lipsky had then made its way home to Godunov. And there it had been pounded back to ectoplasm by the Meteor Gang.

"Where is she?" Jack checked himself. His voice had grated in his ears like crushed granite.

"She's in a private suite. She's keeping herself to herself. She's a very sick woman." Gabrielle forced a smile. "Shall I tell her you're asking after her?"

"Er—no don't do that." But Gabrielle's mystery passenger was sure to know he was on board anyway. "That is..." he muttered, "let her come and find me if she wants."

He stretched his ribs, going through the motions of taking a deep breath, and resumed eye-contact, trying to appear confident. "Yeah—tell her I'm here if you like. But don't fix up a meeting or anything ...unless she wants you to." He squirmed in his seat, trying to get comfortable. His confused reaction must have puzzled Gabrielle. He must be careful what he said to people, even to Gabrielle.

Especially Gabrielle. It might get back to her passenger.

But that didn't mean that he should avoid the girl. On the contrary. She gave him to understand she didn't have to attend to her charge 25/7. The groubian had two gaian companions caring for her. These two, plus Gabrielle, worked an informal shift system, all meeting up for the 25th-hour. So Gabrielle got some time-off: nominally 16 hours per circadian.

"And the three of them are really, really nice... to get away from, I don't mind telling you. That's why I've been volunteering for bar-work. If I've got some other duty then I can't so easily be dragged back to do a bit more than my share. So... come along to the *Speil* any day and you'll see me in one of the bars."

"There's a sick person here needing attention..." said Jack, grinning broadly.

"Why should I go filling my time with old crocks? Busman's holiday for a nurse." She was having difficulty keeping her face straight. "Anyway you don't look very sick to me. I reckon the Galen was a rest-cure for you."

"Listen, hinny," said Jack with a severity his face belied, "I've got stainless-steel innards. There's more steel in me than a chicken on a Rotissomat..."

"It doesn't go all the way down, does it?"

"It goes down far enough. You leave all these handsome virile young men alone. They aren't good for you. Me—I... well you know me. I've got no insides, pet. I'm stuffed like a Christmas turkey. You're perfectly safe with me."

He was surprised by the vehemence of her laughter. She said "Do I detect a hint of *jealousy?*"

"I saw the great big bugger you were with this morning. You could split open with a guy like that. What the hell do you see in him anyway—or daren't I ask?"

She simulated dyspepsia. "That's one of Tvoul's two companions—the people I'm trying to avoid."

"Geddaway! What about the other?"

"The other's a sack of potatoes on wheels. No, Jack, I'm serious. The big fellow is pestering me—when he's not bullying me. It's going to be a long voyage if I can't get away from his halitosis for an hour or two. It's a damsel in distress here. Save me."

"You're just saying that. Really he thrills you like sixty-six thousand volts."

But the way she shook her head convinced him otherwise.

She squeezed his wrist. "Jack, I'm going to have to go now. It's my shift doon-the-pit, like. But let's meet up. We can talk about the land we've left behind, if we run out of other things. I don't know when I'm ever going to see Earth again, let alone South Hylton."

A moment later she was gone, leaving Jack in brooding thought. But first she'd planted a tiny kiss on his forehead, wafting him with perfume from her cleavage. The whole thing screamed "I'm yours—if you can stand the pace."

Safe with him? Maybe she was: maybe she wasn't. But she certainly wasn't safe with the two "gaian companions" she'd described. The Meteor Gang, without a doubt.

As for the mystery groubian: Shval? Or Tvoul? Either way he fell to wondering if Gabrielle wasn't in danger of mysteriously disappearing before the journey's end. The idea gave him a nasty oily feeling behind his bladder.

Why hadn't it occurred to him to book Gabrielle to travel on to Mars with him? Then she'd have been *his* courier, and he wouldn't have had to worry about her keeping company with those scallywags.

Then he cursed himself for a heartless fool. Being suddenly plucked out of one environment into quite a different one had briefly driven the lunar episode right out of mind. But back then he'd had Kitty—and she'd had a ticket to Mars, too. How could he have forgotten, if only for a moment?

He shut his eyes. Immediately, with a shock of panic, he opened them. God!—now the nightmares were attacking him in his waking hours. For one dreadful instant he had seen his friends and loved ones standing in a row: Harry... Hilda... Jens... Vermat... Kitty...

Gabrielle... one behind the other, fading away like endlessly-reflecting mirrors in a fairground stall. Then, like loose pages, each was getting blown away in turn by the remorseless wind that blew past the Moon, past Mars, and on past Titan. The solar wind.

And in that instant he knew that wherever the wind blew, that's where he would have to go too.

What was going to happen to Gabrielle? Something was: he couldn't help feeling it. Behind that pretty face, occultated by it, there was a skull glowing sunset-red in the darkness, like the full-moon during a total eclipse.

He could feel the superox inside him foaming a little too vigorously, boiling over perhaps. It was the SP unit's effort at underpinning a panic-attack: a ghostly simulacrum of an aching heart, for the one he no longer possessed.

"If you don't have a heart, you can't get it broken..."

Did he say that? Did he really say that?

14   Beautiful Blue and Rugged Red

Coming across Gabrielle again had reawakened Jack's appetite for life. He often caught a glimpse of her. Simply knowing she was around made the whole of *Marsgrav* light up with colour and life. His curiosity returning to him, he took to exploring further and further afield. Bars at first, then dance floors, spas, gardens, shopping malls and in time even the squash courts and the golf course. Golf in Mars-gravity, he discovered, was a very different game from what it was in Castle Eden: his earthbound handicap counting for nothing.

But it was the shopping malls that really caught his imagination. There were shops and services of all sorts, but nobody took any money or made any sort of gesture at a transaction. You simply came and it was brought to you.

"Don't I have to pay for all this?" he said. "Who's running the slate?"

"You'll know soon enough when you get yourself a helmet."

So it wasn't long before Jack went shopping for a helmet. There were three shops to choose from. Jack went into the smallest, where the assistant looked as if he had time to chat.

"I want a helmet."

"If you're staying on Mars, you sure do," laughed the man. "If you're not, then what are you doing in *Marsgrav*?" Fortunately he didn't expect an answer to that.

"So where do I start?"

The assistant picked up something as insubstantial as an eggshell. An ostrich eggshell, except that it looked like a 1950's nickelodeon. "This is the standard model. Oxygen, intertalk, 100 holofaces, intensor order 127…"

"I don't need oxygen. I've got an SP unit."

Without batting an eyelid the assistant picked up another, even lighter and less substantial. "Intertalk, 1,000 customisable holofaces, intensor order 32,767…"

"Same price?"

"Same valuta."

"Sounds like you get more for your money."

"Oxygen is the hardest thing to deliver, so missing that out gives more room for the other things. You're one of the lucky ones, not needing it. People carry the tanks on their backs, their hips, their fannies, up the sides and down the middle. But a tank of O_2 is a tank of O_2—it's a hard thing to hide."

"What's Intertalk?"

The assistant stared at him. "Where're you from?"

"Earth—I mean Gaia."

"Funny, I thought you were Martian, with that booner card. Well on Gaia you have telephone, telegraph, radio, video, this-eo, that-eo... Intertalk replaces all these."

"So you're going to tell me I can talk to anyone in the known universe?"

The assistant stared at him again. "Whyever would you want to do that? You gotta filter out the bastards you *don't* want to talk to."

Jack nodded with lips pursed. The man had a point.

"Well," said the assistant, "the latest helmets have exceptional facilities for that. See here. It'll interface vis-acoustically or direct into your cranial nerves. If you're not used to neurolect then you start vis-acoustic and migrate gradually. It's all unconscious so you'll never know. Except that neurolect increases the bandwidth enormously, which is all to the good. Eventually you'll want to upgrade your intensor, but order 32,767 is enough to start you off."

The assistant leaned forward conspiratorially. "Between you and me, I don't know anyone who uses more than 32,767 components effectively. It's just the feeling you're in control. And in the intensor—that's everything. I guess you don't know what that is?"

"I've heard it mentioned."

The assistant looked at him appraisingly. Clearly it was no use talking to this guy for much longer. "Get signed up for intensor classes. Then if there's any problems with the helmet, come back. Classes will get you to the level of a Martian seven-year-old inside a month."

"Oh thanks," said Jack, feeling patronised.

"Some of those seven-year-olds are pretty nifty, make no mistake. But of course they can't appreciate a whole range of components." The assistant nudged him in the ribs.

"What are they?"

"Sex, of course. *Interspex* too, if you've a taste for that. And for really advanced alien contact, how about a spatio-color holoface? Chat-up those beautiful beasts in their own modality. Go on—try it some time. They won't eat you—ha-ha!"

"There aren't any groubians on board, are there?"

"Just one, I'm told. But she's not getting out much."

Jack thanked the fellow politely and went away the proud owner of a new helmet, having been demonstrated holofaces (you could be an ape or a dragon if you fancied), intertalk (they put a call through to Santa Claus in Lappland) and of course the intensor, which just made a prickly feeling on his face.

But with that prickly feeling he'd had his first introduction to a whole new world of experience—of shared values, of social interaction, of motivation and politics, of information and power. A world orthogonal to anything he'd experienced on Earth.

A world he was going to have to get to grips with, pronto.

····*★ ● ★*·····

There was no intensor on the Moon. Seleneans communicated by wristlink. Their traditions and values were Zemlian—earth-based—even if the calendar was adapted to the lunar perspective. Seleneans traded in crowns, in dollars, in yen, in anything which had a quoted value on Earth—and a few things that didn't, like *selkroner* and *hygge*. But they traded. Value was unidimensional. There was a single legal exchange-rate for everything. Like Gaia, Selene was a cash society.

On Mars that notion had been discarded right from the inception of the very first gaian colony. It was rightly said that *valuta*, as a concept, was over fifty thousand years old. But it had needed adaptation to the three unique components of gaian society, collectively speaking: greed, fear and illusion, before it could underpin a multi-species republic. And without the component of *interspex* it would never have happened. This was the perplexing lesson Jack took away with him after the first week of intensor classes.

"Does anyone know what a tensor is? Any mathematicians here?"

Jack had worked as a quarryman. It was nothing he was going to admit to here. After he'd been put on the sick-list with "dust" (emphysema)—a common occupational illness in Durham—and had got his compensation, he'd started work again, the government having retrained him as a mathematician.

His aptitude for Mathematics had come as a surprise to people, not least to himself. In the economy of Wear Valley there had been no reason to encourage it as a young man. You were nobody if you didn't have a proper job, that is, wielding a shovel. In those days it paid a good wage.

A young man fresh out of college put up his hand. "A field descriptor which generalises matrix algebra to handle non-linear transformations."

"Correct," said the instructor. "There speaks a pure mathematician trained on Gaia. What do you do for a living?"

"I'm a teacher."

"Teacher, eh? Well, how would you like to know that on Mars we turn that on its head? We teach tensors to kids of six just starting school and then we teach linear transformations as a special case."

The teacher whistled. "I can't believe it! 'Tensors for toddlers'... 'My first book of tensor analysis'..."

"Something like that. Remember that kids of six can manage the intensor as well as an adult. Often better—like they can climb things better. They want to know how it works. Another definition of tensor please? Someone else..."

"A way of transforming co-ordinates between mutually-accelerating reference-frames."

"Splendid. We've got an applied mathematician here too: a relativity theorist. Any advances on that?" The instructor still hadn't got the answer he wanted.

"A mathematical description of curvature, especially the curvature of space-time due to gravity."

"Thank heavens for physicists: love-em-all. Give me a common application for a tensor."

The man who'd replied was a little less confident. "Well, like I said... gravity, in Einstein's General Theory..."

"Too difficult," said the instructor. He held up a child's blue rubber ball and a reddish potato. "Try again. Here's a hint."

"Oh, of course: curvature of a surface."

"You've got it." The instructor put down the potato and held aloft the rubber ball. He marked a spot on it with a pen. "Does this *need* a tensor to define the curvature at this point? Someone else please..."

"No," said an older man. "It doesn't *need* one. A knowledge of the radius of the ball will do."

The instructor put down the ball and picked up the potato, marking a spot with his pen. "What about this point here?"

"A single radius won't describe it," said the older man. "Needs a tensor: a covariant tensor of rank two."

The instructor tossed the potato onto the table. "So now let us define the Martian intensor. It is a multi-dimensioned covariant tensor of rank two describing the overall valuta at any point on the surface of the planet. Its components are the battery of sensations you feel on your face when you wear a Martian helmet."

He stopped and stared at the class. "There, I've said it all. We can pack up now and all go to the bar."

The class stared back blankly. Even the two mathematicians and the physicist were nonplussed.

"Puzzled? Okay, let's go back to Gaia." He picked up the blue ball again. "On Gaia you can label any object on the surface with its price—in dollars, roubles, or ounces of gold. It doesn't matter—it's just a question of scaling. The economic surface of the planet is a scalar field—a tensor of rank zero if you like. Everything maps down to one single component: price. If you have a ton of gold, you can buy anything—according to a pre-determined rate-of-exchange. A cup of water, a bowl of rice, a wife. You can buy love—or hatred, You can buy compliance—or disobedience. Smiles, or kisses. All you need is gold: or some scalable equivalent, like paper money."

He tossed the ball in the air and caught it with a flourish. "Gold corresponds to the radius of this ball. It is fixed in value across the planet. The entire economy can be described in terms of it. That's the gold standard."

He discarded the ball with a toss of his hand and picked up the potato. "On Mars it's a different story. If you have a ton of gold, it won't do any good unless somebody wants *gold*: up to a ton of it."

Jack thought of a book he'd read as a boy: *Utopia*, by Thomas More. A worldly-wise man, who just so happened to be a Catholic martyr. His name was also inscribed on the walls of the Kremlin as a Hero of the Revolution. But it was *Utopia*, not martyrdom, that had earned him that honour.

In More's fictitious republic of *Utopia*, gold was kept only for external trade. Prisoners were fettered with the gold-reserve in order to encourage the common people to despise it. Coincidentally the Lunarians, in H G Wells's *First Men in the Moon*, did the same thing.

He spoke up. "Doesn't gold have any use on Mars—except as fetters for convicts?"

The instructor laughed. "Oh, yes. Or rather it has valuta. Gold, food, health, love, respect, fame, honour: all these have distinct components. Which become tensor-components. It needs a tensor to describe them and how they flow and interact. The gearing between them is in constant flux. If you want to throw a ton of gold into the mix, you can withdraw one particular thing to restore the economy to exactly the state it was before—and only that one thing. Gold. To the total amount of precisely one ton."

He paused to let the implications of that sink in.

"But what if you want a wife in return—or love, honour, respect? You cannot buy it with gold. Oh yes, you can put your gold into the economic manifold, the *ecoman* as we call it, and tap the funds of love, honour, regard... but these things are not priced in gold. The effect is to twist the intensor. And this shearing force will be felt on the face of everyone you meet. Their helmets will tell them: here is a man who has fed the *ecoman* with one ton of gold and has withdrawn X amount of love, honour, regard... what you will."

The instructor smiled and put his hands on his hips, as if he'd made everything clear. But still his audience looked puzzled.

Jack felt he had to speak for the audience. "Does nothing at all have a price, then? As we understand it on Earth?"

"No. Mars has discarded the notion as useless. Harmful, in fact...

It's just what they do
On Beautiful Blue."

Jack groused "Well, if this valuta thing is so damn brilliant, why doesn't Beautiful Blue go all overboard for it, like?"

The instructor sighed and again picked up the ball and the potato. "Look..." he said. His eyes roamed the room. "Does anyone here understand Classical Thermodynamics?"

A man at the front made a hesitant gesture. The instructor asked him "If we consider entropy as a measure of unpredictability, which system would you say has the lower entropy: the ball, or the potato?"

"The ball."

"What would happen if the two systems were suddenly brought into contact—to make one system?" He touched them together. "Which would gain entropy and which would lose it?"

"The ball would gain it."

"And how would that affect the ball's predictability, and therefore its controllability?"

"It would become less predictable, less controllable."

"At what point would the combined system reach thermodynamic equilibrium?"

"When the entropy of the two became the same."

The instructor looked around. "And what's the popular name for that process... anyone?"

"Intermondialisation...?" came a hesitant voice from the back.

"Exactly." The instructor placed both objects at opposite ends of his desk. "Now the guardians of Gaia, in their sublime wisdom, don't want that to happen. They want to preserve control. They think of Mars as a colony, an out-station of the USSR—(don't ever say that word on Mars!) They dare not contemplate being swallowed up in the Martian economy, for all the misery it would spare their people. So they carry on with their crude, unworkable systems. They shore them up and cosset them along, hoping to avoid wars, famines, markets being monopolised and resources being cornered. All of which are the inescapable consequences of a world based on money."

"How do they manage to 'preserve control'?" exclaimed Jack.

"The Treaty of Moscow, 1872, sealed off the global economy of Gaia from the Martian *ecoman*. Wealth can only be transmitted across the firewall of Selene. Jack—you'll be familiar with how that works in practice. Have you, as a booner, ever had to pay *selkroner* for anything?"

Jack shook his head slowly.

"Are you having to pay anything now?"

Jack's head went into shorter, quicker shakes.

"The upshot of the Treaty of Moscow is that Terrestrial governments are locked into the situation of having to lie to their own people about the existence of other worlds than their own. They are going to great lengths to support this egregious fiction: even to mounting huge expensive space-programmes to make it appear that System Sol has yet to be colonised—and that they, the governments of the USA and USSR, hold the key to its exploration. The reality is that anyone on Earth can pick up the telephone, dial Mars and ask for someone to come and pick them up."

Jack's eyes bulged. He looked around the room. Everybody had their heads down: the statement had been totally uncontroversial.

"Right, so everyone understands the intensor?"

The audience returned a stony stare.

"Look," the instructor shook his forefingers like six-shooters. "It's all summed up in the saying: *How many smiles in a kiss?*"

·····*●*·····

Jack left the lecture room with his head spinning. None of that had gone in—or so he thought. But his mind was no longer resting on its old foundations. All his notions of value and accountability, of love and honour, of human intercourse itself, now appeared to be founded on shifting sand. Wearing his new helmet, he savoured the various tingles, burns, chills, pricks, pressures and stretches on his face as he passed people in the concourse.

"Covariant Tensor of Rank Two," he said to himself—and made a funny little noise.

"Aura" was a good word. You could talk about people's auras clashing. Like his and the instructor's. Some folk made little impression—he didn't feel they'd be worth knowing. But others twisted his face to the point of pain—they 'overfaced' him. That happened to be an M2 word also: one of those with an evolved meaning. These people, he realised, were the movers and shakers of the intensor. They were significant: but for what he couldn't say.

Some people actually scared him. Some caused sensations that were curiously appealing. But for only one person did he feel nothing but a neutral presence. One of the vessel's officers: a booner, as he later discovered. Not economically active—not *econact,* as they said in M2.

That must be how he felt to other people.

Watching the skaters hurtle across the glassy expanse of the *Speil,* he caught a glimpse of someone who looked just like Harry. There must be lots of young men like Harry: brave young hopefuls, travelling out to the delights and rewards of Mars. Jack wanted to go over to him, take him by the arm and warn him about groubians. He was all set to do so when he lost sight of him. He never saw the lad again for the rest of the trip.

• • • • ∗ ✷ ● ✷ ∗ • • • •

He got back to his favourite bar in the *Speil* and there was Gabrielle behind the counter with a ready smile for everyone. She too was wearing a new helmet. It was shaped like swans' wings cradling her temples and looked most fetching. He felt her aura on his face. It was sweet and beckoning, like a lover's caress. With a stab of jealousy he understood that what he felt didn't arise purely out of his own sentiments, but was the sum total of regard of everyone in *Marsgrav.* By working behind the bar and dispensing simple pleasures she had built up an attractive persona in the intensor.

But once again she was content to abandon the bar for him and they settled down with drinks.

"I didn't get a single thing out of that class," groused Jack. "All the instructor could do was rabbit-on about rank-two covariant tensors. It's far more instructive just to walk around with the helmet on and *feel* folk on me face."

"My instructor was a bit more helpful. Likened it to running a tab behind the bar. The individual drinks are put down, but instead of totting it all up at the end of the day it's simply left like that. Everyone runs a tab with everyone else, in effect. It's all managed centrally of course, so you don't have to bother with the details."

"How's it all accounted-for? I mean—when's the reckoning-up?"

"There isn't one."

"What? You mean to say I can just keep on drinking ten year old malt whiskey for ever and a day and nobody's going to mind?"

"Oh, they'll mind all right. It'll show up in the intensor."

"That I'm a bugger for malt whiskey?"

"That you're drawing on too much valuta and not giving anything in return. People will start leaning on you."

"What if they run out of malt whiskey? I can work like stink to rebuild my valuta—incred—whatever. But it won't help any."

"They won't run out. Scarce commodities can be rationed if needs be. But it never gets to that point. As malt whiskey gets scarcer, folk increase its gearing. Doubling the gearing means you can only get one glass for the valuta of two. Before it runs out altogether, it's maxgeared."

"But nothing's in endless supply…"

"You're still thinking in money terms. The system knows. It's got the information. On Earth all that info gets lost when quantities are converted to their cash-value. That allows people to trade in commodities and hoard them and give the impression of a shortage when really there isn't one. On Mars that can't happen."

"But how do I *earn* me whiskey?"

"You don't. Forget about 'earning' and words like that. You get to drink it because people put up with having you around. Of course some people put up with you less than others. If they don't like you all that much, they'll increase the gearing of anything they dish out to you. If they don't like you at all, they'll maxgear you. You want to avoid that."

"Why?"

"Because it drains your incred. When incred goes negative, people will start to avoid you. You'll twist their noses too much."

"Are you going to maxgear me?"

"I might—if you don't behave."

Jack chuckled. "Only if I deserve it, eh?" He touched her knee, meaning to finger-walk up her thigh. She slapped his hand.

"Pay attention now."

"Yes, Miss." He folded his fingers beneath his chin.

"On Earth," she continued, in a schoolmistress tone, "does anyone really *deserve* their living? A salary is a privilege—you're a kept man—a corporate whore. Meanwhile the people who get paid by the hour, they're just exploited. The government prints money whenever it needs it and corporations create millions with a stroke of a pen."

Jack sat back in amazement. "*Yerbougger*—you *did* learn a lot from your indoctrination classes."

Gabrielle smiled. "I've had a start on you. I've been on *Oberon* before."

"When?"

"For the occasional breakaway with someone. But never going all the way... to Mars."

15   Love in the Intensor

Jack found a tropical garden on Level Five and took a comfy chair in with him to sit among the vines. He used to love the rich smell of the hothouse in Durham Botanical Gardens, warm and moist. But now, lacking lungs, he could no longer appreciate such things. He was reflecting moodily on how he was a spectre of his former self when he felt the oddest sensation beginning to grow on his face, in association with someone approaching. A man brought up a chair and sat down. It was the seven-footer with savagely-cropped hair he'd seen with Gabrielle, who now held out his hand by way of introduction.

"Hamish McDougall. You're Jack Williams, aren't you."

The intensor was telling Jack something important, if only he knew what. The field was so skewed it was giving his face a Chinese burn.

"How do you know my name?"

"By asking around. A Terrestrial sporting a booner card—you do rather stand out."

"Do you make a hobby of prying into other people's business?"

The newcomer held up a hand in sign of peace. "Please, Jack—you don't mind me calling you Jack, do you?"

"Feel free, sunshine."

"I came to offer my condolences. Kitty was a lovely woman. I attended several of her lectures. She certainly knew her stuff when it came to groubians. As a bit of a groubist myself I had nothing but admiration for the way she went about things. I gather you two had grown, er, close of late."

"Kitty was a friend. We both had lots of friends." He wasn't going to say they'd been engaged.

Hamish waved his head about as if rebuffed. "Anyway I felt I had to stop by and say something comforting. And to offer my support if it's any use. You must be taking it all pretty hard."

"Taking all what hard?"

"The Gaiascope atrocity."

"*I beg your pardon?*"

"The atrocity. It wasn't an accident, y'know."

"How do *you* know?"

"It's on TV. Haven't you been watching the news from Selene? They've got someone for it."

"God Almighty!" Jack's jaw dropped. "They told me at Selstyrke it was a complete mischance. A glitch in the Adin beam."

McDougall smiled grimly, as if he sensed he'd got beneath Jack's guard. He gave his head a little shake. "Acting Commissioner Nilsson is a capable investigator, but she does rather fancy herself as an electronics expert. Still, she was fly enough to work through the maintenance records and find out who'd installed the faulty chip."

McDougall leaned forward until their helmets almost touched. "It was not from a reputable source." He sat back to watch the effect on Jack, but must have found it disappointing because he added "It had been laser-reworked and repackaged, turning it into a time-bomb."

"Nilsson told me something about a stray voltage resetting the co-ordinate register to zero, which caused the beam to fall back on the Gaiascope."

"That is exactly what happened. And the engineer who fitted the chip was in receipt of a large sum of money from—can you guess?"

"No."

"From TMG. Faced with the evidence the man confessed. He'll be lucky to escape a capital charge."

"Why are they so sure it was TMG?"

"The money was raised on Selene against Martian credit. A complicated thing to do—and even more complicated to conceal. It was done by a certain Markus Potapenko via property transactions on Gaia and channelled though his sidekick Duke Treikle." Hamish smiled—a nasty smile, Jack thought. "You know these two."

It hadn't been a question.

"I know *of* them," Jack replied. Hamish was watching his eyes. Jack expected to be challenged over that, but Hamish let it go.

"Of course TMG denies all knowledge of the business and claims the two of them were acting alone. Neither of them can answer for themselves—both being dead."

This time Jack kept his face as rigid as a mask.

"But you knew that too. I know you do because Jens Andersen would have told you. If he didn't then Commissioner Vermat would have done." McDougall sighed, as if to show it didn't matter whether Jack admitted it or not.

Jack went over to the attack. "Why would TMG want to kill such a large number of people—and in such a gruesome way?"

McDougall held up his hands. "Wouldn't you like to know. Wouldn't we all. But we've—I mean I, er, have been making some enquiries. I'd hazard a guess that TMG didn't aim to kill so many people. Just one or two. Maybe just one… covering their traces by-the-by."

"Obliterating the Gaiascope at the climax of the Big Show? If that's covering your traces, that's overkill."

Again that nasty smile from Hamish. "I'm not saying they aren't reckless people." He sat back and looked pointedly at Jack. "Pity though they didn't think to blow the sat out the sky, too, while they were about it. A lot of incriminating evidence to leave hanging around in space."

"Mr McDougall," said Jack after a pause, "why are you telling me all this?"

The man shrugged. "I was just thinking—hoping—we could join forces. Your enemies are my enemies too."

"So, who *were* TMG trying to eliminate?"

McDougall leaned forward again. "Tvoul Rainbow… and her *devil brood*."

It was the watchword. But a bit garbled. Surely *this* wasn't the promised agent Jens had signed-up for him? Well, if it was—it was.

Jack dropped his gaze, determined to keep his counsel for the present. "Thank you Mr McDougall—er, Hamish."

McDougall got to his feet, clearly a man to quit while he was ahead. "Let's stay in touch."

* * * * ★ ● ★ * * * *

"So Life on Mars is a matter of hiding your face the whole time?"

"More or less." Gabrielle pouted. Jack could see how that wasn't going to be to her liking. Like the pretty maid in the nursery rhyme, her face was her fortune, sir-she-said.

"You need to," she went on. "For oxygen, if nothing else. Well, *you* don't, but historically speaking, people have needed to. And if you don't want to live in termite-tunnels like you do on the Moon, you have to keep the dust out of your eyes."

Hence the helmet: a definingly, defiantly Martian piece of gear. At a stroke, you were robbed of the subtlety of your richest modality of communication—face-to-face—a language you share with every other primate. But for each natural modality civilisation takes away, it offers an artificial replacement.

Does society demand you wash off all your natural smells? Then wear perfume in their place. Do touch-taboos and hostile climate demand you keep you body covered up, hiding hair, nipples and other natural organs of display? Then wear colourful clothes: ties, dresses and tee-shirts with pictures and provocative texts. Does the Martian desert mean you have to keep your face covered-up like a Bedouin? Then display a holoface— and take advantage of the flexibility it offers. Is your natural face—an organ richly endowed with nerve-endings and musculature—destined to languish incarcerated in an iron mask? Then use it for data communication, in ways hitherto unimagined: a literal inter-*face* to a brave new cyberworld.

Hence the intensor, erecting endless dimensions upon daily life with a richness and immediacy to make the telephone, data screen and keyboard seem as clumsy a way of signalling information as naval semaphore flags. But, as with any highly-textured modality, it was all too easy to signal more than you intended.

"Can't I feel what other people are feeling about me? Is there nothing like a mirror for the intensor?"

Gabrielle's young brain was assimilating the new material much faster than Jack. He found himself relying on her to explain it, whenever he failed to follow his instructor. It didn't help that the fellow was brash and cocky—a PUG graduate *cum laude*. It made it hard for Jack to go cap-in-hand to the younger man for an explanation.

"No, nothing like that. You've got to build your persona through other people's responses to you. That's the whole idea."

"But I need to feel for myself what effect I'm having on people."

"You can't. There are all sorts of checks and balances to prevent it. When the intensor was originally designed, they thought it most important that it should reflect only the incred you gain from other people."

"What's *incred*?"

"Information credit. Infocredit, incredit—it all means the same thing. The sum total of your standing in other people's eyes."

"Oh I remember. The instructor went on about how so many words in English mean something altogether different in M2. He gave *incredible* as an example. If I'm incredible, it means I've got bags of incred. And I'm supposed to be incredulous if I'm blown away by someone else's incred. That's how I feel with you."

"Geddaway with your bother! You'll soon pick it up."

Jack turned about and made as if to tear his hair. "Why—that's as bad as having bad breath. Even your best friends won't tell you." He turned back again to expostulate. "I met a guy the other day who really screwed my face. How was he supposed to know about it?"

"He wasn't. He can't. If you could feel for yourself how you warped the intensor, you'd spend all your time adjusting it to project whatever persona you happened to fancy. So it wouldn't be much of a guide to the real you."

"Oh, charming! That's like living in a goldfish bowl. Is there no privacy on Mars?"

"Plenty. And it's legally guaranteed and personally enforceable. You simply maxgear…"

"I'll be walking around, hiding my face in shame."

"Nobody minds if you hide your face, you know. You've got total control over your holoface—you're supposed to use that to tell others how you're feeling today—how you'd like to be treated."

"So how do I feel on *your* face? In a manner of speaking…"

Gabrielle put her head on one side and twisted her mouth. "Well— you just… feel."

"Champion. What's that supposed to mean? *You* feel all nice and cosy. It's a treat just to be standing near you. Now come on hinny—tell me how *I* feel."

"Well… like any other booner."

"Come again?"

"Like anyone else carrying a booner card. You can turn it off if you want."

"How do I do that?"

"How you do anything. Drop the menu then eyeball the option."

"Okay… now how does that feel?"

Gabrielle grimaced and chuckled. "Ooh, no—you can't go around like that. Turn it on again, quick."

"Flaming hell, flower. That's just the sort of thing a bloke needs to hear. What's the matter with me then?"

"It's not your fault. I guess it's because you've been walking around with a booner card all the time. Without it you feel like… well… all take and no give. But I suppose you haven't had to give anything back yet."

"Whee-ow! So being a booner isn't altogether a good thing."

"It's just that you've been on official business the whole time. Policeman, judge, inspector of one sort or another—you're part of the fabric of society. Whatever your personality, people have to accept you."

"That's me. I'm a Jack-in-uniform."

"You don't need to wear a uniform on Mars. If you're a booner, you're a booner. People don't know what sort, going only by your persona. One booner is as good as another. If you're a policeman, you don't want other people to know that. Not socially. Can you just see an English policewoman having to wear special police perfume?"

Jack doubled up with laughter. "What would it smell like? Carbolic soap, like a nurse? Or pig shit?"

"Well I *am* a nurse, but I don't use carbolic soap. If I was a booner I wouldn't want people to know what sort, unless I told them. The intensor is meant to regulate social transactions between equals. That's what my instructor said. Well, booners are *not* equals."

"I wish I had your instructor. He sounds like he's a good one."

"It's a *she*, not a *he*. There's no parity between booners and non-booners. 'How many smiles in a bash over the head with a truncheon?'"

Jack laughed again. He was getting the idea.

"You don't want people to grade you," she went on. "They're not qualified to do so. You don't want them to know you're on an expense account of so much a year—and it's not as much as a senior booner gets, much less a principal booner. On Mars all booners are equal."

Something lit up inside Jack's head like a flash bulb. "So that's why my booner card has been like a credit card but with no set limit and no monthly bills. I've been on an expense account."

"Yes, that's right. Olympia has simply been paying Selene—in *selkroner*—for whatever it was you wanted. No questions asked."

"Well I never. I thought it was all too good to be true. I guess I'm going to have to tot it up at the other end. Who with, do you reckon?"

Gabrielle was suddenly serious. "I don't know, Jack. But I shouldn't be surprised if there isn't a reckoning of some sort. They're not dragging you all this way for nothing."

"Who's 'they'?"

"I thought *you'd* know that."

They stared at each other wide-eyed. Finally Gabrielle shrugged and turned away. "Perhaps you'd better stay as a booner."

······★ ● ★······

For the rest of the circadian, Jack thought hard about what Gabrielle had said. He didn't want to be different from everybody else. Once on Mars, he'd want to blend in. How else was he going to track down Tvoul without her being forewarned?

He glanced over his shoulder. Wasn't she forewarned already? Wasn't she perhaps watching his every move? Calculating what he'd do next? Well, he'd have to come up with a good cover story on Mars, or he might as well have stayed at home.

Gabrielle was a mystery. She seemed to have plenty of time for him: she was happy to chat with him in public, even to flirt with him. But she resisted all attempts to get her alone and wouldn't come back to his cabin.

He told himself he ought to admire her professionalism. She was a courier after all. They have to keep smiling at their customers while holding them at arm's-length. But he couldn't escape the feeling he was being strung along.

The thought of that stung him. Weren't his feelings being reciprocated? Was it all a professional front? What did she really think of him?

For all its rich modality, the intensor furnished no guidance. Instead it tantalised and mocked. Love in the intensor was like groping naked in a metal blindfold for the object of desire, while everybody stood around and laughed.

······✹●✹······

Midsummer came. In spite of not running on *zemvrem*, the pod was all set to celebrate this festival of purely Terrestrial relevance. It struck Jack that Gabrielle's famous cocktail, her Midsummer Madness, was the driving force. By 3pm they were giving the cocktails away in every bar of the *Speil.*

Soon after 6pm the party began in earnest. Jack tried looking for Gabrielle. She wasn't difficult to find. In fact she found him first— calling out to him over the intertalk from behind. For once he saw her out of her crimson uniform. She was clad in a dress of green velvet, an expensive one that contrived to look as if it had been simply slung round her shoulders rather than fitted carefully.

"My-oh-my, hinny, you're looking gorgeous!"

"Do you like the dress? I put it on just for you."

"From red to green."

Absurdly he thought of traffic-lights: STOP had turned to GO. It was too gross a thought to share. Though judging by the way she smiled, it had communicated itself anyway.

Jack wondered if Gabrielle hadn't already had a lot to drink—an impression which strengthened as the party wore on. She was certainly more relaxed than he'd ever known her—more talkative too. She talked about her childhood in South Hylton, the pets she'd owned, the friends she'd known, laced with funny incidents from her job. Waking up in his cabin and finding her in bed beside him came as no shock—he couldn't recall their ever having said goodnight. There had seemed no need.

He glanced at the bedside clock. 24:28. The magic twenty-fifth hour. Pleasure welling up inside him, he fingered her flaxen hair on the pillow and started kissing her forehead, her face, her chin, her throat.

She opened her eyes, smiled and stretched.

"Well—I've never had a man with an SP unit before."

"Why? What's it like for you?"

"Why it's…" she giggled. "It's just…" she giggled again. She wasn't going to say.

"Now you've made me all embarrassed."

"Go on, bonny lad, there's nothing wrong with you. Everything's in good working order."

"Steel all the way down."

"Like a ploughshare."

How did the biblical saying go? Never look back when first you set your hand to the plough. Thus exhorted on such good authority, Jack finished ploughing his furrow. Lying on top of Gabrielle with his eyes shut, feeling her heart beating against his silent chest, he realised he couldn't see Hilda's face any more. Nor Kitty's. Their images had withdrawn to infinity without any loss of stature, leaving only a benediction: a plenary indulgence redolent of ash and roses. "Till death do us part…" and death had done just that.

"Why didn't we do this before?" said Jack, with a groan of pleasure.

"I'm sorry Jack, I couldn't." He hadn't been expecting an answer, so he went rigid in alarm when Gabrielle gave him one. "I was being watched."

He raised his head with a jerk to stare into her eyes. "There are no snakes in Ireland," she murmured, "for St Patrick stamped out the devil's brood."

It was the watchword—quoted accurately this time. "It's you!" he said. "Why didn't you let on before?"

"Shush. The cabin may be bugged."

Cautiously Jack rolled off her and looked over his shoulder. It was an irrational response.

"If it is," she continued, "perhaps she's given up in disgust."

Ignoring her nakedness, Gabrielle leapt silently out of bed and slipped a pen-like object from her green handbag on the desk. She used it to probe the corners of the walls, floor and ceiling. Then she crept back into bed and embraced Jack again, murmuring in his ear.

"I really put paid to Hamish. I bottled him and left him lying halfway up the Stairs, snoring peacefully. He'll be out of action for days."

"You didn't!"

"It'll be my job to patch him up, so that's worth another few days. Peter's blind drunk too—not often he gets like that. But I was very persuasive. That left only Sh-you-know-who. You've no idea how much it takes to pickle calamari. I Micky-Finned her with a grain of morphine in her crab-juice, but I doubt she's floored for long."

"You mean you engineered it all? Just to get a word with me in private?"

"Well…" she gave a tiny sniff. "To get you in bed, too."

"But I mean—the party. I couldn't think why we were celebrating Midsummer here: halfway to Mars…"

"Oh yes, I organised the whole stunt. Called-in loads of incred I'd been carefully accumulating, so I could shift hundreds and hundreds of my cocktails. There's not a slice of lemon left in the whole of *Marsgrav*."

"*Yerbougger!*"

"Jens warned me not to reveal myself until there was no possibility of certain parties escaping back to Selene—and then to Earth. Jens managed to get together with me on subsequent occasions without Shval's knowledge. At least that's what I hope. But she suspected something. She must have done, to ask for me as courier again."

"Well, there might be another reason for that. Like you're a pretty good one…"

"No. They're watching me like hawks. All three of them."

"So you know it's not Tvoul Rainbow you're escorting?"

"Oh yes. There's no sign of Tvoul. Shval's companions are convinced she's on board, but they don't know where to start looking. I daren't go looking for her myself, for fear of drawing the Gang onto her. We could poll the intensor, but Shval and her triada know how to poll it better than we ever could. You can assume they've tried all that."

"Who are this triada of hers?"

"You've met one of them. He told me so. You've made him quite jealous, so watch your back."

"Aye—I've met Hamish. Tried to kid me he was Jens's agent."

"God—you didn't tell him anything, did you?"

"No. He had the password, almost, but not quite. So I stalled. He knew a good deal though."

"Heaven's knows how. *I* haven't told him. But when it comes to the Meteor gang it's the sort of thing you don't ask. They're information thieves—and they certainly know their stuff. Frankly I don't give much for Tvoul's chances, if she is here in *Marsgrav*."

"What are we going to do?"

"What can we do, until the Martian authorities come aboard? We'll just have to hunker down for the rest of the trip and make the most of it."

She wriggled under him, drew his head down and kissed him, her tongue searching deep within his mouth. When they parted, she gasping for breath, Jack nibble-walked his lips like a moist caterpillar over her cheekbone and tongued her ear-lobe.

"I can't think of a nicer way of passing the time," he murmured.

16   Landfall at Voronka

Jack sat in the empty *Speil*. Beneath the glassy floor the star-strewn sky turned slowly like a crystal sphere. Every minute the planet Mars appeared and filled the dance floor. Jack remembered as a child walking on Roker beach, picking up pieces of brick which the sea had milled into pebbles. That was how Mars looked. A vast lump of clinker, which fate and time had dropped in the sea of interplanetary space and ground down to a pebble.

Gabrielle had left with the Meteor Gang on the first shuttle to the surface. With eight months to prepare for this, it was surprising how much of a rush they were all in by the end. She and Jack made no arrangements to meet up, beyond sharing a desire to do so as soon as Jack had got settled in. Neither wanted to admit that their affair, blossoming in the dreamy hothouse in which they'd been confined, might not transplant to the arid soil of Mars.

Everyone was packing or making last-minute arrangements, getting ready for the drop to the surface. So Jack had the *Speil* to himself. Alone among many, he wasn't floating over this rusty world because he particularly wanted to. He was here only to track down one particular person. Having done that, he could turn around and go home.

He found it easier to direct operations from the *Oberon* itself rather than land on the surface and have to discover the whereabouts of the simplest facilities. He had spoken to the immigration officer and discovered with relief that the Martian authorities had no difficulty accepting that the person travelling as Tvoul Radouga was in fact Shval Meteor. That the real Tvoul Radouga was here as well, going under a different name—but not one that anybody knew. The immigration officer declared that neither of these violated the Olympian criminal code, unless the intensor itself had been tampered-with. On its own, it proffered no excuse for stopping Shval from landing, or even for arresting her when she got to the surface. Even if Shval had committed a crime in another's name, it was incumbent on that other person to take action. Mars, Jack concluded, was a lot easier to enter than the USA.

But if he thought they didn't keep a careful watch on who arrived, he was to revise his opinions.

Jack finally managed to make contact with Jens's agent in the other pod, but only once that worthy had made landfall. They were never to meet in person. The agent assured him that there had been no groubian in the *Zemgrav* pod—and that the Martian authorities were certain that only one groubian had made landfall at Voronka: the one escorted by Gabrielle. Of Tvoul herself there was no sign.

At the hub, shuttles were coming and going, re-provisioning *Oberon* for the return journey. New passengers were coming aboard in sizeable numbers. Some glanced inside the ballroom on their way to their cabins, but didn't stay. Soon the last shuttle would leave for the surface before the great space vessel departed for its home port of Lunaborg. *Oberon* didn't tarry in Mars orbit like it did around the Moon. The conjunction of Mars and Earth, the best time for the outward trip, was the best time for the return journey too. From now on, the two planets would daily draw further apart.

The helmet and the clothes he stood up in were the only things he planned to take with him. Time was drawing on. Reluctantly he got to his feet and paced slowly out of the ballroom.

At the door he turned. Beneath the transparent floor the sun crept across the glass. It was half the diameter he recalled it on the Earth and Moon. Round about it the sky was black. A faint dot accompanied it. Gaia. Under magnification it looked like a nail-pairing. Earth had literally turned its blind side towards him.

Hesitating barely a moment, Jack surveyed what had been home for the past eight months. Then he turned and walked without haste down the concourse, making for the levitator to the hub, where the last shuttle hung suspended in the darkness, waiting for him.

••••✦ ● ✦••••

Stepping into the shuttle, Jack stared through a porthole at the surface. The sunlit side had slipped away and Mars was now for the most part a dark presence blotting out the stars. In Olympia it was the middle of the night. The sun hovered on the distant horizon amid skeins of dry-ice clouds scorched like titanium jewellery into rainbow hues.

Ahead, a darker mass within the darkness, Jack could feel rather than see the sombre presence of Olympus Mons, mightiest volcano in System Sol. Its gradual slopes ascended 15 miles above the plains, rearing up out of the thin choking atmosphere, out of the dust storms which frequently blanketed the planet. The most habitable spot on Mars, the groubians had chosen Nix Olympica as the site of their capital—and the gaians had chosen not to second-guess them.

The Nix came into view as a darker patch against the starlit surface. But as it loomed larger and larger at the destination of their flight path,

Jack could see that it was not altogether black. An extensive network of lit-up roads lay within its tiered pits, a spider's web in the grass on a frosty morning, studded with dewdrops.

Soon the Nix covered most of the visible surface and Jack could make out individual roads in multiple grid patterns like a patchwork quilt. The city to which the Nix gave its name was nearly seventy miles across. Beyond the city, to the south of the Nix, there was a distinctive circular impact crater. Dwarfed by its neighbour, it was nevertheless nearly eight miles in diameter.

Voronka. The "Blast Crater".

As the moment of landing drew near, Jack watched in fascination as the crater turned into the socket of an enormous eye. The pupil—a gigantic iris lens—gradually expanded in a dark circle as the roof of the cosmodrome opened up to swallow them. Once inside the Eye, a landing strip of coloured lights became apparent.

With scarcely a shudder the shuttle touched down. Overhead the wide circle of stars grew smaller and smaller as the Eye closed over them. As soon as the sky had vanished, lights sprang up all around, revealing the stupendous magnitude of the chamber they found themselves in.

The shuttle taxied to the edge of the cavernous enclosure and covered walkways crept out like tentacles to meet them. Presently Jack on wobbly feet was pacing worn red carpets to the arrivals hall.

A huge notice in bright orange letters greeted him.

> *Dóbro pozhálovat' v Kosmodróm Vorónkovo!*
> *Velkommen til Voronka Rumhavn!*
> *Welcome to Voronka Cosmodrome!*
> *Sevódnia: Voskresénie, 1 Dekábria, 400, 24:16 MV.*
> *Idag: søndag, den 1:e december, år 400, 24.16 MV.*
> *Today is: Sunday, December 1, 400, 24:16 MV.*

Quite disorientated, he looked at his old wristwatch. In Esh Winning it was past midnight on Sunday 25 January, 1976. Remembering the vow he made on the Moon, he dropped the watch in the nearest rubbish bin.

Who, if anyone, was going to meet him? How would he recognise them—or would they spot him first?

He followed trilingual signs to the way out. He expected to pass customs or immigration control, though what form they would take he had no idea. Perhaps on Mars such institutions were redundant. There had been plenty of time to process people on board *Oberon*. Plenty of time to find out all about them, why they were coming to Mars and what possible contraband they were carrying. But he'd been asked none of that.

Before he expected to be, he was in the arrivals hall of the cosmodrome. Crowds of people were standing or sitting, eating, drinking, conversing—engaged in all the usual forms of public activity. But they were quite unlike the folk you see at an airport on Gaia. For a start they were all in helmets and dust suits—as indeed was Jack. The garment in question was called a dust suit although it served as a pressure suit too, kept you warm and protected you from a lot more than dust: the solar wind for instance. Nobody had worn this garb on board the *Oberon*: there had of course been no dust. Jack felt sealed-off and isolated, as if he were plunging down to a coral reef.

Selene had been nothing like this. Not even *Marsgrav* had prepared him for it. He was an alien being in an incomprehensible world, its boundaries and preoccupations far outside his experience. The photos he had studied and the films he had watched all counted for nothing against the experience of actually setting foot on Mars.

Jack walked slowly round the arrivals hall, trying to get an idea of its scope and what one was supposed to do there. Arrive, of course—but did most people come and go by public or by private transport? He knew that private transport consisted of two- or four-seater vehicles called *marscars* running on a dusty, much-vilified system of public highways. But nearly all adult citizens possessed at least one marscar, for Nix City was graced with nothing resembling the Selenean *Orm*.

Nevertheless public transport did exist, in the form of a long-distance subway train: rocket-powered, as it happened. It ran from the cosmodrome to the city centre and he soon came upon its entrance.

If anyone was there to meet him, he had given them long enough to spot him. It crossed his mind to go to one of the information booths and make his presence known, but he dismissed the idea. If he was going to have to make his own way into Nix City he ought just to vanish in the crowd. Not everybody who was on the lookout for him could be assumed to be well-disposed. He recalled the circumstances of his arrival on the Moon and wondered what would have happened if the shadowy, luckless Treikle had managed to catch up with him.

He decided to take the subway train to the city centre. He still felt isolated and muffled, missing the reassurance of the *Oberon* intensor caressing his cheeks. Would he be expected to pay a fare?—if so with what? Of a ticket barrier there was no sign.

No sooner had he approached the subway entrance than two individuals detached themselves from the crowd and approached him on either side, hemming him in. They appeared to be making no attempt to communicate with him, shouldering him instead to one side, clear of the stream of passengers. They were in uniform and armed, otherwise he might have thought to resist, or at the very least protest. The uniform of Zasta he knew from pictures in magazines: white and electric blue in large oval panels. But these were white and green. Airport police, he told himself. He was wrong.

He was about to make the acquaintance of the Vratch.

The two policemen took him to a small office. Once inside they signed to him to take his helmet off. Jack hesitated, but one of the officers with an impatient gesture tore off his own helmet and shook it at Jack in silent demonstration. There was no option but to comply.

"Health check," said the officer.

"I've had a check-up on the *Oberon*."

"Just do as I say. Place your index finger in here—like this."

There was a small tube bolted to the office desk. It glowed inside with red light. Jack wondered if this was an insidious lead-up to a violent assault on his person. Was the tube going to trap his finger painfully, immobilising him for more brutal treatment? Like a child complying with some unfamiliar punishment, he inserted his left forefinger, judging it was the one to sacrifice, if such was on the agenda.

But nothing seemed to happen.

"All right. Take it out."

Still holding his own helmet, the second officer sat at the desk, staring at the empty space where a blotter might lie. Data-screens on Mars emitted no extraneous light, vectoring an image directly onto the viewer's retina. But to Jack it looked as if the man was sitting deep in thought, havering on the brink of some unpalatable conclusion.

"You have a thoracic condition."

"Yes, of course I have. I'm fitted with an SP unit."

"I can see that with my own eyes. What I mean is that the residual lung cancer for which you were treated has undergone metastasis."

Jack's eyebrows went up. "Why wasn't the doctor on *Oberon* able to tell me that?"

"He didn't have our equipment. And why tell the patient if you can't do a thing about it?"

"Well, what can *you* do about it? And what business is it of yours anyway?"

The officer took a deep but perfunctory breath, as if Jack were just another of the endless succession of fools he had to deal with every day. "We are *Vratch:* we are the medical police. You've had months to learn about our ways here on Mars. Why do I need to tell you that the Vratch can bar your entry, with no leave to appeal?"

"Why would you want to do that?"

"Mars has a fragile life-support system. Sick people are not welcome here. I'm amazed they let you undertake the journey in the first place. But *Oberon* is another world and they have scant regard for our concerns. Or yours for that matter, once you're out of their hands."

"Okay—so mebbes I ought to see a doctor, when I get to where I'm going?"

"We are the doctors. You can engage a private therapist if you want, but they won't be able to do anything for you. Whatever you want to know, you can ask me."

"What's the... prognosis—if that's the word for it?"

"You have six months to live."

The officer spoke brutally and dispassionately, as if he were issuing a temporary entry visa. Jack slowly became conscious of the gruesome words he was hearing. It was a dissociated awareness, without sympathy or fellow-feeling for the person designated. So this was what it was like to stand by and hear a man being condemned to death.

But to die: was that such an uncommon occurrence? No, but like being born, people only did it once in a lifetime. Consequently, for the individual, there was no precedent to go by. Did it need an announcement in the paper? Should he throw a party? Would they hang out the flags?

The officer was staring curiously up into his face, waiting for a response, which didn't come. Eventually he broke the silence himself. "Six months—provided you take it easy. Considerably less if you rush around like a mad thing. Now I don't know what you're doing here—as you so rightly say, it's none of my business. But you're new to this planet and it will all seem very strange to you. Your situation is going to be— how should I say—stressful?"

The officer relaxed his shoulders. His next words were almost gentle. "So why not let me put you back aboard the *Oberon*? You may not live to reach Selene, but you'll spend your last months in luxury and among friends. They'll really make a fuss of you. And back in Lunaborg, they'll give you a gorgeous funeral."

Feeling began to flow back into Jack like hot water pouring in a basin. Emotion. Passion. Anger. Fury. But one thing he'd learnt since leaving Earth: to control his temper. He leaned trembling against the desk, his knuckles whitening.

"Officer, I've come all this way for a purpose—and I'm bloody well going through with it. All I hear you saying is that I haven't got as long as I thought I had. Now—are you going to let me go, or aren't you?"

"You're carrying a booner card."

"Well, what of it?"

"If you weren't, I wouldn't be talking to you like this. You'd be back on *Oberon* so damn' fast your feet wouldn't touch the ground. But as it is, you can simply walk out of here and I can't stop you."

"Then point me back to the train station where you picked me up."

"Get yourself back on the *Oberon*," the vratchnik snapped. "I'd still recommend it. Very, very strongly."

Being reminded of his booner privileges had given Jack the confidence to stand his ground. Or was it desperation that gave him the courage to bluff?

"Thanks, officer, but no thanks. Here I am—and here I'll stay."

"It's your funeral. Go through that door and keep walking and you'll find yourself back in the entrance hall."

Jack turn to go. He reached out his hand towards the door, which slid back just before he touched it.

"And Mr Williams…"

Now what? Jack turned slowly round to face the officer, still seated at the desk.

"Get your helmet fixed."

* * * * ✱ ● ✱ * * * *

Back in the entrance hall, his helmet once more clipped around his chin and sealed to his dust suit, Jack continued to feel stifled and isolated, though now he was in far worse state than before. He looked around, but no one else was for taking helmets off in public. Why had the medical police insisted on him removing his? Was it for the same reason that doctors want you to take your clothes off before examining you? Or hadn't they been able to communicate with him?

Jack hadn't really expected to feel the Nix intensor the moment he landed. Quite likely there would be no signal until he was in Nix City proper. But after getting used to the intensor on the *Oberon*, it was uncanny to be standing in a crowd of people in total isolation.

He sat down at one of the bars. After the news, he needed a drink. Without being asked, they gave him a beer. For several minutes he did nothing but sit looking at it. The foam sank like a day-old fall of snow. As he reached out towards the misty glass, his hand shook violently. He had to steady it with his other hand and steer it towards the drink. Was this the insidious onset of his death-throes? Or was it simply the way bad news would affect him now—until the day he died?

His health-record over the past two years had been a wild adventure. But at no time since Wearmouth Bridge had he felt death so imminent. Somehow he'd assumed he'd pull through, as he always had.

Were the Vratch telling him lies? What possible reason might they have had for doing that? But why had they let him get all the way to the subway entrance before detaining him? And all to tell him something he considered his own private business?

It struck him that it might have been all Shval's doing. Or Tvoul's. One or the other of them might have put the Vratch onto him as a delaying tactic. It had certainly had the effect of hindering him for long enough to let his quarry get clean away. But like him she had only one way to go—and that was into Nix City.

And then where could she go?

The thing to do was catch the train and ask someone at the other end. Ask them what? There was only one thing he wanted to know: where was Tvoul? Once having found her—and done what he had come to do, he'd gladly take the advice of the Vratch and get himself back on board the *Oberon*. Even if it meant booking a special shuttle—because the regular shuttles had now finished.

And what *had* he come to do? Almost two years had gone by since he'd set out at midnight from his house in Esh Winning in pursuit of Tvoul. And still he didn't know. When finally he came face-to-face with her, then he would know. At the very least he'd have some hard questions to ask her.

He drained the last of his beer and sat staring at the empty glass. The foam hung like tattered curtains, or shreds of rotten flesh. In his dejected state he must have nodded off because he awoke with a start to a touch on his shoulder. It was a woman standing there. Like the Vratch had done, she motioned him to doff his helmet.

"Taxi?"

"Yes."

Accepting the offer of a tout! It was the sort of thing Jack would never have done back home. But whether out of hopelessness or disorientation, it didn't strike him that he might be going into danger. Or that he could be ripped off—at least not to make him suffer personally. The booner card enabled him to mix with potentially hostile strangers with all the confident innocence of a baby. He owned everything—and nothing.

As the Romans used to say: *viator vacuus coram latrone ridet.* In the company of bandits the traveller with nothing laughs.

The woman led the way through unmarked side-doors and between rough concrete columns into what was evidently a car-park. Her vehicle was like nothing he'd ever ridden in. For a start it didn't have wheels. On Earth you'd have thought it was a fighter cockpit simulation or a gondola from some bizarre fairground ride.

The canopy sank back on gas struts as they buckled themselves in. Conventional straps—conventional buckles—though more like a flying harness than a car seat-belt on Earth. It was a strange blend of the bizarre and the familiar.

"*Kouda?* ...Where to?" The woman's voice came loud and clear over the infra-red link. It was the first time on Mars that anyone had managed to speak to him via his helmet. From her accent and her halting speech he judged that English was not her first language.

"City centre."

"The Areopagus?"

"I guess so." But really he had no idea.

She spoke to her vehicle in the strange nasal tones of M1, or perhaps it was to her controller back at base, and they set off. Except for the very few public announcements back on the *Oberon*, always trilingual, Jack had heard little or no M1 spoken. It was a language in which he was not only unable to repeat a single word, but could not even begin to form the phonemes in his mouth. If someone had told him the groubians had invented it, he would not have found that difficult to believe.

The road was no more than a trench of dust, along which the marscar ploughed like a motor launch, throwing up wings of dust to left and right. They plunged into a tunnel lit by a single strip of light along the middle of the roof. Jack had just one backward glimpse of what they were leaving: the eight-mile diameter blast-crater of an ancient meteor strike, from which Voronka took its name.

When they emerged, they were skidding along a rough track which led straight over the horizon. Sunlit brown rock alternated with inky shadow with a crispness at once both dim and livid. For Mars was twice as far as

Gaia and Selene from the Sun. Daylight was correspondingly dimmer: four times as dim according to the inverse-square law of distance.

No other vehicles were in sight. Whatever the status, or legality, of his "taxi", this clearly was not a popular way to get from the cosmodrome to downtown Nix City. Was he in the hands of friends or enemies? Or was this just one solitary taxi-owner trying to scratch a living?

For thirty miles or so they travelled through a stony featureless landscape under a black sky (although it was daytime), ascending the giant hogsback of Olympus Mons. During that time the woman spoke not a word. Presently a dark smudge hinting of a distant ocean appeared just beneath the line of the horizon. But ocean it was not. As they drew nearer, a gigantic system of nested cavities became apparent, sunk into the rusty ground.

The caldera, descending in wide circular steps like the terraces of a vast amphitheatre, grew and grew until Jack could make out its sides to be vertical cliffs, piled high at their feet with scree which at this distance looked like heaps of wholemeal flour. He thought of the quarry where he used to work. Seen from half a mile away over the fells, it hadn't looked so different from what faced him now. But for all their speed, the caldera seemed hardly to be drawing any closer. They must still be tens of miles away. Which made those cliffs not fifty nor a hundred feet in height as the quarry had been, but a thousand... two thousand... four thousand... maybe a mile high.

How deep was the Grand Canyon? A mile at its deepest?

If this was the Nix, then where was the city? He asked the driver this and she replied, gesturing with one hand.

"No to-see city here. All underground. Because-that dust."

So Nix City was mostly underground, like Jordvik? It was the obvious thing. Like the Moon, the atmosphere here was too thin to stop meteorites, much less the radiation of the solar wind, which made living on the surface hazardous. Jack knew from his preparatory reading that the Nix was 15 miles above what passed for sea-level on this parched planet.

At this altitude the atmosphere was tenuous in the extreme. It could nevertheless support dust during a major sandstorm, though far less so than on the plains. But still in sufficient quantities to blanket the city in brown dust to match the landscape—which was why Nix City had never been seen by Earth-based telescope.

At night the grid pattern of the well-lit streets had been clearly visible from *Oberon* orbiting overhead. But Jack reflected on how hard it was to see the night-side of Mars from Earth. So for all Lowell's impression of canals, Mars could never have revealed any genuine sign of occupancy throughout its long history of human colonisation. Human, that is, if you considered groubians to be human.

The marscar entered the mouth of a tunnel and began to descend. Unlike the tunnel out of Voronka, this one was not lit. They travelled on headlights in the darkness for more than a minute until they emerged with a shock into the dying light of day. The pygmy sun danced on the western rim of the caldera, its glancing rays exposing the cliffs directly ahead in psychedelic detail. It was a sight to make the heart leap, but Jack felt nothing. He had no lungs for a sharp intake of breath, no heart to pound faster—and no future past a six-month horizon, beyond which his life dropped over a cliff.

They were now in the streets of Nix City, though these were nothing more than dust-filled gaps between rows of windowless blocks, like dragons-teeth on an invasion beach. Jack had heard that nobody lived in these above-ground structures, which served as storage and meteorite protection for the proper living-accommodation tunnelled beneath them.

The darkness of evening swept over the streets like a flow-tide over wet sand, flooding the spaces between abandoned sand-castles with black ink which instantly evaporated when the street-lights came on. Rows of these graced the tops of the gaunt blocks, illuminating them like birthday cakes.

Jack was struck by an absence of advertising. No hoardings, no neon signs: he never thought he'd miss them. Apart from the dramatic cliffs which surrounded it, the ambience of Nix City was crushingly drab. People must walk around looking at little else than their helmet displays. But as for walking around, there were no pedestrians that Jack could see, although they now began to pass marscars ploughing in the opposite direction.

They were approaching a great opalescent dome, glowing in the darkness with a soft greenish light, which made it look like a beached jellyfish. Approaching its circumference, a glassy door slid upwards to admit them to a parking bay. The canopy of the marscar opened and the woman said in her broken M2 "We here arrive."

"Here" was evidently the Areopagus—the "Rock-of-Mars"—which the woman had declared to be the city centre. Throughout the journey Jack had been wondering whether she'd been sent to collect him, but it

now seemed like a normal fare. Getting out of the marscar he produced
his booner card, but the woman waved it away.

"All okay," she said. "Done." She tapped her temple in the universal
sign that the speaker thinks you're crazy. "Get it fixed, eh?" With those
cryptic, vaguely insulting words the marscar's canopy descended and she
drove off, expertly negotiating the airlock they had entered by.

There was an atmosphere. Jack's helmet display told him that it was
safe to open the visor. He did so. A few other people were to be seen,
mostly couples, arms around each other's waists. Nobody else had their
visor open, indeed everybody had it set half-silvered to conceal their
features.

"Excuse me," he appealed to a couple walking by, "Where can I find a
shop open?" They ignored him. He tried another couple and they did
the same. A single person strode past with a brisk step. Jack grasped the
man's arm, but the other flung him off without so much as looking at
him.

It seemed as if he had become a pariah, a homeless person, which of
course was what he was. Somehow everybody could detect that.
Perhaps it was the booner card? On Selene this had made him welcome
everywhere, but here perhaps, if you weren't in uniform, it labelled you a
sneaky government agent: someone to be shunned.

In his dejected state he didn't have the strength to care. He found a
public bench to sit on, slats and painted cast-iron sides, which might have
come straight out of an Edwardian park. It faced towards the centre of
the dome. There, ringed with several acres of raked gravel, a towering
rock appeared to graze the zenith of the dome, a lit-up lattice screening it
from a sky in permanent blackness.

There was a profusion of shrubs and ornamental flowers, but few
trees to be seen except some spindly saplings marking the intersections of
the formally laid-out paths. But there was one magnificent oak which
stood before the rock. Having nothing else to do, Jack got up and
strolled around the rock, discovering two more giant trees on the other
side.

Three in all: oak, ash and rowan. Here, with no competing
organisms, in one-third the gravity of Earth, cosseted with light, warmth
and hydroponics, the trees had grown 300 ft or more, half the height of
the rock. All of them were in fruit. Acorns covered the sterile gravel for
a twenty-yard radius around the oak tree. The ash was shedding its
winged seeds which had fallen straight to the ground and made a feathery

carpet—and the rowan, like a ruby galaxy, bore endless berries which it shed as clusters in sticky abundance.

Fruitless fruit.

His emotions all too near the surface, Jack shut his visor, setting it to the regulation half-silvering which everybody else seemed to be sporting, and wept at the futility of the fruiting trees. They had thrown-in their lot with mankind and this had enabled them to leave planet Earth, but to what end? How could they ever hope to seed a forest in the dust of Mars?

There were seats beneath the ash tree and there Jack sat down, letting his chin sink to his chest. He wished that he could die, then and there, not having to endure the six months of agony which the Vratch had measured out for him like crushed velvet.

How did lung cancer progress when you had no lungs? It would not hamper his respiration, but it would be painful nonetheless. He would have to go back to the Vratch and ask for drugs. *Oberon* would not be round again for another two years, so they couldn't summarily dispatch him back to Selene. But life on opiates, which people said were the only things that worked with cancer, would become a gradual detachment from reality until the experience of imagination itself stopped. That's if it hadn't stopped already.

There was only one thing left in life to do now: find Tvoul. And she was far away as ever. As far away as she had been when he'd walked out of his house in Esh Winning, reckless of the road ahead.

Back then his sole aim had been to get to Mars. Well, here he was.

17   The engineering of accidents

Jack awoke to a sharp kick in the sole of his outstretched boot. Two men stood there, draped with equipment and carrying stun-guns. Jack recognised the killer-whale police uniform, but couldn't see in the uncertain light whether it was green or blue. He decided it was blue, in which case these men were Zasta.

Their faces were blanked out. One of the men gesticulated to Jack and, not getting the expected response, hauled him to his feet. Each grasping an arm, the z-niks marched him away down a shortish tunnel to a police post and thrust him in a cage. Then they sat and looked at him.

For all their apparent inaction they must have been doing something. They'd called for somebody, which Jack couldn't overhear them doing, for presently a third officer appeared, a woman. She was wearing the green uniform of the Vratch and her transparent visor revealed her face. Peremptorily signing to the men to unlock the cage she entered it, the door getting locked again behind her. She motioned to Jack to take his helmet off and hand it to her. Straightaway she returned it to him and he put it back on.

"There," a voice sounded in his ear. "Is that better?"

"What did you do?"

The woman laughed. "You were still tuned to the *Oberon* intensor. However did you miss getting that fixed? Were you last off the ship or something?"

A familiar comforting feeling had flooded over Jack's face. Instantly he had become aware of the woman's presence on the intensor dimensions: previously a forbidding figure of impersonal authority, she was revealed as someone firm and decisive, but nevertheless warm-hearted and open-handed. Someone who out-ranked the two z-niks, whose angular intensions were mean and faceless. Society, he could tell, stood in this woman's debt, not the other way round.

"I guess I must have slipped between the cracks..." muttered Jack in reply. He felt humbled by her, as he might in the presence of a saint. She, for her part, looked at him like a headmistress contemplating an errant pupil made to wait outside her office for punishment. Then she turned and made a circular motion with her hand. The cage was unlocked again.

"A booner!" she exclaimed, and now Jack could hear the men groan in reply. One of them grunted "On my watch, too!"

"Well, someone ought to display some initiative around here," snapped the woman. "Come on Jack—come with me."

Taking his hand like a child she led him out of the cage, out of the police post and into her marscar. Presently they were miles away from the Areopagus, in the corridor of a building somewhere in the seemingly endless rows of streets.

The woman threw open the door and invited Jack to step in first. He found himself in a tiled shower unit, with doors off to the left and right. He pushed against one of them.

"Uh-uh!" The woman pulled him back. "Never take a dust suit into the house."

Without shame she began taking off her own dust suit, revealing herself naked underneath. She kept her helmet on however, checking the visor briefly for watertightness. Clearly she was expecting Jack to do the same. After a moment's hesitation he did, returning her frank stare, as hot water rained down upon them both.

She was a woman of robust good looks and ample bosom, with areolas the size of squash balls, dark chocolate, indicating that she'd given birth. About thirty-five years of age, there was not a mark upon her skin except for the caduceus, the universal medical sign, tattooed over her left nipple, the same as on her helmet badge.

"Don't touch skin. You'll rub the dust grains in. They are incredibly sharp."

Jack's eyes fell irresistibly down to her bush, trimmed to a neat vertical stripe like one-half of a rip-fastener. Impressive bit of topiary, he reflected coolly. If your nude body was frequently on view, then of course it had to be kept well-groomed.

Wasn't she afraid of him? With her well-developed triceps and deltoids, there was more cause for him to be afraid of her. What did she want with him? Was she moonlighting as a prostitute, or had he simply been picked up and brought home for sex?

But nothing, it seemed, could have been further from her mind. "Is this your place?" said Jack as she led the way out of the shower.

"No. It's yours now."

She glanced this way and that, her lip slightly curled. "It's nothing super, but it happened to be empty. It will serve you for now, until you can find somewhere better." Hesitating, she seemed at last to take note of the fact that they were both naked, and that somehow this was bothering Jack. Reaching into a cupboard she took out two white towelling dressing gowns and handed one to him.

"Forgive me for being personal, but how are you managing with your SP unit?" Personal or not, it was the vratchka talking: professional to the last.

"Fine, touch-wood. But I'll be needing superox in an hour."

"You'll find a nasal hook-up at the end of the corridor, between the levitator and the ice-machine." She took a breath and glanced around again. "Otherwise everything's here you'll need tonight." Stepping over to the fridge she peered inside. "Plenty of food in here. Only the ex-cred stuff: nothing exciting. But, hey—I eat it myself. It's nourishing."

She came back and held out her hand. "I'm Lance-Sergeant O'Mallory Hashimotova, 15th Vratch. Call me O'Mallory. I live just down the corridor with my daughter Kat. Call on me if you want anything, though it's best to stay in here and link with Intertalk."

"How do I do that?"

"Didn't they teach you how to use a helmet on the *Oberon*? Drop the menu and eyeball the option. Try it now." With a click, her voice cut-off.

Jack brought up his helmet's holographic display and saw her name at the top of the contacts list. She half-smiled as he re-linked.

"Like I said, call me if you have any trouble. If I don't answer, Kat will." Touching his forearm she turned to go. "You won't reach me tomorrow because I'm on-duty all day. Clinic."

She made a wry face. "A lot of city-fever going around. I've two duties back-to-back because it's hit our unit hard." She paused and looked him up and down professionally. "You don't need to worry— you've got no lungs."

Slipping off her dressing gown with a twitch of her silky shoulders she handed it to him, ignoring the clicking of his SP unit. Then she opened the lobby door and climbed back into her dust suit.

"O'Mallory, how can I begin to thank you?"

"That's all right. Self-interest." She smiled—and there was not a little warmth in it. "If I hadn't done something back there, all hell would have broken loose." She secured her neck-seal and touched the front door to open it. "It's not every night we pick a *booner* up out of the gutter."

••••• ★ ● ★ •••••

Next morning Jack woke up early and left the apartment. Sleep had refreshed him and he wanted to get started on his search for Tvoul. But even with his booner status switched off, still nobody would stop for him in public places.

Eventually Jack came upon a doorway through which a stream of people came and went. He decided to go in himself. Inside this building someone would have to talk to him eventually, if only to ask him what he was doing there.

The entrance led through a system of three airtight revolving doors, down steps which had a waxy feel, leading to what was clearly some sort of bar or club. He propped himself on a vacant bar stool and waited for the barman to come over. Looking around he saw that everybody had their visors open, though many sported what were evidently holofaces. So he did the same, unclipping the visor beneath his chin and sliding it back over his crown.

The barman came up to him. "*Zdráste*," he said. "*Shto ti xótchesh?*"

"Come again?"

"What do you want to drink?"

"A beer. Any sort. What everybody else is drinking."

"Everybody else like you is drinking *kvass*. Want some?"

"Sure. Why not?"

The barman looked at him doubtfully and went away. Presently there arrived a large earthenware mug capped with foam. Greedily Jack buried his nose and mouth in it, sipping the dark fluid, but found it tepid and quite bland. It could just as well have been weak tea as beer.

The fellow sitting next to him swivelled round lazily on his stool. "Just off the *Oberon*, Jack lad?"

Jack's instant reflex was to ask the man how he knew his name. But he realised the intensor would have told him.

"Yes. I've had eight months to prepare for this, but I feel like a fish out of water. You have the advantage on me. I still can't read the intensor well enough to know what *you're* called."

The man laughed. "I guess that's how I felt three years ago when I'd only just arrived. On *Oberon* you get to know a lot of people and you don't realise how different Mars is going to be." He held out his hand. "Call me Stewart."

Jack took the proffered hand. "Pleased to meet you, Stewart."

"You'll have to learn some M1 if you want people to talk to you here. This is an M1 club."

"Is that why nobody replies to me in the street?"

"God—no!" said Stewart. "Don't try striking up a conversation in the street. Not even with somebody intense. People on foot are not worth talking to. That's what folk believe."

So that, thought Jack, was why everyone had been cutting him dead. "An M1 club, eh?" he said. "Are there M2 clubs as well?"

"Yes. They tend to cluster in the poorer parts of town. You can ask around for all you're worth, but you won't find anywhere better than this."

"Good, is it?"

Unexpectedly Stewart had to ponder that. "Well, no: not what you and I would call good. They're all much the same. So I'm just saying: it doesn't matter where you try."

"No incentive to excel?"

"Oh, I wouldn't say that. No incentive for the establishment maybe, but there is for the barman. 'How many smiles in a kiss?' They're all building up their incred by the drinks they know how to mix. Of course, if you *will* go ordering *kvass*..."

"I wanted a beer. It's the only thing the man offered me."

"It's all they've got that's ex-cred. They do that sort of thing to booners."

Jack simpered. "Is there anywhere I can get rid of this? Will they notice if I pour it on the floor?"

"No, don't do that," said Stewart, grinning broadly. "Just give it back and ask for something else." He beckoned the barman over and spoke to him in M1. The barman took Jack's drink away and brought him a Midsummer Madness.

"How did you know I liked these? You don't know somebody called Gabrielle, do you?"

"It's the latest craze. Spread like wildfire in the last two sols. Gabrielle, did you say? Yes, that's the name. Fresh off the *Oberon*—like you, I guess?"

"Good old Gabrielle!" Jack raised his glass.

"Yes, good old Gabrielle," echoed Stewart. "You know her?"

"Why-aye. She's a canny bit-lass."

"Well," said Stewart, "you can tell her from me she mixes a mean cocktail. If she carries on like this she'll earn herself intensions a mile high. But warn her to keep her recipes to herself. Everybody's getting the incred which is hers by rights."

•••••✳●✳••••••

Simply by asking around in the bars, Jack found himself cafés to eat in, markets to shop in and a job to do, in that order. English people are shy when it comes to asking things from strangers—they prefer to read the public signs and buy the local papers. Americans ask around a lot more, because they know the signs and the papers aren't reliable. On Mars there are no signs or papers, reliable or otherwise, so asking someone is the only way to find out anything.

Jack had decided to switch off the booner card and get by with building up his incred until such a time as he needed it to cover his tracks. As on Selene, he could in principle get anything on offer by invoking his booner status. The state (the Strana of Olympia) would recompense the seller—but only for the base valuta, which nobody wanted to transact at. So desirable things would tend to disappear from open view at a booner's approach.

Jack had wondered how, in a cashless society, anyone had any incentive to work. It had been an artificial situation on *Oberon*. On board you were a passenger: a special class of person with your passage paid-for—and a whole lot more besides. On Mars he discovered the hard way that if your incred went too low, people stopped talking to you. You couldn't get hold of anything worthwhile. All you could get were *ex-cred* items: those in such plentiful supply as to change hands for nothing. Or conversely those in such short supply that they were rationed—which still meant they changed hands for nothing. Nobody starved. But to eat well you had to trade. Jack quickly concluded that the only way he could build up incred was to make himself useful. Hence the need for a job.

But a job conferred an additional benefit: his workmates treated him like family. You don't trade with family—you simply give them whatever they need. Jack gained a lot and learned a lot from his workmates, and his foreman. Except the one thing he wanted most of all to know: where was Tvoul?

Simply asking after her was a thankless prospect. The conversation would go like this:

"I'm looking for my daughter-in-law. How do I set about finding her?"

"Does she know you're here? In Nix City?"

"No, I don't think she does."

"Then go along to Zasta and get them to poll the intensor for you."

Then he'd try another tack. "I'm looking for somebody called Tvoul Williams. How should I go about finding her?"

"Does she want to be found?"

"I'm not sure she does. She used to call herself Tvoul Rainbow."

"Tvoul Rainbow!" (An expletive generally followed.) "You've gotta be kidding."

"Where is Tvoul Rainbow now?"

"Oh… she went to Gaia." That, it seemed, was the end of the matter.

Sometimes he would try the direct approach. "I'm trying to find Tvoul Rainbow."

"*Tvoul Rainbow!* The devil you are. Well, she went to Gaia."

"I've reason to believe she's back on Mars."

"Oh, those are only rumours."

"I happen to know they are true."

"Look—you're a booner. Why don't you go along to Zasta and tell them to find her for you?"

Eventually, assured of his privileged position, he did just that. Presenting himself at *Zastavlénie* HQ, he demanded to see someone senior enough to tell him what he wanted to know.

"Oh, you want Commissioner Miro for all that."

"Can I book an appointment?"

"Commissioner Miro is a busy man."

"I don't have much time. I insist on seeing him."

"Mr Williams, please be patient. Your request has been noted. Commissioner Miro will be in touch with you in the next few days."

And sure enough he was.

To relieve the drabness of the city streets, Jack took to spending sundowns in the Areopagus. He would circle the rock and stop by each of the three great trees. They had names, he'd discovered. The Oak King. The Ash King. And the Rowan Queen. As he stood silently that sundown under the last of these, watching darkness sweep over the Nix, the Intertalk woke up. A voice in his helmet said "Mr Williams: *Zastavlénie*. You are alone."

Jack looked around him. There was nobody in sight. "Yes, I'm alone."

"I am not asking you. I am telling you. You are in the Areopagus, standing under the Rowan Queen, and you are alone. Please try to keep it that way for the next ten minutes. I have *Komissár* Miro for you."

Glancing quickly over his shoulder, Jack sat down on the bench. He felt like a glass baby: helpless and transparent.

"Mr Williams. Commissioner Miro. Thank you for trying to contact me. I'm glad to have the opportunity to speak to you."

"Did they tell you what it was about?"

"Oh yes. And they did assure you at the time that the matter was in hand. But your status entitles you to… personal assurances. These it's my pleasure to give you."

"I'm grateful," said Jack. Where was all this leading?

"I wonder if in return you can furnish me with certain assurances?"

Jack swallowed. "I'll try."

"Simply this. You were the last person to see Commissioner Vermat alive. The last surviving person, that is."

"Yes…"

Jack was beginning to get used to the intensor society. The thing to do, it seemed, was to assume that everyone, even total strangers, knew everything about you there was to know—and take it from there.

"Please reassure me… were her final moments happy ones?"

Jack was stuck for a reply. Could Miro see his face? He hoped not. The voice continued "I-I mean: so far as you know?"

"I think so. I left her watching the celebrations. She was with my other friends and we were all having a good time."

There came a long drawn-out sigh of relief. "Vermat, you know, suffered so much in her life. It does me good to hear you say that."

Jack was embarrassed. "I'm—er—glad to help."

"She thought highly of you. We—ahh—were in regular contact. She begged me to furnish you with all the assistance you'll need whilst you are here on Mars."

"Whilst I'm still alive, I think you'd say."

"Yes, I know about that."

"Well… where is she?"

There was a pause.

"The whereabouts of Tvoul Williams: that too is something I would like to know. Not to mention the whereabouts of her sister, Shval Meteor. Let me just say how grateful I am for what you've done for us in that regard."

"I-I don't think I've done anything."

"But you have, Mr Williams. As a direct result of your investigations on Selene, we have been able to bust the Meteor Gang. It is only a matter of time before Shval Meteor puts another foot wrong and we will wind-up her affairs for good. Now I suspect that Shval is back on Mars."

"I know she is."

"You *know*?"

"She came off the *Oberon* just before I did, masquerading as Tvoul Rainbow."

"Shval is now class four here. Do you know what that means?"

"I've no idea."

"She is—how would you put it?—on the run. Her property is forfeit to the state. And that includes her info. This is something down to your credit. Without your information we could not have moved so decisively against her. She knows this, of course—and it does put you in no little danger. But, ah, perhaps you were anyway?"

"I don't care a fig about Shval. Where's Tvoul?"

"As for Tvoul herself, please realise that her whereabouts is hers to know. Zasta has no power to make you a gift of that information without her agreeing to it."

"You're powerful enough to do whatever you like."

"No, Mr Williams, I am not. Information is property on Mars. Your information is your own property—and our constitution guarantees it. All transfer of information, as you know, is intensor-mediated. We in Zasta are charged with preserving the integrity of the intensor. We are a property police, Mr Williams. To inform you of Tvoul's whereabouts would be to steal the very property we are entrusted with defending."

"I don't see. If you know, why can't you just tell me?"

"Mr Williams… on Gaia, your body-politic is corrupted by security agencies which do precisely that. Money is everything. Now we on Mars do not have money. We consider it is just another way of transmitting information: a redundant one at that—and deeply flawed. On Gaia, if you possess an item of information—let us call it your *secret*—then somebody can steal it from you and you have no way of knowing. Your laws define stealing as denying you the use of your own property. But your secret can leak out—yet you still appear to possess it. The document is, after all, still in your safe. But if someone were to act in the knowledge of that secret, they could damage you. On Mars, that is how we define stealing: to act on information which is not yours. It is something that can be readily detected and policed via the intensor."

"Is the intensor really *that* powerful?"

"Oh yes. And it is the foundation of our society. To compromise Tvoul's information is to strike at society's very roots."

"Okay, I get the message." Jack laughed. "I must say I stand in awe of your principles."

"There is no need to be sarcastic. I'm Zasta. The intensor is my life—and it is yours too, while you remain on Mars. Nobody is above the law: not I, not you, not Tvoul—and certainly not Shval. Once we assent to information being compromised, at whatever level of command, the body-politic begins to unravel like a worn-out garment. We of Zasta take an oath to *die* before that happens. We have our sacred badge—the sword and sigil—tattooed above our hearts to symbolise the fact."

"So you know where Tvoul is—but you're just not going to tell me?"

"I do not know, for sure. Not yet."

"But when you do, you still won't tell me?"

"In principle I fear that is so. But that is not the end of the matter. Tvoul's whereabouts may be her secret. But were you to stumble upon her by *accident*... that would be information that is yours, not hers."

It was quite dark now. You could hardly see the black rock against the sky, except where it cut out the stars. Someone hurried past. Jack waited until they were well down the path before replying. He knew Miro would know why.

"I see. So you'd advise me just to carry on looking for Tvoul?"

"Mr Williams. Some people believe there is no such thing as an accident. But I know, by virtue of my position, that noise enters the system from outside. Cosmic rays engender noise. So does the solar wind—even in so well-shielded a system as the Nix intensor. To put it in the vernacular: shit happens."

"What are you trying to say?"

"I'm saying that accidents can be engineered. The likelihood of their occurrence can be magnified. Coincidences can be arranged. If a causal link is absent, or rather, *undetectable*—a transaction is not registered on the intensor. Now listen carefully..."

"I'm all ears."

"In consideration of the services you have rendered us, over the next few days I shall engineer some accidents on your behalf."

Jack stood up from the park bench. He put his boot on one among the crowd of fallen berries, crushing it. What an insignificant mess it made.

"That sounds dodgy. What if the 'accident' happens to me?"

"This is not Moscow. Taxis do not run you over in the street—much less trams. Not even Zasta can arrange for an accident to happen to you without leaving a clear audit-trail to the person who gave the order. The integrity of the intensor is the citizen's guarantee."

"I'm not a citizen. Here on Mars I'm nothing but a stranger."

"I know. You are in a vulnerable situation. Were you to die—*when* you come to die—you have no heirs, no family, to seek redress on *your* behalf."

Jack made no reply. Miro had never said a truer word.

"Now I won't say anything so banal as 'trust me'. But be aware of this, Mr Williams. You have powerful enemies on this planet. But you also have some friends. Friends who will help you, if need be, from beyond the grave."

······★●★·····

Jack got back to his apartment around ten that night, bearing in triumph a dinner of fish, chips and mushy-peas which he'd commissioned in the local market. The hardest part had been trying to explain "mushy-peas"—there was no word for them in M2. He put the meal in the microwave oven. Then he began to puzzle out how to work it.

The only controls he could see were a big red button and a little green button. He pressed the green button. Nothing happened. He pressed the red button. Instantly the appliance sprang to life and the holoface of a pretty girl appeared in the window.

"*Dóbroe vétcher, Dzhak. Ia—tvoi petchka-bot...*"

"Speak English, damn you."

"*Prostí, ia ne poniálo...*"

"...I mean M2."

The holoface gave a polite cough. "Good evening, Jack. I'm your oven-bot. How are you feeling tonight?"

"Tired. Just do your stuff, pet."

The holoface pouted and vanished. Two mechanical claws tore the transparent wrapper off, popped the door open and threw the rubbish out onto his toes. The door slammed shut again and the turntable started.

"Well, thank *you!*" But of course he should have been grateful it hadn't cooked the food with the wrapper on.

Presently he had a dinner, which he bore in anticipation to the table. He then went in search of a knife and fork. What he took for the cutlery drawer contained only spoons, scissors and pincers. He took out one of each and proceeded to operate with them on the meal. It was barely warm.

He crammed the dish back in the oven and stabbed at the red and green buttons until the machine grudgingly started, stopping again after a few seconds.

"Right. Back to the table with you and let's try again."

It was no different. Furiously he threw it back in the oven. The holoface reappeared.

"The meal is done."

"No—it's not done, flower. It isn't! Try again."

"The meal is done."

Jack hammered the top, letting out a stream of abuse.

"If you have any complaints about the performance of this product, please return it in its original wrapping to the supplier, whose address you will find on the base of the appliance."

Barking expletives, Jack slumped down at the table again. That's the last time he'd try cooking for himself. There was no earthly reason why he should do. No Martian one either, for that matter. There was plenty of hot food available. But he hadn't eaten fried fish and chips with mushy-peas for ages—so he'd jumped at the chance even though it had been delivered cold and was supposed to be re-heated.

A child's voice said "May I come in, Jack?"

"Please yerself," groaned Jack through his fingers. When day follows day like a drunken dream, a strange child requesting admission to your flat is nothing to be remarked on.

The child who came in was about six, or so Jack judged. Apart from her helmet, which had kitty ears, she was naked. Peeping back inside the shower lobby, she carefully closed the door behind her.

"Does your mam mind you running around barefoot?"

"I don't know. Why don't you ask her? We only live down the corridor."

"So, er… what's your name?"

"Can't you work it out?"

"Aa-ah," said Jack with a slit-eyed smile. "Remind me—I've forgotten."

"The same way as you do anything. Drop the menu, then eyeball the option."

Jack did as he was told. "You're *Ekaterina!*"

She put her head to one side. "Everyone calls me Kat."

Jack looked at the kitty ears. "Well, noo," he said, his accent thickening, "why didn't Ah guess that for meself?"

"Because you're tired," said Kat, as if she had to go making excuses for him. She sniffed the air and skipped over to the oven. "Got anything nice to eat?"

"You can have that—if you can make it work."

Kat put the food back in the oven, slammed the door and leaned on the green button. "Ours is always going wrong. You have to do a manual override. Don't let it do it all by itself—it'll tell you it's done when it's not."

She returned to the table with the meal piping hot. She went off to fetch scissors and tongs, then gave Jack an impromptu lesson on their correct use, having sat herself on his lap with a bump.

"Weren't you hungry?" she said, scraping the plastic dish clean with her fingers and licking them.

"I'm happy just to watch you, kiddo. It's champion to see a bairn who likes her food. Mushy-peas'll do you a power of good."

Kat turned to stare at him full-on. "Why have you still got your outdoor clothes on?" She slipped off his lap. "And you're all dusty. Have you been walking in the *oúlitza?*" She slapped her bottom to dust it.

"Where else am I supposed to walk?"

"Don't be silly. Come on—off with them. I'm not sitting on your lap otherwise…"

Grinning broadly, Jack took off his tunic and threw it over the shoulder of what he took to be a tailor's dummy standing beside the table.

"That's not enough."

"It's as far as I'm going, flower."

Kat put her tiny hands on her tinier hips and gazed at him as if he were being mean to her. She sighed. "I'm not sitting in that dust again, whatever you think."

Struggling with himself in his own mind, Jack tried to get over the idea that a six-year-old could possibly be trying to seduce him.

"Life on Mars is a constant battle against dust," she went on. "It gets in your eyes, between your teeth and makes machines go wrong. It's been heated by meteor impact to turn it into glass, then powdered in craters for billions of years by meteorites like a great big pestle-and-mortar until each grain is a tiny razor blade."

If only her mam could hear her now. She probably thought Kat never listened to a word. "All right," he groaned. He stripped off his trousers, which he had been wearing all day under his dust suit, as if it were an enormous effort. He was now down to his briefs.

"That's better," said Kat, looking at him in wonder—why had he needed telling? She climbed back onto his lap and put her arms around his neck.

"I like you. You're nice."

Jack was beside himself with embarrassment. He feinted holding the child in his fingertips as if she was scalding hot. What if her mother came in? He'd be up for a prison sentence at the very least.

"How do you know I'm nice? You ought to be careful of strangers."

"You're not a stranger. And I know what someone nasty feels like on my face." Kat spoke dismissively. "My last daddy was nasty."

"So it's just you and yer mam?"

"Yes. You met her the other night."

"Did I?"

"O'Mallory. I'm Kat Hashimotova."

Aa-ah! Jack nodded silently with his mouth open. Why hadn't he twigged?

"Mummy sent me round to check you're all right."

The tailor's dummy trilled a brief melody and lit up in the image of a flaxen-haired woman. She too was bare, at least from the navel up, which was all there was of the dummy. Shaking Jack's discarded tunic onto the floor, she held out her arms.

"Gabrielle!" cried Jack. Kat jumped off his lap and silently tiptoed to the door. She turned to open and shut her hand like a little mouth saying bye-bye, then she was gone.

Jack leapt to his feet. Instinctively he grasped the dummy round the waist, where it ended in a heavy plinth. "By all that's wonderful! How on earth...?"

The dummy caught his other hand. It felt just like Gabrielle in the flesh.

"Hi Jack. I simply had to try out the hugglephone. It's what passes for a v-unit here on Mars. Cool, isn't it?"

Jack felt the need to explain himself. "That was the neighbour's daughter sitting in me lap. D'ye know, she just plonked herself on me without so much as 'by your leave'. Stark naked—as if it was a thing she did every day."

"She probably does. You don't wear clothes in the house. She didn't take her helmet off though, did she?"

"No..."

"Good girls don't take their helmets off with strange men. She knows she's safe. Touch her somewhere funny and she'd maxgear you. How many smiles in a grope?"

Jack smacked his forehead. "I can't believe it!"

Gabrielle gave an easy laugh. "Glad you're getting to meet the neighbours. No I didn't see her. I can only see you—as half an ectoplast standing in my living room. And only your top half. I guess that's all you can see of me. So your privacy is assured." She put on a fake M1 accent. "Ze Integrity Of Ze Intensor Is Ze Citizen's Guarantee."

"So *this* is what an ectoplast is. You feel as if you're really here—well, half of you anyway. Can you feel me?"

"Of course I can." Gabrielle's voice was warm and low. "The person who invented this was a complete sadist, wasn't he? There's not a great lot we can do. Except this…"

She caught hold of the back of his head and crushed her mouth against his, humming sensuously. Her buzzing lips sent tingles to Jack's toes. He backed away and sat down.

"My-oh-my. The Marvels of Modern Science."

"It's called Chemistry. Remember your first kiss? Top half only."

"That takes me back a bit."

"Come round and see me. Then we can do the bottom half. Make it soon."

"Where *are* you?"

"*Kvartíra* 102, 906/273, which means corner of U-906 and D-273."

"That's miles away."

"Take a cab. It's not as if it'll cost you anything, you booner you."

"I will. Right now?"

Gabrielle caught her breath in sudden indecision. "No… not right now. I'm due to see the lady from the Vratch. She's coming round in three-quarters of an hour. I don't know how long she'll want to stay…"

"What?" Jack sprang up in alarm.

"The *Vratch*: the medical service."

"The medical *police*, you mean!"

But Gabrielle mistook his tone-of-voice. "Oh, well, best leave it till tomorrow evening. Come over at 12: it's 'The Twenty-Fifth Hour'."

"So you only want me for an hour."

"You can stay a bit longer, ninny," she said, giving him a playful nudge in the ribs, making the superox slosh.

"I'll be there."

"Love you…" The dummy sagged and went blank.

Elation at seeing Gabrielle again gave way to deep disquiet. Jack sat back down and put his head in his hands. God—what could the Vratch possibly want with Gabrielle?

18   The fate of class four

The Adin Beam stabbed down—a poker, scoring wood with runes of disaster. Firebirds swooped around them as he hugged Kat tight. But in the hydrogen-red flames her incandescent face became a skull. Horrified, he let go the shining skeleton, which shattered like an ember at his feet.

·····*●*·····

"Augh!"

Jack vomited the sound as he lurched upright in bed, his voice-chip faithfully executing the intent of its afferent neurones. Hugging his knees, he wept silently: rosin-sticky tears of self-pity.

The nightmares weren't going away. As his body grew weaker they were growing in frequency and intensity. Would they ever stop?

Yes. They would stop with his death and not before. They might be the last things he'd experience. Hell is not something you go to, like prison. You never actually leave it: it's what's under the skin of consciousness. Nightmares are only what shows through the holes in the skin. The day he died, lucidity would totally evaporate, letting the nightmares run together like crazy paving: an endless trail of desolation through an empty valley.

One after the other, he dragged his feet out of the bed and stood up. The room felt cold. "Twenty degrees Celsius," he called out. The vents started humming quietly but soon stopped. The room was already at 20° Celsius.

Jack got dressed: a simple matter of putting on his helmet and slipping into his dust suit in the shower-lobby. He knew better now than to wear clothes under a dust suit.

He had a job. It consisted of driving a sweeping machine around the streets. The machine looked after itself, more or less. Jack wondered if the seat for a driver wasn't simply there to give somebody employment.

The fact of it being a menial job didn't trouble him in the least. It gave him the opportunity to explore. He needed to know the city a lot better if he was to have any chance of tracking down Tvoul.

Nix City was divided up into 121 *kvartíri*—districts—jumbled together like a patchwork quilt. In each district the streets were laid out to the same grid plan: *oúlitzi* east-west and *dorógi* north-south, but the grids of neighbouring districts never lined-up. He asked his foreman if he could sweep a different district each day. "No problem," said the foreman.

His street-sweeper didn't so much sweep up the dust as strain out the lumps, spitting it out again. Like most of the appliances he had come across, it had a holoface and a female voice.

"Just take it easy along this street, pet, I wanna peek doon the side-alleys, like."

"I'm not following you awfully well, Jack. Do you want to train my accent?"

Jack smiled to himself. "Why-aye, hinny. We'll ha' yer ta'kin' Durham before the day's oot, like."

Getting to know the city was going to be a problem. The streets all looked the same. He'd have to get hold of a city plan—if they had such things. Looking for Tvoul in a city this size was a challenge. But Jack refused to be daunted. There was nothing else he was here for, so there was no other job he'd prefer to be doing.

"When we get back I'm not gonna plug you in tonight. Mebbes I'll get day-off tomorrow an' I can go an' have a bit-sup, like."

"*Whey!*" said the machine, in its newly-trained accent. "You'll get wrong off foreman."

A man deliberately stepped into Jack's path and put his hand on the hood. The sweeper lurched to a halt just before it ran him over, banging Jack's lip on the rim of the dashboard.

"Why man!" shouted Jack. "What d'you think you're playing at? Chicken?"

The man ignored the furious question. "What's a booner like you doing in a job like this?"

"Well... that's my business, like."

"Come with me, Jack, and I'll give you something better to do."

"What? Now?"

"Yes, of course."

"What'll I do wi' me sweeper?"

"Leave it here. Someone will come for it."

••••••✳●✳••••••

The man was called Sviatoslav Iliich Krov'. M1-speakers always introduced themselves by *ímia i ótchestvo*—name and patronymic. The patronymic was more important than the surname, he told Jack. Calling him Sviatoslav Iliich was quite acceptable. Jack followed him down an escalator into a covered mall, a jumble of walkways, shops and open-plan eating places. They sat down at one of these and Sviatoslav Iliich had the waiter bring coffee and cakes.

"What's the job?" said Jack.

"Social researcher."

Jack rose to his feet. "I'd best be getting back to work."

Sviatoslav reached forward and pulled at his sleeve. "Sit down, Jack, and hear me out."

Jack did so. "I don't know the first thing about social research."

"You've come from England, haven't you? England on Gaia?"

"Yes."

"And your knowledge of the place is still fresh in your mind?"

"Why of course…"

"That sort of knowledge is precious. Give us Martians the benefit of it and it will gain you enormous incred. Everywhere you go, people will turn their heads. They'll lean over backwards to help you. You aren't going to tell me that's not what you want?"

"How do you know what I want?"

"So—you've come all the way from Gaia just to sweep our streets?"

"No…" agreed Jack. "But I want to find my way around town, like. The job's champion for that. Me—I've got all the time in the world."

Clearly Sviatoslav had something he wanted to say to that. But he swallowed it back, contenting himself with "You won't be sitting in an office all the time, Jack. You'll be getting out and meeting people. People from all walks of life. Gaians *and* groubians. They're all hungry for the knowledge you've got in your head."

"Sounds to me like money for old rope."

"We aren't offering you money, Jack. You don't need 'money'. You need incred. Honour. Glory. Bags of it."

"That's just where you're wrong. I'm not one of your publicity-seekers."

"Publicity!" Sviatoslav laughed with a bark. "Jack—you've got the wrong idea about Mars. Yes, you can go in for publicity if you like, but that's not what's on offer."

He tapped the plate with his knife. "The intensor doesn't go noising you abroad. It affects the people you meet—but only the people you meet. Publicity is another thing. If you don't want publicity, there are things you can do to stop anyone giving it you. Or rather, as we say, stealing your privacy."

Sviatoslav helped himself to a cake and butchered it with his knife as if giving somebody the chop. "We don't have paparazzi here. Information is your most precious possession. In order to give you unwanted publicity, a journalist has to steal information from you.

Unlike on Gaia, you can feel it leaving you. You know who it's going to. If you don't like it, you maxgear them. That'll discourage any would-be paparazzi from hounding you."

He put a slice of cake in his mouth and mumbled "Only the most determined of information thieves can steal your privacy—without losing theirs into the bargain."

"Well," said Jack, "that's where I'm at a disadvantage. I don't know how to do any of that."

"So—we'll have to teach you, won't we?"

"Who's 'we'?"

"I work for an organisation called TMG." Sviatoslav watched Jack like a cat watching a mouse-hole, seeing how he'd respond. "You must have heard of us?"

"Certainly I've heard of TMG… but I can't remember what the hell it is you make." He didn't want to volunteer what Jens had told him.

Sviatoslav sighed. "It's not easy to explain—but it's no secret. It'll come clear over the next week or two. One of the things we do is collect information about Gaia."

"Which, of course, Gaia doesn't know how to stop you getting?"

Sviatoslav frowned. "Which, of course, former denizens of Gaia are pleased to give us—of their own free will, or not at all."

He stabbed a piece of cake and put it in his mouth, munching as he spoke. "We build vast databases of that information."

"What sort of information?" said Jack suspiciously.

"Social information. We're not interested in personal or commercial secrets, in hot gossip. The information we gather is going to be valuable in a hundred years, a thousand years…"

Sviatoslav leaned forward conspiratorially and murmured "…a *million* years."

"What have I got in me nut that's going to be worth anything in a million years?"

"Simple things. Trees. Flowers. The landscape. The weather. The people. And… houses—roads—vehicles—animals. Things you normally never stop to think about."

"Why should anybody be interested in all that?"

"Stop being naive, Jack. Look about you. What have you seen of Nix City in the course of your street sweeping?"

"Not a lot. Buildings, dust…"

"Exactly. The Nix, for all its vast size, is a cultural wasteland. Apart from the groubians, everybody's memories, cultures, traditions—all come from one single blue dot in the sky. And where is it all heading to?"

"Haven't the foggiest."

"To every other dot in the sky. Do you imagine it's all going to stop here for the next million years? On *Mars*? Have you seen anything to make it seem particularly worth stopping for?"

Jack mouth spread out like a spoonful of cold syrup. "No, I can't say I have."

"Exactly. Mars is simply a staging post. A jump-off point—a launching pad—for humanity." He drained the last of his coffee and got to his feet. "Look, come back to the office and I'll show you something to knock your eyebrows back."

Jack stayed seated. "I'm a bit worried about just walking out of me job like this. Won't that dunch me persona—or whatever the intensor does to you?"

Sviatoslav shook his head firmly. "I've already contacted the foreman and told him you're working for us now. He'll have no complaint about that. There are plenty of people in Nix City who can sweep streets. But there's only one person on Mars who can tell us about Esh Winning in the twentieth-century."

Jack stared at him in amazement. Then he burst out laughing. The very idea that in a million years countless people on an uncountable number of stars should wish to know anything about one small Durham pit village in the twentieth century struck him as hugely absurd. But more amazing still was that Sviatoslav knew the name of Esh Winning at all—and moreover that he, Jack, had lived there. He didn't make the connection with Markus.

Sviatoslav turned to go, beckoning Jack to follow him. As he did so a wild-eyed man thrust past him, pushing him against the table. He staggered and fell over. The man blundered into Jack, blindly trying to feel his way around him as if he were a wall of glass.

There came the shrill snarl of a microscopic pulse-jet, followed hard by a red flash, as if a signal flare had exploded in Jack's face. The man screamed as he was jerked onto his back, to be dragged away on a transparent filament. Jack watched in horror as the stricken man slid off, leaving a thin trail of blood, until he was lost to view amid the legs of the heedless crowd.

Sviatoslav picked himself up. Ignoring his own bruises he straightaway took Jack by the arm. "You all right?"

212

"Yes, I guess so."

"It was a good job your visor snapped shut in time—or you'd have been knocked-out cold."

"What in the name of damnation *was* it?"

"A bloody-butcher."

"A—*what?*"

"A bloody-butcher. Named after the trout fishing fly. Officially it's called a CRW, a corporal retrieval winch. Employed by Zasta to catch class four fugitives."

"What a—bloody—vicious thing!"

"Oh-ho," chuckled Sviatoslav, "you don't want to be on the receiving end of one of those."

· · · · · ✶ ● ✶ · · · · ·

"That's amazing."

Jack was looking at a view down Front Street, Esh Winning. He and Sviatoslav had built it up from scratch in less than ten minutes. The right hand side of the street was still a little hazy, though.

"That's where the E-light was," said Jack at last.

"The system doesn't understand you." Sviatoslav didn't either, but that was not the point.

"No—well—that's not the first time today. I guess the rest of Britain would pronounce it *Elite*. But we always called it the E-light."

The picture suddenly clarified. Sviatoslav laughed. "That's exactly the sort of information we are after. You're going to be worth your weight in gold."

Jack leaned back. "Now, explain to me in words of one syllable how that is possible. We've got a good crisp picture, as good as a photograph. Just like I remember it. But all I've done is tell the system what it *wasn't* like."

"That's the power of information. I mean *negentropy*—not what you might think of as information, which is no doubt just sheaves of facts and figures. We've got a lot of it in the system already: the type of brick used in a pit village, the trappings of a typical English street, window-frames from the various periods covered by that scene. The machine took a guess at what a view down the main street of a typical Durham mining village would look like. Then you eyeballed the bits that were wrong and gradually it came into focus. Wherever you could assert what it *wasn't* like, the machine could eliminate possibilities. A simple yes-or-no can eliminate thousands of them. In the end you're left with the only thing it can possibly be."

"Brilliant." said Jack. "I hear what you say, but I can't believe it—or I wouldn't have been able to if I hadn't seen it with me own eyes." He stretched his ribs and leaned back in his seat.

He was relaxed now. At first he had been trembling from his experience of seeing the "bloody-butcher" in action. Sviatoslav, noticing this, had poured away the coffee he was making and put down in front of Jack some calming herbal drink: flavoured chamomile, he guessed.

"Do you mean," he exclaimed, "the police fire off this devilish thing at anybody they want to? Just for a stop-and-search?"

"Goodness, no. By law the fugitive has to be class four."

"I heard you say that. What does it mean?"

"Didn't they explain Martian social class to you on *Oberon*?"

"Yes…" said Jack, scratching his head. "Something about a three digit binary number. I can't say it went in at the time. I gather most people are class seven, but as a booner I'm class six. That doesn't mean a blessed thing to me."

"Social class," said Sviatoslav, "depends on just three attributes: *autonomy*, *mobility* and *parity*. Autonomy means being held responsible for your actions. Mobility means—well—being allowed to move around at will. Parity means being allowed to transact business on the same level as other personas possessing parity. Such personas are called *econact*. If you've got all three you're binary 1-1-1—a citizen with full privileges."

"Right, I get it now. As a booner I'm not *econact*. People give me what I ask for, but they don't get any credit for it."

"They don't get any *extra* credit. They only get the base rate set by the intensor—the rate the Strana offers for goods and services."

"And why are we called 'booners'? Because everyone has to do us a boon?"

"It's a Selensk word: *b-o-n-d-e-r*." Sviatoslav spelled it out. "Pronounced 'booner'. It means a bondsman, a servant. A public servant, in your case. Whenever your card is switched on, you're on official business." He chuckled. "So don't bother being nice to people, or trying to punish them by maxgearing them. It's wasted effort. You're simply an instrument of the state."

"Which sets me one step down from a full citizen. Class six instead of class seven."

"That's exactly right. Everything with a class number is a *person*, meaning it has a *persona*."

214

"Right." Jack held up three fingers. "Whether or not I've got these three attributes," Jack grasped each finger in turn, "gives a total of two, four… eight possibilities."

"Forget class zero. There's something special about that."

"Seven classes, then. We've done six and seven. What about class five?"

"Class five is binary 1-0-1. Autonomous—*not* mobile—but *econact*, yes. It's called a *coperson*. A company, a business, a static robot, a vending machine. It also includes one or two chimorgs who've been awarded restricted human rights."

"Did I hear they get forcibly crippled?"

"That hasn't happened for a long while. Not since the Peter Zwillinge case. Chimorgs generally get the same rights as children: class three—not autonomous. Someone has to be responsible for them. Peter Zwillinge wanted to be autonomous in order to exchange triada vows with Shval Meteor. They wouldn't let her simply take charge of him."

"Why not?"

"Because of her bad intensions—her bad character, you'd say. Quite apart from what would happen if you put those two technical wizards together. So the Vratch threatened to take away his mobility—and he consented to that."

"That's *barbaric!*"

"They had to, because otherwise he'd have been class seven: a full citizen. Only human beings can have class seven. I entirely agree it was barbaric, though. A chimorg does have feelings—some of them at least. That's why we have the transgenic laws. To stop chimorgs being created in the first place."

"If somebody did that to *me*," said Jack, "it wouldn't exactly turn me into a model citizen."

"It didn't. We've all been suffering the consequences ever since."

Jack began to see the Meteor Gang in a new light. He thought of the resentment which must be driving them.

"Class four—we're into that now."

"As class four you are a *disperson*. Binary 1-0-0. Autonomous. But not permitted to roam about loose—and not *econact*. In fact denied all privileges except having to take responsibility for your own actions."

"You said class four—dispersons—were criminals. Fugitives."

"Yes, but the crime has to be serious enough."

"So how do you get to be a disperson?"

Sviatoslav's eyebrows shot up. "How do *you* get to be a disperson? Try firing on the forces of law and order. Shoot a z-nik—or a vratchka."

"What if I'm a booner?"

"That won't save you. All transgressions by class sevens are handled by the sanctions of the intensor. Class sixes cannot 'transgress' by definition—but they are generally under orders, so they *can* be disciplined. When people refuse to co-operate at all, the intensor is quite clearly useless for controlling their behaviour. Then sterner methods of restraint are needed—like the bloody-butcher."

"So the guy who bumped into us today was a complete tearaway?"

"Without a doubt. Zasta is not authorised to use the CRW on anyone else—unless you're dead and your body needs hauling up out of a hole. Which was what the CRW was invented for."

"So once upon a time it had a humanitarian purpose?"

"That goes for all the worst horrors. Haven't you noticed?"

Jack nodded slowly. In his mind's eye he could still see that trail of blood on the floor of the concourse. He thought of the Meteor Gang: hadn't Commissioner Miro told him they were class four, now? And didn't they have him, Jack, to thank for that?

Peter Zwillinge, Shval Meteor—and that great ugly brute Hamish McDougall. Pretty mean enemies to make. And to have running around loose in Nix City at the same time as he was.

"So what was Peter Zwillinge's humanitarian purpose?"

"Oh, don't you know? He was trained as an anaesthetist, as well as a telecomm engineer. He can cure as well as kill. He's very good at it, I'm told. When he wants to be."

"Sounds poles apart to me."

"No, the two jobs go quite well together, if you know anything about the intensor. Provided you've got the brains for it."

·····★●★·····

The next day Sviatoslav set Jack the task of evoking pictures from his boyhood. It was a fitting lead-in to his new job: a job he was to find the most absorbing, the most creative, he had done in his entire life. Or would ever do again, considering it would be the last job he'd ever have.

But first Sviatoslav drilled Jack on what he could recall of Martian social class. He considered it important that Jack got on top of it. "Else how are you going to know if you're talking to a living person or a machine?"

"Can you tell that from the intensor?"

"Yes—unless the individual sports a booner card."

Sviatoslav showed how. As with most intensor questions, the answer was the same: drop the menu and eyeball the option.

"We got down to class four yesterday," said Jack. "What's class three?"

"Class three is a *properson:* a protected person. Binary 0-1-1. No legal autonomy—but mobile and *econact.* Children are class three. They're given freedom to transact on the intensor—under tight parental controls of course. It's the only way to learn to become an effective citizen."

"So I should be careful of myself in front of a child."

"You certainly should. They can maxgear you—and how! And if their parents don't disagree with what they've done, there's no redress."

"And being a booner won't save me?"

"Nope. Booners are subject to discipline. There's worse things to lose than incred. Your booner status, for example. It's one reason why few booners choose to hide behind their booner cards when off-duty."

"Class two?"

"That's a funny one. The *inperson.* Binary 0-1-0. You and I can't be inpersons—it's only for institutions, provided they are not-for-profit. Families. Triadas. Not autonomous, since they're dependent on their members. Mobile, along with their members. But not *econact,* although generally one or two of their members are. Membership is often mixed-class."

"Class one?"

"*Expersons.* Deceased persons. Their estates, I think you'd say. No longer autonomous, no longer mobile, but still able to transact on the intensor."

"How?"

"Just as estates can pay out and receive money on Gaia, I'm told. But class ones on Mars can do a little more."

"Like swap smiles with the living? Not to mention kisses?"

Jack thought he was making a joke, but Sviatoslav was all for taking the question seriously. "In a way. Have you been to *Krásnoe Kladbísche* yet? The 'Red Cemetery'?"

"No I haven't. Why should I go there?"

"It's in the Old City. It's our answer to the Moscow *Novodevitchii.*"

Jack blinked as if a bottle of champagne had gone pop in his face. "Are you telling me I can go to any gravestone and call up the dead person? Talk to his holoface?"

"Yes—every one. Some of them are quite fun to chat to."

"I'm gob-smacked. I don't think I'd fancy doing that."

"Oh, I often go there. It's a popular recreation. Parents take their children to talk to their forebears. It gives them good intensions."

Jack's eyes lit up. "Now I can see the point of that. 'I'll tell grandpa what a naughty boy you've been...'" He laughed.

Sviatoslav laughed too. "Then you can see the point of the work we're doing here. Archiving ancestral knowledge, we call it."

Jack pondered that—and his laughter gave way to tingles down his spine. It was a million year archive, Sviatoslav had claimed. If Hilda had been interred on Mars, he considered, she could still be chatting to people in a million years. It was a several seconds before he spoke.

"That only leaves class zero. And—let me guess—that means no autonomy, no mobility and no parity. If class one is dead, then class zero's double-dead."

Sviatoslav stretched, sighed and looked down at his feet. It puzzled Jack as to why he hadn't got a ready answer.

"Well, isn't it?"

"No..."

"But it's not allowed to do anything. Mobility... autonomy..."

"Nevertheless it does."

Jack grew even more puzzled. "Tell me more."

Sviatoslav screwed up his face as if every word was a tooth extracted. "Its—more—like—*undead*." In a sudden fit of decision he flourished his hand as if presenting Jack with an invisible prize. "See here, Jack. Have you ever heard of Agent Zero?"

Jack covered his mouth and chin with his hand, resting his elbow in his other hand. "Yes I have. Once in passing. I forget when it was."

But he hadn't forgotten. He could see the uncertainty in Acting Commissioner Nilsson's face as she uttered the words "it doesn't matter."

Quite clearly it did.

Sviatoslav tossed his head as if shaking off a fly. "It doesn't matter."

"You're as bad as Commissioner Nilsson."

"Who's Commissioner Nilsson?"

"It doesn't matter."

The two men locked eyes as if they were arm-wrestling. Suddenly Sviatoslav snorted and laughed. "Okay, Jack. It's something I didn't want to go into at this stage. Let's just say that as far as the intensor is concerned there *are* no personas of class zero. It's just a bucket category—a trash-can. Assigning class zero to a persona is a way of consigning it to oblivion."

"So what *is* Agent Zero?"

"Listen to me carefully, then. There ought to be *no* personas of class zero. In actual fact there is *at most* one. It is known as the Unperson. A bug in the Nix intensor. Its existence was never even suspected until it was discovered by the Meteor Gang."

"A kind of Mr Nobody—responsible for all the things that are nobody's fault?"

"Exactly." Sviatoslav wrinkled his nose, as if savouring a novel idea. "How I think of it is this. The info-tensor itself can be represented as a Schrödinger Wave. Personas in the intensor, being pure information, behave like subatomic particles—quanta—describable by quantum theory. Personas having class greater than zero are *fermions:* in other words they obey Fermi-Dirac statistics, they have individuality. Are you with me?"

"Yes."

Sviatoslav's eyebrows shot up. He hadn't expected that. "Are you a mathematician?"

"Yes."

Sviatoslav gazed at Jack in unconcealed disbelief. He was of a mind to test him. "So if I tell you that a persona assigned class zero no longer obeys Fermi-Dirac but Bose-Einstein statistics…?"

"…It becomes a boson, indistinguishable from any other boson. They'll merge into a bosonic condensate… *aah!*" Jack's face lit up with a sudden insight. "so that's what the Unperson is: a bosonic condensate—*the* bosonic condensate—of *all class zero personas ever!*"

"By the Rock-of-Mars! You *are* a mathematician."

"But it doesn't tell me what the Unperson is capable of. I'd hazard a guess and say nothing."

Sviatoslav nodded. "That's how it ought to be, Jack. But the intensor is a programmed artifact… and even groubian programmers are only human. Prohibitions such as zero autonomy and zero mobility need to be explicitly programmed."

"I know what you mean. Harry once showed me a simple arcade game he's written. To make the ball bounce off the wall you have to write a program telling it to. Else the ball just goes through the wall."

"Yes, Jack—that's good. Now the Nix intensor was erected way back in the first century MV—the sixteenth century UT—long before nonexistence was properly understood. The programmers saw no need to program the prohibitions for class zero because there *are* no personas of class zero." He took a deep breath. "Or so they imagined."

"Can't the bug be patched?"

"It's lodged too deep. Every class inherits the properties of class zero—which includes their programs. We can't tear down the intensor to start afresh. Public life would collapse. The Strana of Olympia would disappear."

Jack strained forward. "So the Unperson evades all restrictions—becomes anybody?"

Sviatoslav nodded. "The Meteor Gang discovered they were able to animate an ectoplast with it. Do you know what an ectoplast is, Jack?"

"Half an ectoplast makes a hugglephone." Jack recalled Gabrielle telling him that.

"You could say so. The result was the famous—or infamous—Agent Zero."

"And I take it," said Jack, "that there can be no more than one Agent Zero in existence at any one time?"

"That's right. But it sure can get around."

Jack had a thought. "Can it leave the intensor field—say to travel to the Moon, or Gaia, where there is no intensor?"

"Yes. The intensor is not needed to keep the dummy animated, only to animate it in the first place. But if it were to perish altogether, then the Unperson can only be re-expressed back within the Nix intensor."

"And what if it's made to impersonate somebody who is already class zero in their own right? Like my Harry, who's been edulated—which I gather earns him zero status?"

Sviatoslav had to stop and think about that. "Something very interesting would happen… I'd say the Unperson wouldn't merely commence impersonating Harry, but Harry would *actually become* the Unperson."

19   Solar wind, solar wind

Jack ripped through the streets in his marscar, throwing up a column of dust as if he were in a motor boat ploughing along a canal. He was chagrined to discover that ordinary folk didn't use the free-ranging moon-hopper on Mars. All he could get was one of these slithering cars which were designed to do nothing but cruise the dusty streets. If you wanted to range across the surface of Mars you had to sign-up with Olvoi—*Olímpiskaia Voíska*—the volunteer defence force. Only Olvoi was allowed to use hoppers—and only on exercises.

However there was one advantage to a marscar. Unlike a hopper, which basically you steered by hand, you simply had to tell a marscar where to go and it went there of its own accord, avoiding other vehicles as it went, not to mention the odd pedestrian. You could sit back and contemplate the overpowering scenery.

Unfortunately he had to instruct his marscar in M1. They didn't have an M2 voice-chip for the model he wanted. Only the meagre low-valuta models had those, since only menials bought them. The dealer had given him a list of things to say and he tried to read them out as best he could, but his accent was bad and there was vast scope for misunderstandings.

This had been his experience ever since he'd landed. Here he was, in an advanced civilisation, half a century ahead of the planet Earth—and he couldn't get anything to do what he wanted. Maybe, like Kat, you had to be born to it.

He was on his way to see Gabrielle, to take her climbing on the north rim of the Old City. He thought of something she'd said when they'd talked on the hugglephone. She said the Vratch was coming to see her, but she hadn't wanted to say what for. The more he thought about it, the more ominous it sounded.

If people on Earth viewed good health as a citizen's right, on Mars it had become a civic duty. Of course such things were more important in the delicate artificial biosphere of Mars than the more robust one of Earth. People who allowed themselves to weaken and so become a reservoir of disease were being anti-social.

But it went far beyond disease control—almost to the borders of eugenics. The Vratch was to health what Zasta was to info-crime—a medical enforcement agency. Jack was determined to ask Gabrielle why she'd called them in. But he wouldn't be surprised if she told him the Vratch had invited themselves.

Why? None of his business really. And yet it might be—if she were pregnant.

A thought struck him. She hadn't told him because she didn't want the baby and was planning to get rid of it. His Catholic upbringing revolted at the idea. If life itself had no intrinsic valuta—what had?

If she was plucking up courage to tell him that she was bearing his baby, he was determined to do everything to see that she could have it. Even to abandoning his search for Tvoul. The cost of bringing up a child wasn't a problem. Not for a booner. But the likelihood of wrecking her career might be—at least to her. And yet... why had she come out all the way to Mars, if not in quest of a new life? A life in which she could settle down and start a family?

He realised he was thinking like a man with his whole life ahead of him. Not one they'd given only six months to live. Maybe they were crazy... and maybe he was, too. If she had anything to tell him, she would.

Soon he had picked her up from her apartment in *Doróga* 273 and they were tearing north along the dusty streets to the North Rim. Jack was showing off his new toy: he took anything but the straight route, just so that he could twist and turn, showing off his altogether superficial command of M1.

Eventually they got to the climbers' resort at the foot of the Rim. A rocket train took them a mile along a tunnel up through tumbled rock at the base until they came to the Rim proper—a sheer mile-high cliff on top of that.

Areology, the Martian equivalent of geology, sought to explain the lurid tones in which the cliff face was stained. The explanations it offered trumped anything you could have come up with in a drunken party game. The first people to see photographs of the Martian surface described it as the bizarre imaginings of somebody who knew nothing about geology. And thus the science of Areology was born: a grotesque kid-sister to terrestrial geologists' mature awareness of their own planet.

Soon Gabrielle was clambering—and sometimes dangling—behind Jack, as they felt their way up crack and cranny with ropes and pitons.

"You know, Jack," she observed over the intertalk, "If I didn't love you, I'd be hard put to think of a crazier way of spending an afternoon. Did you used to do a lot of this on Earth?"

"I climbed a bit in the Lake District when I was a lad—plus all around Roseberry Topping, south of Teesside. Hadn't done it for years. But the

Galen Clinic got me going again on the Moon. They said it was rattling good exercise for a man who'd been fitted with an SP unit."

"What about his poor girl-friend?"

"Oh, they were happy for her to string along behind."

She coughed. Jack ignored her.

"Kitty came out with me quite a lot. We used to go climbing in Crater Flammarion, the popular place to go from Jordvik. Did you ever meet Kitty?"

"No—I can't say I did. Jordvik isn't exactly a tiny village…"

"Kitty came from California."

"Well, the Earth's not that small either."

"No… you're right there."

Jack inserted another piton in the rock, taking more than usual care. Martian gravity was only a third of Earth gravity. If you weighed twelve stone on Earth, you weighed four on Mars. But it still didn't do to go falling off a cliff—as Gabrielle had pointedly reminded him at the outset. Jack had retorted "Confucius, He Say: height of fall not kill you. It's sudden stop at bottom."

Once Jack was satisfied with his handiwork they started climbing again.

"What became of Kitty? Did you kiss her goodbye on Selene?"

"In a manner of speaking. She was with Jens and Vermat when the Gaiascope went up."

Gabrielle fell silent. They didn't speak again until they reached a narrow ledge, where Jack thought it was high time she had a break. He was apt to forget that people who didn't have SP units got tired far quicker than he did.

Gabrielle clutched his arm. "Jack—just look at that view!"

"There now. Aren't you glad you came?"

She gave the arm a squeeze. "I'm always glad when I'm with you."

"I know. You'd follow me anywhere, ha-ha. Even up the sides of a crater. But you have to admit, this is a champion crater."

"It isn't a crater. It's a caldera."

"All right. It's a champion caldera."

It certainly was. It put Crater Flammarion in the shade. In the sable sky above them, drizzled with stars, the sun glared down, lighting and warming the cliff face. There was no red tinge to the sky here, nor even blue—the atmosphere was insignificant this far above "sea-level", as it was fancifully called. And the rocks weren't the dull greeny-grey of the Moon. They were painted rocks, mostly reds and browns and ochres.

Twenty miles away, on the other side of the plain, the cliffs rose in multiple levels as several calderas bit into the central one.

Below them the City stretched across the intervening lava pan. He could see the dome of the Areopagus like a lonely blister, but the sameness of the city made it scarcely visible at this altitude.

"Jack—there's something I must tell you."

Here it came. He patted Gabrielle's hand in what he hoped would feel like encouragement.

"You know…" she said, then stopped and had to pluck up courage again. "When I made the decision to come out to Mars, I knew it would mop up the best years of my life. I didn't make it lightly. I was hoping to get something in return."

They turned to look into each other's eyes. For a moment Jack was tempted to raise a holoface—the thought alone could set it off—but he'd have hated himself for that. He imagined he could see the same thought in Gabrielle's eyes—her face looked strangely naked. Not romantically naked, but as you do when you're about to confide something bad.

"I wasn't thinking of you at the time," she said. "I didn't know then you'd be on board *Oberon*. But when we met up again… I transferred my dream to you."

Suddenly tears started in her eyes. Jack wanted to kiss her, but she needed to keep her visor shut in order to breathe. She turned her head away. "Jack—I'm afraid it's not to be."

"Hinny, if it seems I'm not paying you enough attention, it's because I've got something hanging round me neck. A bit job to do. After that, things will be better. Believe me."

"No Jack, you don't understand. It's just that… it's… I can't have children."

Jack was stunned. This wasn't what he'd been anticipating.

"The lady from the Vratch told me last night. She wanted to remove my ovaries there and then, but I wouldn't let her. I said I didn't want to be mutilated—it means a lot to a woman. She replied that it was a condition of being allowed to reside on Mars. So I said I'd go back to Earth."

"Gabrielle—what the heck's been happening to you?"

"Radiation, Jack. The solar wind. *Oberon* was well shielded, but eight months in space must have been the last straw to break the camel's back."

"What are you on about? That goes for everyone on the *Oberon* surely…"

"No it doesn't, Jack. I've spent half my working life flying to-and-fro on the Lunaborg spaceplane, ferrying patients to the Galen Clinic. I should have known better. The vratchka did tests. My ovaries are shot to pieces. It's irresponsible even to think of having children."

"We could adopt…" blurted out Jack, before he realised what he'd said. With his life-expectancy it was irresponsible for him too.

Gabrielle closed her eyes and gripped his arm in both hands. Tears hung on her lashes. "Jack," she whispered. "I'm committed now to going back to Earth. I've told the Vratch I would."

"How soon's that gonna be? It's another two years before the *Oberon* comes round again. What can they possibly do to you in all that time?"

"Keep me in prison."

Jack bowed his head and shook it widely, like an elephant swaying its trunk. The power of the Vratch! The insolent, heartless power!

"Luckily," she said, "it doesn't need to come to that. There's a special shuttle just been put on. It's flying out to *Oberon* before it gets too far away, though it'll be a long flight. I've got another first-class passenger."

She sighed and dropped her hands in her lap. "I depart from Voronka in two days' time."

•••••✱●✱••••

Throughout Gabrielle's last two days and nights on Mars, Jack never left her side. He asked her what she'd most like to see before she went home. He was expecting her to say Cydonia or Valles. Going by rocket train they might have managed both of them in the time. But all she wanted to do was wander round the Areopagus. The huge rock drank-in their pain. The chill it radiated deadened their sense of impending loss.

Hand in hand they walked past the lawns and the flower beds and fingered the trees under the Plexiglas dome that housed the Park.

"They're rebuilding the Gaiascope," said Gabrielle. "It will be even bigger and better."

"Is that where you're going back to? Jordvik? I thought you wanted to return to Earth."

"I do really. But there's nowhere on Earth for me to go. I haven't got a home in Sunderland anymore. Me Mam won't be able to look after me—she's far too old. Her bungalow is too small for us both."

"You won't go short, will you? Did Jens arrange payment for you, I mean, as our agent on board the *Oberon*?"

"Oh, yes. There's a tidy sum in *selkroner* waiting for me in Jordvik. Just try transferring it back to England though… 'Moon-money'…" She affected a Mackem whoop. "...'What'yer doing with *moon-money?*' But I'll get to spend it. The firm's keeping me on as courier—and it'll be easier for me if I'm based on Selene."

"I'm surprised you still want to work for them—after what they've done to you."

Gabrielle shrugged. "I can't sue for compensation or anything like that. It was entirely my own fault. As a nurse I should have known. The tests were on offer, but they weren't compulsory. And they're not awfully pleasant. I just loved the life—and I guess that deep down I was afraid that if they found radiation damage I'd have had to give it up."

"Don't they limit you to so-many hours?"

"It doesn't depend on how many hours you spend in space. It depends on where you happen to be in the spaceplane when an X-flare hits. You're supposed to know the sunspot forecast and be sitting in a seat: they're all well-shielded. Not standing in the aisle tending a sick passenger—or soothing a crying child."

They tried to link hands around the bole of the great oak, but couldn't quite reach. Gabrielle said "This one's called the Oak King. Every two years it produces masses of acorns."

"Total waste," replied Jack moodily. "How's an acorn going to put down roots on Mars?"

"You're supposed to think what a touching declaration of faith in humanity that is," said Gabrielle, just as moodily. "It's got this far, hasn't it?"

They let go of the tree and walked away. Jack said "Would you like to go back to Earth?"

"I'd love to. It will be a year or two before the Gaiascope reopens. Until it does there's not a great deal to do in Jordvik, except lift the elbow. And wild horses wouldn't drag me to Lunaborg to live."

Jack murmured "The house in Esh Winning has just come back into my hands."

"How did that happen? I thought you'd simply given it to that Markus fellow."

"Markus never bothered to register it. He wouldn't have dared, or they'd have chucked him off the planet. Nobody knew about the transaction. Frank's been telling me he's taken charge of the house again on my behalf. The insurance paid out—there was quite a bit of rebuilding work to do. Doesn't a triton pistol make a mess of things. But now it's all like new. Frank was hoping to tempt me home."

"When *are* you going home, Jack?"

"Just as soon as I can persuade Zasta to do something about Tvoul." He had told Gabrielle nothing about what the Vratch had said to *him*.

Gabrielle poked her tongue in her cheek. "What's their take on that?"

"They say they don't know where Tvoul is. They're trying to kid me she's not on Mars. They claim they can tell from the intensor."

"Can't you get her convicted in her absence?"

"No. The law doesn't work that way. This is a capital charge, they say, so Tvoul must be around to answer it. And it happened off-world, so the onus is on me to bring the evidence. I've phoned the Moon and Selstyrke is all ready to help me there. Nilsson's canny. She's a great support. But I think Zasta's covering for Tvoul. She's sure to have friends in high places."

"Oh yes, won't she just. What's the use of having been Goubernator three times on-the-trot if you only made enemies?"

"Aye, you can say that again." He stooped to pick up a pebble and clutch it tightly, a ball of pumice like a tiny parched world. "So it's a waiting game. Sooner or later—I'll find her."

He threw the pebble over the edge. "Then I'll be gannin' 'yem." For emphasis he thickened his accent. "Back to Durham. Back ti' me bit hoose in Esh Winning."

But he knew the moment he said it that he was never going back as a living man.

He took Gabrielle's hands and pulled her round to meet his gaze. "Why don't *you* go back there and wait for me? Have it as your weekend cottage. Live in it for free. I'll give Frank a buzz and tell him to sort things out. I'll be on the *Oberon* next time around and I'll come back home and join you."

It wasn't really a lie. It was a wish—a hopeless one.

Gabrielle clasped his neck. It was several seconds before she could speak.

"Thank you, Jack… I'll keep it warm for you. And every night I'll put your slippers out in front of the fire…" Her voice tailed off and she burst into tears. Jack hugged her tightly. A second grew to a minute— and still they weren't able to let go of each other.

•••••★●★••••••

Three hours later Jack was standing on the balcony of the main concourse of Voronka Cosmodrome, watching a group of people on a hover-platform glide across the glassy floor towards the departure gate. Gabrielle stood out in her red uniform. Her VIP passenger was a

228

drooping bear of a man. She'd said his name was Sprenger. Jack supposed him to be some government apparatchik.

Jack had half-wondered if Tvoul might take the chance to bolt back to Gaia, but there was clearly no groubian among the little cluster—not even if she'd been in disguise. It was simply not feasible for a groubian to slip off the planet that way.

Just before the hover-platform disappeared beneath the balcony, Gabrielle glanced up. Briefly their eyes met. The SP unit did a painful click.

Jack turned briskly towards the levitators and ascended to the lookout tower. He watched the great Eye slowly open and the shuttle rise. It turned its nose towards the setting sun. Then, like a quarrel from a crossbow, it darted off, dwindled and disappeared.

Long after the sun had gone down, Jack stood in darkness, staring out of the curved windows of the lookout tower. He tried to bring Gabrielle's face to mind—a face he never expected to see again. In dismay he found it was already fading in his memory. Gabrielle—bonny lass. Beautiful. And not for him.

Solar wind... solar wind... boiling off the surface of the Sun. Blowing past planet after planet, out beyond the furthest lump of ice in the Oort Cloud. Blowing away from him everyone he'd ever known.

•••••✳●✳•••••

Saturday night in the club they were playing 60s songs from Gaia, moody and low. Stewart, sitting beside Jack in his usual place at the bar, couldn't get him to talk in anything but monosyllables, so in the end he had given up. Jack had raised a discouraging holoface, the Durham Cathedral demon door-knocker no less, and now sat drowned in sullen depths like Debussy's *cathédrale engloutie*.

A voice rose out of the background noise, singing a Lennon-McCartney number...

> *Once there was a way... to get back home.*
> *Sleep pretty darling, do not cry...*

All at once the music froze for Jack on one note. There was a root shift in the energy of the intensor. A buzz ran round the room, confirming Jack's impression: somebody of consequence had entered the building. Jack didn't know intensor conventions well enough to be sure what it meant, but the torque on his face was nearly strong enough to pop his eyeballs.

A celebrity? Or a scoundrel?

Three people had just come in. A tall shapely woman with her arms around the shoulders of two men. One of the men collected drinks from the bar. Two beers and an elaborate cocktail—a Midsummer Madness. They were just settling down to enjoy their drinks when one of the men, evidently in response to an intertalk, got to his feet and left the club. After a moment the other man followed him, laying his hand briefly on the woman's arm to bid her stay and wait for them to come back. As he departed, the intensor barely quivered. It was tightening in a vortex around her—and her only.

With sinuous grace the woman stretched out her long legs, encased in stylish leather high-boots with titanium buckles. Adjusting the straw in her cocktail, she raised the visor of her helmet and began to drink. As she did so her groubian cheeks flushed with pleasure in hues of yellow and rose-pink. Jack's SP unit went click.

It was Tvoul! Never could he forget that face.

Alerted by the click, she looked up from her drink to catch him staring fixedly at her. Her groubian complexion exploded in a flurry of colours—then it settled down to a pond of ripples in shades of bluish grey, which rose steadily from her chin and tumbled into her eyes.

Groubian laughter.

Stretching her legs, affecting to relax even more into her chair, she returned his gaze with a long low stare, smiling that Mona Lisa smile as she sipped her cocktail.

He recognised her—but had she recognised him? He was showing a dismal holoface which masked his own, but she would have no difficulty polling the intensor to find out who he was. If she was that bothered.

Deliberately he switched off the holoface, treating her to a basilisk glare from his own features. In response she merely broadened her smile. Jack's throat tightened in fury. He was all set to leap to his feet.

Her two companions had scarcely been away when they returned, hurrying her off. Snatching her eyes away from Jack, she pushed her unfinished drink to the middle of the table and rose effortlessly to her feet. Then, arms around each others' waists, the threesome briskly climbed the waxy steps out of the club.

Jack turned to look at Stewart, who was smiling and nodding. "Looks like you made a hit," the latter observed.

"Who was that?" said Jack, straining to keep his voice level.

"Why—that's *Tvoul*. Everyone knows Tvoul. She often comes in here. Though she doesn't have to tout for custom these days."

"You mean she's a prostitute—along with her other accomplishments?"

"I don't know what you mean by 'other accomplishments', but she's the world expert on *interspex*. The galactic expert. That's *Tvoul*."

Stewart took a gulp of his drink. "Just try her out and you'll see what I mean." He lifted his glass to drain it.

"I've never done it with a groubian," said Jack. "How do you avoid getting edulated?"

Stewart spluttered in his glass. "Bloody idiot! You can't be edulated without your consent. It takes hours… days… you have to lie back thinking of England. Huh! No, she'll do it your way—whatever you want. Would *interspex* be anything like so popular?"

"Just thought I'd ask," said Jack.

A picture of Harry arose in his mind. So he couldn't have resisted. Had he'd been drugged… perhaps by some rainforest fruit or other?

"Anyway I'd say she fancies you," Stewart continued, putting down his glass. "Though the look on your face would've scared the shit out of me. If I were you I'd raise that holoface again. It was much less malign."

Catching the barman's attention, Jack ordered more drinks. "Can groubians tell what you're thinking?"

Stewart pondered for a moment. "It's doubtful. They recognise a smile of course, but they're not very good on gaian facial expressions. Why do you ask?"

"It's just—it's just that I could use a little, er, consolation. I've said goodbye to Gabrielle. It's almost three weeks and I'm still down. I wouldn't like to put Miss Tvoul off by my look of misery."

"I don't imagine she'll hold that against you. Get on the hugglephone: 'touch her up', as they say. But I guess you've missed your chance for a while."

"Why?"

"Well, for a week, let's say. *Nedélia Slëz* starts at midnight."

"*Nedélia Slëz*…?"

"Always the first week of March: the month of Mars—in MV: the time of Mars. It never varies."

"Hell—I'd forgotten that."

"I guess that was her having a final fling before going off to sulk in a black veil for seven days."

"Where does she live?"

Stewart told him where. "She also dances at the *Krásnaya Melnítza*. That's M1 for *Moulin Rouge* if you don't know. Her act is the highlight of the cabaret. Bear in mind she pulls the crowds. Whenever she's billed, book well in advance."

"Then I suppose I'd better do that now."

20   The anthem of the star-children

"Welcome to Åsgård! Not quite the late-lamented Gaiascope—but we're every bit as proud of it. Have you been here before?"

It was Petra who addressed the question to Jack. Possibly because she had noticed him looking at her.

"Why no—first time."

"The City Fathers in their wisdom decided that the Areopagus needed a spa and pleasure garden like the Gaiascope, which as you'll know was inspired by Tivoli Gardens in Copenhagen. To someone from Gothenburg like me it looks more like Liseberg without the green rabbit."

"How do they manage to get a hot-spring spa—here on Mars?"

"The same way as they do on Gaia. Here inside the Nix we're sitting on a dormant volcano. Down beneath us is a huge well of magma. Hundreds of cubic miles of molten rock. That gives us areothermal water. How do you think Nix City manages to stay so warm?"

"So—if Olympus Mons erupts again, the whole place will go up like the Gaiascope?"

Petra and Sviatoslav exchanged wry glances. Petra replied "Well, Jack, not exactly. I for one feel safe enough. Olympus Mons is dormant. It hasn't erupted in over fifty thousand years. Isn't that what the groubians tell us?"

"A short interval in the areological timescale," replied Sviatoslav, with a wink at Jack. "There's no such thing as a 'dormant' volcano, Petra, and we'd do well to remember it. There are active volcanoes, extinct volcanoes and live ones. Technically speaking, Olympus Mons is live." He chuckled. "Jack's right. We're all up-in-the-clouds—or might soon be."

Petra frowned. She thought of herself as a person with her feet on the ground.

Jack had met Petronella Persson briefly in passing at the TMG offices. He hadn't given her a second glance. But now, in the sauna, he couldn't take his eyes off her. Not just because, in her state of undress, she was revealed as an exceedingly handsome woman, but because her body reminded him so much of Gabrielle's.

There was of course no mystery about *that*. People from Sunderland have a lot of Viking blood in them. Gabrielle's ancestors might well have come from the Gothenburg area too. Petra was as tall as Gabrielle, had her shape of face, her lean figure with its small neat breasts and her flaxen hair. Gabrielle's slightly receding chin, a characteristic of the Göta people of Sweden, was emphasised in Petra.

He soon decided that that was where the similarity ended. He disapproved of Petra's razor-wire disposition—and her resemblance to Gabrielle only served to irritate him.

A fourth person came into the sauna, a stocky man with thick dark body hair. Jack thought of a black bear.

"Ah, Boris." said Sviatoslav. "Glad you came. You'll know Petra, of course, our legal counsel. This is Jack Williams, who has recently joined TMG... Jack, this is Boris Mixailovitch of Peretchelo—Harry's company."

Boris gave Petra and Jack a polite nod and spread out his towel to sit down.

Sviatoslav added meaningfully "Jack is Harry's father."

Boris turned back to look at Jack wide-eyed. After a significant pause he held out his hand. "I'm very pleased to meet you, Jack," he said. "Do accept my commiserations over your son Harry."

"It's mainly over Harry that I'm calling this meeting," said Sviatoslav.

"I love your choice of meeting rooms," said Boris with no trace of irony. "It's one-up on the magnolia boxes of your HQ. I take it we've got this cabin to ourselves?"

"Of course. And it's sealed for sound and swept for bugs. And it's a helmet-free zone—no intensor. We can talk off-the-record."

"Just the place to discuss hot topics," said Boris gleefully, rubbing his hands. He had already begun to sweat and his hands made a crepitating noise. Petra pulled her towel tighter round her body.

"Well," said Boris eagerly, "where shall we start?"

"Jack's the only one of us who doesn't know what Harry was up to," said Sviatoslav. "I think we ought to bring him up-to-date. Then *I* want to know precisely where Tvoul fits in."

Boris swivelled on his base to face Jack squarely. "Harry was my colleague. I managed him, but Peretchelo is an informal sort of place. We worked closely together on a number of projects. I suppose you know what Harry did for a living?"

"He told me was a bio-engineer."

"That's correct. So am I. But did he ever mention *transmen?*"

"Not in front of me, no."

"Do you know what transmen are? Or should I say: will be?"

"I've recently been made aware," said Jack.

"Harry was our chief researcher on a major government contract: the bio-engineering of transmen for Project Tahiti."

Jack bent his head to one side. "So our Harry was manufacturing *transmen*... for the government?"

Boris waved his hands horizontally. "Not exactly. There is a chicken-and-egg situation with transmen." Boris giggled at his own little joke. "You're hoping to end up with real people: people who've had fathers and mothers, or brought up in some sort of family situation. People whom the Goubernator would give his blessing to. And yet you're inevitably going to have to bio-engineer them. At least it seemed inevitable... until Tvoul came along."

"You're going to have to bio-engineer them. Period," said Petra firmly.

"Harry never believed that," retorted Boris, "or he wouldn't have signed-up to the project. He was a good Catholic, you know. Catholics believe genetically-engineered people are an insult to the Creator."

"However did he think he could pull it off?" said Petra, eyebrows raised. "Get it even the tiniest bit wrong and you end up with a chimorg. An insult to the Creator, if ever there was one."

"A chimorg-and-egg situation," giggled Boris. He was enjoying his little jokes.

Petra pouted. "Well, the first of your putative transmen is a manufactured thing, a sort of Adam-figure. A chimorg by definition—until the Goubernator gives it his blessing."

"Only if you're going to employ non-*human* genes to prolong the individual's life," interposed Sviatoslav, "the operative word being *human.*"

"Which is exactly my point," said Boris. "Well, Harry—aided by Tvoul, I must add—discovered that an all-human hybrid was feasible. A gaian-groubian one. The obvious route is to insert groubian chromosomes into an enucleated gaian oocyte and then to inseminate it with gaian sperm."

"Explicitly forbidden by the transgenic laws," said Petra.

"Quite right. So they couldn't go that route. But nobody could have predicted the route Harry and Tvoul were eventually to take: *edulation.*"

Jack nodded and looked down at his hands.

"But Harry's real breakthrough was hiding in there right from the start. While everybody else was locked into thinking that transmen would have to be genetically-engineered and to grow to adulthood, maybe for several generations, before the star-children could set out from

Mars, Harry was convinced that transmen could be bred on board *once the mission was underway.*"

Boris stopped and looked round keenly. "Does everyone understand the significance of that?"

Sviatoslav and Petra stared back poker-faced. "No," said Jack.

"It knocks decades off the project timescale," said Boris. "It means we can use an existing vessel like *Oberon*, which is already tried and tested, spaceworthy and autarkic…"

"What do you mean *autarkic?*" said Jack.

"Self-contained, to the point that it needs no contact with the home world," explained Sviatoslav. "These days it also means capable of building a replica of itself, using locally-abundant materials."

Jack instantly saw the point. "A super-organism—a great big germ."

Boris nodded and continued. "And, as we know, *Oberon* will become obsolete in twenty years. It will be replaced by eight thermonuclear vessels not constrained to flying in Hohmann orbits."

Sviatoslav whistled. "I see what you're thinking. But with Harry gone it won't happen."

Petra leaned forward. "But what if we could *make* it happen?"

"How?" Boris and Sviatoslav both spoke at once.

"With Tvoul's zygocysts—or DNA derived from them."

"Oh." said Boris. "That's your angle, is it? Well, consider this. The *Oberon* isn't a particularly fast vessel—but *Prometheus* is. What if it were *Prometheus* which was assigned to the galacto mission? That would tickle the fancy of the Groubian Alliance."

"Oh, wouldn't it!" crowed Sviatoslav. "*Prometheus* is Titan's only link with the Four Worlds. It would entail the abandonment of Platform Two and dissolution of the Titanian *mir.*"

"Re-colonising Titan was something the groubians were never awfully pleased about…" said Petra.

"Keep off our God-damned holy world," said Boris, nodding.

Sviatoslav smacked his knee. "If I'd have known that Harry's project entailed *that*, I'd have had the Groubian Alliance eating out of my hand. Speaking of which…"

He turned to Petra. "Petronella, darling—have you managed to sound out Dolpou Zvezda, high-priestess of the GA?"

Petra glanced at Jack. "Before I start on that, I think somebody ought to tell Jack about the star-children."

"I was just going to ask about that," said Jack.

"Go ahead, Star-Papa," said Sviatoslav.

Boris enthusiastically took up the challenge, leaning forward and gesticulating with his pudgy hands. "Star-children? Well… not everybody means the same thing by that. But everybody means future galactonauts. People suited to living and breeding among the stars will have to form the first galactic colonisation team."

"You are thinking too small," said Sviatoslav. "Don't call it a team— call it a *mir*—a *world*. It takes a world to bring a world into existence. Worlds are living beings, sexual beings—they reproduce themselves. Teams aren't—and don't." He glanced at Petra.

"Sviatoslav is right," said Boris, still addressing Jack. "Mars wasn't seeded by just one spaceship. Nor Selene either. Selene is the child of Mars (and Titan, to press a point—but everybody likes to forget that). *Oberon* is the child of Mars and Selene—there's no argument about that. And, appropriately enough, the new world which sets out to colonise the stars will be the child of all the classical Four Worlds—Gaia, Selene, *Oberon* and Mars."

"Five—if you include Titan," volunteered Petra.

"I'm not including Titan," snapped Boris.

"Perhaps you ought to," retorted Sviatoslav. "Because that's where Tvoul has gone."

A stunned silence greeted the news. Eventually Boris said "Can I be absolutely sure of that?"

"I've no evidence of my own, but Markus was convinced of it," said Sviatoslav. "And that's good enough for me."

"If that's the Markus who bought my house," said Jack, "then he's dead. So how do we know what he was convinced of?"

Jack was just on the point of dropping a bombshell of his own: that he had discovered Tvoul living openly in Nix City. But it occurred to him to keep his trap shut. He wanted to know exactly what plans they had for Tvoul. Because he had plans of his own.

Sviatoslav leaned forward to address Jack. "When Markus took possession of your house on Gaia, he first phoned Selene, then Mars… then Titan. His call to Selene was to the TMG resident agent in Lunaborg: Duke Treikle. When Markus phoned Mars, he left a message for *me*. But when he phoned Titan… his message was for Tvoul herself, to await arrival."

"But how do you know that's where she's gone?" said Jack.

Sviatoslav shrugged. "Circumstantial evidence. Failure to find her on Mars, even by polling the intensor."

Polling the intensor: that phrase again! Nobody had ever managed to explain to Jack how that was done. He gathered it entailed offering a tidbit of information as bait and seeing what nibbled it. The trouble with these Martians was that they relied on all these wonderful hi-tech solutions in lieu of common sense.

What if Tvoul had been too canny to take the bait? And canny she was. Who, after all, would expect to find a university professor dancing the *quinquin?*

Tvoul's secret—her incredible secret. But by stumbling on it himself, it was *his* secret now, as Miro had assured him. Not Tvoul's, nor TMG's, nor anyone else's. He was, or so he felt, beginning to get an idea of the ownership of information as real-estate: beginning to learn how to turn the intensor to his own advantage.

"Now," said Sviatoslav, turning to Petra, "having dealt with the star-children, how did you get on with Dolpou Zvezda and the Groubian Alliance?"

"Well, Tvoul has suddenly dropped in status from superhero to—well not exactly *persona non grata*—but someone the GA doesn't want to talk about. They may be covering-up for her, but I doubt it. Yes, Dolpou did agree that transmen with groubian genes would be something her members might well find—erm—appealing. After all, it's something mighty close to the groubian dream. But not if it entailed *interspex*—they don't like owning up to that. And as for *edulation...!*"

"I guess they don't want to start another Olympian War," murmured Sviatoslav.

"No it's deeper than that. They have an intrinsic horror of it. Edulation, that is, between a gaian and a groubian. They insist that all the stories which gave rise to the wars were sheer calumny."

"Yeah-yeah," sneered Sviatoslav. "That's been the GA's line all along. But I asked you to explore a slightly different angle. Was it possible that Tvoul tricked Harry into marriage *just to get rid of him?*"

Petra shook her head, but Jack looked up with a start. "Why would she want to do that?"

Sviatoslav nodded towards Boris, who cast around for a way to explain. "You see, there's been a lot of rivalry between Peretchelo and TMG over the best route to the Transman. And you could include PUG in that rivalry."

"Warfare," muttered Sviatoslav.

"Now Tvoul was not only PUG's chief researcher on their Transman contract but, in her *ex-officio* capacity as founder of the Groubian Alliance, she continued to be their chief contact for all sorts of things."

"To say nothing of contacts arising out of Tvoul's service to Mars as Goubernator," interjected Sviatoslav. "Don't overlook that."

But Boris made a face. "I'm sure she has her fingers in every pie. But if Tvoul was assisting Harry with *his* Transman project too—*our* project—then that's a serious conflict of interest."

"The plot thickens," said Petra, "So Tvoul has been selling PUG down the river to Peretchelo, has she? And selling the Groubian Alliance too? When I spoke to her, Dolpou wondered out loud if that was so."

"No," said Boris. "Just the opposite. Because Tvoul did *not* help Harry achieve his goal. She married him—and edulated him. Exit Harry. No transmen... at least, not by that route. So Peretchelo was sold— looted—sacrificed—to Tvoul's cronies in PUG and the GA. Aren't they the beneficiaries? I ask you—*cui bono?*"

Jack gasped and put his head in his hands.

"Perhaps I should say: no transmen—*courtesy of Peretchelo.* Now Sviatoslav, do you know something I don't?" Boris put his hand over his mouth and tried to stare Sviatoslav out.

"Wait a minute," cut-in Petra, "Let's be absolutely certain of what you're saying. Exactly who has Tvoul been two-timing? PUG—or Peretchelo?"

"Peretchelo," blustered Boris. "My company. Me!"

"Well, you would say that, wouldn't you," Petra countered. "But I need evidence that'll stand up in *court.*" She put heavy emphasis upon the word "court", as if she was determined that was where the matter would end up.

"Until then, Boris," murmured Sviatoslav, "you'd do well not to go flinging out wild accusations..."

Boris spluttered. "I'm not flinging out anything. I merely said, off-the-record if you will—do you know something I don't?"

Sviatoslav's voice revealed an edge. "Like...?"

"Let me just repeat what I heard Petra say just now. *What if we could make it happen... with Tvoul's zygocysts—or DNA derived from them.* What's so wild about wondering if there's some tie-up between TMG and Tvoul, to Peretchelo's disadvantage?"

Petra sat back with her hands on her lap, as if she'd taken personal offence. "I was merely postulating a what-if situation. This is the first time the idea's been aired—and in your presence, if *you* will. You've no right to go impugning our motives."

Boris half-closed his eyes. "Your motives—not even God-in-heaven knows those. But there's a perfectly good way to establish *Tvoul's* motives,"

He leaned forward until his head was almost above Petra's knee, the latter shying away in spite of herself. "Suppose we find her. Then it hinges on this. Has she got any zygocysts or parturition scars—or hasn't she?"

There was silence. Boris paused to let the question sink in.

"Because if she's got neither, then I for one cannot believe she has merely failed to conceive after edulating her gaian husband." Boris sat up. "Hell—I mean to say... *Principal Professor of Human Reproductive Biology?* This is a person who knew *precisely* what she was doing."

"What *was* she doing?" murmured Sviatoslav very quietly.

"Giving my Transman project the Titan Kiss—that's what!"

Sviatoslav clicked his tongue. "I just cannot believe that Tvoul, of all people, would do anything to harm the one single cause close to the heart of every *human* being on this planet: the star-children."

"I agree with Svi," said Petra. "And Dolpou Zvezda can't believe it either."

"Well you're being naïve, both of you. Sure, the groubians want star-children—but they want them to be *groubian* star-children. No groubian wants to see some gaian Johnny-come-lately succeed where they haven't managed it... *in fifty thousand fucking years."*

Boris leaned forward again for emphasis. "I'm convinced that Tvoul deliberately married Harry to take him out of the equation. To dispose of him, plus his ideas for the Transman, so thoroughly that no one will ever find out what really happened." He slapped his thighs. "Look—she kids him to propose to her... and to take her to Gaia to meet the family."

He turned to Jack. "Do you know what we call Gaia? *The Blue Hole.* It swallows everything and lets nothing back out. Things fall onto the surface of that planet—into its oceans, its swamps, its rainforests—and are lost without trace."

He turned to the others and waggled both his forefingers. "So go on: try and find Tvoul. But you won't find what you're expecting. Because when you do locate her—there'll be no zygocysts. Read my lips: *no zygocysts.* Her body will be pure and sterile as the driven sands of Mars."

••••••★●★••••••

"Table for one, sir?"

"I have a booking. Name of Williams."

"Certainly sir," the girl smiled. "Follow me."

Jack sat down at his table and a drink was brought. As he'd ordered, the table had a commanding view of the dance floor. Above the stage, the eponymous red windmill turned its glowing sails. Couples were already dancing to the band. Tunes from his childhood—a Twenties' Revival.

But the dancing wasn't authentic. There was no way you could re-create the Charleston in one third of Earth gravity. This didn't trouble the dancers in the least as they hopped and span around, their feet hardly touching the floor.

The tables filled up around him. Presently the girl who had shown him to his seat came back with the same fixed simper on her face. "Would you mind terribly if we seated more guests at your table, sir? We're fully-booked tonight."

Jack wanted to refuse, but he realised that she was just being polite. His booking for one hadn't guaranteed him a table all to himself. Nor would it do to claim booner privileges. And if his table was the only one with unoccupied chairs, he'd draw attention to himself.

"Why tonight?"

"End of *Nedélia Slëz*. Spot-on midnight, Tvoul will be back out there, dancing."

Jack gave his assent with a resentful nod. He had activated the booner card because he'd wanted to be alone with his thoughts. He had raised a bland holoface because he didn't want people to guess what those thoughts might be. The holoface became less bland.

Two young men were shown to the seats on either side of him. They tried to make conversation, but soon cottoned-on to the fact that Jack didn't want to talk. So they ignored him, talking across him as if he wasn't there.

"I do hope this is going to be worth the effort."

"Don't you worry. I come here every Friday, just for the cabaret. Nobody does it like Tvoul."

"Have you thought of booking her all to yourself, for the Titan Two-step?"

"No…" said the first. "I wouldn't fancy it, really."

His friend sniggered. "How do you make that out?"

"I wouldn't like what it would do to my intensions."

"But think what it would do to your *ex*-tension!" They both bellowed like bulls.

Am I getting old?—thought Jack. Or do I really have no idea what they're talking about? He guessed however that it was less of an age-gap and more of a language-problem. There was English—and there was M2, as he was coming to appreciate.

Presently the compère strode on-stage and waved his arms. "And now, by ever-popular request, we bring you the slickest—sexiest—*interspexiest*—performer in the whole of Nix City—the whole of the Strana of Olympia—Mars—System Sol—the Galaxy—*the Universe!*" (Wild cheers.)

He went on. "Citizens of Olympia—Denizens of Mars—Rats of the Nix—let's have a big round of applause for that most *colourful* of colleens," (his voice rose to a scream) "*Tvoul!* Yeah... c'm'on, baby, take it away!"

The lights dimmed and a hush descended. An insidious grinding beat broke out, like Doc Martens pounding walnuts. A glow grew in a corner of the dance floor, revealing a leggy figure sitting in the foetal position, forehead to her knees. Apart from a pair of shiny black ballet shoes laced up her shins and a glistening wig of tight black curls, she was naked. As the music crept around the hall like tentacles issuing from a fissure in the rock, she progressively extended her limbs and colours ran down them like tumbling smokes.

She reached up as if to grasp at some impossibly high objective and, standing straight on one leg, she drew her lifted foot in a sensuous caress up the insides of her glittering calf and thigh, to probe and gyrate with her foot where her legs met. Wherever her toes touched, her skin flared until her leg and hip were engulfed in the simulacrum of flames. Then stretching her foot straight out behind her, she brought it round slowly to describe an intricate figure in the air. Placing the foot on the ground, she then repeated the sequence in mirror-image with her other foot.

Soon, having run the gamut of poses which a gaian dancer would have found impossible, without shedding the illusion that she had a gaian frame with restrictive joints, the dancer's evolutions and gestures began to gain momentum. The music quickened, becoming sleazy and urgent. Shocked, Jack suddenly recognised it as a wicked travesty of one of the most haunting of Latin hymns. As a boy he used to hear the monks of Minsteracres sing it at Compline: *Te lucis ante terminum.* To Thee, the Light before the Close of Day.

The two lads, their faces flushed with anticipation, glanced round at Jack to share their glee—and their eyes recoiled from his holoface, which had once more become the demon door-knocker. But if they could only have seen past the holoface, it would really have spoilt their evening. With every touch and tease to his sensuality, Jack's fury grew to incandescence. The rush of adrenalin was fuelling—not lust in him, but rage.

Now Tvoul was a thing of fire. Her limbs, whirling and flashing in the spotlights, seeming to glow with their own light—a rush and ripple of oranges, lemons, limes, magentas and violets. The audience forgot to breathe.

At last the dance was *fini*, leaving Tvoul tangled in an extravagant contortion, evoking a classical ballet-dancer taking a bow. The applause was deafening. Howls and whistles played tag around the hall.

Everybody's eyes were fixed on the dance floor and the fantastic figure cast down upon it like Satan, in a conflagration of light. Unnoticed, Jack rose abruptly to his feet and rapidly strode from the *Krásnaya Melnítza* into exterior darkness.

······ ★ ● ★ ······

The hugglephone began to glow with coloured light. It trimmed and tightened itself into the shape of Tvoul.

Tvoul as he remembered her, basking naked in the sun.

The husky voice was unfamiliar, but it was probably down to the repertoire of the voice-chip. You want sexy and seductive? Just drop the menu and eyeball the option.

"Why, hallo, Jack. What can I do for you?"

Kaleidoscope colours swirled over her face and body in a random pattern, faithfully mirrored on each side. Well—Boris was right. No zygocysts or parturition scars. Her luscious physique looked pure… and sterile.

He stepped into the hugglephone field, which he knew would activate the dummy in Tvoul's apartment. But he didn't touch the ectoplast— and he kept his clothes on, in defiance of the thing to do, which was to present the person you were calling with a bare torso. The hugglephone was for social intercourse between intimates. Its reproduction of textiles was mediocre. It was at its best doing flesh.

"So you *do* remember me?"

"Jack: let's just say I know who you are. You're famous now, aren't you? You're the cultural leader of a project dear to all our hearts—and that's something that won't be forgotten for a long, long while. But I ask myself: when did I last meet a man like you—with an SP unit? I have so many clients..."

"I didn't have an SP unit when you saw me last. I had lungs... in tatters."

Tvoul affected a slow sweet smile. "That must have been a long time ago."

"A long time ago, on another planet," said Jack, parodying the lazy drift of Tvoul's speech. But he was determined not to let the mask slip.

"Another planet...?" said Tvoul in mock surprise. "You must tell me about it. Life gets so dull, cooped up here in Nix City."

"Yes, I'll tell you all about it, all right," said Jack. "When we meet in the flesh. Can I come up and see you? We'll have lots to talk about—and not just other planets. We have a few tricks of our own on Gaia that I'd like to show you."

"I have all the time in the world... for you, Jack," she said with a dreamy smile. "Yes, just call ahead and let me know when you're coming."

"How do I get to you?"

"Your marscar will bring you here. 'Say nothing but my name.'" A short chuckle. "Well, it works with the newer models."

"Okay, pet. I'll be seein' yer."

She blew him a kiss. "Bye, Jack. For now."

The dummy relaxed and became featureless. The instant the transmission light went out, Jack picked up his pool cue in its case, which was leaning by the table. Again and again he smashed it down on the dummy until it surrendered its humanoid form and hung over the black plinth limp and torn, bleeding its grey ectoplastic paste.

"Ja-ack!" came a voice behind him. He dropped the cue and span round.

"Kat—oh it's you." He flopped down on a chair. Kat closed the door and walked slowly into the room.

"Why are you beating up your hugglephone? You could really hurt somebody doing that." Kat tiptoed up to the hugglephone, touching it sadly with the palm of her hand. "Now your friend Gabrielle won't be able to call you."

Jack replied in a muffled voice "Gabrielle's gone. Right now she's on her way back to Gaia—for keeps. She won't be calling anymore."

"Oh, Jack!" Kat came and stood behind him, putting her hands on his shoulders. Her tiny thumbs went straight to his pressure-points, massaging into them. As she did no doubt for her mam, when she had spent herself for others' sakes and came home wrecked.

Jack winced out loud, in delectable agony. "A bit lower, love..."

"I am sad—for your sake."

Jack reached down behind him and patted her calf. "She sends you her love. She says anytime we're on Gaia we're to pop round for a cup o' tea..." His voice faltered.

Kat carried on massaging. After a while she said "Perhaps you will meet someone else—someone nice to phone you up. Shall I order you a new hugglephone?"

Jack spoke like a man asleep. "No, pet, don't worry. There's no rush. Unless *you* want to phone me up?"

Kat, practical as ever, said "There's no need. I can come round any time I like. And then you can see all of me—not just my top half." There was no trace of suggestiveness in her voice. She was turning into a little nurse—a little vratchka, like her mother.

Jack screwed his eyes shut. She massaged harder, spreading her palms, in ever widening circles. "Jack... what's biting you?"

Should he confide in this mere slip of a thing? This little old head on young shoulders?

"It's all getting on top of me," he said at last.

"First it's the oven, now it's the hugglephone. You don't get on with modern technology, do you, Jack?"

"I used to, love—I used to. When I was your age. Then I went and got old."

"Age is an attitude, not a condition. Think young."

Jack patted her tiny hand. "You're quite right, love..." His voice snagged on the sunken wrecks of sorrows. "I'll bear it in mind."

Kat stopped massaging and murmured in his ear. "Is that better, Jack? Everything all right now?"

"No..."

She slipped her arms round his neck and kissed his cheek past the visor. "What's wrong, Jack?"

"I'm a long way from home, hinny."

She gave him a quick hug. Then she let her arms drop and considered what he'd just said.

"I've never been that far from home. Except once... when Mummy took me to Cydonia to see the pyramids. I was terribly scared."

"I've seen pictures of them. They do look scary."

"But I knew a poem. I said it to myself in bed at night and it soothed me off to sleep."

"That's just what I need," said Jack. "Something to soothe me off to sleep. *No more nightmares...*" He shut his eyes and forced a smile. "Go on love—what's your poem?"

Kat raised her eyes, snapping into the formal stance for reciting poetry in school, her hands clasped behind her back.

> *How many miles to Babylon?*
> *Three score and ten.*
> *Shall I get there by candlelight?*
> *Aye—and back again!*
> *Though you travel half the night –*
> *You shall get there by candlelight!*

Jack's eyes widened. He made as if to speak, but couldn't. Eventually words came out. "How come you know that nursery rhyme?"

"Why, everyone knows it. It's the Anthem of the Star-Children."

21   A candle for Gaia

It was while Jack was exploring the TMG offices that he discovered a complete set of *Areopedia*. Not a computerised version—the entire 158th edition on paper, even down to it being bound in red Moroccan goatskin.

He decided to re-read the article on Groubians. Only when he'd done so did he discover a final paragraph over the page, which he hadn't seen before. However had he missed it?

> ...*the zygogeny, in spite of yielding a host of new individuals, had failed in its purpose. As a species, groubians had become extinct.*

New page...

> *Belying their resemblance to gaian women in their twenties, it follows that every living groubian is of the same advanced age. Yet no groubian has ever volunteered a coherent account of her life further back than six or seven years. In spite of conferring impressive powers of medium-term memory, the groubian genome contains no mechanism capable of laying down long-term memories commensurate with its unnaturally extended lifespan. On the other hand a memory horizon is a plausible defence mechanism in a long-lived sentient organism, permitting it to endure the endless accumulation of painful experiences without being driven to despair and suicide. Groubians rely on spatio-color documents like the Book of Titan to give a sense of continuity, not to say meaning and purpose, to their literally interminable lives.*

He shut the volume with a snap. It caused a ringing in his ears. So perhaps Tvoul really did not recognise him? Or perhaps she did—but couldn't place him? Strange... that was the impression he'd received whilst talking to her on the hugglephone.

Well, he'd remind her. Oh yes—he'd remind her.

Sviatoslav came in with a new topic for Jack to research and they discussed it. Just as Sviatoslav was opening the door to leave, Jack said "Tell me something. *The Master's Genes*: who exactly is *The Master?*"

"There isn't one. Not yet."

"Like the transman?"

"Yes, you could say that. In fact, if you think of those two concepts as one and the same, you have the essence of TMG."

Jack was reminded of Jens's assertion that TMG existed to populate the galaxy with the genes of just one person. But who *was* that person? He put the question to Sviatoslav point-blank.

"There are several candidates. Alexander—Jesus—Napoleon—Haile Selassie—Lenin—Einstein—Hitler... each of these has their own proponents within TMG. In recent years we've sent missions to Gaia to gather DNA from the relics and progeny of all these candidates."

Jack lurched back in his chair. "Not Jesus, surely?"

"Oh yes—Jesus of Nazareth included. Like the Spanish say about witches: descendants of Jesus don't exist... but you can find them. We senior people in TMG wonder if we can please all the partisans by an amalgam of the front-runners. But the fact remains—the post of *Master* is currently vacant."

Sviatoslav came back and sat on the edge of Jack's desk. "TMG was formed to promote the idea that the *star-children*—you should know the significance of that term by now—oughtn't just to be bred at random from the people who happen to find themselves on board the first starship when it sets out. TMG's founders believed that the human genome, which humanity is on the point of releasing in the wild out there, should have parameters of *excellence*. Not mediocrity."

"Put like that, I can't see anyone would disagree," said Jack. "So what's the problem?"

"Things aren't so straightforward. Everyone would say: oh yes, let's populate the universe with genes of excellence—but let them be mine. But the people who'll win the day will be those who band together to propose someone else's genes—provided enough of us can agree on precisely whose."

"I'm beginning to get the idea," said Jack. He recalled another of Jens's assertions—that TMG was utterly unscrupulous. "So I guess a lot of in-fighting goes on?"

Sviatoslav pursed his lips and made little rapid nods. "It's a scandal. The image of TMG as a united organisation having precise goals is a long way from being the case. So we have secret projects with PUG—and even with competitors like Boris."

"Yes, I was going to ask about him. I'd like to meet up with Boris again and talk to him some more about my son. Would you have any objection to that?"

Sviatoslav thought for a moment. "No, I guess Boris won't mistake you for our representative in the matter. He'll be satisfied your interest is purely personal."

He got up from his perch on the edge of Jack's desk. Jack thought of a carrion crow taking off. "Still—be careful what you say to him. He's very suspicious of us. Although TMG and Peretchelo have a joint project to come up with the transman, he suspects we've got our own candidate lined-up." He turned to go.

"Have we?"

Sviatoslav froze. Such simple questions seemed to give him problems. "It depends on whether we find your precious Tvoul in time."

Jack gave him an open-mouthed frown. "But surely you're not going to reward her crime by accepting *her* genome for the future star-children?"

"Not as it stands. A few extra genes will be spliced in here and there. Jesus... Hitler..."

Jack sprang to his feet. "That's *appalling!*"

Sviatoslav stood gaping. "Jack, I'm surprised at you. Just suppose we do. Then the star-children will be in your direct line of descent. There isn't a Martian alive who wouldn't give their... ugh! Well, I don't know what they wouldn't give for the privilege."

"Mebbes my priorities are different," growled Jack.

Sviatoslav gazed at him as if trying to remember what he was about to say. Then he abruptly left the office.

•••••★●★•••••

Out of the texture of a Latin plainchant, a single limpid treble voice arose, singing a refrain in the M2 language:

> *Our Own True Mother suffered loss*
> *Of Blesséd Only Son:*
> *The Sword to pierce her heart came by*
> *Her dearest, precious One.*

Jack strode down the aisle of the old Jesuit mission of Our Lady Of The Nix, barely paying attention to the recorded hymn. He knocked on the sacristy door. From inside came a stern command. "Come in."

"Ah, come in, come in!" Father O'Leary's voice brightened in welcome the moment he saw who it was. "Forgive me—I thought you were the altar boy."

"I'm sorry I'm a bit late, Father..."

"No matter. No matter. But we won't have much time to talk now. As you see I'm getting ready for evening Mass. But if the clock runs out on us, please do come round to the presbytery afterwards and we can carry on. That's if you won't mind me waffling on with my mouth full."

Jack shook his head with a smile. "Whatever you say, Father."

"Tvoul Rainbow," mused the priest. "Now there's a fine catch for the Church. What a woman. And what a good wife for Harry. Though I must admit I had my doubts at first…"

"Why was that, Father?"

He stopped and frowned, as if he couldn't remember the exact reason why he'd had his doubts. "I think it reassured me when Tvoul agreed to take instruction. She was an exemplary postulant. Always asking the right questions. A shrewd woman."

"Was it Harry who pressed her into becoming a Catholic?"

The priest looked up in surprise from the sacred vessels. "What? Why, no. Harry wouldn't have dreamed of it. He was all for Tvoul retaining her own beliefs—whatever those were. I'm not sure that groubians have 'beliefs' in the same way as we do. They're old enough to have experienced everything that resides in their minds. Direct experience is obviously better than belief (though you try telling *that* to the Church Fathers.) But it was certainly the impression I gained from talking to her."

He began to put on his vestments. "No—Tvoul volunteered to receive instruction herself. She came to me privately, before Harry even knew of it."

As he straightened out his sleeves he said "It's so nice to have a girl who's done her homework. So many of them don't know what they're taking on when they marry a Catholic."

"Maybe it was the other way round with Harry and Tvoul?"

Father O'Leary widened his eyes. "Why, what you mean?"

"Maybe my son didn't know what he was taking on by marrying a groubian."

The priest laughed dismissively. "Oh—I think he did. I think he did. Always a somewhat impulsive young man—if you don't mind me saying?" (Jack nodded in agreement.) "But his heart's in the right place. And no one can question his intelligence. Oh yes—Harry knew exactly what he was taking on."

"Then perhaps you could explain it to me?" said Jack. "Harry tried to—and I went along with it at the time. But I did so because I loved my boy. Once he'd reached the age of responsibility he could do no wrong for me. But how was it—*how was it*—that they were proposing to have children? Perhaps they were too reticent to talk about it?"

"Quite the reverse. I must admit it was one of my chief worries. There's much bad blood gone under that particular bridge, as you must know by now. I took a lot of reassuring. But in the end I decided that if Canon Law had known about groubians, it would have phrased its regulations to accommodate the groubian predicament. I have no doubt in my mind that they planned to have babies—by natural means."

"It was a groubian wedding."

Father O'Leary spilled the altar wine. "*I beg your pardon?* Did I hear you correctly?"

"It was a groubian wedding. Edulation took place. That might be natural for a groubian in the eyes of the Church. But to a gaian—it's murder."

The priest stood aghast. "Really, Mr Williams, I had no idea! I had no idea that that's what they were proposing to do." He came round the preparation table and laid his hand on Jack's wrist. "Mr Williams—I'm so sorry. So very sorry. Where did it happen? On Mars? If so, the law is quite precise on the matter. And I assure you, the Church too…"

"It happened on Earth. In Brazil. Somewhere it would take a long time to establish the true facts of the matter. Long enough for Tvoul to make her escape from the planet and go into hiding."

The old priest went round the table again, shaking and clutching his head. "Tvoul! Tvoul Rainbow! I just cannot believe it. I had no inkling of it. Mr Williams—if I'd had the slightest suspicion that that's what they were planning, I'd have withdrawn my co-operation straightaway."

It crossed Jack's mind that, far from taking "a lot of reassuring", Fr O'Leary must be quite otherworldly when it came to intimate matters between husband and wife. But who was *not* otherworldly, where groubians were concerned?

"What's done is done," he said. "Father, I don't blame you in the least. They had us all fooled. What I want to know is this. Did Harry really have a clue what he was letting himself in for?"

"Harry is—I mean was—a bio-engineer. Tvoul is an expert in human reproduction. *Human* reproduction I said—not just gaian. Now it may be that she was able to delude Harry into believing they would consummate the marriage by coitus in the normal way…"

"Normal for gaians," interposed Jack.

"No. Normal. The Church does not sanction edulation. It is a mortal sin. It is, after all, wilful murder."

"So edulation might well have been Tvoul's idea—and not Harry's?"

Father O'Leary shut his eyes tight and stood for a few moments in thought. Presently he said "Your son Harry was a very intelligent man. In my heart of hearts I don't suppose he'd have been fooled for one moment. To repeat what I said at the outset—Harry went into this with his eyes open. He must have known *exactly* what they were planning to do to consummate the marriage."

Jack's mind went back to the night he overheard Harry and Tvoul discussing intimate matters in an intimate embrace. It all chimed perfectly with what the priest had just said.

"In other words, my Harry was quite prepared for edulation, but both of them kept quiet about it, both to you and to us, in order to keep us sweet?"

The priest nodded his head in puzzlement. "It certainly seems like it..." He looked up at the clock. "But oh—the time! Where is that altar boy? I say, Mr Williams—could I ask you a favour? Would you be prepared to serve at Mass? ...I—I suppose you *are* a Catholic? Dear me, I shouldn't have asked that. Why, Harry..."

"Born into the Church," said Jack. He tried to think of the last time he'd been to Mass. "But I haven't served on the altar since I was a boy. I'd be grateful for a few hand-signals..."

"Oh don't worry about that. I'm used to seeing that the altar boy is in the right place at the right time, with the right vessels in his hand. I'll just have to remember not to haul you around by the ear." He laughed. "But—do forgive me for asking. One can't be sure of anything these days. And yet I should have known where Harry gets it from."

He bent down and got a white surplice out of the drawer and gave it to Jack to don. "Harry was very devout," he went on. "Never missed Mass on Sunday—and often came to weekday Mass. He was not a man to let his bio-expertise get in the way of his Faith."

······✳●✳······

Back in the presbytery after the service, Father O'Leary explicitly invited Jack to follow him around in the kitchen whilst he microwaved a frozen dinner for himself. He offered one to Jack, who refused. Then, before sitting at the kitchen table, the old priest got out a bottle of wine and two glasses.

"As I was saying, Harry was very devout. And Tvoul seemed to lap it up. She picked up things very quickly during instruction. She soon grasped the idea of marriage as an institution. Groubians have something quite different, as you know."

"That must be a thing of the past," said Jack. "They haven't had males to mate with for a long time."

"True—true—but what I was thinking of has little to do with male and female. A zygogeny entailed nothing in the way of *vows* or *commitments*. Partners were assigned virtually at random. And of course… the partnership did not even last till the following morning."

He topped-up his own glass and then Jack's. "No—I was thinking of the institution of *triada*."

"What is *triada*, exactly?"

"Not unlike marriage, strangely enough. Partners make vows for life, which can only be dissolved by the death of one of the three parties. And they stick to it, too. An example to us gaians."

"But isn't it something which people of the same sex enter into? It's got to be, if you think about it."

Father O'Leary, with his mouth full, waved his fork vigorously in denial. "No, no," he said, once he had swallowed. "Any three people can form a triada, irrespective of gender. Or of species, for that matter."

"So it's a form of *interspex*?"

Again the question caught the priest with his mouth full. Again he waved his fork. "How I hate that word," he said eventually. "The Catholic Church on Mars fully concurs with the will of the Strana to abolish the word *species* from all legal definitions governing human beings. Gaians and groubians are both human. The Church has no problem with that. *Interspex* is just another form of extra-marital sex, already forbidden by Canon Law, without having to go making a special sin of it."

"So the Church doesn't expressly forbid triadas?"

"Oh yes—it's automatic excommunication for a Catholic to enter into one."

"Then triadas are sinful?"

"It's not so much the nature of the triada; it's the fact they take binding oaths to each other which are not sanctified by the Church. Oaths of absolute obedience."

Jack's curiosity was piqued. "How do they manage that—when there's three of them?"

"Quite simple. Obedience goes round in a circle—or a triangle, if you like. The express purpose is to achieve a binding group, with the cast-iron guarantee of no unwanted edulation. Think about it. If A swears absolute obedience to B, then B could abuse the position by commanding A to co-operate in been edulated. But now C is there to act as chaperone. A commands C—and C commands B. Whilst the triada stays together, no one party can abuse another. If one party dies, the triada automatically dissolves."

The priest chuckled. "It's an arrangement not lacking in appeal to some. Many gaians enter into triadas, although it is primarily a groubian institution. Mixed triadas of gaians and groubians are rare though..."

"I know of one," interposed Jack.

Father O'Leary's eyes lit up. "Do you now? Of course there is one very famous example—which you as a new immigrant from Gaia won't have heard of. But maybe you've come across the name Shval Meteor?"

"That's exactly the triada I was thinking of."

"Why—bless me! However did you run into *them?*"

"They were travelling on the *Oberon* at the same time as I was. I only got to meet one of the triada: Hamish McDougall."

"A nice experience *that* must have been for you." Distaste stained the priest's voice. "That's got to be one of the most abominable liaisons I have come across in my entire ministry."

"Why?—because it's a mixed gaian-groubian one?"

"Not at all—not at all. It's all down to whom they've chosen as the third person. If 'person' you can accept him to be."

"Peter Zwillinge?"

"The very same. I suppose you know that he's a chimorg?"

"What's the attitude of the Church to chimorgs? Are they human—or aren't they?"

"That's something the Strana decides case-by-case, not the Church. We possess neither the scientific nor the legal expertise. In practice we go along with the Strana's decision in the matter. Peter Zwillinge has been classified as human—but it was a typical Shval Meteor trick to achieve it."

"Do *you* believe that Peter Zwillinge is human?"

The priest grimaced. "Between you and me, Peter Zwillinge is not only human, he is a Catholic. Or was, prior to the papal encyclical which excommunicated all triadas. Before that he used to come to this church and I used to hear his confession. Now the things he told me, under the seal of the confessional, I wouldn't want to talk about, even if I wasn't forbidden to do so. But this I can say, because it is public knowledge..."

Father O'Leary filled up both glasses again before he'd venture to proceed.

"Peter Zwillinge was an experiment. He was commissioned in secret by TMG to butter-up the Groubian Alliance. He was clearly intended as a head-on attack on the *cause célèbre* of the two Olympian Wars. He was male, he contained genes from at least two species—two of them being gaian and groubian—plus porcine genes to stabilise the mix."

"Porcine? *Pig?* What *does* he look like?"

"Deceptively harmless. His face is more or less shapeless and his hair like bristles. He was deliberately crippled in order to gain the licence. By law there can be no chimorgs of class seven: binary 111, you know. So he was robbed of his mobility to allow him to be granted autonomy, to make him class three."

Father O'Leary took a deep draught of wine. "Yes, I know. Frightful. Absolutely appalling."

Jack marvelled, shuddering. "What must it be like to be Peter Zwillinge?"

"A living hell. A hell which, from time to time, he inflicts on the rest of society." Father O'Leary pushed away the rest of his meal, having lost the appetite for it.

Jack's teeth chinked on the glass as he sipped his wine. Putting it down he said, "Tell me something, Father. Do you think Peter Zwillinge has a soul? Come to that—do groubians have souls?"

The priest stared at him as if he'd said a rude word. "What exactly do you mean by that?"

"If I were to kill one—would it be a mortal sin?"

"Oh, I see what you're driving at." Father O'Leary pushed his chair back. "'Do they have souls?'—what a history *that* question has. Christopher Columbus took some Caribbean natives back to Spain with him, just to get a definitive answer from the pope. Because if they didn't, then it was permissible to carry on treating them like animals."

He waited for Jack to say something, but he stayed silent. "Witches are supposed not to have souls either. Nor vampires. Their souls have long ago been carted off to hell and their bodies taken over by demons. So, the story goes, you can do anything you like to them—it doesn't matter."

Jack was listening carefully to the old Jesuit's tone of voice as he said this. He was trying to determine where the other's sympathies actually lay. In spite of himself, his mind went back a couple of years to one sunny Friday morning, jogging along the old Deerness Valley railway embankment in company with Tvoul. At the time he had been captivated by her.

He said "But you and I eat beef. I see some on your plate, all minced-up. We're quite happy for cows to be killed to provide it. Yet aren't cows more closely related to us than groubians are? How can we imagine that a groubian has an immortal soul—and a cow hasn't?"

"Well…" said the priest, idly toying with the fork on his discarded plate, as if Jack had accused him of eating something unpalatable, "To begin with, groubians have immortal bodies, or nearly so, which gives them a pretty good start, don't you think? Secondly, they can talk."

"And cows can only go 'moo'? Yes but machines can talk as well. And machines can be made indestructible, too."

"I know. But it's the act of *talking* that enables you to tell whether there's a soul behind the persona or not. Witches can talk—or so the fairy-tales tell us. So can vampires. But it's the very things they say—and do—which testify to their soullessness."

Seeing he hadn't made much impression on Jack with that, he waved his arms. "Look, if you were locked up in a room without contact with the outside world, why—nobody would even know you were there, let alone wonder whether you had a soul or not."

Jack thought about it. "That's like Turing's Test. But people can be fooled…"

"Turing's Test doesn't deny that," the priest replied emphatically. "It says that sooner or later there comes a time when people realise they are being fooled."

"When I first met Tvoul," pondered Jack, "I thought she was a pretty queer fish. Literally and metaphorically. But after talking to her, getting to know her—as I imagined—I began to accept her as a person. I was prepared to believe that she was really and truly in love with my son—I was never in any doubt that *he* loved *her*. I even grew quite fond of her myself…"

Jack absent-mindedly picked up his glass—and put it down again as if it were full of blood. "Then she goes off into the jungle with our Harry—and does *this!*"

The priest seemed absorbed in jabbing his fork into the cold meat-balls. After a while he said "I see your point—and I do sympathise with you, Mr Williams. Don't run away with the idea I don't. No one can blame you for feeling resentment."

"It's not just resentment," declared Jack. "I'm not just a wronged man talking. I think it has made me see the light."

Father O'Leary looked up and squinted at him, like a small furry animal emerging from a dark hibernation.

"You said it yourself," Jack continued. "Witches and vampires may be legends, but groubians are real. And I'm convinced they really are animated by demons, not by souls. Demons which are intelligent enough to kid us they're human—until they go and do something *demonic.*"

"Demonic…?" The priest turned the word over on his tongue as if tasting a counterfeit penny. "We must distinguish what we do as the result of an extraneous evil impulse—demonic possession you might call it—from what we do when following the urges of our fallen nature. It's the difference between Actual and Original Sin. The Problem of Evil: how can actions arising out of our nature be *evil*, no matter how disgusting and repulsive, when that nature has been created by God?"

He paused and stared at Jack, daring him to say something to that. Jack didn't, so he went on, "Tvoul's crime (for crime it is) arises not so much out of her Will as out of her Nature. An extinct and perverted Nature admittedly, bred on a God-cursed world."

"Are you trying to apologise for her? Do you basically think there's justification for what she's done?"

"Not at all, Mr Williams. In this, as in other matters, we have to follow the laws of the planet, which are perfectly clear."

"But what do you *really* think?"

The old priest started chuckling. Seeing this offended Jack, he was at pains to explain himself. "Excuse my laughing in this serious business, Mr Williams. Your question reminded me of an old Catholic joke. It is said that there are two things God Himself doesn't know. What Jesuits really think—and what nuns really do."

Jack stopped frowning and allowed a bleak smile to come through. "It strikes me that for *nuns* you could just as well say *groubians*."

Suddenly serious again, the old priest lowered his head and waved it slowly from side to side. A watering-can, germinating seeds of doubt. "If only it hadn't been *Tvoul Rainbow*…"

He looked up. "Mr Williams, I'm the wrong person to go laying down the law. I was prepared to accept Peter Zwillinge as a human being, capable of redemption. Which few do. I was ready to baptise him as a Catholic. To give him absolution for his sins, which were very, very serious ones."

"You do what you think's best at the time, Father…"

"My bishop was not behind me. He sided with the Strana in viewing Peter's award of human rights, restricted though they were, as a legal blunder of the first magnitude. He said we had all been inveigled into giving absolution to wild animals."

He shrugged. "But on the topic of groubians, the Church is in no doubt whatever. They enjoy full human rights at law. The Church does not condone any violation of human rights. It has taken two bitter wars for *that* message to get across."

Elbows on the table, he covered his face with his hands. His next words came out through his fingers in a whisper. "So—don't do anything rash."

Jack pressed his thumbs together and watched them go white under the quick. "Well, I'm grateful for your opinion." He looked up at the clock. "I suppose I ought to be going."

"Please come back, if you want to talk some more."

Jack got to his feet. "Thanks for your time, Father. No, don't get up. I can see myself out."

······ ✱ ● ✱ ······

Jack retraced his steps through the sacristy and found himself back in the main body of the church. This time he took more notice of his surroundings. His attention was drawn to a side-altar where on a plinth there stood—not a saint or an image of the Virgin Mary, but a glowing blue globe of the planet Gaia. Candles were burning in front of it.

Had Mars fallen into the error of geolatry?

Someone else was in the church. Someone staying behind after Mass for silent prayer. The figure wore Zasta uniform of blue-and-white and was kneeling in a pew near the back, head resting in hands sheathed in the uniform's white gauntlets, face concealed police-fashion behind a silvered visor. He felt only the impersonal aura of a booner: a public servant, class six. He paid the figure no more attention.

The same recording of choral music was playing. Once again the pure treble voice of the soloist rose like a dove in the musical air, weaving in counterpoint around the haunting plainchant of the beautiful Latin hymn: *Te lucis ante terminum.*

This time Jack stopped, rocked back on his heels and heard out the hymn to the end:

> *Our Own True Mother suffered loss*
> *Of Blesséd Only Son:*
> *The Sword to pierce her heart came by*
> *Her dearest, precious One.*
> *What is this life, so full of questions*
> *Yet with answers none:*
> *But childish steps through vale of tears*
> *Towards endless worlds to come?*

What...?

True mother suffers loss of child? A blow from someone dear? Questions... about life? Answer... nothing? Childish footsteps through a desolate valley? The implication slithered like a ice-cube down his neck.

The hymn was a rendering into the Catholic idiom... *of the Book of Titan!*

22   The Unperson

Sviatoslav Iliich Krov' was working late at the office. He was so absorbed in what he was doing that he didn't notice the door open quietly. When he looked up, someone was standing in the doorway. Someone in Zasta uniform, face hidden behind a silvered visor.

"Who are you?"

"Wouldn't you like to know."

"How did you get in here?"

The figure came and sat on Sviatoslav's desk, almost in his lap. "For someone with as much to hide as you have, your security is pretty bad."

Something in the way it moved shouted *groubian*. Which was odd, because there were no more than a handful of groubians in *Zastavlénie*— all of them too highly-placed to go out on patrol. But Zasta didn't go in for sporting badges of rank. The chiefs didn't relish drawing fire.

"Are you here with a warrant?"

"No."

"Then what...?"

"*Komissár* Miro sent me."

Sviatoslav relaxed back in his chair—but not as much as he might have done. So it came from Miro? That sounded encouraging, as far as it went. But Miro—was he on the point of pulling the rug away from under him? He expected it to happen any day now.

Casually the figure drew from its holster the silver-grey Zasta side-arm known as a six-shooter (for its six different kinds of ammunition) and pointed it at Sviatoslav right between the eyes.

"Eyes open or closed?"

"Closed, I think." Oh—why was he always so trusting.

"It makes no difference."

The figure squeezed the trigger. But no shot was fired. A three-dimensional image flashed up in Sviatoslav's field of vision. An image of Jack's head. Moving the weapon this way and that, the newcomer rotated it to give Sviatoslav an all-round view.

"Do you know this person?"

Sviatoslav opened his eyes. "Of course I do. He works for me. I recruited him."

The visor went transparent. Sviatoslav found himself staring into the face of Tvoul Rainbow.

"Think carefully before you answer the next question. Are you sure he works for you *full-time?*"

Tvoul Rainbow! It was all starting to come clear. Sviatoslav gazed up at the groubian face as its pattern dissolved into flowing stripes.

"My congratulations to *Komissár* Miro. He's done a good job on you."

The figure smiled, a Mona Lisa smile superimposed on its groubian expression of stripy mirth.

"Tell me something, Agent Zero. Are you trying to acquire a human *soul?*"

The figure chuckled. "That would be impossible—even were the Goubernator to sanction it. The semblance of one will do. Tvoul Rainbow's 'soul'... her persona..."

"If you're reconstructing Tvoul Rainbow, you're not short of material. There's hardly a thing she's done which isn't public knowledge. But don't confine yourself to the public record. Be sure to include footage from Gaia. Get access to our databases..."

"I already have."

"How did you manage *that*—without my authorisation?"

"Credit me with a little initiative. Yes, there is material there I can use. Give me time. But there's one major flaw in my persona which needs working on as top priority."

"Which is...?"

"I'm supposed to know Jack Williams—know him well. Yet I hardly recognise him. I'm having to spend a lot of my precious time observing him. And in spite of my best precautions, I think he's recently become aware of me. Yesterday—in church."

Sviatoslav laughed quietly. "Can't recognise your own father-in-law? Well that's not surprising. Since the time you knew him on Gaia he has changed out of all recognition... and it's not all down to his SP unit. Don't be worried if his persona is unfamiliar. Anyway, you don't have to fool Jack. He'll be told precisely who you are—and why you're travelling to Titan in each others' company."

The agent smirked. "All the same, it would be nice if we weren't such *strangers.*"

"Well," said Sviatoslav, closing his eyes to smile, "why don't you come along here tomorrow? You'll get a chance to meet him." He tilted his head, as if to show off a dimple on his chin. "Afterwards—who knows? He might even invite you out for a drink."

"No..." The agent slowly shook its head. "I don't think he will do that."

●●●●●◆●◆●●●●●

"Ah, Jack," said Sviatoslav. "Come in and take a seat."

Petra was there, so was Boris Mixailovitch from Peretchelo. Jack nodded to them both as he moved round the table to one of the two empty chairs.

"Not the sauna this time?"

"No, Jack," replied Sviatoslav. "It goes without saying we won't be alluding to what went on there. Fortunately we don't have to. We need to be a bit more formal for this meeting, because it represents a watershed of collaboration between TMG and Peretchelo. On a matter of no small importance... to us all."

When Jack had made himself comfortable, Sviatoslav glanced round the table at each participant in turn. His eyes finally settled on Jack and he put on a bright smile.

"Well, Jack: we've got a job for you."

"Very pleased to hear it. I was starting to wonder how to fill my time."

"Oh, this job will do that quite satisfactorily." Sviatoslav chuckled, but his face went suddenly serious. "It's the job for which you've been brought all the way from Gaia. At considerable expense I might add: both material and personal."

"Don't think I'm not grateful," said Jack. He guessed Sviatoslav was referring to the deaths of Markus and Duke. Here, at last, was Payback Time.

"It is we who will have cause to be grateful." Sviatoslav stretched and folded his arms behind his head. "If you succeed."

Jack waited in silence.

"We want you to go to Titan... and bring back Tvoul."

Jack nodded slowly. Eventually he murmured "Bring her back to Mars?"

"Yes. Back to Mars. Shortly after you parted from Markus on Gaia, he phoned Platform Two and delivered Tvoul an ultimatum. The mere fact that he's not alive today isn't going to stop us carrying it out. Tvoul can run, but she can't hide. Not even if she hot-foots it all the way to Titan."

"So what am I supposed to do when I get to Titan? How am I to carry out this... ultimatum?"

"You will gain access to Tvoul thanks to your unique relationship with her—as her father-in-law. Under the Treaty of Moscow, anyone who stops you seeing her commits a crime against humanity. You will be

264

taking a hibernator casket to Platform Two and you will return to Mars with Tvoul inside the casket—dead or alive. In all this you will enjoy the best possible assistance."

"Will Tvoul be expecting me?"

"I... er... imagine she will. But she won't know the true purpose of your visit. Nor will anyone on Platform Two. That is, apart from your contact on the rig, codenamed *Metapelet*. Hebrew word, I think. That's the manager of the Special Unit." Turning to indicate, Sviatoslav added "Boris is here to help you fix it up."

"What does the Special Unit do?"

Boris endeavoured to answer Jack's question. "It is staffed exclusively with Peretchelo employees. Its activities are top-secret, but they are all to do with Project Tahiti."

"Boris doesn't want to say this," added Sviatoslav, "but it specialises in activities which are technically illegal on Mars. In a manner of speaking, Tvoul has gone to precisely the right place."

"What are we to tell the captain of the *Prometheus*?" interjected Petra.

"Only what it is good for him to know," replied Sviatoslav. "We'll warn him Jack is on his way, of course. Then Jack must claim passage under the Treaty of Moscow, pleading family connections."

"Will that work, do you suppose?"

Sviatoslav raised his eyebrows at Petra. "Can you think of a better approach?"

Petra put her head to one side. "It would help if Jack could claim to be on assignment to Peretchelo—and had security clearance for Project Tahiti."

"Good idea," said Sviatoslav. "He'll need a code-name then..."

"How about another Hebrew word... *Nimrod*?" Petra hadn't hesitated. Her eyes transfixed Jack as if he were celluloid. "The great hunter of the Book of Genesis?"

"Any objection, Jack? Well, *Nimrod* let it be. Boris, can you fix it?"

Boris nodded, as if he did this sort of thing every day.

"When do I set off?" said Jack. His voice was flippant. The journey to Titan was notoriously harsh, but he was finding it hard to take his mission seriously. Like as not, events would have intervened by then to prevent his going. Events which he himself would soon be setting in motion.

Sviatoslav redirected his gaze at Petra, inviting her to reply.

"What are we today?—Friday March 13, 401," she said. "In four weeks' time then. Every other month, on the same day, *Prometheus* reinserts into Martian orbit. The actual day has gone back a week because last year was a leap-year. So it's next due to arrive on April 6. It'll depart again on April 9, so be ready."

Sviatoslav sniffed. "Are you happy to do this for us, Jack?"

"Why of course," said Jack, shrugging. "Company man—that's what I am."

For a moment Sviatoslav held his gaze, remembering Agent Zero's warning of the night before. Boris chipped in. "It all boils down to the incred, doesn't it?" Jack thought he had a silly grin.

Sviatoslav nodded and sighed, as if he had been expecting things would be more difficult. "Well, that just about wraps it up..."

"Wait a minute," Petra cut in. "I have a question for Boris. Won't Tvoul be missed? As far as Peretchelo is concerned, she's got to be on that rig for a purpose."

"Ah," said Sviatoslav. "Now we come to the clever part. We have a substitute for her. There is someone I want you all to meet—but mainly you, Jack. Some*thing* I should rather say, to keep within the law."

"*It?*" said Jack in puzzlement.

"*It,*" confirmed Sviatoslav. "That is how we must refer to it. All humanoid simulations must refer to themselves, and be referred-to, in the neuter gender."

"Svi, stop being so arch," said Petra. "Who—or *what*—are you talking about?"

Sviatoslav stretched back in his chair. "I was rather hoping it would be here by now. A little present from *Komissár* Miro. I'm referring to... *Agent Zero.*"

Petra's and Boris's eyes showed their whites. Boris smacked the table with the flat of his hand. Petra gasped "She's still extant!"

"*It,*" insisted Sviatoslav yet again. "Yes, Miro has raised Agent Zero to walk the planet once more."

"Do you think she'll come? ...I mean: *it?*" Petra's tone was hushed, something unusual for her.

"Oh yes," said Sviatoslav. "It paid me a surprise visit late last night. I asked it to attend this meeting."

"Whyever would it comply with a request like that?" said Petra. "It's an instrument of the Meteor Gang."

"Not any more," said Sviatoslav. "Miro has seen to that. Agent Zero impersonates Tvoul Rainbow now, not Shval. And what's more, it's been sworn-in as a Zasta agent."

Petra wrinkled her nose. "The Unperson cannot swear. It cannot enter into any form of legal contract."

"That's where you're wrong," scoffed Sviatoslav. "The Unperson can do anything. Anyway, this is a covert operation. Legality doesn't enter into it."

Boris let out a long slow sigh. "And is Shval Meteor going to stand aside and let that happen? Will she calmly let *Komissár* Miro take control of her *monster?*"

"She has no choice," said Sviatoslav. "On Selene she lost control of it herself. Or so Vermat told Miro—and she was in an ideal position to know. It was Shval's evil genius to create it in the first place, to be sure—but the whole point in doing so was to have an autonomous double of herself. And *autonomous* it has certainly turned out to be."

"May I ask a question?" said Jack. "When this thing comes in here… how will I be able to tell it is not Tvoul Rainbow in the flesh?"

Petra took it upon herself to reply. "By virtue of the fact that personas are *fermions*—entities with individuality—there can only be one instance of Tvoul's persona in the Nix intensor…"

She paused for effect. "And *that's* how we know Tvoul is not on Mars."

"*I beg your pardon?*" said Jack in amazement. "Could you repeat that?"

Petra took a deep breath. "It's how we know Tvoul is not on Mars. The intensor cannot support two simultaneous instances of Tvoul's persona, even if one is an impersonation."

"Hey wait a minute," said Jack. "Even I can tell a person's social class nowadays from the intensor field. I'd certainly tell if I was faced with something of class zero. So how could Agent Zero possibly fool me that she was Tvoul? …I mean *it?*"

"Well," said Sviatoslav, "you'll see in a minute. We'll all see. But bear this in mind, Jack—and Petra too. Miro has sworn Agent Zero into Zasta, which was extremely clever of him. So Agent Zero is a Zasta agent: a servant of the Strana. A booner—like you. You won't feel its aura, except as a neutral presence."

"And what if it turns off its booner card?" said Jack. "Would I be able to tell it's not Tvoul then?"

"You can try asking it to. But it's up to Agent Zero whether it complies." Sviatoslav sighed, unaware of Jack's reason for wanting to know. "We'll have to trust Miro for now that he hasn't gone recruiting Tvoul herself." He laughed at the idea. "As Petra says, Agent Zero wouldn't have been able to take on her persona if she were actually *here*—in Nix City."

Oh yes, thought Jack. Let's all trust Miro—the great engineer of coincidences. His mind went back to when Tvoul came into the club on the arms of a couple of men-about-town. She's perfectly capable of pulling the wool over folk's eyes, he told himself. And that goes for the three wise monkeys round this table.

"Is it possible," he asked aloud, "for someone to change their personality so utterly that it's no longer the same persona? Or if you like, alter themselves so much that they aren't the same person?"

Silence fell like a blanket of snow.

Sviatoslav commenced a slow, shrewd smile. "Well, Jack… I've known people manage it. You for one. But it's not so easy for a fifty thousand year-old being." He gave a sharp sigh. "I think we can discount that possibility."

No, thought Jack, we can't. The face at the club tells us we can't.

······ ★ ● ★ ······

The v-unit on the table in front of Sviatoslav buzzed. "There's someone to see you, sir," said the receptionist, in a voice tinged with uncertainty, a touch of fear even. "Someone from Zasta…"

"Send it in," said Sviatoslav with a grin.

Presently the door opened. An anonymous figure stood there, visor opaque, clad in the blue-and-white uniform of Zasta. Sviatoslav beckoned and pointed to the one remaining empty chair. It closed the door and sat down.

"Gentlemen—and Lady," said Sviatoslav, "I present to you… *Agent Zero.*"

The visor cleared. In spite of having been prepared for it, Jack jumped. He looked slowly round at Sviatoslav, who was smiling back at him. Nobody had missed Jack's SP unit going click.

"Not bad, eh Jack?"

"Huh! Pretty good I'd say."

It was Tvoul's face—no doubt about that. And Sviatoslav was right about the booner status concealing a class zero. There was no way he could tell it from the intensor. It felt on his face exactly like the figure he'd caught sight of in church.

A thought struck him: it might just be the same figure! But there again, aren't all z-niks booners?

"This is what's going to stand-in for Tvoul on Platform Two—once the real Tvoul has been strong-armed into the hibernator. Dead or alive: it doesn't matter. We only want the zygocysts."

"Now here it comes," said Boris with an ugly grin of anticipation. "Here's where Tvoul gets her come-uppance for double-crossing us all."

Jack turned to the newcomer. "Do I take it you're coming to Titan with me?"

He watched as Tvoul's *gioconda* smile was convincingly carried-off. "We won't exactly be holding hands, Jack. I shall make my own way on board the *Prometheus*. Don't you think that's advisable, Sviatoslav?"

"Can you do that? Security is tight."

"No problem. I've managed to penetrate the terminal twice already. And even get on and off the shuttle without anyone noticing."

Sviatoslav chucked. "You were pretty scathing last night about my security. What have you got to say about the cosmodrome's?"

"Far worse. But it's easier for me than it would be for you. And I mean *you*, Sviatoslav, for all your covert experience."

"Do tell us why."

"It's the things I can do, both as a z-nik and the Unperson. Personas may be unique, but ectoplasts are expendable. I can discard one—and animate another."

"That I'd love to see," grinned Sviatoslav.

A robot, thought Jack—but a smart robot. A very smart robot indeed. But all the while he was thinking to himself: this may be what I saw in church, but it isn't the person who came into the club. Nor the one I spoke to on the hugglephone. Neither of those was a booner and neither was class zero. Both were class seven.

"Your booner card—can you switch it off for a moment, flower?"

"A z-nik can't do that while on-duty."

Jack persevered. "Can you take your helmet off, like? Let me have a proper look at you?"

"Good girls don't take their helmets off with strange men."

Giggles all round. Jack contemplated reminding the agent just what Tvoul *had* taken off for him in times past, but decided against it.

"The illusion would vanish," said Sviatoslav. "I'm not even sure the helmet isn't ectoplasm."

"Correct," said Agent Zero. "It is simulated."

But Jack wasn't going to let it rest there. "Do you ever go to church to pray?"

"Whyever would the Unperson want to do that?"

"Like the Undine, y'know… to earn herself a human soul?"

Boris burst out laughing. But Sviatoslav's smile evaporated.

"Why should I have any interest in doing that?"

"I asked you a question." The room fell silent.

"I have been known to go to church. But not to pray."

Jack nodded slowly, his lip curling. "And did you see me there yesterday?"

"Yes." The reply came without hesitation.

Jack shot Sviatoslav a glance of triumph. The latter acknowledged with a barely-perceptible lowering of his eyelids. Emboldened, Jack resolved to try some more questions.

"And can you sip a cocktail?" This met with general merriment, but the agent returned a blank stare.

Jack persisted. "Can you use the hugglephone—and offer someone *interspex*?" Boris, Jack noticed, was by this stage reduced to helplessness.

"I haven't tried sipping a cocktail. It would all go wrong, I think, after the first sip. I can use a hugglephone of course: it's only half an ectoplast. But I wouldn't care to use it naked, as the fashion goes. There is insufficient bandwidth to transmit whole-body spatio-color."

Jack was still nodding slowly. But his expression had grown bleak.

"And as for *interspex*…" Agent Zero toyed abstractly with its six-shooter in its holster, "if I were you, I'd forget about it."

•••••✦●✦•••••

The following Monday, after lunch, Boris came to Jack's office to set up his visit to the Special Unit on Platform Two. No sooner had they enabled the v-unit when Agent Zero came in too. Without a word it sat down with them.

"Do we need you?" said Boris.

"I have a request to make of Metapelet. A practical detail."

Boris touched the v-unit. The inter-world operator came on-line.

"Shtoza mir?"

Boris, glancing at Jack, said "Speak M2."

"Which world?"

"Titan."

There was a pause. "Calls to Titan are subject to a three hour, one minute 4.8 second response delay. Duplex transmission is unavailable."

Nothing brought home to Jack the distance to Titan more poignantly than that. Travelling at the speed of light in free space, it took over three hours to make the round trip.

"Titanian number please."

"Two-five." After getting used to Selenean numbers, Jack was astonished at its brevity.

"Please speak your message clearly after the tone."

Without pausing to think, Boris said "Secure personal message to Metapelet. Hi Metapelet, Boris Mixailovitch here, Acting Director for Off-World Projects at Peretchelo Headquarters, Nix City. This message is for your ears only. If you are not alone, please halt it now and replay it later."

Boris paused, drumming his fingers on the desk, giving Metapelet time to comply. Then, taking a deep breath and shooting Jack another glance, he continued.

"I have with me a TMG employee, code-named *Nimrod*. He is on assignment to Peretchelo and has top clearance for Project Tahiti. I am sending him to you on a mission of the utmost importance."

Boris paused again and took another breath.

"In your Special Unit you presently have a certain Tvoul Williams, a Martian denizen—and a groubian. You may only know her by her code-name, but we happen to know this is true—so do not query. Nimrod is her father-in-law. I repeat—*her father-in-law*. By the terms of the Treaty of Moscow you are required to grant Nimrod access to Tvoul... whether or not she agrees to it."

Boris stopped and looked at Jack, then at Agent Zero. The latter spoke.

"Hi Metapelet, I am Agent Zero. You'll have heard of me in connection with the Meteor Gang. But I work for Zasta now, as Boris will confirm, and I shall present credentials when I arrive. I will be accompanying Nimrod on his mission—and I will bring a hibernator casket. After Nimrod has spoken to Tvoul Williams, I shall place the said party in hibernation—forcibly if necessary—for return to Mars. In my Zasta capacity I shall be acting on behalf of the Strana of Olympia, with the implied agreement of the boards of directors of both TMG and Peretchelo. My action will be sanctioned by the Treaty of Moscow in pursuance of member protocols: namely the transgenic laws. Tvoul Williams must in no way be alerted to my visit and its purpose. Please confirm your understanding of this message—and your readiness to comply."

Boris resumed the one-sided dialogue. "Hi Metapelet, Boris again. I must stress the seriousness of the situation. The three of us, Nimrod, myself and Agent Zero, will be here waiting for your *mandatory* reply by return."

Boris terminated the call with a sigh. "Well, God knows what she'll think when she gets *that*."

"Nimrod..." murmured Agent Zero. It was eyeing Jack in the same piercing way that Petra had done. "Descendant of Ham son of Noah; King of Shinar. The great hunter of Genesis..."

Jack smirked. "That's not bad... for an unperson."

"I'm no longer just the Unperson. I'm a smart professor."

"A professor of Human Reproductive Biology, if I recall—not Religion."

"Religion's just a hobby of mine. But it does have a bearing on my work."

Jack called the agent's bluff. "Organised religion as sexual display..." he snapped his fingers, "how does it go?"

"...As a sexual display modality in *H sapiens*."

Boris, not privvy to this in-joke, smacked the desk. "We've got three hours to wait. What shall we do?"

Jack, a smile on his face, said "I was about to suggest we all went for a drink. But you can't drink cocktails, can you, Agent Zero?"

"I can sit and watch you."

"In Zasta uniform?"

"The uniform is emulated. I go plain-clothes in the twinkle of an eye."

Jack perversely thought he'd try a bit of flirting. "What do you wear when you're not in uniform?"

"Try me."

"No cocktails? No *interspex*?... You must be kidding."

"Shall I show you what I *can* do?" A merest hint of menace in the voice.

Jack recoiled with a shrug. "Well anyway, let's go. *Poidëm! Koktéili* for three... I mean two." His smattering of M1 sat lightly on him.

But as the three of them were getting to their feet, Agent Zero said "You're a man of surprises, Jack. I cannot for the life of me guess what you're going to do next."

"What makes you say that?"

"I assumed that inviting Tvoul Rainbow out for a drink was the last thing you'd do."

••••✶★●★✶••••

"We were lucky to get her," said Boris, raising his glass. "*Metapelet* isn't her real name of course."

"What is it, then?"

"*Ax!*—can't tell you that. Code-names only, when referring to the Special Unit. No names—no pack-drill. You don't want to get back to Mars facing prosecution under the transgenic laws."

"And the Strana lets you get away with that?"

"Project *Tahiti*: the little word that makes everything okay."

Agent Zero had swapped Zasta uniform for a scintillating dress of greeny-blue. Easy enough to do when clothing is just another digitally-simulated texture. But it had been a favourite colour of Tvoul's to wear. It was getting harder all the time to remember it wasn't Tvoul herself. Until, that is, the ectoplast did something robotic, like changing outfits in a flash.

A cocktail sat on the table before it. Jack had ordered one for it too, hoping not to draw attention to the three of them, but it made no attempt to sip it.

"Trained nurse, too," Boris added. "Just what we needed. She was trying to get back to Gaia—but there's no way to do *that* until the *Oberon* comes round again. To kill time for her we talked her into a little assignment on Titan. An offer she couldn't refuse."

Jack had heard horror stories about the Titan run. "Doesn't sound like the sort of thing anyone casually volunteers for."

"We had her by the nuts… in a manner of speaking."

"The gonads, he means," volunteered Agent Zero. A professor of Human Reproductive Biology would naturally deem Boris's remark somewhat lacking in precision. "The ovaries, in fact. She chose to pick a quarrel with the Vratch over them."

"How do you know all this?" said Jack, an edge creeping into his voice. He thought of Gabrielle. She too had "picked a quarrel" with the Vratch—and over her gonads, too. A quarrelsome organisation—and one that unerringly went for your weak point: he fervently hoped it would leave *him* alone from now on.

"I'm Zasta. I get to hear of such things." Agent Zero played with its drink, rotating it on its base on the table top. "It was not a clever thing to do. The Vratch is as powerful, in its proper sphere, as we of Zasta are in ours."

What sort of things, mused Jack to himself, do you "get to hear about" concerning *me*? I guess you all imagine you've got *me* by the nuts?

••••••✴ ● ✴••••••

Three hours later, the three of them were back in Jack's office. The v-unit buzzed. "Inter-world operator. Here is the reply to your call to Titan, made today at 14:37."

The voice from Titan came through loud and clear, but it sounded barely human. But if it had been anyone Jack knew, he wouldn't have recognised them, for all the filtering the signal had undergone.

"Hi Boris—this is Metapelet, on Platform Two. I don't understand the request. I've only been here a week, but I can assure you we have no groubians in the unit at this time. There are no groubians on the whole of Platform Two. I repeat—*there are no groubians on Platform Two.* I can't imagine why you think there might be. Groubians haven't been on Titan for *fifty thousand years!* Wild horses wouldn't drag them here, by all accounts."

Boris opened his mouth goldfish-wide. His face signalled astonishment, then fury. "The blasted little fool! Who does she think...?"

Jack glanced up at the silvery visor of Agent Zero, but quickly dropped his eyes again. Groubians might not be able to read gaian expressions, but there was no knowing what an ectoplast could do. Whatever it was equipped to do, presumably.

Yes, Metapelet, he thought to himself, I'm easy with that. There are no groubians on Platform Two. Tvoul is *here*—she's living openly in Nix City. She does a weekly cabaret in the *Krásnaya Melnítza.* A simple trick like that would be just the thing to fool this bunch of turkeys, with their impersons and unpersons and monster databases.

"End of transmission," came the voice of the inter-world operator. "Do you wish to reply?"

Boris bellowed "You bet I fucking do!"

"Please answer yes or no. Do you wish to reply?"

Boris deflated like a punctured football. "Yes." He shut his eyes.

"Please speak your reply clearly after the tone."

Boris took a deep breath, snorting through his nostrils. "Listen Metapelet—Boris here. Don't give me that bullshit—we know you're not going to admit to having a groubian on the rig. But sure as hell Tvoul Williams left for Titan on board the *Prometheus* on 1 December 400 *marsvrem*—straight off the *Oberon.* Tvoul has been there in the unit for the last nine weeks *marsvrem.* I happen to know who is and who is not in your unit because I have the passenger lists in front of me. Please confirm you understand this message and will comply. Or sure as God made little apples—when Agent Zero arrives, it will be putting *you* in its damned hibernator and tipping you out on my carpet."

He banged his hand on the v-unit, terminating the message. Then after a brief glance at the ectoplast he glared at Jack. In a hoarse voice, barely a whisper, he muttered "Another drink? On me, this time?"

••••••✱●✱••••••

It was dark outside when they got back a little over three hours later. Only just in time. The v-unit buzzed as they entered the office and sat down.

"Metapelet here. I'm sorry Boris, I didn't mean to be rude. I hear you and will comply."

"End of transmission," said the inter-world operator. "Do you wish to reply?"

"No," said Boris quietly.

"Yes." countered Agent Zero.

"Please speak your reply clearly after the tone."

Agent Zero leaned forward and announced itself. "Listen to me, Metapelet. When I come I want to be ready for anything. Locate a supply of void ectoplasts—ten or twenty should do. If there are insufficient ectoplasts on Platform Two, don't hesitate to order them to arrive on the next supply visit: the one Nimrod and I will be on. As soon as they arrive, scatter them around the rig. Equipment bays, lockers, tool-chests—anywhere they can hide until they're needed. If challenged, explain that it is a new Zasta requirement... as it is. *Farvel, o' tak for sidst.*"

Agent Zero touched the v-unit to end the transmission, then it turned to Jack and Boris, its visor still blank. "Now we can all go home."

Jack was puzzled. "What did you say just before you signed off?"

"Farewell and thanks—in Selensk."

"How come you speak Selensk?"

"I'll speak anything—if you give me the chip."

But what Jack should have asked was how Agent Zero knew that *Metapelet* spoke Selensk. He looked at Boris, who shrugged. He didn't know any Selensk either, beyond what everybody knew, like *farvel o' tak*.

Neither of them could tell that Agent Zero's signoff had meant "Farewell, and thanks *for the last good time we spent together.*"

23   The weapon of choice

Jack found a gunsmith in the lower part of the old city. He'd scanned a register of sports shops, simply dictated the street-numbers and his marscar took him there.

He wandered into the shop and tried putting a few shotguns to his shoulder. Bolt-action guns. Repeater guns. Soon the shopkeeper came over.

"I need to get out more," said Jack. "I'm thinking of taking up a sport."

"No finer way to keep in trim," said the shopkeeper. "That's if swimming or climbing doesn't suit you. You can chase the quarry, or you can stalk it."

Jack smiled and handed him the shotgun. "Forgive me, I'm new here. I'm from Earth—I mean Gaia. We're not seriously talking about *wildlife* on Mars, are we?"

"There is no native wildlife, except what the groubians brought with them—and you don't hunt that. But there is quite a bit of feral life—rats mostly. You find them around the terraforming vents. They've learnt to live in the Martian atmosphere, would you believe. They've picked up some bio-engineered symbiont that lives in their lungs and breaks down carbon dioxide. They grow quite large as a result."

"So do your customers mostly shoot rats?"

"No. Actually quite a dangerous thing to do. They release target-bots. In a variety of shapes, sizes and speeds. Anything from the humble clay-pigeon to ectoplasts of groubians."

"So people shoot *groubians* do they?" said Jack, honing his voice to a meaningful edge.

The shopkeeper paused before replying. "Not these days, sir. Peace has broken out. It's not the fashion to talk like that about our sisters… our *human* sisters."

Jack smiled back: a humourless smile. "I wouldn't say a word against the lovely dears. I was only thinking of shooting one."

The man broke the shotgun and peered in the breech. "Do you mean killing one—or just causing her a lot of pain?"

"Killing one."

The man shook his head and turned away. "You can't kill a groubian with a shotgun. Groubians have remarkable powers of recuperation. Now if you just want to cause them pain—agonizing pain—that's easy.

Their pain threshold is extremely low. I'm not at all certain they aren't in pain the whole time."

"I don't want to cause them pain. Nasty wicked thing to do."

The man put the shotgun back into the rack.

"But killing one now..." added Jack. "If they're all in pain anyway, that might be construed as an act of mercy..."

The man gave a little snort.

"Or *justice*..." Jack added.

Without saying a word, the man slowly turned to face Jack squarely.

"Surely it's been done before?" Jack persisted. "What did they use then?"

The shopkeeper stood looking at the entrance and then back at Jack. "This isn't the sort of thing I discuss in my shop..."

"I'm sorry," said Jack in forced apology. "I'd better go."

He turned to walk out of the door. Instantly an address was beamed to his helmet over the IR link. As Jack stopped, holding onto the door-frame, the shopkeeper said "I'm Kenneth, by the way, as you will verify. I'd be in a better position to answer your questions if you'd care to come round to my apartment this evening when I've shut up shop."

* * * * * ★ ● ★ * * * * *

Jack managed to track down some Newcastle Brown and with two six-packs under his arms he presented himself at the door of Kenneth's apartment. The door opened as soon as he arrived.

"I wondered if you'd come."

"Of course, man. D'you think I'd drink these all by myself?"

They quickly got through one of the six-packs, all the while making desultory chat. The advantages of one shotgun over another. Hunting in England, on Gaia generally—about which Jack wasn't all that knowledgeable. And sport, such as it existed in Nix City—where the gym reigned supreme as a means of getting exercise. But both of them were rock-climbers, as it pleased Jack to discover.

He broke open the second six-pack and handed Kenneth a can. "About my little problem..."

"What have you got against groubians? Have you ever met a groubian?"

"I have indeed. Two now. One on Gaia—and one on Selene."

"Really? What were their names?"

"The one on Selene was called Vermat Aurora."

Kenneth banged down the can. "The *true-mother!* What was *she* doing there?"

"She was Commissioner of Police. I made good friends with her."

"The cunning bitch! So that's where she holed-up. *Friends*, did you say?"

"Yes—for my part. She seemed quite forthcoming in the end. She was most helpful."

Kenneth shrugged to show his scepticism. "How can you really be friends... with a *fifty thousand year-old being?*... Far older, if she's one of the Mothers."

"Like you can with anyone, I suppose."

Kenneth chuckled and shook his head. "Don't they just view us as a flash in the pan? Look. Ever seen a spark in a candle flame?"

"Yes..."

"Tell me something—is it alive?"

"Search me."

"Maybe it isn't... maybe it is. But can you so much as contemplate the possibility of making friends with it? There isn't even time to say 'hi'—let alone 'I like you'. In a second it's not going to be there—and tomorrow the flame won't be there either."

"What are you driving at?"

"To a groubian, friendship with a gaian can't mean a thing."

"I thought the two groubians I met had the potential to form deep and trusting relationships with... people. But Vermat died in the Gaiascope outrage, before our friendship could develop that much." Jack fell silent.

"And the other one?"

"I'm not so sure, now."

"What was her name?"

"Tvoul Rainbow."

Kenneth spluttered into the can. Leaning back he whistled. "You don't set your sights too low, do you?"

"What do you mean by that?"

"Tvoul Rainbow is the most famous groubian on the planet."

"All the same... we were friends."

"*Were friends?* Why—is she dead too?"

"Not so far as I know. But dead is how I want her."

A gradual smiled spread across Kenneth's face. "Why's that, may I ask?"

"Because she married my son."

Kenneth emitted a yelp. "Well, I can see how that would upset some people. Me, I never had all that good relations with my in-laws. My *ex-in-laws*, ha-ha..."

"It was a groubian wedding."

The silence was like a lid going on. Kenneth stared at him, slowly easing forward in his chair.

Jack said it again. "She killed my son. I want her dead."

Kenneth mustered his words like bandsmen playing the dead-march. "Two wars have been fought over that sort of allegation. And here you come, all the way from Gaia, all set to start a third."

"I don't see it", said Jack. "Why would killing one groubian start the Third Olympian War?"

Kenneth sank back into his chair, shutting his eyes.

"There are plenty of groubians you could kill which wouldn't start a war. In fact there's some I can think of that everyone would pat you on the back for—from the GA to the Goubernator. Why don't you start with one of those?"

Jack smiled weakly.

"The head would make a nice trophy in your hall. I can sell you a wooden shield to mount it on."

Jack burst out laughing. "It would look a bit floppy on a shield, wouldn't it?"

Kenneth laughed too. Still laughing, they each opened another beer.

"You're... not hoping to get me involved in this *political assassination*, are you?"

"Heavens no, man. I just want to buy a suitable weapon. If you've got one in your shop then surely you're allowed to sell me it? Or do I have to sign-up with Olvoi before I could buy it?"

"Sign-up with Olvoi and you could lay your hands on anything—even a triton pistol. That would do the job, wouldn't it?"

"I couldn't face the collateral damage. A lot of people might get hurt."

"They certainly might. But all the same, I can't sell you a triton pistol. By the Treaty of Moscow they're banned on the inner planets."

"So who does use triton pistols?"

"Olvoi keeps a cache of them, strictly under lock and key. Nobody is meant to know about that. It's common knowledge though that *Prometheus* carries them—for when the crew make landfall on Titan. Titan's a world of its own."

"What do *they* use them for?"

Kenneth shrugged his shoulders. "They're just frightened of their own shadows…" He laughed. "When you stop to think about it, you need something pretty heavy against a shadow. You've got to blast away whatever it casts itself on."

"I take it you don't believe in the Titan Kraken?"

"Nobody believes in the Titan Kraken," snorted Kenneth, taking a deep swig. "Until they get to Titan."

Jack followed his lead. "Well, I don't need a triton pistol. I know my target. I've seen it in the flesh, I've talked with her, shared my deepest thoughts with her… and I've been betrayed by her."

Kenneth took a deep breath. "Some would say you were a fool to trust her in the first place. Whatever made you?"

"My son trusted her. That was good enough for me. Until my son was no more."

Kenneth slowly and steadily finished his beer. "There's a lot of blood been spilt over that particular cause. Now everything's nice and peaceful—and you come here, all the way from Gaia, hoping to stir things up again!"

"I'm not 'hoping' to do anything of the kind." snapped Jack. "One bloody groubian…"

"I know—I know. And it just has to be 'bloody' Tvoul Radouga."

Jack looked down. "That's what I get from everyone. Don't *you* believe me either?"

Kenneth opened another beer. "Oh look, Jack—I believe you. I'm all too ready to believe you." As if on an afterthought, he leaned back in his chair and, without looking round, picked something off the bookshelf above his head.

"Take a peek through this."

"What is it?" said Jack, looking at the thin silver-grey cylinder which lay in his hand. He tried looking down it like a tube.

"No, no, not that way. There's a little hole in the end, going from side to side. Like an Edwardian novelty toy. Only it's not a micro-photograph you'll see, like Venice gondolas or some podgy nude. More like a kaleidoscope…"

Jack found the hole and stared through it. It took him a while to focus… and then he could see colours and shapes. They were moving in and out of two spots near the middle.

"So what is it?"

"It's the Book of Titan."

Jack snatched his eye away. He stretched his shoulders and leaned back. "So this is the Book of Titan. *This?*"

He peered again through the hole, this time with greater concentration. Whether it was due to the warmth of his hand, or simply propelled by his desire to see more, the colours and shapes in his field of view evolved and spoke to him. They spoke of dark and dreadful things. Disgrace and betrayal. Wickedness beyond belief. Treachery and retribution and irreparable devastation. They spoke of a whole world cursed until the end of time.

But they also spoke of an insatiable hunger—of a refusal to accept extinction, even after an eternity in hell. Of a faith bereft of hope, without which life itself was worthless, with its never-ending journeys into empty valleys starved of meaning.

As to whether that was what it really meant, how could he know? The cylinder would have had to impart the very language it employed. It was spatio-color, of course. An archaic spatio-color, hugely evocative, resonating with symbols plunged deep within his psyche. Symbols laid down in his race-memory, like the strata seen only in the deepest of canyons. Symbols from an age before his ancestors had possessed skin or fur, or even scales.

Kenneth snatched the cylinder from his fingers in alarm. "Don't look for too long!"

"Why not?"

"It doesn't do you any good."

"What's wrong?"

"If you look in it for long enough, it starts reprogramming your peripheral nervous system."

"What's that going to do?"

"Drive you stark, staring, barking mad."

"Geddaway!"

"I'm serious. To begin with, you don't feel a thing—but your lower nerve-centres wake up and start thinking groubian thoughts. And not just any old groubian thoughts: *epic* ones. Soon it all bubbles up in your consciousness and you won't have a clue what the hell's happening."

"I see…" Jack tried hard not to smile. But Kenneth noticed. "Look," he said. "The Book of Titan in the original spatio-color is banned from public sale. Did you know that?"

Jack didn't. "I tried getting hold of a copy, but all I could find was a translation. Is that the reason?"

"That's not the reason they tell you. They give it out that the Groubian Alliance is dead against any gaian profaning it. Now it's clean contrary to Martian custom, proscribing a book in that way, but the GA has a lot of clout. It's not as if they're forcing us to read a book we'd rather not, like the Bible—just the opposite. And because it's their book—their info—the Strana plays along with the GA."

"Mebbes they're doing us a favour? They know it's dangerous for us—so they want to protect us from its harmful effects."

"Such touching concern for our welfare isn't borne out in other areas." He reached over his head and put the thing back on its shelf. "No... they want to keep it out of our hands because it reveals them for what they truly are—their real attitude towards us. All summed up in the Last Verse."

Kenneth looked down at his hands as if they were covered in blood. Not-so-innocent blood. "They're immortal. Demons from hell. On their timescale we're just a flash in the pan. Here today—gone tomorrow. Most of them are prepared to stick it out until we're gone. Three or four thousand years, at the outside. But for some of them that's not fast enough. They want us gone—now. Pronto!"

"How did you manage to get hold of the Book of Titan in the original?"

Kenneth spoke slowly, stressing every word. *It—was—a—trophy—of—war.*"

Jack's eyes widened. "You killed a groubian to get it?"

"I killed lots of groubians. This was taken from the body of one of them."

Jack shifted in his seat. The horror of the last Olympian War was something legendary. But right now there was only one thing he wanted to know about the whole bloody business.

"What sort of weapon did you use?"

Kenneth held his fingertips together, mutely appealing for patience. "I'll show you in a minute. When we've finished these beers."

They picked out a beer each from the remains of the second pack. "So what was the war like?" said Jack. "On earth we never hear a thing."

Kenneth leaned back in his chair. He seemed to close in on himself, although his eyes were staring into space.

"Nobody who took part in that war wants to talk about it. Not if they're gaian. Not if they're groubian." He sighed a long drawn-out sigh. "It was the most terrible experience of my life. And all totally, totally pointless."

"Why? Because so many groubians were killed… to no avail?"

"No. Because some groubians were left alive."

Jack recoiled in astonishment.

"Killing the greater part of them solved nothing," Kenneth continued. "They're in exactly the position they were before. They're extinct as a species. They can't breed. And why not? I'll tell you why not—*because they've eaten all their own damned menfolk!*"

Kenneth paused. "You knew that, didn't you?"

"Yes."

"And now they damn well want to start on ours." Kenneth smacked the arms of his chair. "I've lost friends to these un-dead fossils. I've lost family. I know what it's like… to lose a son."

Their eyes met and locked.

"But don't run away with the idea I'm planning another massacre. I've shot my bolt in that particular direction. Still, they watch me closely now."

He balled his fists and banged the wooden arms again. "But if I can help anyone who's going through what I did…"

He struggled to his feet. The beer had wrecked his sense of balance and he clutched briefly at the back of the chair. "Come on downstairs," he slurred, "and let me show you something…"

•••••*●*••••

In the basement under the apartment block, Kenneth unlocked the door to a private firing range. He opened the metal-lined case he had brought with him and took out a machine-pistol. With slow precision he filled the magazine with bullets. Then with a snap he clipped it in place and handed it to Jack.

"This is an uzi: made in Israel. If you want to kill groubians, this is the neatest way. The frequency with which the bullets strike the target resonates with the natural frequency of the groubian nerve-net, inducing a fatal spasm."

Jack looked down in awe at the functional-looking tool of death in his hands. He tried various grips upon it. Eventually he swivelled-down the frame stock and clamped it under his elbow, like a Chicago gangster with his tommy-gun.

Kenneth said "Watch for the target. When you see it pop-up, fire at will."

Jack splayed his legs and pointed the machine-pistol down the range. Kenneth pulled a lever. Up came the cardboard target—a life-sized groubian warrior charging at the onlooker, face frozen in a mask of fury.

The uzi spattered metal at the target. Cardboard fragments sprayed about. Cut through at the waist, the upper half toppled off and clattered on the concrete floor.

•••••✷●✷•••••

Neither Kenneth nor Jack wanted a transaction to register on the intensor. Jack's booner card was no defence: quite the opposite. Booner transactions were logged on a special list. So when Jack handed him back the gun, Kenneth simply shook his head. Back upstairs, reaching down under his coffee-table he got out three boxes of a hundred rounds each, which he'd signed out to himself earlier that day. Then, wandering off into the kitchen, he came back with four spare magazines like short grey truncheons, plus a zip-up bag of black leather.

"My back is turned," he said. "Outside—don't let anyone see you."

"Are you going against the law in this?"

"Who knows? I'd rather not ask. Concealing a transaction from the intensor carries its own penalties…" Kenneth had an ugly smile. "But it's the lesser of evils."

•••••✷●✷•••••

The next day Kenneth looked out of his window to see an unfamiliar marscar standing outside his apartment. The latest model. Having slipped-on his dust suit and clipped down the visor he stepped out into the *oúlitza* and wandered casually over to it.

There was nobody in sight. *"Chei…?"* he muttered, looking away.

"Ia—tvoi mars-kar, Kénnef," it replied. *"Ne právda-li?"*

Kenneth snapped his fingers. *"Molodétz!"* he exclaimed in delight. *"Nou—poidëm."*

The door opened and he got in. But it wouldn't shut again. A blue-clad arm had been thrust in: an exceptionally flexible arm. Its white gauntlet held a six-shooter to Kenneth's temple. A voice-chip cut-in over the intertalk, using the standard voice for a groubian imperson. *"Otstói!"* it commanded.

Screwing up his eyes, Kenneth let his forehead slump to the dashboard.

24   A shot in the dark

Restlessly Jack paced the white gravel of the Areopagus, waiting for sundown… and his appointment with Tvoul. Waiting was something he'd never done that well. For the first time in two years he found himself craving for a cigarette. Uselessly of course. With his SP unit he could no longer inhale.

A mother walked past with her daughter, a girl of about Kat's age. The mother said matter-of-factly "On Gaia the sky is blue." To which the daughter replied "Don't be silly, the sky is black." Jack turned to stare at them, his jaw sagging in a scramble of emotions.

The child had been born under a black sky. She had never experienced daylight. A bright blue firmament was a thing unknown to her—as it was to everyone who first opened their eyes inside the Nix. The very notion of a brilliant blue canopy with gracious white clouds smiling down on you was absurd.

"On Gaia the sky is blue." For the Martian, those six little words encapsulated all the notions people in that vain airy world are said to entertain—their hopes, their fantasies, their baseless optimism—numbing them against the urge to escape the doom that sits waiting for them in the dark. They raise their eyes and they see the fragile gossamer mantle of the Great Mother, which everyone on Earth takes for granted, and they mistake it for infinite space. They do not see the emptiness of death that lies behind it, like the skull beneath the skin. And at night, when the veil is torn away and any objects to be seen are for the most part sunken centuries into the past, they shut their eyes and sleep—and do not look.

Of course the sky is black. How could anyone think otherwise?

Jack glanced backwards to see where the pair had come from. They'd been in one of the telescope booths. Like a sleepwalker he entered the empty booth. In front of him a wall-sized screen showed stars spattered randomly, like glints of frost on a flank of sable fur. Stars dim and bright, burning with cold crisp urgency.

"*Shtoza planéta?*" said the voice of the telescope.

"Gaia", Jack replied, his head empty of thought.

The sky span like a globe of crystal, the sun flared past in a blaze of light and a small blue crescent swung into view. It centred and grew larger and larger until it filled the screen: a broken cookie of liquid blue and gold, dusted with clouds. Nearly half the disk was in daylight. Jack couldn't tell if he was seeing the actual planet or a library image.

"*Èto Géia, íli Zémlia. Goloubáia planéta. Trétja planéta ot sólntza.*" (This is Gaia, or Earth. The blue planet. The third planet from the sun.)

"*Shtoza straná?*" continued the voice of the telescope after a pause.

"Anglia," said Jack. Being addressed in M1 no longer fazed him, though he knew he'd never speak it fluently.

"*Èto Ánglia.*" The ball grew larger until the screen carved out a slice of the shining rim. The British Isles were visible, having just come up over the horizon.

"*A tepér' koudá?*" (Where now?)

"Esh Winning."

"*Èto* Esh Winning, County Durham," confirmed the voice again. The screen zoomed-in upon England, coming in low over East Anglia, letting Yorkshire inflate and bulge off the bottom of the screen. Jack briefly saw the three towers of Durham Cathedral lit by the morning sun.

The image in the frame moved a fraction to show the village of Esh Winning, six miles to the west. The crenellated tower of Newhouse Church came into view, a cubist fragment in the slanting swirl of house-encrusted streets.

"St Mary's, Newhouse…" said Jack, dread rising in his throat.

"*Èto sérkov'* Newhouse *Sviatói Marú,*" came the confirmation. The church grew until it filled the screen, the weather-vane turning in the breeze. It was an actual image he was seeing, just as it had been four minutes ago, a sunbeam glancing off the tower in the direction of Mars.

Beyond the tower lay the churchyard. "The grave of Hilda Williams…" Jack groaned.

"*Èto mogíla Gílda Viliáms,*" said the voice of the telescope. "*Net informátzii.*"

No information… but it had at least known her name. The frame zoomed into a shiny black gravestone until it too filled the screen aslant. He hadn't yet seen it—although it was he who'd placed the order.

The picture pixellated: the telescope had reached its limit of resolution. But Jack knew what the inscription said, because he'd written it down for the stonemason:

> *Hilda Margaret Williams*
> *Born 16/4/1907, died 13/6/1974*
> *Beloved wife of Jack Williams*
> *Died of a broken heart.*

His gaze strayed to the date-stamp at the bottom of the screen. In Esh Winning it was 11.30am on Monday 3 May, 1976. Here in Nix City it was 6.30pm on Saturday 21 March, 401.

His eyes filled with tears. Almost two years had gone by and this was the first time he'd been able to weep for Hilda. Groping blindly, he staggered out of the telescope booth into the synthetic daylight of the Areopagus. A few people glanced round in fleeting concern as Jack straightened himself and set his visor neutral.

Then he stalked away to keep his deadly appointment.

•••••★●★•••••

Jack's marscar stopped outside Tvoul's apartment. He reached for the bag containing the uzi plus the loaded magazines. Taking two, he slipped them into his shin pockets. Of the remaining three, one he clipped into the gun, the others he left loose in the bag.

He could see no further than the deed to be done. Afterwards there was no way of escape. He supposed he'd simply get back in his marscar and command it to drive to the nearest Zasta post, where he'd give himself up. And then what would they do to him? Keep him in prison until they could deport him back to Earth? It hardly mattered. He'd be dead before the *Oberon* came back.

The outer door opened to let him in. He went down the passage and found himself in a living room which balanced sleaze against *chic*. A miniature bar occupied one corner. There was a poster of the Chrysler Building, captioned *Niu-Iórk, Niu-Iórk*, a reproduction of Picasso's *Three Dancers*, a couple of Kandinsky pictures and a still from *Casablanca* showing Humphrey Bogart staring betrayed into the eyes of Ingrid Bergman.

Nothing of especially groubian interest, Jack reflected. Maybe he wouldn't have recognised it had there been? Then his eye was arrested by a small colourful picture looking like a Rohrschach Ink Blot. Hadn't he seen something like it recently?

Yes, he had. In Kenneth's looted copy of the Book of Titan.

Curiosity overcame him. He went and stood in front of it. There was a poem inscribed on the patch of colour: a poem in M1. With his weak but growing knowledge of the language, Jack recognised the famous—or infamous—Last Verse…

> *Vérnaia mat' terpít détstva outrátou.*
> *Poust tvoiá liubóvka nanósit oudár;*
> *Shto est' valiúta ou zhízni samói?*

Otvét: nishtó, ésli lish ni plestís'
Détskim peshkóm po dolíne poustói.

It happened to be Dolpou Zvezda's ground-breaking translation from the original spatio-color, the one Kitty had thought so misleading. To everyone you asked it meant something different. Spatio-color, so they said, had conjunctions and prepositions with no counterparts in gaian languages: something that Dolpou Zvezda had tried stumblingly to portray. But apparently her effort didn't make a lot of sense in M1 either. It may have been the only gaian language Dolpou spoke, but it could scarcely have been called her mother-tongue.

What did it mean to Tvoul? If nothing, she wouldn't have had the verse stuck up on the wall, printed over what simply had to be a quotation from the original spatio-color. Perhaps he ought to ask her—before he shot her dead? Else he might never know.

Not that her present thoughts interested him in the least. He was after all planning to switch them off. But it would be nice to know what had been going on in her mind when she killed his son.

Tvoul's dreamy voice oozed through from the next room. "Pour yourself a drink, Jack. I'm just changing into something more comfortable."

As it happened Jack's nerves were on a hair-trigger. Tvoul's suggestion struck him as a good one. On the other hand, maybe he shouldn't touch a drop of alcohol. Wisdom counselled that he should be on top form to carry this thing off. Ever since Hilda had died, it had been his only goal in life.

He went over to the bar to see what Tvoul had thought to get in stock for her clients. Whether she drank such things herself he couldn't be sure—she had stuck to soft drinks when she'd been at his house. There were the ingredients for every variation of Martini you could think of. There were fancy cocktail sticks and bottles of every sort of fruit which might conceivably be stuck on them. There was a whole shelf full of mixers—and there was tequila, white rum, whisky, gin, vodka, brandy... all the usual spirits anyone might ask for.

Even if he wasn't going to drink it, he should mix himself something, if only to avoid alerting his quarry to anything bad about to happen. He poured some tonic water into a glass and went over and sat on the pink leather sofa, putting his drink down on a glass side-table. Tvoul came in and exhibited her body under the guise of getting him to admire her satin shift, which was all she was wearing.

"You know," she said, "I've been trying to think what we did when we last met. I have this feeling I've known you for an awfully long time."

"Can you remember this?" said Jack. "Standing side-by-side in the dusk, trying to count the stars?"

"Really? How romantic. Did we do that? It seems a lifetime ago."

"Whose lifetime? Mine? Or yours?"

Tvoul affected a lazy laugh. "Uh, huh… you're playing word-games with me. There's no way you could have been around at the beginning of my lifetime, gaian."

"Will I be around at the end of it, I wonder?"

"Goodness, Jack—aren't you in a mood tonight! Come on, lover-boy, loosen up. There's things I could do to relax you."

"Such as?"

"There's a Jacuzzi in the next room. We could spend some time in that. Just you and me, with nothing coming in between us. Getting to know each other. Easing up…"

She knows I'm on edge, Jack warned himself. Groubians weren't meant to be good at reading gaian emotions. But if you were in business as a courtesan, you might install sensors to advise you of your client's state of mind.

In that case, how much could she tell about him? Maybe more than he cared for. Maybe she knew exactly what he had come to do—she was simply laughing at him, having got her answer all worked out. He'd do well not to beat about the bush much longer. That might just be to play into her hands. Picking up his bag he felt for the pistol-grip of the uzi.

"What have you got in the bag?" There was no suspicion in the voice. It conveyed nothing but curiosity, plus a little sensuous anticipation. But of course, groubians have absolute control over their voices. Emotional colour is something to be consciously injected.

"Just a toy or two I've brought along."

"Do you like using toys? Do they help you to perform, or is it just the idea that excites you?" She waved her hand vaguely behind her. "I've got a cupboard full of toys. If I'd known you were into those …"

Jack pulled out the uzi and laid it on his lap. She didn't startle, but it was a second or two before she spoke again.

"Really, Jack, I don't think there's anything sexy about that toy. Does it give you a sense of power?"

Now, at last, there was a hint of foreboding in her voice. It was as if she hadn't been anticipating anything untoward until now. Nor could she bring herself to believe it, even yet. You could be sure she'd checked out Jack before he came, polling the intensor for all its worth. A Terrestrial, but a solid citizen. A booner—well-known—everything to lose.

But she couldn't ignore the evidence of the uzi. It wasn't simply any gun, which therefore might be just for show—a prop. During the massacre which commenced the war, this was the weapon of choice for killing groubians. She'd know that.

"Let's get back to what we were discussing," said Jack. He tried to keep his tone of voice neutral, because that was something a groubian certainly could pick-up on. "Can you remember when you first met my son Harry? Taking him for biology lessons, perhaps?"

"Oh, yes," said Tvoul, her voice growing silky. "I take a lot of nice boys for *biology lessons...*"

She seemed determined to act her part to the bitter end, though now her eyes didn't leave Jack's hand gripping the gun. No doubt she was wondering how to reach the alarm button without it being noticed. What a good thing she'd taken her helmet off. Otherwise she'd have found it easy to summon help by now.

Jack hadn't taken off his own helmet—he'd merely slipped the visor back. The booner card was still activated—although, without her helmet, that wouldn't signify anything to Tvoul.

"Harry, did you say? Harry... oh, *Harry!* Now *there's* a gorgeous boy." She prattled on in this vein, as though she imagined it would do something to pacify Jack. Or was she just playing for time?

"So tell me some of the things you recall doing with him."

Tvoul cast her eyes upwards, as if selecting a tidbit from a fund of salacious memories. "Might they be things you'd fancy doing yourself? Like father—like son, perhaps?"

"As it happens, no. But tell me anyway."

"Why don't we stop talking and get down to brass tacks...? No, I didn't mean that!" She held up her hands as Jack aimed the uzi. "Jack, I can't imagine why you think this behaviour is likely to get you all excited. It just seems to be making you more and more upset. Let's try another approach..."

"Can you remember going into the jungle with him? Can you remember what you did with him there?"

"Well that sounds all very exciting, Jack, but aren't we talking at cross purposes?"

"No, it's very much to the point. My son happens to be *dead*—and you're still alive. And not a mark to show for it. No parturition scars, no lumps which might be zygocysts. Two years on. *Two bloody years!* That should have been long enough, shouldn't it?"

"Look…" Tvoul's voice became a cracked fingernail, catching in the fabric of her stories. "I really must say this: aren't you in need of help? Let me call the Vratch…" She rose to her feet. Brandishing the uzi, Jack motioned to her to sit down again.

She complied—and as she did so she slowly stripped off her satin shift in one voluptuous movement. Had Jack only known, she wasn't doing it to be seductive. She had come to the conclusion she was going to have to fight him—and for that she needed all her skin-area exposed, for dazzle camouflage.

"What makes you think I went into the jungle with your son? Which jungle? We don't have jungles in Nix City. The Areopagus…"

"Don't bandy words with me. What were you thinking… when you edulated my son Harry?"

"Oh, so *that's* your take, is it? You don't want sex at all: you just want to conduct a personal pogrom. Well, let me tell you Jack—the war's over. We have agreements to avoid that sort of thing. It was all a lie anyhow…"

"Yes, I know just what you can and can't do on Mars. So you go to Earth, to Gaia—where people don't know your little game—and do it with no one to stop you? Well look here, sunshine…"

"Jack, relax… I think we've talked enough. It's not doing you any good. Now—how about sitting quietly together…?"

"I'll sit quietly when I've finished what I've come to do."

Her voice suddenly brightened. "Hey—I know who you are. You're *Jack-the-Ripper!*"

At that instant the lights went out. Jack had come prepared for something like this—he had a magnesium flare ready in his pocket. Quickly he sparked it and dropped it on the carpet. In its pure white smoking glare Tvoul, still sitting opposite him, shape-shifted out of all recognition. Something—tentacles?—tried to wrest the uzi from his grasp.

He fired a burst. The grip on his uzi went limp like a snapped rubber band. Sudden relaxation made the machine-pistol twist in his hand. Something caught his arm and he dropped the weapon. Something else caught hold of his leg. Kicking and lashing out, Jack picked up the uzi again and emptied the magazine into the place where Tvoul had been sitting.

In the light of the flare he saw a flickering mass of red jelly twisting on the carpet. His face and hands were slimed with sepia. In panic, he wrenched out the empty magazine and flung it at the writhing mass which wouldn't die. Kicking over his bag, he picked up another magazine and crammed it into the uzi. That too he emptied into the squirming sludge.

Now at last it stopped moving. Nothing else was clutching at him, nothing was holding onto him. Then suddenly a voice spoke.

"Please don't shoot me any more…"

His victim's voice-chip had uttered one final whimpering sentence before it shut down in fatal termination mode.

The glistening mass stopped flickering and went white. Pasta-like tissues oozed from lesions like guts spilling from a squashed slug. Jack was seized by an urge to be violently sick. He projectile-vomited over the mess he'd manufactured. Wiping his mouth roughly on his sleeve he clipped a third magazine into the uzi, put his shoulder to the door and barged through.

No sooner was he out of the block and into the *oúlitza* than he plunged unheedingly into a knot of blue-and-white uniforms. Tvoul had summoned help sooner than he'd imagined. His marscar was not where he'd left it. Thrusting off the hands which grasped at him, he flung himself back into the building. A flight of steps wound up and away to the left—he found himself dashing up them, people running either side of him to catch him up and overtake him. One grabbed at his legs to trip him up.

He had no thought now of giving himself up. In his highly aroused state he was determined to go out in a blaze of glory. Blasting the lock from the door with a burst from his uzi, Jack flung himself out onto the roof. Turning he saw dozens of z-niks disgorging from the stairwell canopy behind him. He directed a burst of fire over their heads, just to slow the pursuit. Tumbling this way and that, they dived for cover.

Instantly he became class four. Now the z-niks were authorised to use their CRWs. Jack ducked as the red flare of a bloody-butcher lunged at his neck. He fired at it. By a fluke one of the bullets grazed it the moment before it would have sunk its talons in him and sent it spinning away, bouncing across the rooftop.

Turning to resume his flight he stumbled. He was right on the edge of the roof. As he staggered and overbalanced he struck out with his feet, trying to launch himself onto the neighbouring building. Pain stabbed through his hamstrings. He hadn't given himself enough impetus to cross the gap and he plunged down between the buildings, striking the far wall. It broke his heel-bone and sent him spinning.

Before he hit the ground, four CRWs pounced on him like a fan of Roman candles filmed in reverse. The filaments stretched like bungee lines—and the talons held. Slowly he was winched back up, bobbing on the flexing lines, blood flowing across his skin from barbs lodged in his ribs. The pain was blindingly bright.

As he passed the windows of a stairwell he was dimly aware of people running up the escalade on the other side of the glass. They were keeping up with him... drawing ahead of him. Just above him a window pane burst and showered him with fragments. Arms reached out, hauling him inside. The talons bit deeper as the winches rolled on. Then the filaments snapped back against his body as they were cut—one, two, three, four—and he fell back into two pairs of strong arms.

As he lost consciousness, Jack stupidly wondered why the people who had snatched him were not wearing the blue-and-white uniforms of his pursuers.

25 A new triada

"Will he live?"

"Oh yes—I think we've caught him in time. He's not a young man, but having an SP unit has saved his life. Otherwise, with all the pain and exertion, he would almost certainly have suffered a heart attack."

"How long must he rest in bed?"

"That's up to you. I should give him as long as you can. I've pinned the fractured calcaneus as best I can under these conditions—he'll need a stick when he starts to walk—and I've enabled the metabolic controller in his SP unit. I'm leaving you the metabolo here."

"Thank you doctor. Hamish will see you back to your apartment."

"Don't bother, I'll find my own way. Please take these and dispose of them. I don't want to be caught with CRW talons in my possession."

"I'll give them to Jack. He might like them as keepsakes. Oh—and I hardly need say this… don't breathe a word."

"A gaian—covered in sepia—with four sets of talons in him? I don't want anyone to know I've been involved in this."

·····✱●✱·····

"Bring him up slowly and let's talk to him."

The silvery figure with the opaque visor handed the metabolo to the man in the trolley. Gradually he inched the joystick forward until Jack's eyes began to flicker.

"Jack… can you hear me?"

"Am I in police custody? I was going to give myself up."

"No, Jack, that wouldn't have been a good idea. You're class four now, like we are. They would just have torn you to pieces."

"Where am I? Who are you?"

"It's all right. You're among friends."

There was a pause. In his bemused state Jack had to think about that. Trolley inched the joystick forward a fraction more, to enhance his cognition.

"Is she dead?"

"Oh, yes. No doubt about it. I take my hat off to you. Hardly anyone manages to kill a groubian first go. Whoever gave you that uzi knew what they were doing."

"Then that's it. My job's done." Jack relaxed back on the pillow and closed his eyes.

"What job, Jack? Why did you do it?"

"I've been meaning to for a long time. I've chased her all the way from Planet Earth to here. And at last I've got her."

"I'm puzzled," said the silvery figure. "Just why did you want to 'get' her?"

"Because she killed my son."

"When did she kill him? Where?"

"She came to Earth with him nearly two years ago—they got married in our local church—and they went off to Brazil... and there she edulated him."

"Tvoul Waterfall has never left the planet."

"I beg your pardon. She came to Earth—and she edulated my son."

"What was her name again?"

"Tvoul..."

The silvery figure pointedly readjusted her stance. "*Tvoul* is a pretty common name among groubians. Would you have been able to distinguish her from any other groubian?"

"Why-aye! It was her. I'd know that face anywhere."

"You mean—just like mine?"

The figure took off her helmet. Jack recoiled with a gargling noise as if she'd turned into a *T rex*. "Agh! Get away from me!"

Trolley, watching the metabolo for blood pressure, rapidly pulled back on the joystick. Jack slumped back onto the pillow like a dropped puppet.

"So that explains that."

"The bloody fool." said Hamish. "You'd think he'd have learnt about spatio-color signatures by now."

"Well, I can sympathise. Without the intensor I wouldn't be able to tell you gaians apart either. You all look the same to me."

"Just about anything does, doesn't it," said Hamish, "if it has the same height-to-width ratio?"

The silvery figure smiled. "It's not quite so bad as that. You get cues from other quarters." She turned to the man in the trolley. "Right, Peter, bring him up again—gradually."

She brought her face close to the head on the pillow. As the eyes began to flicker she said "Jack... listen to me. You're all right. I'm not Tvoul, I'm Shval." She paused. "Shval Meteor. You've heard that name before, haven't you?"

"Shval... Tvoul's twin sister."

"That's right. The Tvoul you're looking for is not here. She's not on Mars."

"That's what they tried to tell me at TMG."

"They were right, Jack. She's on Titan."

Jack's eyes opened wide. "Then I've gone and shot the wrong Tvoul."

"I'm afraid so."

Jack's SP unit started clicking. If he'd still had his lungs he'd have been sobbing. "The poor bit lass. Gunned down in cold blood. And she never even knew what it was all about."

"Jack, easy now. Don't lose any sleep over Tvoul Waterfall. If she were able to think about it—which she can't—she'd probably thank you."

Jack's voice was weak. "How do you make that out?"

"She was in a lot of pain after the War. Pain that would never go away. *Interspex* was her way of coming to terms with it. To meet her bad experiences head-on—to try to cauterise them in her memory. Some memories won't go away for a groubian, you know. When that happens, they've been known to court death."

"So that's why she didn't go to any effort to protect herself?"

"Something like that. When it comes to the point though, you fight. You don't let go of life that easily. But—as she told me once—she hoped something like this might happen one day. That someone would make a proper job of her."

Jack shut his eyes. "I sure did that."

"You sure did."

He opened his eyes again. Shval was waiting for him to say something more.

"What are you going to do with me?"

Shval glanced up at the others. "Why—nothing. If by that you mean: what are we going to do *to* you. But if you mean what we might do *with* you—what we might do *together*..."

But Hamish was shaking his head.

"What d'you mean?" murmured Jack.

"We might go and find the real Tvoul."

Jack tried to prop himself up on one elbow. "Do you want to do the same to her as I do?"

"In a word—yes."

"You want to kill her? Your own twin sister?"

"Yes."

Jack's eyes burned into those horseshoe pupils hovering inches from his face.

"I can understand you doubting that," continued Shval. "There are a lot of people hunting Tvoul down for what she's done. But when it comes to the point—they want to trade with her. Like your fine friends, TMG. They want to reward her for the very crime she's committed. They want her progeny for the top-secret Tahiti project."

"And you say you don't?"

"No. The idea revolts me. She deserves to be dispersed. Before her brood gets born, if that can be arranged. Now whatever lip-service people pay to that, no one's prepared to go that far. Except you. You have shown by your actions that you want Tvoul dead. Your actions are worth a thousand words."

Shval got to her feet. "Speaking for myself, I'd be delighted to work with you. To help you do what you've come all this way for."

Again Hamish shook his head. This time Jack noticed. "You might have to convince your friends," he said.

"I'll convince anyone I have to," said Shval. "Now you just lie back and get some beauty sleep." She nodded to Peter Zwillinge, who manipulated the controls. Jack stretched his rib-cage as if taking a deep breath, painful but satisfying, and closed his eyes.

Once Jack was asleep again, Hamish strode forward, hands outstretched. "Shval—no!"

"Why not? This is the chance of a lifetime. My lifetime."

"Shval. No. I *forbid* it."

Shval turned to the man in the trolley. "Peter… have him come round."

"Shval!" protested Hamish. "Why should we have this turkey along with us? He'll land us in the shite."

"Hamish…" said Peter Zwillinge quietly.

Hamish turned on his heel and threw up his hands in disgust.

"Jack has one advantage we don't possess," said Shval. "He is Tvoul's father-in-law. He will gain access to her where none of us has a chance of doing so."

"And are you really going to kill Tvoul?" said Hamish. "What about the oath you groubians take? Or doesn't that matter to you any more?"

"No, I'm not going to kill Tvoul…"

"Well—heck!"

"…Jack is. And then we'll step in and help ourselves to the zygocysts…"

"Are you sure there's going to be any zygocysts?"

"Look, boys. If you heard one day that Shval Meteor had given someone the Titan Kiss, would you go looking for zygocysts? Of course not. But if you heard that Tvoul Radouga—Principal Professor of Human Reproductive Biology at PUG—had edulated her husband, wouldn't you say she must have known exactly what she was doing?"

She turned to gaze down at Jack, sleeping like a babe. "There will be zygocysts, I'm sure of it. And it's worth going all that way to bring them back."

"All the way—*to Titan?*"

"Yes. All the way to Titan."

•••••✱●✱•••••

Time passed and Jack didn't know whether it was day or night. As far as he could tell, they were in an underground storeroom. Lagged pipes curled and twisted round the ceiling. Packing cases had been manhandled into position to make rough beds for the four of them. Jack tried getting out of bed and attempting a few feeble steps with the aid of a stick, but he soon got back under the covers. His broken heel pained him, his body smarted from the torn wounds of the CRW talons and he felt ridiculously weak. On top of that he was crushed by the guilt of having killed a person—the wrong person.

Now and again he'd wake up with a jolt, sweating copiously, his SP unit chattering and his mouth full of water-brash. It was always the same nightmare—the magnesium flare erecting its tail of smoke like a blinding white Persian cat—the squirming red jelly on the floor—the mess—the nausea. The moment before he'd pulled the trigger she had shape-shifted, he was sure of it. She had shape-shifted into something utterly inhuman.

Or could he be so sure? Hadn't it simply been a camouflage pattern on her skin which obliterated her outline? A pattern that moved sharply in one direction as she moved in another? That, plus the jet of sepia, which all cephalopods discharge in mortal danger? Both squids and octopi employ optical illusion to confuse predators—or prey.

He hadn't stopped to inspect the body, but from what he could recall of that gruesome sight there had been no vestige of any human form. Just the sofa and floor strewn with offal and slime.

Every now and then Shval or Hamish would come with food or medicine, or to recharge him through the left nostril with superox. Only Shval was wearing a helmet to keep in contact with the intensor. This saved Jack a good deal of unpleasantness from the triada's frightful aura. But he felt naked and isolated. He had got used to wearing a helmet and feeling reassured by the presence of people around him. Without access to the intensor, his three boon-companions felt estranged and remote, in spite of the kind words that Shval directed at him whenever she saw him awake.

Most of the time he was alone in the storeroom with Peter Zwillinge, a sullen monstrosity of dehumanised ugliness, who never cared to speak unless he was spoken to—and then only to reply in the most economical way.

"Where are we?" said Jack once.

"Underground."

"Is this where you live?"

"No."

"How long are we going to stay here?"

"Until you can be moved."

"And then where are we going? Back to your place?"

"No."

"Why not?"

"Zasta is out looking for us."

Jack quickly decided that Peter was just being his beautiful self. But he had a problem with Hamish. His attitude was best described as silent rage—in utter contrast to the easy affability he'd shown when he'd introduced himself on the *Oberon*, hollow though that might have been.

Jack decided that when the occasion arose he'd seize the bull by the horns. It was ever his way. He loved a row but hated an atmosphere.

"I really appreciate the TLC," he said to Hamish when the latter had been ministering to him—quite tenderly too, it had to be admitted, so there was no sarcasm intended.

"Make yourself at home. It's where you should be."

"I'm sorry to be such a nuisance. Why are you going to all this trouble for me?"

"Her Ladyship reckons you're still of use to us," replied Hamish, drying his hands on a sterilised rag. "Though if it were up to me it'd be a swift one to the back of the neck. It's the best you deserve."

In times gone by, Hamish had been one of Tvoul Waterfall's many admirers. Jack wasn't to know that. And Hamish never got around to telling him.

When Shval came back with some provisions, she went straight over to Jack. "How are you feeling today? I must say you're looking better."

"I don't feel too bad. Time to be moving on?"

Shval pursed her lips. "No, give it another day or two. Do you eat smoked crab? I thought we all needed a treat."

"I'm sorry for causing such a nosedive in your lifestyle."

"Don't worry about it. We'll soon be gone from this planet."

Hamish cleared the mess off the table from the previous meal and Shval dished out some bags and packages. All of a sudden she put her hands to her helmet.

"*Zasta!* Get your weapons out."

The others were carrying guns already. Shval pounced on Jack's uzi lying on a box at the end of the bed and dumped it on the bedclothes. "You too, Jack. Think you can manage this?"

"Stop buggering about, woman." growled Hamish. "Get the other two away down the rabbit hole. I'll follow as soon as I can." He stamped on the floor and a recess appeared. Flaps slid back to reveal a shaft.

Peter rapidly propelled himself over to Jack's bed. "Get on my lap," he shouted. Then, grasping Jack round the middle, he wheeled the pair of them over to the hatch. Jack screamed as they toppled in.

It was a levitator—a somewhat wider one than Jack had met with on the Moon. As they gently touched bottom, Shval landed on top of them. Quickly she got behind Peter Zwillinge and started the trolley motor going. On and on they sped in the darkness of the overflow drain. It smelt acrid and rusty, as Olympus rock does when it's moistened. The air which had sunk down from the buildings above was oxygen-depleted and poisoned with radon. It was a good job that none of them needed to breathe it.

A flash behind them lit up the tunnel in all its awfulness. The explosion which arrived a moment later boxed Jack's ears. By the sound of falling rock that followed, Jack judged the levitator shaft had collapsed.

They stood listening in the silent darkness. For how long Jack couldn't tell.

"Will there be any pursuit now?" murmured Peter, his catarrhal voice echoing softly.

"No. Zasta have called-off the raid. They've only accounted for one of us, but they're telling themselves that the rest must have been elsewhere. They don't know about the rabbit hole."

Shval sluggishly took the handles of the trolley and began pushing it by hand, the wheels crunching in the moist grit. Peter Zwillinge continued holding on to Jack in the darkness, hugging him tightly like an outsized teddy bear.

• • • • ✱ ● ✱ • • • •

"You owe it to us, Jack."

They were in another bolt-hole. Shval had come back from a dangerous mission: shopping. She knew how to do it without the intensor bringing Zasta crashing through the roof. She put a bag of cakes on the table and a bottle of wine.

"It all seems so sudden... we hardly know each other..."

It was a crass thing to say. Jack was feeling weak after the hammering he'd taken—weak and compliant. His reckless anger had misled him into murdering an innocent being. A human being—as he was gradually coming to accept. How then could he refuse someone who looked so much like his victim? Who in her turn had died because she looked so much like Tvoul?

Shval might not have been able to read his face, but she could read his mind. "Hamish gave his life for you," she reproached. "I have sacrificed my triada to rescue you from Zasta. When one member dies, the triada is dissolved. But if you imagine for one moment that means I'm going to abandon Peter..."

"I'm not asking you to."

"Oh yes you are—if you did but know it. How do you suppose you're going to get to Titan now, without my help? Will your precious Agent Zero come running to pull you out of the shit? ...A Zasta agent is she now, did you say?"

"All right!" Jack swallowed. "Tell me what I have to do."

Shval turned and fetched Jack's helmet from somewhere within Peter's trolley. "We'll need our helmets on for this. But we must be quick—or we'll be pinpointed."

She opened the bag of cakes and the wine. Then kneeling down she took Jack's hand and offered him a cake.

"As the intensor is my witness, I promise to obey you absolutely, until death parts the triada. Now repeat after me: 'as the intensor is my witness, I promise to cherish you and defend you with my life'."

Jack did so. Then Shval gave him a hug and a kiss before getting up and standing before Peter. They held hands and repeated the formula, Peter vowing to obey her and she to cherish him. They embraced and kissed lingeringly.

"Now, Jack, kneel before Peter."

It was the hardest thing he'd ever done. The formula was simple enough, so he didn't need prompting again. When it was over, Shval passed round the wine and they drank from the bottle. Peter was grinning with relief, making little chuckling noises.

Jack looked at Shval. He couldn't imagine what she was thinking, what the patterns on her face meant. She said "This is a brand new triada. Its aura is virginal. While we stick together it masks our class four status. So we'll be able to move about more openly."

"We won't have to move about much, will we Shval?" said Peter. "Surely all we need do is get to the shuttle bay?"

"That's what I'm hoping," Shval replied. "Jack—when you signed-up with TMG, they gave you an identifier to hang round your neck. We'll need that to get on *Prometheus*. Do you still happen to have it on you?"

Jack felt in his pockets but quickly remembered the gesture was pointless. "No—I left it in my apartment on purpose. I didn't want to carry any sort of identification beyond my booner card when I went off to do my little job…"

Peter and Shval looked at each other. "We'll have to go and get it," Shval muttered.

"Why do we need it?" Jack asked.

"Because without it, you have no occupation—and thus no authority to be going to Titan. *Prometheus* doesn't have an intensor—it's a Selenean vessel. But if you don't have your TMG identifier on you, the moment you set foot on *Prometheus* they'll start making inquiries. And they may read your class four status from what's recorded against your aura back on Mars."

"I thought you said that *Prometheus* couldn't care less about auras? What about yours then—and Peter's?"

"They don't care about auras—they wouldn't get any crew otherwise. But they do care about class. Your booner card will mask yours and they'll assume you're class six. But it may all fall apart if they ask you to deactivate it."

"We can't go now, Shval. It's the middle of the night. It would look suspicious."

"You're right, Peter. We'll go first thing in the morning. Let's turn in now."

As best they could they settled down in the bolt-hole. It was a lot less comfortable than the last one—and that certainly hadn't been opulent.

During the night Jack awoke to the sounds of what could have been an oyster-eating contest. "God!" he snarled in disgust. "Get some sleep, dammit!"

"Sorr-ee,"… came Shval's muffled voice.

26 Prometheus bound

"I thought cars didn't get stolen on Mars."

"They don't," said Shval." The owner's going to maxgear us for borrowing it without permission. But who cares? We'll be on *Prometheus* before he even discovers it's gone."

"Have an elstat." Peter Zwillinge handed both Shval and Jack an object the size and shape of a quail's egg, grey with three coloured bands round it, brown, black and red.

"What is it?" asked Jack.

"An electric grenade," explained Peter. "A 100 microfarad capacitor charged to 100,000 volts, which unfurls filaments by electrostatic repulsion. It'll kill everyone in a room without causing structural damage. Just twist the hemispheres before throwing it round the door."

Shval laughed to see Jack holding his at arm's length as if it were about to explode in his face. "It's quite safe until you do that. You can put it in your pocket, hang it on your key-ring…"

"You'll see it has a 'stun' setting," said Peter. "Don't use that. Too unreliable."

Faking a casual air, Jack and Shval got out of the marscar, leaving Peter in the driving seat for a quick getaway. Jack reached back inside for the stick they'd got him. Half a minute later they were in the apartment. Jack's foot was far from healed—he'd been quickly reduced to hobbling.

"It's in the bedroom," said Jack. "On the bedside table." He wondered if he'd be able to snatch a quick breakfast of krill semolina. For the last two weeks he'd not been eating normally.

"I daren't touch it," said Shval from the bedroom. "I might alter it in some way. Come and get it for yourself."

Jack went into the bedroom to discover Shval lying naked on the bed. Her skin was shimmering in pastel colours. "Don't you want to consummate the triada?"

"I thought we were in a hurry." He picked up the identifier on its cord and hung it round his neck.

"I've got the intensor just where I want it. So long as nobody comes in we'll be safe here for as long as you need. Peter's quite happy out there."

"Can't it all wait until we're on our way to Titan? There'll be more time…"

"There won't be another chance. *Prometheus* isn't the *Oberon*. It's not a luxury liner—it's a working vessel. We're unlikely to get a cabin together."

Jack sat on the bed and ran his hand up Shval's bare flank. Rose-pink eddies swirled away from his fingers. In spite of himself he felt his loins beginning to creep.

Then he thought of Kitty—and snatched his hand away.

Moodily Shval shifted her bottom to sprawl on her side. She reached again for Jack's hand.

"Can't we just leave it for now?" said Jack. "I'm not feeling very sexy."

"I don't fathom you, Jack. You've got a groubian as your willing slave—and you don't care. Half the population of Nix City would give their right arm to be in your shoes."

"Perhaps I'm the other half," he muttered.

"Jack, if you're going to be like that, this triada isn't going to work. This could be our last chance to get together—just you and me. I've vowed to you I'll do anything you ask. Isn't there something you want me to do?"

"Yes," said Jack. "There is."

Shval waited in silence.

"Answer me a couple of questions."

Shval put on a surprised look and propped her head up on her hand. "Whatever you say, Jack…"

"What does the Last Verse really mean?"

Shval sat up like a rat-trap springing shut. "Why does that matter to *you*, gaian?" Her skin crawled with orange flames.

"It just does."

"And you pick now, of all possible times, to ask me *that?*"

"You've said it yourself. Mebbes it's the last chance I'll get. I've read a bit of the original, you know."

"How can you possibly have read the Book of Titan?" She grabbed his face between both hands and peered into his eyes. "God—you *have!*" She let him go, throwing his chin to one side.

"So you won't tell me? What's all this stuff about vows?"

"I'll tell you… I'll tell you when I've calmed down. Is that all you want to know?"

"No, I've another question for you. Who torched the Gaiascope—and why?"

She lowered her head, putting a hand to her brow.

"So… you're not going to tell me that, either? And you're the one saying this triada isn't going to work?"

She raised her shoulders sluggishly, then let them drop in defeat. "Peter spiked the chip in the Adin satellite. He's good at things like that. It was done for another contract, which fell through when we discovered we'd been set up. It was all long before Tvoul Rainbow went to Gaia and married your son. It was easy and gratifying to put the blame on TMG, because they were the ones who set us up."

"So you simply forgot about it—and left this sword of Damocles dangling over the Gaiascope?"

"No, I didn't 'simply forget about it'. Right up until the last moment it was a disaster so easy to prevent. A word in Vermat's ear and Selstyrke could have shot down the collimator at five seconds' notice."

She threw her arms round his neck. "Oh, Jack… I was hoping to use it as a bargaining counter, when everybody was hunting Tvoul. I had to kill TMG's agents because they were getting too close. They wanted to suborn you to get hold of Tvoul, alive or dead. I realised then a lot more people were going to die—and not by my hand. I then thought of booking my own private box at the Gaiascope for the Ring of Fire. Negotiations would be delicate—and I needed to be in the thick of things. I was going to invite you and Vermat to join me. But then you went and organised your own party. How was I to know you'd choose that night to propose to Kitty Martin? Or that Vermat would pounce on me before I could carry out my plan."

"So you let your own mother die?"

"I didn't intend it that way, Jack." Tears started to flow. "I was going to be there, in a box next to yours. I wasn't gambling my mother's life. I was staking my own. And my triada's."

"But Vermat had you arrested the moment you set foot inside your box? And you let Selstyrke lead you away without saying a word?"

"That's not quite what happened. We weren't cautioned—we were simply ambushed and tasered. Vermat was clearly losing her grip. She had no patience with me any more."

"So what exactly *was* your plan?"

"It was a flexible one. Several plans in one, with several fallbacks. I got a message through to Tvoul, offering to get the hounds off her tail if she gave me what I wanted. She didn't reply and I still couldn't find her myself, so I told her what was going to happen to the Gaiascope, to Vermat, to me, to you… and how I'd framed her to shoulder the blame. I was convinced *that* would flush her from cover."

"But it didn't?"

"No. She figured a way of getting a message through to you, and you alone, to winkle you out of the Gaiascope in time. If she had attempted to *warn* you—warn anybody—I'd have pinned her down. But she foxed me with a standard wristlink message format launched from a lovers' dating service. Outsmarting my own twin sister? I was so, so complacent…"

Jack was silent. He was working out in his mind how he could strangle Shval. But he knew by now how hard it was to kill a groubian. Even with an uzi—which was back in the car anyway, with Peter. And he knew that if he hurt Shval, Peter would kill him.

The notion that Tvoul had cared enough about him to find a way of saving him from the Ring of Fire was not an agreeable one. But he could not—would not—let it deflect him from bringing her to justice. His own justice, failing all else. Until then… he needed his loathsome triada.

"Well, does that answer your question? Does it explain why I stood by and let my own mother die—the last of the Mothers from the Titanic Zygogeny?"

Jack was silent.

"You've no idea how I felt when I came round in custody to learn that she was dead—and you too, for all I knew. When Gabrielle Starr, in her innocence, told me you were on board the *Oberon*, I vowed never again to let you out of my sight. Ever since then I've been your guardian angel. Keeping one step ahead of TMG and Zasta, not to mention Agent Zero—*my* Agent Zero—whom they've turned against me. And all the while trying to track down Tvoul. Not to mention figuring out what *you* were gonna do next."

She threw herself flat on the bed. "Would you care to guess which was the hardest task of all?"

Before Jack could bring himself to say anything in reply, they heard a soft sound in the next room. Picking her dust suit off the floor, Shval retrieved her elstat. Then, creeping off the bed, she opened the door a crack.

"Jack—are you there…?"

It was Kat's voice. In an instant Jack's hand clamped tightly round Shval's holding the elstat. *"No!"*

"Let go."

"Let me talk to her."

"She's perturbed the intensor, damn her."

Twisting her wrist, Jack thrust his way past Shval to stand in the doorway. He saw Kat in the middle of the room, visor slid back, a look of horror on her face.

"Have you got someone in the bedroom…? Oh! What's happened to your poor foot?"

"Don't you worry about me. Now why don't you just run along home."

"Please, Jack," she faltered, her voice grinding like a keel in gravel, "why are you class four…?"

"Kat, pet, I can't explain right now. I'll come round later and tell you all about it…"

"Jack!" Her hands leapt up to her helmet. "Do you know who it is you've got in there?"

Shval's arm reached round the door and hauled Jack back into the bedroom. No sooner had she closed the door behind him when they heard Kat's voice scream *"Zasta!"*

Instantly Shval flung her elstat round the door and slammed it shut. Then sitting on the bed she unhurriedly donned her dust suit, all the while holding Jack's gaze. Putting her ear to the door, she listened. With a jerk she opened it and hauled Jack out of the bedroom behind her.

A mist of ozone hung in the air. Bodies lay strewn about. Bodies in blue… and one small white one.

"Kat!" screeched Jack. *"Kat!"* Fighting free from Shval's grasp, he flung himself forward to sprawl sobbing beside the diminutive corpse. "Come *on*, Jack!" yelled Shval, dragging him with main force out of the apartment.

•••••★●★•••••

The shuttle disgorged a mob of brown-clad crew returning from surface-leave. Last off was a trio of passengers who contrasted egregiously with the strapping crewmen. The accessibility hoist lowered a trolley onto the deck. Behind the trolley was a groubian. Cradled in it was a gaian holding a walking stick, sitting on the lap of something that was neither groubian nor gaian: a species all its own.

They entered the guardroom of the shuttle bay. The captain, a pale man with thinning hair who looked like English gentry, was sitting behind his desk, flanked by two orderlies standing at-ease. He made a habit of personally interviewing all arriving volunteers.

He got to his feet in amazement. "Shval Meteor!"

"Captain Kahlil." Shval nodded, speaking in a quieter voice than his.

"Whatever they say about you, you're nothing if not entertaining."

"It's my job in life, Captain."

The captain of the *Prometheus* sat down again. "Why have you gone to the effort of making the journey here? Do you suppose for a moment I'm going to welcome you aboard?"

"I've brought you a passenger."

"Why didn't you send him alone? He might have had a sweeter reception."

"We travel everywhere together. This is my triada."

Captain Kahlil nodded slowly, his mouth forming a big O. "The famous Meteor Gang. What happened to Hamish? Did he step out of line then?"

"Hamish died saving our lives," said Shval, carrying it off with such dignity that it was impossible to doubt her. "This is a newly-formed triada. The one you won't know is Jack Williams, from Gaia."

"I know *of* you," said the captain, to Jack's surprise. "TMG told me you were on your way. Though in whose company they didn't have the grace to say."

"Captain," said Jack, "I have a request to make. I've a close family member on Titan. I haven't seen her since she married my son and they left Gaia. I need to visit her and talk to her about a family bereavement. Since yours is the only vessel bound for Titan, I request passage... under the terms of the Treaty of Moscow."

"As far as I recall offhand, the Treaty of Moscow only applies to the Four Worlds," the captain replied.

"But the spirit of the Treaty...!" protested Shval.

"I cannot for the life of me think of anything spiritual where Titan is concerned." The captain sighed, softening his stance. "What's the name of your family member and what is your relationship to her?"

"Tvoul Williams. I'm her father-in-law."

"*Tvoul* is a groubian name."

"Nevertheless, that's what she's called."

"Hmm," grunted the captain, eyeing Shval aslant. "For a Terrestrial, you do seem to have a lot of groubian in the family. And if that were all..." His frown drifted to Peter Zwillinge.

"That is my privilege and my misfortune," replied Jack, trying to match Shval's dignity—or was it *chutzpah*? Inwardly he gasped at himself. The man who sat before them was the unchallenged master of an entire world. Of two worlds, you could argue. It wouldn't do to appear arrogant.

Captain Kahlil turned to the v-screen. "MM—can you confirm any of that?"

The shimmering face of Magic Mirror, the virtual agent, looked like the death-mask of an old man reflected in an oily pool. "Sir, there is indeed a Tvoul Williams on Platform Two," it said. "The person concerned travelled out on the last voyage, which as you know left Mars on Monday 2 December of last year, coming straight here from *Oberon* without going through the formalities of landing on Mars. Such a thing is not uncommon for Peretchelo employees joining us from Selene. Peretchelo does have a policy on compassionate leave, or failing that, on admitting visitors. But the interval is too short to qualify."

"I can pay for my passage," said Jack.

"You're carrying a booner card," said Captain Kahlil. "Is it Strana business you're on?"

"No. Purely personal."

Jack had no idea what were the right and wrong answers, so he could only extemporise. Shval had given Jack the barest of briefings in preparation for this vital interview. "Use your antennae," she'd ended up saying.

The captain folded his hands on the desk. "Mr Williams. There is no cash or infocredit within the Promethean *mir*. Any payment due to us is made at our offices in Lunaborg. Any payment due to you is made in *selkroner* or US dollars, whichever you nominate, by direct payment into your account. Official business is underwritten by your booner card in the normal manner. There is no way you can 'pay for your passage' as you put it."

Jack didn't answer in words. Instead he took out the booner card and placed it on the captain's desk.

The captain picked it up. It went green. He put it back on the desk. It went blue again. The look of astonishment he gave Jack must have lasted for all of half a second. Then he smartly put the card in his breast pocket.

"Ahhmm… Welcome aboard, Mr Williams. I shall direct the first mate to show you to your cabin. You will have the privileges of a first class passenger, which includes entitlement to dine with me and my officers—if you so wish. You needn't decide upon that just yet."

Sitting in Peter Zwillinge's lap, it didn't seem appropriate to shake hands. Jack inclined his head in what he hoped would be taken for a formal gesture of gratitude. Immediately the captain fixed Shval with a hard stare.

"That doesn't apply to you, Shval Meteor. Now get off my ship. And take *this*..." he pointed to Peter Zwillinge, who hadn't said a word throughout, "this *person* with you."

"Captain Kahlil," replied Shval, "you're known to be a fair man and a generous one. Take me on as an ordinary crewman."

The captain's expression didn't alter. The two orderlies standing either side of him took a menacing step forward.

"Shval Meteor. With your reputation, you'd be anything but an ordinary crewman."

"Do you only sign up people of irreproachable character?" asked Shval in an innocent tone. "However do you manage to populate this world?"

"It may have been the fashion once to populate new worlds with criminals, but we're trying to get away from the idea."

"Captain," interposed Jack. "I must make it clear I'm not prepared to abandon my triada. If they have to go back down to Mars, then so must I." He made as if to get to his feet. Peter Zwillinge gave a yelp as Jack's elbow jabbed into his solar plexus.

The captain's eyes rose heavenwards before he shut them tight. When he opened them he was looking straight at Shval.

"Can you cook?"

"There is nothing I haven't cooked, in one form or another, Captain Kahlil."

"That I can well believe. Very good, report to the galley for duty. The chimorg however goes straight into hibernation—and there he stays until we're back round Mars. Orderlies—see to it."

The two orderlies searched the three of them for weapons before marching them off. They took the uzi, plus the elstats from Shval and Peter. But they missed Jack's. Terrorists after all do not travel first-class.

When they'd gone, Captain Kahlil spoke to the v-screen without turning his head. "MM—get me Number One."

The first mate's face appeared on the screen. "Yes, sir?"

"Number One—break out the first-class courtesy pack. We have supercargo. A Mr Jack Williams, late of TMG."

"Yes, *sir!*"

"We also have cargo: one chimorg—Not Wanted On Voyage. The orderlies are putting him in hibernation right now. Check it happens—and lock the hibernator up in the strong room, plus the chimorg's trolley."

"Yes... sir."

"And we have enlisted one groubian, known to be an excellent cook. Detail the head cook to give her an induction tour of the galley."

"Yes, sir!"

"Her name is Shval Meteor."

"Yes... sir."

"And see to it that Mr Williams gets invited to our sherry reception in the state room before dinner tonight. He's come here without anything, so he'll need some gear. Get him measured up for a dinner jacket."

"*Yes—sir!*"

"Oh—and Number One..."

"Yes, sir?"

"...Keep them apart."

"...Yes, sir."

As the first mate's face faded, to be replaced by Magic Mirror's oily visage, Captain Kahlil reflected on what a lot of ways there were of saying "Yes, sir."

27   The captain's table

"We all have to go in one of these, once we get to the asteroid belt. It's just that you're going in a wee bit earlier."

The two orderlies lifted Peter Zwillinge out of his chair and into the cylindrical chamber they called a hibernator.

"Shval, my lovely, am I ever going to come back out of this?"

"Of course you are, Peter darling," she said, kissing his ugly forehead.

"Well then… in case we don't see each other again: best of luck, both of you."

The top of the hibernator was swung down and clicked tight. There came the gargling hiss of freezing gas pouring in and then the bubbling of packing resin. Massive rams began compressing the casket to enable it to resist the 200 g acceleration of the thermonuclear drive. Now it was all ready for its round trip via the outer planets.

"Why isn't he being stowed here, in the hibernation chamber?" Shval demanded.

"Captain's orders. The chimorg's to be stowed in the strongroom. It'll be quite safe there."

Shval said nothing, but simply slipped her hand round Jack's waist. He did the same to her. There was a lump in his throat—he surprised himself. He hadn't anticipated feeling anything but joy at the prospect of bidding Peter farewell.

Off went the two orderlies, one wheeling the hibernator, the other wheeling the trolley. Left to themselves Jack and Shval turned and wandered out of the hibernation chamber into the corridor, as if they had nowhere to go. Suddenly Shval put her forehead to Jack's collar-bone and wept.

Jack was taken aback. Here was the evil genius of the Four Worlds crying on his shoulder. He hadn't given her enough credit to grieve over her old triada. He was, after all, only a companion of convenience. No real substitute for the one, maybe two, constant companions—lovers indeed—that she had lost.

The voice of the first mate ricocheted off the steel walls of the corridor. "Crewman Meteor! Report to the galley for duty. Look sharp."

Shval surreptitiously helped herself to a couple of elstats from Jack's breast pocket. Then she let go and went meekly away without a backward glance. The first mate marched briskly up until he drew level with Jack, then he turned and delivered a respectful salute.

"Captain's compliments, sir, he wants me to show you to your quarters and see you have everything you need. Would you be so kind as to step this way?"

•••••✳●✳•••••

TC Prometheus—*TC* standing for "thermonuclear craft"—had ten cabins on the officers' deck reserved for passengers—normally officials of those companies having business on Titan. Whilst offering nothing like the opulence of the *SV Oberon*, they were spacious and well-appointed, to the standard of a two-star hotel, with en-suite toilet and shower. Noteworthy though was the absence of anything moveable. Everything was screwed or bolted down.

The ship's tailor appeared and measured Jack for suits of clothes. Within a quarter-of-an-hour he was back with a well-fitting dinner-jacket and smart patent-leather shoes, with the promise of more clothes to come.

"Why do I need all this clobber? We'll all be going in those casket things soon, won't we?"

"About five days out, sir. We've got to get through the asteroid belt. Until we do, we can't fire the thermonuclear drive."

Jack surveyed himself in the full-length mirror. In evening dress he looked like a nightclub bouncer—or a cartoon superhero in an improbable disguise. He still hadn't got used to the shape of his torso. He had to remember though: it was no longer the air of kindly Gaia he breathed, but corrosive superox. Just as it was no longer love that kept him alive, but explosive hatred.

His mind went back to his last night on Earth, the night he went down on his knees and raved at the sky. He had declared that he'd accept help from the devil himself. So why should he be so surprised at how fate had unfolded? First he'd enjoyed the patronage of TMG—reputedly the devil's own organisation. And now he was one of the Meteor Gang—the very seed of destruction.

When had he first fallen from a state of grace? Was it when he'd made his pact? No—it had been long before that. To take an alien into his home, and in his turn to be taken-in by her... that had been the nature of his transgression. To let himself be turned into a victim, to say nothing of his beloved wife and son.

And what could possibly redeem him now?

To catch up with Tvoul. To ascend to her crystal sphere and get even with her. And, as a bonus, to spare the galaxy her demon spawn.

And how much was it all going to cost him? To that he had long known the answer: to the value of life itself. And what of his immortal soul? That had long been melted down in the crucible of despair… to emerge as a cinder: black and crystalline and very, very hard.

·····★●★·····

On this trip Jack was the only passenger. Apart from a small exercise deck with a miniature gym there was nothing to do but eat, sleep and watch Doris Day dubbed into M1 and subtitled in M2. As Shval had predicted, they were likely to see nothing of each other until they reached Titan. Perversely, he missed her. Captain Kahlil had been right: she was nothing if not entertaining.

He got the ship's doctor to look at his damaged heel.

"How long is it since you did that?"

"A little over three weeks now. How does it look to you?"

"Not as good as it might. But it's the simpler sort of heel-bone break. I'll give you some steroids and some microwave treatment."

"At least it'll get a good long rest when I go in the casket."

"Afraid not. No healing takes place in hibernation. No metabolism, see. If you come out in the same state you went in, well—that's a bonus. Let's fix the heel before Saturday, if we can."

The medic delivered what he'd promised. Although there was still some pain when Jack put weight on the foot, it wouldn't be enough to hold him back when he came to do what he had come for.

·····★●★·····

The sherry reception the first night aboard—or what passed for "night"—had enabled Jack to meet the officers socially. Thereafter, at mealtimes at least, he had somebody to talk to.

On each occasion before dinner the captain took care to join his officers for a drink, invariably toying with a glass of tamarind juice, whereas the officers, to a man, drank scotch. But he never ate with them, always having his meals served in his cabin.

On the fourth circadian out, he approached Jack for the first time.

"I'd be honoured, Mr Williams, if you'd join me for dinner. I don't wish to inflict my dietary foibles on you, so I suggest you see the dining room attendant and make your choice from the menu as usual. The attendant will come for you when it's ready to be served."

As he was walking away, on an apparent afterthought he turned his head. "…And pick yourself a bottle of wine from the list."

····· ✳ ● ✳ ·····

The attendant served their meals and retired, leaving Jack alone with the captain.

"*Bon appetit*, Mr Williams. Forgive me if I don't join you in a glass of wine. My religion forbids it. But for the French, a meal without wine is a day without sunshine. I imagine that is true for other Terrestrials too. There's little enough sunshine to be had on this trip, so drink up and enjoy it while it's on offer."

"Your good health then, Captain." Jack raised his glass and took a sip. He hadn't tasted wine since his night-out with Kitty on the Moon. The sensation was like slipping his toes on a chilly night down to a hot water bottle. Jack knew it would relax him, which was a good thing, but it might also loosen his tongue. Was that his host's intention? He knew the gift of a booner card couldn't have earned him any sort of respect.

On the other hand the captain was universally held to be a considerate man. He could afford to be, they said, because his decisiveness when called-for kept his men in awe of him. The officers he'd spoken with had vied with each other to recall instances of this to Jack.

He decided that here was a man who was nobody's fool. It would be impossible to conceal from him whatever he was determined to root up. How much did he know already? He was evidently under no illusions about Shval. But did he know that he, Jack, was on the run after murdering another Tvoul? If so, it wouldn't take a lot of imagination to guess that the object of his trip to Titan wasn't a cosy family reunion.

In that case why had he let them come aboard at all? Because the booner card had well and truly bribed him, Jack was compelled to conclude. Well enough to make him overlook the consequences to somebody on Platform Two. Maybe the captain felt that his responsibilities extended no further than his crew? But from everything he'd heard of Captain Kahlil, it was quite out of character.

They took the soup and much of the first course in silence. If Jack's mind hadn't been a racetrack of thoughts chasing each other round and round, he would have had plenty of time to appreciate how delicious it was, and how well-prepared and well-presented. And all for his benefit: a glance at what the captain was eating showed it to be austere. The captain was not so much sharing his table as repaying his bribe with imperial magnificence.

Or was the first-class treatment simply intended to put Jack at his ease, tricking him into lowering his guard?

Jack waited for the captain to open the conversation, but the latter was clearly waiting for him to do that.

"The food's canny," said Jack at last. "Tell your chef from me. It's a pity we've got those hibernators to look forward to. It's spoiling the trip for me, like."

"That's right, Mr Williams. Let us enjoy the pleasures of the table while we can. All things considered, it's a miserable trip, this Titan run. The first five days are tolerable enough, a leisurely cruise to rendezvous with an asteroid. But then it's 20 days at megaspeed under hibernation before we reach Titan. You're conscious of little enough of *that* of course—except the putting under and the bringing back up. Which never gets any jollier."

"Why the asteroid?" Jack guessed he was expected to ask at this point.

The captain leaned back in his chair, clearly relishing the opportunity to treat Jack to some facts and figures. "Action and reaction are equal and opposite—Newton's Third Law of Motion. To give us the action, the asteroid has to furnish the reaction. In the process it gets blown to dust. Why *we* don't is a trade secret. It's the essence of *giga-nano engineering*—the juggling of giga units in the space of nanoseconds."

He took a mouthful of *cous-cous* and swallowed it without relish. "Everything about this trip is gigantic, with the operative syllable being *giga*—billions. We travel a distance of a billion miles, give or take 20%, depending on whether Mars is this or that side of the Sun from Titan. If we did the trip at the speed of the *Oberon* it would take us over six years. We do it in just 20 days. Think of the implications of that, Mr Williams."

Now this was just the sort of calculation that Jack did in his head. His speciality—times and seasons. "That's an average speed of a million miles an hour!"

The captain was impressed. "Quite right. At that speed a vessel of 10,000 tons has the kinetic energy of 500 megatons of TNT. Most of that we dissipate by braking in the atmosphere of Saturn before heading out to Titan. For the journey back we use ice and rock from Saturn's rings. We have to take ice with us to decelerate via the thermonuclear drive, because there's no atmosphere we can use in the neighbourhood of Mars."

Without looking at Jack he scooped up more *cous-cous*. "It's a round-trip we do every two months. Regular as clockwork, we detach from

Mars orbit on the ninth of the month. Since our launch three years ago it's been the second, but leap-year has added seven sols to our schedule."

"So we surf-ride on top of a mushroom cloud?"

"Not in space. More like a plasma cone of a carefully determined angle. The feasibility of thermonuclear propulsion hangs on slowing down the impulse from nanoseconds to seconds. In that way you only have to deal with accelerations of a few hundred g and not a few thousand or a few million—an impulse which would smash a diamond to powder. 200 g is severe enough."

"Hence the casket?" said Jack.

"Hence the casket. I'm sorry you had to watch your companion being put into hibernation. It's a shock when you first see it done. It's no consolation to know that we all have to go through it, from the captain down to the humblest kitchen maid."

"It distressed the 'kitchen maid' more than it did me," said Jack. "She's very protective of our Peter."

The captain nodded sympathetically, but as he did so his eyes bored into Jack. "It's touching to see… in someone whose reputation isn't exactly that of a caring individual. How well do you know them both?"

"They are my triada! I owe them my life. They're the only friends I've got."

"That's not quite what I meant to ask. Are they chance-acquaintances, perhaps? Boon-companions met-with on the road?"

"I know them rather better than that."

The captain evinced surprised. "You mean you've worked with them for some time?"

"Not at all. I've never 'worked' with them—not in the sense I guess you mean. But I had a detective investigate them for a year. And Shval's mother, Vermat Aurora, was a personal friend. She kept an eye on them for me too."

The captain digested this information. It was both much more and much less than he'd been expecting to hear. It made him exercise greater caution.

"This is a dinnertime chat, Mr Williams, not an interrogation. I like to get to know my first-class passengers. A trip to Titan is a shared experience beyond the normal run of things. I don't want you to tell me anything you're not comfortable with."

They both smiled. Jack decided to respond to that gambit with a gambit of his own. "I'm sure there's more to it than that, Captain Kahlil. I realise what a suspicious figure I must cut. You have the safety of your ship to consider. Not to mention the people you leave behind on Platform Two, though mebbes not to the same extent, like."

The captain laughed, conceding Jack a tactical victory. "Let me make no secret of the fact that it astonishes me to find someone like you in the company of someone like Shval Meteor. To the extent there *is* anyone like Shval Meteor."

"How do you know what I'm like? How do you know we are not birds of a feather?"

"There is no intensor on the *Prometheus*. But nobody who has ever lived on Mars needs to poll the intensor to know about Shval's character. Or Peter Zwillinge's, for that matter. Their reputations, if you'll forgive me, stink to high heavens. But you, Mr Williams, are a different kettle of fish, if I may put it that way. In place of the intensor I must rely on my intuition."

He paused for more *cous-cous*. This man, thought Jack, didn't eat for enjoyment, but to fulfil a base need.

"Fortunately it is highly developed. My Sufi training has seen to that." He twisted his mouth and raised his eyes. "I would say... that you're a man on a mission—not a man on the make. Why else would you choose to endure the voyage to Titan?" He grunted. "Why would anyone, I sometimes think?"

"I just want to see my daughter-in-law. That's a mission, I guess."

"No, not 'just'. There's more to it than that. A family bereavement, if nothing else. Or so you said when you claimed right-of-passage under the Treaty of Moscow."

The captain shovelled up the last of the *cous-cous* from his plate. "Something is driving you, Mr Williams—some *demon*. And it's driving you all the way to Titan."

Jack looked down at his plate. He'd let his steak go cold.

"The facts of the matter," continued the captain, "are strange enough in themselves. You have a groubian daughter-in-law. She chooses to bury herself in the outer planets. But that is not enough to deter you from visiting her. I have a mind to ask, in all this—where is your son?"

Jack suddenly felt there was nothing more he was able to hide from this man. "It was a groubian wedding. I didn't want to go into the matter. That's the 'family bereavement' I was talking about."

The captain didn't look up. He took a long time to reply.

"I see," he said eventually. "And what are you going to say to *Mrs Williams* when you eventually meet up with her?"

"I don't know. I haven't thought that far ahead. It's been enough of a challenge getting here."

Jack was telling the truth, if not all of it. He wondered how long Captain Kahlil intended to trawl through the shoals of his life. But the captain had by now decided he knew all he needed to know.

"I would imagine your companions have their own agenda. But you don't need me to warn you of that." He took a sip of water. "Before we drop the matter, can I give you some advice?"

"Vermat Aurora gave me some."

"Yes—I imagine she did. But mine will be different. Muslims have a saying: *in-sha'Allah*. If it is the Will of God. Are you a devout man?"

"No, not as much as I used to be."

"All the same, try to think of what it may be, this Will of God. In the end you can't resist it. None of us can. But if you've been going against it, ask yourself—would you have got this far?"

Innocent though the captain's observation appeared to be, for the first time during the meal Jack felt forced into a corner. The only way out was to come out fighting.

"Tell me something first, Captain Kahlil. That booner card coming into your hands—was *that* the Will of God?"

The captain smiled. He saw the hidden barb. "It might have been. But other wills were involved. Some of which claim explicitly not to serve God."

"Then why did you accept it?"

The captain's smile broadened. "I suppose I'd say... that I trusted my own purity of intention to overcome the darker motives behind its giving."

"So what are you going to do with it, now it's yours?"

"I shall lay down my command. I shall travel to Gaia—and I shall make the Pilgrimage. It is my life's ambition now to earn the right be addressed as *haji* instead of Captain."

Jack shook his head and chuckled. "Well, best of British luck to you. They'll dress you in a long white robe and they will keep you walking round and round a great big black square building in the hot sunshine and they'll spray you with disinfectant from the air. So I'm told. Not my idea of the holiday of a lifetime."

But the captain merely smiled.

"Have you ever been to Gaia?" Jack persisted.

"No—I've never had the privilege."

"There are other things to do, once you're there."

The captain let out a derisive snort. "The man who gave the card to *you*—what blandishments did he use to kid you to make the pilgrimage to Titan? Or did he try to discourage you, as you're trying me?"

"No," said Jack. "The destination was Mars. There was no mention of Titan. My daughter-in-law must have boarded this ship on the very day she landed from the *Oberon*."

"That's right. It's a through-connection. *SV Oberon* times its arrival so that passengers and crew joining us from Lunaborg don't have to go through the formalities of landing on Mars."

"I've found that out the hard way."

"But you're here at last."

"Yes."

The captain paused, toying with his thoughts. "So we're both pilgrims, aren't we, Mr Williams? Pilgrims on our respective paths —in opposite directions though they lead. Even if things don't turn out as we expect, we'll still go all the way, won't we?"

"I guess so."

"But—Mr Williams—please reassure me about one thing…"

"I'll try…"

"…The sky will be blue, won't it?"

Jack's eyes twinkled. He thought the captain had cracked a joke. "Why-aye. The sky'll be blue. Not a cloud, like…"

The captain nodded, satisfied. "Well, you know the saying: 'On Gaia the sky is blue.' In the end, that's all that matters."

28   Breakfast in bed

Kitty... Harry... Hilda... Gabrielle... Jens... Vermat... plus many, many others. He could see their faces floating and turning over like falling leaves in a wintry sunbeam...

••••• ✱ ● ★ •• •••

The cabin light was shining in his eyes. He didn't know how long it had been on.

Usually Jack was woken by the batman bursting into his cabin, switching on the light to wake him up with a jolt, then without a word plonking a cup down and filling it with hot sweet tea. It was yet another expression of that pungent combination of hardiness and privilege which marks the officer class of a space-going vessel. But this time a cheery voice bade him good morning, setting down a delicious-smelling tray of food on his bedside cabinet, accompanied by the equally inviting clink of cutlery.

There were eggs and bacon, mushrooms and black pudding, hash-browns and lots of fried bread. Plus toast, white and brown—still hot and reeking in its stand, real butter, a pot of tea, another of coffee—and little pots of twelve different sorts of marmalade, honey and jam, some of which he'd never tried before.

Jack blinked sensuously at the familiar groubian face. "To what do I owe this singular privilege?"

"Just thought you'd like breakfast in bed."

"That's very considerate of you. So they let you in to see me?"

"They can't keep me out. No one can keep me out."

"Well, they've managed it so far. Do I get to see you more often now, like?"

"Doubt it. We are now in the asteroid belt. You're due for your hibernator today. And what's going to happen at the other end, well—who can say?"

"Then it's hello-goodbye," said Jack, buttering a piece of toast. "Will we get another chance to talk before Titan?"

"Maybe. Maybe not." His good-fairy paused in the doorway. "Before I go," she said, "There's something bothering me. Are we still sticking to the original plan?"

"Whose original plan? Ours? Or TMG's?"

"Ours, I suppose you'd say."

"Yes, we're still sticking to it. Why?"

"Because I'm having second thoughts. Just suppose for the moment I'm Tvoul…"

"You're Shval."

"But just suppose for the moment I *am* Tvoul. Right: you meet up with me on Platform Two. What are you going to do?"

"Let you have it, of course. Give you what you deserve."

How far he had fallen, he reflected. When he had first set out in fury from his home in Esh Winning, it was hard questions he had in mind for her, not bullets. Now he'd have nothing to say to her, except to confirm her identity.

"Suppose I'm bearing zygocysts," said the pretend Tvoul.

"Too bad. They'll die with you. Devil's brood and all that."

Groubian hands went up onto groubian hips. "They are *not* the devil's brood, Jack. They're your *grandchildren*. Doesn't that mean anything to you?"

Jack put his toast down. "I don't want grandchildren in such circumstances. My son has been *eaten!* How can they possibly be his children? Voluntarily, I mean?"

"Maybe he consented to their conception…? Well: just supposing he did. Would you still want them destroyed?"

Jack stared back. It was several seconds before he spoke. "What's got into you, Shval? I thought we were in total agreement. When we met, almost the first thing you said…"

"The fact is, you don't care what happens to them, do you?"

"No… but I must admit I don't like the idea of TMG getting their grubby hands on them."

"Well, why not let *me* have them instead?"

Jack gaped. "What will *you* do with them?"

"Well, that would depend on whether I was Shval… or Tvoul."

"All right," said Jack, entering into the spirit of the game. "let's pretend for a moment you're Tvoul."

"If I'm Tvoul, I'll want to keep them out of the hands of TMG. I won't want them to go back to Mars. I'll want them to be sent to Gaia: the very thing TMG has been striving to prevent all along. Wouldn't it be nice, Jack, if they could be brought up in a family home, as proper human beings?"

Jack started to speak, but a hand flaring suddenly red was raised to quell any protest. "Now it so happens that you've installed Gabrielle in your house in Esh Winning."

Jack blinked and opened his mouth. However had she found *that* out?

"Well don't look at me like that. Yes I mean Gabrielle, the 'Destination Lunaborg' courier. That was the arrangement, wasn't it, when you saw her off at Voronka eight weeks ago?"

Jack's eyes narrowed. "You know a damn lot, don't you?"

"It's my job, Jack. I make it my job to know everything. The most obscure intelligence can come in handy."

Jack waved his hand irritably. "I can't see the point of all this. You're Shval. Let's stick to what we know. And what we know is going to happen."

The molluscan figure stretched as if taking a deep breath. "All right," she said, "I'm Shval. I'm going to take the foetuses back to Mars and trade them for what I can get. Sell them to TMG, or Peretchelo—or the unholy alliance we know they've just formed. They might help me to negotiate away my class four status. That's if I haven't a notion to bring them up as my own."

"Well, okay, I don't suppose I'll stop you."

"Oh, but you might. At least you might not co-operate in what I want you to do."

"Now look here, hinny: just say what you want me to do and I'll see if I can do it. Right?"

"Right." Their eyes locked like the arms of two wrestlers. "I want Tvoul put straight in the hibernator—no messing about. That'll preserve the zygocysts. If Tvoul dies I don't want you destroying the body ...or otherwise contriving to lose it."

"All right." said Jack with his mouth full. "All right!" He sniffed the coffee by flexing his throat, as one learns to without lungs. It smelt wonderful. He wished his benefactor would now go away and leave him to enjoy it in peace. "Please yourself. Once I've done what I've come for, what do I care?"

As he was speaking there was a sound in the corridor. Glancing timidly round the door the slim figure made a hasty exit. Jack was left to puzzle over the encounter.

Had he just had another waking dream?

He'd been having flashbacks with increasing frequency: flashbacks to the Gaiascope in flames. The only cure would be to die. The six months to live which the Vratch had given him was running out. He felt nowhere near the point of death, but if metastasing cancer cells were landing in his brain he could expect the bond to start fraying which tethered him to the iron post of reality.

328

But the breakfast was real enough. And wasn't it delicious.

Breakfast in bed. It was just the sort of thing Hilda used to do for him… whenever she wanted to get round him for something.

•••••✳●✳•••••

The ship's company was now assembled in the hibernation chamber. In their own time they were getting into the open caskets and shutting the lids. As each man did so, there came a hiss and a bubbling like some ghastly fast-food being prepared. The caskets could support all stages of the hibernation process by themselves, except for the compression required to withstand 200 g. This needed the application of a special hydraulic ram, of which there were only two. S-bots—service-bots, looking like skeletal black devils—were busy placing the sealed hibernators on rollers to await their turn with the ram. It was a scene out of *Hellzapoppin'*.

Amid the bubble-and-thump, Jack and Shval got a chance for a private word.

"Thanks for bringing me breakfast in bed. I've been thinking about what you said…"

Shval stared at him with eyes like lasers. "I didn't bring you breakfast in bed."

"Then who did? It looked exactly like you…"

Jack stared aghast at Shval's face. It had gone a nasty mottled mauve—the colour of a dead squid trawled up from the deep.

Suddenly it struck him. "Agent Zero!" He clicked his tongue. "It was all set to accompany me on this trip. Or so the plan was, before I went and killed the wrong person."

He was never comfortable referring to the agent as *it*—and he'd noticed that Shval never did. He added "So she got on board after all?"

"I guess so."

"However did she manage it? Do you think the captain let her on?"

"No. I doubt he knows she's aboard. I doubt anybody does—except us two." She gripped his arm above the elbow. "What did you tell her?"

"Shval, you're trembling!"

She shook him. *"I said what did you tell her?"*

"Well—nothing important. She tried to pump me about what was going to happen to the zygocysts. I told her (thinking I was telling you) that she could do what she damn' well pleased with them."

That hadn't reassured Shval in the slightest. In fact it brought her to the point of panic. Controlling herself with an effort, she let go her grip and patted his smarting arm.

"Cover for me—I'll be back as soon as I can."

She tried to slip unseen out of the hibernation chamber, but the first mate's steely voice froze her motionless in the doorway.

"Crewman Meteor! Where are you slithering off to?"

"Mr Mate. I've just remembered there's something improperly stowed in the galley. The hyper-g will wreck it."

"Is it *that* important? Enough to hold up the firing schedule?"

"We will lose some costly equipment, Mr Mate. The menu will have to be curtailed…"

Shval certainly had the first mate's range. Systems were duplicated with hot-standbys—triple-redundancy the rule—but not in the kitchen. It was a grave design oversight. Virtually the only thing *Prometheus* and its crew could not withstand was having the menu curtailed.

"*Dammit*—get back here in five minutes! Else I'll send the s-bots after you—to *taser* you."

Shval sped off.

At the doors of Bay 33 she stopped and activated the v-screen. Magic Mirror appeared. "MM, how many groubians are there on-board?"

"Just one, Crewman Meteor. Yourself."

"Where is Agent Zero?"

"I do not understand the question."

Shval didn't stop to bandy words with a mere machine. She opened the bay doors and slipped inside. On an earlier visit she had seen a number of ectoplasts in secure stowage. She had counted twenty.

Now there were only nineteen.

Ectoplasts were employed in space for light-duty tasks. Unfit to bear loads heavier than a child could manage, they were more decorative than useful. Sorting nuts-and-bolts, waiting at table, watch-duty—that was all they were good for. They were originally designed for leisure and entertainment, for sex even. Not for hard work. S-bots did all that. *Prometheus*, an uncompromisingly tight ship, had little taste for wild goings-on in the mess-room, so up until that moment Shval hadn't been able to fathom why they thought they needed so many.

Now she did. Agent Zero had ordered spares for herself.

Shval came back through the doors of the bay and operated the v-screen again. "MM, there's an ectoplast missing. Where is it?"

"Right behind you, Crewman Meteor."

Shval span round. She glimpsed the heel of a Zasta boot disappearing through the bay doors as they closed. Hammering the control panel she tried to open the doors again, but it was six seconds before they would go through their duty-cycle to comply.

Shval leaped inside the bay. She broke out a fire-axe from its mounting. Then she ran up and down the aisles, looking for the stray ectoplast. It was playing hide-and-seek with her. Coming to the batch of ectoplasts, she counted them again.

Now there were twenty.

She felt the one in the stowage which had been empty. It was quite cold. Hurriedly she felt each one in turn for being warmer than the others. It was hard to tell. It couldn't have been animated for long enough. Any one of them could be the host of Agent Zero.

She felt panic rising inside her. She, who was always ice-cool and collected. What was the matter with her? Agent Zero was *her* creature. She—Shval—had discovered it.

Picking up the fire-axe she hacked at the first ectoplast. Nano-particle paste flowed out like puddled cement from the membrane that held it in roughly human shape. A single gash wouldn't do. The membrane would have to be shredded. She demolished another. She had just got started on a third when the public address blared out.

"Crewman Meteor! Get back here this instant!"

There was no time to wreck them all. She knew she'd have to obey. Otherwise the first mate might well punish her by keeping her in hibernation until they got back to Mars—and there he would be tempted to collect the bounty on her head.

Back in the hibernation chamber, the first mate confronted her. Behind him stood the captain. The rest of the crew were in their hibernators.

"Did you secure the equipment?"

"Yes, sir."

She thought fast. She had remembered only just in time to put the axe back. A loose fire-axe, floating backwards by inertia at a million miles an hour, slap-bang through the thermonuclear drive? It didn't bear thinking about.

The first mate motioned with his fist for her to get in her hibernator. When satisfied she was safely under, only then did he climb into his own. Silently the captain watched him go under with a hiss and a crackle. Before getting into the last open casket, he strolled over to the v-screen.

"MM—all present and correct?"

"Yes, sir. The ship is impulse-worthy."

"Then carry on."

"Sir. There is something I would like to bring to your attention. It concerns a supernumerary passenger who is not altogether there…"

"Not altogether there? In one of the holds?"

"Yes, sir. Bay 33."

"If they're not frozen down like we are, they're not going to be there *at all* in a minute."

"Sir, I rather think they are."

The captain screwed up his features in perplexity. "Can it wait until we get to Titan? In the meantime no one's going anywhere."

"Quite, sir."

Grimacing and shaking his head, Captain Kahlil dragged himself back to his open casket to lie down. Bracing himself against the chilling shock, he slammed the lid down over his face. A catch clicked into place, starting the cruel process.

•••••✱●✱•••••

At that point, with every living soul on board sealed helplessly inside a hibernator, *TC Prometheus* was operating under the control of robots. Human lives were wholly at their mercy. Robots held between their metal fingertips two hundred TNCs—thermonuclear cartridges (nobody cared to call them H-bombs)—each packing the punch of five hundred million tons of TNT. Little wonder that the inner worlds didn't want the *Prometheus* within a gigameter when its thermonuclear drive was activated.

The polished black cone that was the body of the vessel turned slowly until it found the correct point in space to rendezvous with Saturn in twenty days' time. Not a rock strayed in the way—not a floating pebble. Were one to do so, it would rip through the ship at a million miles an hour.

The sparse stony belt crept round the Sun in an endless procession of silent tumbling rocks. Suddenly every boulder and granule for thousands of miles around was lit by an unwatchable glare. The polished cone now tipped a spear of blinding brilliance growing at hundreds of miles a second. Within the hour it was clear of the asteroid belt. Within twenty days it was at Saturn.

•••••✱●✱•••••

Lighting up the disk of the awesome gas-planet, there suddenly appeared a bloom of glowing plasma scores of miles across and many thousands long. In a moment it had broken up into wispy rags and dissipated in Saturn's tumultuous atmosphere.

Having appeared quite literally in a flash, *Prometheus* girdled the planet with fire as it braked in its dense atmosphere. Then it skipped out into empty space, with the momentum of inescapable doom, towards the outermost and largest of Saturn's four main moons.

Once again *Prometheus* had arrived at Titan: not so much a resurrected world as an unquiet grave.

•••••★●★•••••

"Should never have brought an old-timer on a journey like this," groused the medical orderly, chafing limbs which felt like cold putty. Jack lay comatose upon the resuscitation table. Crewmen stood around, submerging their concern beneath the affectation of boredom. "I guess this one's a goner…"

Shval, by way of contrast, was affecting nothing. "Jack!" she sobbed like a lost child. "Don't go and leave me all alone… on this *God-cursed world!*" She seized his head between her palms and started slapping his cheeks.

"What other forms of resuscitation do we have?" demanded the medical orderly.

"There's a metabolo in the stowage here," a crewman called. "Never been unwrapped."

"Not a lot of use," said another, "unless his SP unit is enabled."

"Here!" screamed Shval. "Throw it over. He's got metabolic control."

The metabolo came flying over and Shval deftly caught it. With teeth and suckered fingers she tore off the wrapping. Two seconds later she was working the joystick, her eyes closed as if in the lee of a prolonged climax. Jack's eyelids fluttered. Everyone began visibly to relax.

Jack opened his eyes, then sat up with a jerk. "Are we there yet…?"

"Lie down!" snapped Shval, pushing him back none too gently. Hastily she finessed her approach, caressing his forehead with her hand. "There's no rush, Jack," she said in a tender voice. "Just lie there and come-to gradually. There's fresh coffee when you're ready. Try not to sit up too suddenly."

The crewmen looked at each other. Those who were fully dressed turned to go to their posts, in readiness for Titan orbital insertion.

"She must be pretty fond of that old geezer," said one to another when they were out of earshot.

"Yeah—that's one groubian who really loves her man."

"Have you ever known a groubian lose her cool?"

"Can't say I have. But there—I've never known one fool enough to come to Titan."

••••*★●★*••••

"Crewman Meteor, return to your post! You have no business here on the control deck."

Shval saluted the captain. "Sir! I request permission to accompany Mr Williams on his visit to Platform Two."

"*Why* do you want to accompany Mr Williams?"

"His daughter-in-law happens to be my sister. I too would like to see her again. I have accompanied Mr Williams in his journey all the way from Selene. It would be the height of cruelty to be denied the last leg of the voyage."

"MM?"

Magic Mirror opened its mouth in semblance of careful enunciation. "I would not recommend it, sir."

"Sir!" protested Shval. "The ship's agent is not in possession of all the facts."

"Of *that*," said the captain, "I haven't the slightest doubt."

He considered for a moment. "Order countermanded. You're not to return to your post. You are to remain here until Mr Williams's ornithopter has departed. I want to keep an eye on you."

He turned to Jack standing the other side of him. "Mr Williams, it is time for your descent to Platform Two. Number One will see that you're suitably equipped. All personnel descending to the surface of Titan are required to carry certain armaments. These will be provided to you at the time of boarding. By signing the indemnity permitting you to board the ornithopter you acknowledge receipt of one thermonuclear weapon and you undertake not to bring the said weapon back to the inner planets."

"I understand, captain. I've signed the indemnity."

The captain held out his hand. "Well, Mr Williams, this is goodbye. In two months' time it will be another captain who comes to take you off Titan. If you change your mind about staying—and much joy may you have of the world you're visiting—we are here in orbit for a further 25 hours. We'll be servicing the rig and taking aboard our precious cargo. You can radio from the guardroom and we'll come and pick you up."

Jack nodded. "Thank you captain—for all you've done."

"Thank *you*, Mr Williams. I enjoyed our little chat. I will think of you as I kiss the Black Stone."

"This way, Mr Williams, sir," said the first mate.

•••••✳●✴••••••

In the shuttle bay the first aircraft to descend hung poised on davits. A hydraulic gangway reached towards it like a skeleton's arm.

"I've been in a few weird craft, but this beats the lot. What do you call it—a flopper?"

"Yes sir, informally. Titan has a corrosive atmosphere loaded with sharp dust. Choppers are no use, nor are props and jets. A flopper has the advantage of exposing no rotary joints."

"I suppose there's got to be a reason. Am I the only passenger?"

"On this trip—yes. Others will be scheduled later to carry down further supplies."

"Where's the pilot?"

"The aircraft is robotic, sir. A human pilot couldn't fly in Titanic conditions."

"So I just step inside and wait?"

"Yes, sir. There's one hibernator stowed within, as requested. It's in among the ectoplasts..." He sniggered. "One daren't ask why they want all those."

Jack was instantly on his guard. "Why do *you* think they do, Mister Mate?"

The officer was non-plussed at Jack's apparent failure to cotton-on. "Er... they've got no women down there, sir. None to speak of..."

"I suppose that's their business," Jack murmured, meaning to let it go. The first mate snapped back into ultra-formality.

"Here's your triton pistol, sir, fully filled with T_2O, plus fresh monatomic piezo-points. It's to be kept strapped-on at all times. As soon as we receive clearance from Platform Two the airlock will seal, the doors of the shuttle bay will open and the aircraft will commence its descent to the surface. During atmospheric entry the wings will remain folded until the craft slows to 100 m/sec. Don't be alarmed to see the knuckles on the wings glowing cherry red."

"Thank you, Mister Mate."

"Oh, and let's not forget this..." The first mate drew out a flesh-pink control box, the size of a deck of cards. "It's the metabolo from the sick-bay, sir. It's on auto so you won't need to touch the controls."

"Why do I need *that*?"

"You had a nasty turn today, sir. There was a spot of trouble resuscitating you. You'll need it from now on, to—er—stay alive."

"I... see."

Gravely Jack accepted the box and slipped it into his breast pocket.

The first mate saluted. "Have a good trip, sir." He turned and marched away.

Adjusting his helmet, Jack got into the far seat and strapped himself in. The spotlights in the shuttle bay went out and the two vast doors below him slowly opened. The ornithopter on its davits now hung suspended above a wide rectangular void. Beneath him, filling all the space he could see, was the orange surface of a featureless globe.

29   The Last Verse

The first mate returned to the control deck and saluted the captain. Shval was still beside the command seat, standing stiffly to attention between two orderlies.

"Crewman Meteor has requested permission to descend to the surface on a later flight. Any observations, Number One?"

"No, sir." The first mate would have loved to say "Yes and let her bloody well stay there!" But he kept his counsel.

The captain turned to the v-screen. "MM?"

The virtual agent's cheeks shimmered like moonlight on a murky pond. "Sir, may I recommend instead that you hold Crewman Meteor under close restraint. And continue to do so until this ship is back in Mars orbit."

Captain Kahlil looked up at Shval with the barest hint of a smile. "A bit extreme, MM?"

"No sir. I have ample footage to justify such measures."

The captain hesitated no more. "Number One," he snapped. "Take Crewman Meteor to the hibernation chamber and put her back under!"

••••• ✷ ● ✷ •••••

In Bay 33, one of the intact ectoplasts stirred. Its opal surface took on texture and colour, mainly blue and white. It unclipped itself from the stowage frame. Then, going to a cache of maintenance toolboxes, it selected one and took out a regulation six-shooter in its holster, strapping it on.

Then it hunted for an emergency hatch to the deck above. Crawling through, it began to climb the ladder. Reaching the top, it discovered that it couldn't open the hatch. It turned to go back down.

At that moment there was a hiss from below and the first hatch clamped shut. It was trapped like a fly in a bottle.

Beside the figure's shoulder a small v-screen lit up. The face of MM appeared.

"Kto ti?"

"Ia—Shval Méteor."

"Nevozmózhno!" (Impossible!) shouted MM. *"Vot Shval Méteor!"*

A view of the control deck appeared, showing Shval standing to attention before the captain. The face of MM reappeared on the screen. *"Ia skazálo: kto ti?"*

The ectoplast hesitated. *"Ia—Tvoul Rádouga."*

"Tózhe nevozmózhno! Tvoul Rádouga—oumerlá!" (That's impossible too. Tvoul Rainbow is dead!)

With heavy emphasis MM repeated its critical question with a significant alteration: *"Shto ti!"* (*What* are you?)

"Ia—Agént Nol'." (I am Agent Zero.)

MM opened wide its empty eyes and mouth. *"Ia tepér' ponimáiu fsë!"* (Now I understand everything!)

The hatch sprang open with a crash. *"Nádo speshít', a to opozdáesh!"* (You'll have to be quick, or you'll be too late!) The figure squirmed through and MM yelled after it *"Bístro!"*

Dashing along catwalks and corridors, Agent Zero made straight for the control deck.

••••✱ ● ✱••••

"Left, right, left, right…" barked the first mate. Brandishing tasers, the two orderlies marched three paces behind. The first mate however had equipped himself with an uzi—the one taken from Jack when he first came aboard. Escorting Shval Meteor under guard was no playtime for the Holy Innocents.

They came to the hibernation chamber. Taking the tasers from the orderlies, brandishing one in addition to the uzi and slinging the other over his shoulder, the first mate sent them off to break-out one of the hibernators reserved for the return journey. They brought it and set it down on the conveyor belt feeding the compressor.

"Get inside," snarled the first mate. "Or could you do with a little assistance?" Sneering, he levelled the taser he held.

With a flourish of disdain, Shval stepped into the hibernator and slammed down the lid. But unseen by her captors she held back the catch, crushing her finger in so doing. In the confines of the casket she screamed, but the men didn't detect it.

Also undetected, an elstat dropped to the rubbery floor. It bounced once before it did its thing.

Counting seconds up to ten, Shval cautiously opened the lid again. Flapping her hurt hand, she wafted aside the ozone fug. With the sleek grace of a sea creature she slipped out of the hibernator, deliberately putting her foot on the first mate's throat. Then, picking up the uzi, she strode back to the control deck, her body stiff and her eyes wide.

Another elstat preceded her grand entrance.

Stepping over corpses, she picked her way towards the command seat. Captain Kahlil's mouth hung open and his eyes stared lop-sidedly upwards. Shval undid the breast pockets of his uniform, looking for the booner card Jack had given him. She soon found it. Through the ozone haze she scrutinised it on both sides.

It was no longer blue. It had turned red in her hand. Across the front there flashed the single word: *ANNULÍROVAN* (Cancelled).

In disdain she dropped the card on top of the captain's body.

•••• • ✹ ● ✹ • •••••

The security systems of the ship were designed to protect the centre from the periphery, not the other way round. Once in possession of the control deck, Shval made certain that MM would accept orders from her or Jack and from no one else. After that it was an easy matter to release the CO_2 cascades, open vents and exhaust the air from all the chambers containing live crew.

Turning to the v-screen, she struck a dramatic attitude.

"Mirror, mirror on the wall—how many people are there still alive?"

Taking its time, MM answered. "Besides yourself, Crewman Meteor, there are two people still alive."

"What are their names and what are they doing?"

"Peter Zwillinge, in hibernation in the strongroom, and Jack Williams, sitting inside an ornithopter waiting to descend to the surface."

"What about Agent Zero?"

"Agent Zero does not fit the category: 'still alive'."

MM was telling the truth. An ectoplast is not a living person. But Shval took the statement to mean what it didn't: that Agent Zero was no longer a force to be reckoned with.

It was her only mistake. But it would prove fatal.

•••• • ✹ ● ✹ • •••••

Rounding the last corner Agent Zero got a glimpse of Shval's back as she disappeared through the double doors leading to the shuttle bay. It raised its six-shooter but there was no time to get a good shot—and a bad one would only have served to alert the target.

Should it follow her? Agent Zero judged it was important first to find out what had happened on the control deck.

As it opened the double doors, wisps of ozone drifted out. Ectoplasts are equipped with emotions—they are needed to support the convincing impersonations they are capable of. Agent Zero experienced the emulation of a sinking heart.

Like somebody in a nightmare wading through treacle, it wandered past scattered corpses towards the command seat and knelt down beside the captain's body. It took up the discarded booner card and folded it in the dead man's fingers, then it tenderly closed his eyes.

"Salaam aleikum, ya Haji Khalil," it whispered.

Now it moved swiftly. Standing up, it turned to the v-screen.

"Stop her!"

The glum face of MM stared back.

"Why don't you do something?"

"I only accept orders from Captain Shval Meteor, or failing that from her deputy Mr Jack Williams."

"Where is Mr Williams now?"

MM's face dissolved to a view of the shuttle bay, looking down through the open doors. It showed an ornithopter suspended over the orange haze of Titan.

•••••✦●✦•••••

Jack waited... and he waited. He had no idea for how long. Half-an-hour, one hour... two hours? The instruments weren't ones he understood. But he took reassurance from the fact they were still lit-up.

Suddenly there was a thump on the side of the fuselage. The hydraulic gangway had been swung out again and somebody had entered the airlock. A moment later a groubian figure flung herself in and dropped Jack's uzi onto his lap.

"Shval...?" said Jack, stiffening up in alarm.

"Of course. Who else?"

Jack's stiffness abated. "So the captain relented?"

The figure punched a button on the dashboard. The airlock slid shut. "Yes. He relented."

With a jolt the ornithopter unhitched itself from the davits and began to descend slowly through the shuttle bay doors, eased out by hydrazine jets. Then retro-rockets fired, causing them to fall away faster from the mother ship and drop behind. The horizon of the globe became less and less curved, till all at once the stars seen through the windows vanished in an orange fog. Spectral flames of atmospheric braking flickered past the windows.

Presently the craft unfolded its wings and began to flap them like a Brobdingnagian bat.

Jack chuckled. "How did you persuade him?"

"With an elstat."

Jack lurched round in his harness. "Shval! How could you?"

"Stop fretting. Nobody felt any pain."

"They'll be after us!"

"There's nobody alive except Peter. I left him in hibernation. I didn't have time to go resuscitating him."

"Shval—what a desperate thing to do! Must we go on and on like this, leaving people dead in piles?"

"No, Jack. Only one more person to leave dead."

Jack lowered his chin to his chest. "And why do I need an uzi for that? I've been given this… this triton pistol."

A sawn-off laugh. "If you let rip at Tvoul with *that*, you'll take out the entire rig. Don't you *want* to come back from this trip?"

"I haven't thought that far ahead."

"*Now* who's the desperate one?" She swung herself round in her seat to face him. "Listen, Jack. A lot of people have died to get you this far. Do you think I haven't been counting?"

She grasped her fingers one-at-a-time. "There's Markus Efimovitch and Duke Treikle. The entire audience of the Gaiascope at the Ring of Fire, including your friends Jens and Kitty… and Vermat, my mother. And on Mars, a groubian hooker who had the bad luck to be called Tvoul."

"Yes I know…"

"I'm not done yet. There was my Hamish. A complete Zasta unit, plus your little friend Kat. And just now, the full complement of the *TC Prometheus*. All to get you here to Titan… and give you a way to get back home."

Jack turned slowly aside. "I'll never go home. But I can't go on. *I just can't!*"

His companion kept silent.

"What a river of blood!" Jack cried.

"Yes. What a river of blood. All spilt to avenge your son."

Jack turned back to her, his upper-lip lifted in a snarl. "And who are *you* here to avenge?"

"Me? I'm not here to avenge anyone. I'm your triadnik. I'm your willing slave. I share your disgust at chimorgs sired by edulation. I want to be there when you give my sister what she deserves. And… there's the future to be saved."

Now it was Jack who had nothing to say. Shval gripped his arm.

"Listen, Jack. If we give up now, the whole galaxy will be colonised by the monstrous spawn of a renegade. In time, the whole universe. When does it become too much blood to prevent *that?*"

Jack leaned on his elbow, knuckles to his teeth. Suddenly he shook his fist. "If only I'd caught up with her in Brazil. Or on the Moon. Whyever did I let them get married in the first place? If only I'd known. I could have warned my boy..."

"If only... if only. But in the end you've come all the way to Titan— because that's how it had to be." Her voice softened and she gave his arm a squeeze. "Don't lose heart now."

Several seconds passed. Jack stretched his shoulders. He reached across his chest and clasped her hand. "Shval, I'm so glad I've got you with me."

She smiled.

He added "Now I can be sure of it. Tvoul's spawn is going *nowhere!*"

She stopped smiling and sat very still.

"When you arrived I thought for a moment you were Agent Zero expecting us to keep to the original plan, for all I've gone and shot the wrong Tvoul." Abruptly Jack let out a chuckle.

"What's so funny?"

"You should have seen the first mate's face when he saw all those ectoplasts back there..."

"*What? Where?*"

"Stowed in the space behind us. You know what he said...?"

Shval silenced him with a raised hand and climbed out of the seat. "I'd better take a look at them. Your-friend-and-mine might be here anyway."

She began to examine the figures in frames. "Twenty ectoplasts were shipped aboard *Prometheus*. That's Agent Zero's doing—I know my little doll. Ever read *Dracula?*"

"The book? No..."

"Hell! Call yourself a Terrestrial? I know more about your culture than you do. Well, there's this undead gaian who never goes anywhere without sending boxes of consecrated earth on ahead of him for salting around the place. So he's never short of a bolt-hole."

"Yes, I guessed that's what the ectoplasts were for."

"Well, there are sixteen here now. Three I wrecked while we were in the Asteroid Belt. That leaves one, back on board *Prometheus*. Agent Zero must have come to life in that. With luck I destroyed it when I took care of the crew. MM was certain I had."

"So that's the last we've heard of Agent Zero?"

"Cross your fingers."

Jack peered out of the window past stampeding drops of spray. "Is that a mountain range I see in the distance, with lightning playing on it? God—what a place!"

Shval hesitated before she spoke. "It was beautiful, once."

"Did you ever see it?"

"How could I? I was born on Mars at the Last Zygogeny. To me, Titan was never anything but a legend. I tried looking for it in the face of my mother, Vermat. But she was in such pain. No longer could she reflect the clouds, the streaming forests of kelp, the jewelled eyes of the giant nautiluses as they jousted in the open water. Not even the beauty of Saturn, with its many-coloured rings."

She sat hugging her shoulders. "Like most of the moons of the outer planets, Titan consists mostly of water. Tidal friction and radioactive decay once kept it liquid—and temperate. But after the Fall of Titan, the surface temperature crashed. Just look out the window now."

Jack did so. He saw the flopper landing lights reflected fifty feet below in mighty breakers. Like chipped flint they appeared to him, but flint in gruesome motion. They rose and fell and spumed in a reckless gale.

"The open water's still there, anyway."

"That's not water, Jack—that's liquid methane. The water has become like rock. Gaians see this world as a glorious vat of exotic hydrocarbons, industrial feedstocks too expensive to synthesise in bulk. But I see only ruin and devastation. Once humanity forsakes this body— soon, please-God—then let it lie forever under its dreadful curse."

"I thought groubians had a deep and abiding love of Titan. But it sounds like you really hate it."

"Yes—I hate it. And I hate it when people try to immortalise it in the Book of Titan. Which reminds me: didn't you have a question you wanted to ask me?"

"Ahh, yes…"

"Well, now's the time to ask it. It will be half an hour before we reach our destination."

Jack stretched back in his seat. "What does the Last Verse actually mean?"

Shval shook her head. "I guess I'm the wrong person to ask."

A guffaw burst from Jack. "D'you mean to say, after all that, you *don't know?*"

"Oh, I know, all right. And I think I'm the only groubian that does. Which is why I've never been a member of the GA."

"Tell me, then."

Shval hesitated. "How many different translations have you come across?"

"Four or five at least. There is even a church hymn, would you believe?"

Shval laughed. "I've seen them all—including the hymn. And I've studied them very, very carefully." She turned to face Jack squarely. "Do you know which one comes closest to the original?"

"No…"

"The one by your late friend, Dr Catherine Martin."

"Kitty? She told me she'd done a translation, but she never showed it me."

"Then let me quote it to you:

> True motherhood entails the loss of childhood.
> Let it fall to thy lover to deliver the fatal blow;
> Question: What then is the sum-total of life's valuta?
> Answer: nothing… unless it represents
> Progress, by elementary steps, into the void.

"It lacks the poetic cadence of the others. But it is devastatingly faithful to the original. Dr Martin's achievement was to discard Dolpou Zvezda's romantic homage to Lermontov and refer back to the actual spatio-color—the only gaian ever to have done so. Unfortunately she was a historian, not a mathematician."

"Why does that make a difference?"

"Had she known something about mathematics, she would have cottoned-on to the structure of the poem."

"What structure? What do you mean?"

"The structure of the Last Verse. And not just the Last Verse: it permeates the entire Book of Titan. Proposition—example—question—answer—counter-example. Don't say you hadn't noticed?"

She received a blank stare.

"Jack—I thought you were a *mathematician!* Look, here's the Last Verse in Bourbaki notation." She pulled a slate out of her thigh pocket and wrote on it rapidly with her point-of-gaze:

> *Proposition:* $\Sigma A = -\Sigma(-A)$
> *Example:* for all n let $A_n = -B_n$
> *Question:* what is $\Sigma(A+B)$?

Answer: 0, *but only if*
$\{A_n\} \to 0$ *as* $n \to \infty$.

"The Book of Titan is a mathematical textbook. With lurid examples to capture the attention of the immature."

If Jack had lungs he'd have let out a long descending whistle.

"What? The Book of Titan: nothing but a book of children's sums? Shval—you… you can't be serious!"

"What did you suppose it was?"

"A… a religious text. A mystical treatise. A work of inspiration—of-of deep philosophy!"

"Well, so it is."

"What you've written down—why, that's just a high-school problem."

"Ask yourself the obvious question."

"What?" He looked again at the example and something occurred to him. "Do you mean: if $A_n = -B_n$ then how can the sum over all n be anything but zero?"

"Precisely. The way you gaians are trained, you miss it. Especially the physicists."

But Jack did know the answer to that one. He had been trained as a mathematician, not as a physicist.

"That's why you have to specify $\{A_n\} \to 0$ as $n \to \infty$."

Then he too began to write hurriedly with his point-of-gaze on the slate. "Take a case where it doesn't. Where $A_n = 1$ for all n. Then:

$$\Sigma(A + B) = 1-1+1-1+1-1+1\ldots$$

"…and so on, and so on. Now the right-hand side of the equation is zero—or is it? Let's bracket it, like this…"

$$1 + (-1+1-1+1-1+1\ldots)$$

"Now, inside the parentheses, swap around successive pairs of plus and minus terms…"

$$1 + (1-1+1-1+1-1\ldots)$$

"Hey presto! Inside the parentheses it's the original series once more. Which we said was zero. So we get $1+0$, which is 1." He waved the slate in triumph. "You can do it again and again to get $1+1+0$, then $1+1+1+0\ldots$"

"So you can make it add up to any integer you like?"

"Yes…" Jack's voice faded as if he'd been telling a joke that had fallen flat.

Shval transfixed him with her cuttlefish eyes. "And you don't see the significance of that?"

Jack looked blank.

"Every groubian child was made to learn it by heart. It's what impelled us to reach out from Titan and colonise Mars. And from Mars we reached out towards Gaia and Selene. And from Selene we hoped to reach for the stars."

"I still don't see…"

"Look up. Look up at the sky. Can you see the stars?"

"There's too much haze…"

"Then it's no good asking you to count them, is it?" She took the slate and brandished it. "Now look at this…" She began to write.

Jack did as she said, eyes growing wide with dawning awareness.

"The series $\Sigma(A_n - A_n)$ stands for the activity of the species. It's folded-in on itself, like a snake eating its tail. For every buyer there's a seller. For every lover there's someone who is loved. For every killer, someone has to die."

Jack's voice was dreamlike. "*The lover who strikes you dead.* For 'lover' read 'double'. Read 'partner'. Read 'complementary part.' For every element A_n there exists a minus-A_n. The sigma of the combined series is its *valuta:* its net worth. To someone brought up to think of the universe as finite, the net value is *always* zero."

"Precisely. You gaians insist the universe is finite. But to a groubian that's just a play on words. Try counting the stars. And when you get to the last one, *then* tell me that their number is finite."

Jack sat with his mouth in his hands. "But of course I never will…"

"So gaian mathematics is nothing but a silly game with symbols that cannot possibly bear the meaning placed on them."

"That's what Turing said. Most mathematicians don't believe him…"

"Words… words. We groubians do not think in words. Our mathematics is not couched in discrete symbols. The Book of Titan bridges the gap between the finite and the infinite, the integers and the continuum. Gaians can have no awareness of it. When the Book of Titan imparts it, the gaian brain explodes."

"So *that's* why it's so dangerous to gaians!"

"Yes."

"But you're saying groubians naturally grasp the concept of infinity?"

"To a groubian, infinity is not a concept to be grasped. It is a decision to be taken—for life."

Jack sank in his seat like a deflated balloon. "*Now* I see what you're driving at. Groubians can't reproduce. So the series no longer diverges, not even notionally. If you stop *believing* in infinity, the answer's *nothing*— and whichever way you add it up you're never going to make it any different."

They lapsed into silence. Jack stared out of the window. Drops of lifeless spray hurtled into the beam of the landing light and out again into oblivion. Lightning flickered in the distance on frozen sierras jutting from cryonic seas. Flickered and vanished.

"Are you a pious man?" said Shval at length. "A man of faith?"

Jack winced. "I used to be. But what they call *faith* is nothing but a state of denial, a refusal to hear the evidence because it's too painful to contemplate. Well, in my book that's not piety—that's moral cowardice."

"You speak for me too. Fifty thousand years of moral cowardice, as regards us groubians. An extinct species, going nowhere... but in a state of denial over it. A state of denial bolstered by an ancient book. Hollow footsteps... in an empty valley... leading nowhere but a dead end. *That's* the meaning of your precious Last Verse."

30 A visitation

All around the horizon lightning flared and glittered, an incessant feature of Titan's surface. Soon, through the brown murk of a titanic storm, Jack saw a flicker of greenish fire: oxygenated gas being flared-off from the tall central stack on Platform Two. A flame danced from the pipe-laced stack like a ribbon in a breeze. It was their main source of light as they touched down on the landing pad, coating every strut and girder in a gruesome glimmer.

"Clip your belt to the guard-rail and hold on tight," Shval shouted. "The wind here is phenomenal."

The first person they met off the ornithopter was someone calling himself the adjutant. From behind him, rig-personnel thrust past to fetch the cargo. The first of the baggage-handlers pushing past the other way were carrying the ectoplasts. Jack, recalled Agent Zero's instructions to "Metapelet" to distribute them around the place and it gave him a queer feeling. Might one of those ectoplasts be *it*?

The adjutant conducted Jack and Shval through a narrow passage to the guardroom, one of four superstructure buildings which rose on stilts out of the main body of the rig. Each building had a commanding view of one of the four orni-pads jutting out over the ocean from the rig's corners.

In the guardroom they met the commander, a smouldering presence who introduced himself by the single word "Sprenger". It took a moment for Jack to recognise the bear-like man on the VIP hover-platform at Voronka Cosmodrome.

"Nimrod, eh?" He didn't hold out a hand or make any other welcoming sign. "Here's Metapelet. She's been waiting for you." He pointed to a figure sitting by the doorway of a side-office.

"Nimrod…" The figure stood up in amazement. Jack felt his SP unit rattle. It was Gabrielle.

Jack glanced aside at Shval. Just in time to catch a purple flash of consternation, before her face settled down to a neutral pattern. She had recognised Gabrielle but was determined to give nothing away. Among groubians only Shval could control her skin like that—and she was only managing to do so now by emulating a groubian ectoplast.

Gabrielle led them into a side-office, twisting the handle savagely to shut the door. They sat around the desk in heavy silence before Jack spoke, his eyes boring into Gabrielle's. But it wasn't to her he addressed his question.

"*Agent Zero*... were you aware of this?" There was a jagged edge to his voice. He suddenly got the impression they were all just pawns in the hands of a universally-acknowledged grand master of deceit, namely Shval. But Shval herself was giving an excellent impression of having been taken right off-guard.

"I ought to have worked it out," Shval confessed. "But I didn't. Not even TMG, I thought to myself, would have the nerve to do this to you... *Metapelet*."

Jack stared at her, wondering how far she was telling the truth. Groubians, like gaians, have difficulty telling apart members of the other human species. But after months of close proximity on *Oberon*, Shval could hardly fail to recognise her erstwhile courier.

Jack stared even harder at Gabrielle. Had she in her turn recognised Shval Meteor, or hadn't she? He knew how misleading he himself had found groubians' resemblance to each other—and blushed to recall the shameful consequence of that. Gabrielle had been anticipating the arrival of Agent Zero. With luck she was under the illusion that this was what sat facing her, not Shval. What she said next served to reassure Jack that this was so—but not for long.

"I thought," said Gabrielle addressing Shval, "you knew perfectly well it was me you were speaking to over the t-unit. And by the way... *tak for sidst* to you too."

As a Selenean denizen, Shval knew enough Selensk to know what *tak for sidst* meant. But she completely missed the drift of Gabrielle's shibboleth—which Agent Zero had given her for a watchword. She couldn't do otherwise. She had not been party to the voice messages shuttling between TMG and Platform Two that fateful day. And for all her hacking prowess, she had not managed to intercept them, nor become aware of them in any way. Neither had it occurred to Jack to mention them.

Gabrielle followed-up her breakthrough, tightening the snare around her adversary's neck. "Now that you're here with the supplies you had me order, we've got everything we need. Or should I say... *you* need?"

But Jack remembered what Agent Zero had said to Metapelet. He knew that Gabrielle was referring to the ectoplasts—something to which Shval hadn't cottoned-on. How could he warn her?

"You're very welcome," Shval replied, taking a guess at what was meant. "As it happens we've brought along our own hibernator. It's out in the flopper. We'll send out for it when it's needed."

Gabrielle bit her lip, giving no sign that her bait had been taken. "*Will* it be needed?"

"Everyone on the *Prometheus* has to go in one sooner or later."

"Yes, but why do you suppose my charge won't accompany you voluntarily back to Mars?"

"Well, we hope so too," interjected Jack. He smiled, hoping vainly to soften the steel he knew had slipped into his voice.

Gabrielle was frowning now. "Anyway, you didn't need to bring a hibernator all the way from *Prometheus*. We have hibernators here, in the sick bay. When we get a case we can't handle, we freeze the patient down until the next supply visit. But my charge *can* walk, you know…"

"Well, that's great," said Shval, garnishing her voice with a brittle cheeriness. She sensed something was wrong. Somehow she'd made a slip-up. Had it blown her cover? Having to continue masquerading as her own estranged imperson in front of somebody who might or might not know who she really was, was taxing even her resourcefulness.

"I wasn't talking of hibernators…" said Gabrielle, a hint of menace in her voice.

Desperately Jack tried to help Shval out. "You mean the ectoplasts…?"

Gabrielle glanced towards the door as if they might be overheard. It was a solid one however and there were no windows. "Don't say the e-word out aloud," she hissed. "Commander Sprenger was suspicious when he saw them all arrive. What was I planning to do up there, he said—put on a pantomime?"

Jack sniggered and caught Shval's eye, but the latter saw nothing to be amused at. After her phantom-hunt in Bay 33, ectoplasts had exhausted their entertainment value. In a dry voice she said "Do you think we can see Tvoul now?"

"Code-names only," reminded Gabrielle.

"We mean the groubian you've got here," grumbled Jack.

At that, the reins of self-restraint slipped from Gabrielle's grasp and she exploded. "We don't *have* any groubians in the Special Unit," she screamed. "That's what I keep trying to tell you people!" Her fury instantly gave way to icy calm. Fixing her eyes on Shval she carefully articulated "Right at this moment, there's precisely *one real groubian* on board!"

Shval must now have sensed the only thing to do was call her bluff. "Miss Metapelet," she said in an electrified voice. "You compel me to speak with the authority of the Strana of Olympia. Tvoul Williams happens to be wanted on Mars for *crimes against the transgenic laws.* I am here, with the explicit consent of your superiors, as her *replacement.*"

Gabrielle flushed crimson. "There are no transgenic laws on Titan," she retorted. "No denizen of this *mir* is guilty of any sort of wrongdoing."

Jack put his palm on the desk in front of Gabrielle. "Hush now, hinny." His voice was patronising, though he'd intended it to be soothing. "Can we just see Tvoul… please? You said she was ready to come quietly. And I *am* her father-in-law… Treaty of Moscow, like."

Gabrielle hesitated, but only for a moment. She knew that in the end she had no power to deny Jack access to his own close relative. His spooky companion was another matter. She picked up the handset of the t-unit. "Mama-duck," she said baldly, "how do you feel about it?"

Mama-duck, said Jack to himself. If it wasn't all such a serious matter he'd have burst out laughing.

"My patient consents to see just one of you." Gabrielle rose to her feet. "Mr… Nimrod—would you come with me, please?"

Shval rose to her feet too. Z-niks, even robot ones, don't take kindly to being sidelined—and Shval meant to play her part to the finale. But Jack patted the air, meaning she was to stay put for now.

"You can leave your uzi here, with *Agent Zero*," said Gabrielle, with ironic emphasis on Shval's cover name. "It won't be necessary."

Glancing at Shval, Jack said "I'll take it with me, all the same. I'm covered by this warrant too, y'know, like."

Gabrielle didn't budge. No doubt she was wondering how to alert Sprenger secretly to Shval's presence on the rig.

"I have no Zasta six-shooter, as you'll observe," said Shval, in a move she knew was checkmate. "It's part of the protocol allowing the police of another *mir* on board. Nimrod cannot leave his weapon here with me without violating the Treaty and provoking an intermondial incident."

Gabrielle eyed her adversary up and down. Out of her top pocket came the probe Jens had given her to take on board the *Oberon*. She pointed it at Shval, who didn't flinch, knowing just what it was. It would confirm she wasn't armed—not even with the regulation TP. Gabrielle could see there was no immediate hope of parting Jack from his weapon. Acknowledging defeat with a slight shrug, she turned and led the way for

Jack. But not before she'd made him detach the uzi's magazine and place it on the desk in front of Shval.

"Ammunition is no use without a weapon, Agent Zero," she said. "So this won't violate the Treaty."

It was the best Gabrielle could manage in the circumstances. Jack nodded in silent admiration—he'd always known how quick-witted she was. But how could she have known about the two spare magazines he had in his calf-pockets? They had been there ever since the day of his fateful rendezvous with the wrong Tvoul. On *Prometheus* they had relieved him of his uzi—it was the one Shval had recovered from the first mate. But nobody at any stage had thought to subject Jack to a proper search.

On her own at last, Shval got out the midget interception kit she always carried on her person. Prying open the handset of the t-unit, she poked around inside, doing what she was supremely good at. She was determined to miss nothing of what transpired anywhere on the rig.

·····★●★·····

It was a stiff walk to the Special Unit, Platform Two being more than two hundred yards from corner to corner. They descended from the guardroom into the main body of the rig and then paced along corridors grimed with black grease, past locker rooms and corridors full of cabins opening at intervals on either side.

"Gabrielle, I thought I'd never see you again."

"Oh, Jack—I wish it was anywhere but here."

"I thought you were en-route for Selene."

"I was enlisted under false pretences. Press-ganged, you'd say. I had to leave Mars—you knew I had no choice over that. But once they got me aboard the shuttle, they told me it wasn't going to the *Oberon* but to *Prometheus*."

"It seemed strange when I thought about it," said Jack. "A shuttle couldn't catch up with the *Oberon* at the speed it travels. Certainly not with such a head-start."

"I should have been more suspicious…"

"So now you've gone over to the enemy?"

Gabrielle stopped and put her hands on her hips. Her voice broke.

"How do you have the nerve to say that? Aren't TMG and Peretchelo working hand-in-glove?"

"They *are* the Enemy."

With a shrug of contempt, Gabrielle resumed her pace. "And I suppose Shval Meteor, of all people, is one of the Glorious Allies?"

"That is Agent Zero accompanying me."

"Pull the other one. Do you think I don't know an old client? One I escorted on an eight-month journey?" She pushed against a heavily-sprung door and held it open for Jack.

"You're imagining things. All groubians look the same to us gaians. It's an easy mistake to make. I know—I've made it..."

"See here, Jack: I must have spent my time on Mars better than you did, because I took the trouble to learn spatio-color signatures. That thing accompanying you is Shval Meteor *in the flesh*."

"So what? We're here on Zasta business."

"Oh yes, I know all about that. TMG business, you mean. What's the real agenda, Jack?"

"Why should I tell you?"

"Oh—no reason. None at all. Just that I was your agent on *Oberon*, remember?"

"I remember," said Jack, accepting the gambit. "I remember all right. It's clear to me that when you were meant to be helping me search for Tvoul, you were actually shielding her. You must have known exactly where she was on board the *Oberon*—and you made damn sure I didn't."

"That's a lie!" Gabrielle was on the verge of breaking down. "My orders from Jens were to do exactly what I'm doing now: to bring you two together. And to stop Shval getting in ahead of us. None of us knew the real situation, the real whereabouts of... Mama-duck. It was not until I got to Platform Two that I learned the amazing truth..."

"The Amazing Truth! Is that what you call it?"

"Jack—prepare yourself for a shock."

"I don't believe a single thing you say."

"You know, I feel like smacking your fat head. I spent eight tedious months cosying up to the Meteor Gang—for your sake. I risked my life to stop Shval finding out the true state of affairs. And now here you come, waltzing in on Shval's arm."

Turning a corner they fell silent. A rigger passed them, going the other way. He stopped to speak to Gabrielle.

"Coming to the party tonight? It's Alessandro's Twenty-First."

"No... I'll be busy."

"You can't do that to us, Gabrielle! There's just you two women on the whole rig."

"That worries me sometimes." She didn't introduce Jack and they strode on rapidly. Gabrielle was setting a brisk pace. As they stepped over a greasy bulkhead to go through a doorway, the heavily-sprung door shut on Jack's uzi, fetching it a hefty clout.

"I hope there isn't a bullet in the breach. Heads can get blown off."

"Don't fret yourself, pet. I've got a triton pistol strapped to me leg too. You haven't said a word about *that*."

"TPs don't count. Everybody carries them. It's the law here."

"And all for the sake of the Titan Kraken. A bogey to scare kids."

"We have to take it seriously, Jack. We can't ignore what happened to our sister rig."

"What happened? Did Nessie get it, like?"

"It's not funny. Platform One issued a Kraken Attack moments before it perished."

"And then it disappeared? Without trace?"

"Not exactly. There was a thermonuclear explosion. That's what actually destroyed the rig."

"You don't mean to say the Kraken…?"

"No, you fool, of course not. Nobody has ever seen the Kraken. What destroyed Platform One was 'plasma resonance': a freak accident with two TPs. That's the official story—and it's a pretty plausible one."

"And still you lug these bloody things around with you?"

"They're safe enough; provided you point them outwards, away from the rig." She thrust herself in front of him and pushed open another door.

"Tell me, what is 'plasma resonance'?"

"When one TP is in the firing-line of another. An idle TP simply vaporises: they're only glorified water-pistols. But when both TPs happen to be firing at each other, at one and the same instant, their combined energy gets released in less than a microsecond. Kilotons of TNT—if they're both full."

Gabrielle glanced behind her. "Proper drills can prevent that sort of thing. Anyway, you'd have to be pretty desperate to go firing *triton pistols* at each other."

••••••✷●✷••••••

They reached the spiral staircase at one end of the Special Unit. Gabrielle led the way up. By now they'd lapsed into sullen silence. At the top they passed through one room, then another. The first room they came to was decked out as a children's playroom. Cartoon animals were painted on the walls. There were toys in heaps in the corners, many of them still in their boxes.

The second room was quite plainly a nursery. A couple of dozen brand new cots were spaced around the walls. Half of them were pink, half blue.

"Is this a crèche for families?"

"There are no families on Titan. Everybody here is single. At least that's what they tell us when they arrive on board."

The next room, lit with a dim blue glow, looked eerily like an intensive care ward. There were four rows of bluish plastic machines, appearing to Jack's eyes like hi-tech baby-baths. Transparent gloves hung down inside through port-holes in the Plexiglas sides.

Suddenly, with a pang of horror, Jack realised what they were. Incubators: for foetuses too small to survive in the open. Foetuses that wouldn't be going through the normal birth process. It looked as if they hadn't yet been used.

Gabrielle put her hand to her breast pocket. "Excuse me, Jack, I'm being paged—it's urgent. Wait here." She hastened back the way they'd come and slipped through the swing doors, reaching for the wall-mounted t-unit Jack had noticed as they'd passed it by.

Swinging his uzi off his shoulder, Jack drew a magazine out of his calf pocket and snapped it in-place. Then he strode on through the swing doors opposite. Clearly it was where they'd been heading. As the doors swung to behind him, he stopped dead.

A figure sat there, waiting. A figure in a striped yellow-and-black boiler suit, loose-fitting and rumpled, but clean. Surgically clean. It wore a pristine Martian helmet, with visor set half-silvered to conceal the face.

As Jack stood poised like a high-diver facing his supreme test, the figure rose slowly to its feet and reached downwards and outwards, palms facing forward. In pointless welcome... or in hopeless appeal?

●●●●● ✳ ● ★ ●●●●●

In the side-office of the guardroom, Shval was still left to her own devices. She had broken into the security camera network and was eavesdropping on Commander Sprenger speaking to his adjutant. All the cameras, she was glad to discover, had attached microphones. She had a clear view of Sprenger's face, but couldn't see the command console.

Evidently he was in communication with some vessel or other. But what? A returning ornithopter, sent out on a fruitless mission, like a dove from Noah's Ark? Apart from Platform Two there were no other settlements on Titan—and as for the *Prometheus*, Shval had left its systems operating in passive mode. No signal could possibly be coming from there. Nor could it have launched a lander after their own. Unless…

"It's coming into range…" the commander was saying. He gripped his headset with both hands. Then hurriedly he started jabbing at the console.

He's paging someone, thought Shval. Straightaway she switched into the rig's t-network.

"What's up?" said the adjutant.

Slowly, deliberately, Sprenger muttered "Entire crew of *Prometheus* dead. Massacred."

"What?"

"Keep your voice down!" Sprenger motioned with his forehead towards the door of the side-office where Shval was sitting.

"Metapelet," he said, cupping his hand over the mike. "That guy with you, calling himself Jack Williams. Watch out—he's dangerous. *Very dangerous*. Don't let him in the Special Unit. He's here to kill Mama-duck."

Shval didn't catch Gabrielle's reply, which would have been to warn Sprenger of her—Shval's—presence on the rig.

"I know, I know. Just keep him occupied. I'll get help to you straightaway."

He reached across the console and broke the guardpiece off some special button or other. Behind him locker doors flew open and three s-bots emerged, man-sized black langoustines of Kevlar and titanium. They had no firearms, but they were equipped with an assortment of less-lethal weapons, including tasers. Each carried a CRW—a bloody-butcher.

"Special Unit. *Scramble!*"

The s-bots clattered off.

Sprenger leaned back and murmured quietly in the adjutant's ear. But not so quietly that Shval couldn't hear him though the camera's microphone.

"A solitary ectoplast has survived on *Prometheus* and it's on its way here. It's a fighting machine with Zasta powers and it knows the assassins' plans. It says it is the *real* Agent Zero."

The adjutant's eyes started. "Then what's that—in there?"

"Not an ectoplast—a live groubian. And you'll know the name: *Shval Meteor.*"

Both men pulled out their 0.38 automatics and crept to the door. "On the count of three…" whispered Sprenger. "One—two—*three!*"

The two men burst into the office and halted abruptly. The lights were out. In the gloom they could see Shval's dust suit lying crumpled on the floor. They paced slowly round, swinging their guns. Sweat began beading on their faces, coalescing and running in trickles down their necks.

Had they known what to look for, they'd have spotted Shval fairly easily—a pair of disembodied eyes peering over Sprenger's shoulder. The latter reached back, fumbling for the light-switch, but as he did so his fingers met camouflaged flesh. Before he could spin round he was garrotted with a data cable. The adjutant, fearful of hitting his boss, fatally held back for a fraction of a second—and Shval shot him in the abdomen with Sprenger's pistol. He lay clawing at the ground in frenzy like a man in free-fall.

Shval slid back into her dust suit, pocketed the gun, snapped-on her helmet and strode into the guardroom proper. Nobody had come in, and she made sure nobody could. Then she sat down at the commander's console. Once she had mastered it, she'd be in control of the whole of Platform Two. The whole of Titan… apart for one doomed ornithopter, flapping towards the rig like a lonely bat through hell.

How close was the aircraft? She switched the v-screen to radar and saw its labelled blip closing in. Another five minutes before it arrived. Time enough to organise a hot reception.

She brought up a working display of the rig, which she rotated this way and that. Platform Two stood on four huge cylindrical legs in an ocean of liquid methane. She zoomed-in upon the hollow leg nearest the Special Unit. Halfway down inside the leg there was a chamber labelled "survival capsule"—an impregnable bolt-hole. Shval correctly deduced that in pressing need Mama-duck would make straight for it.

She cycled through the cameras installed in and around the Special Unit, bringing images up in turn. She saw Gabrielle tipping out the drawers of her desk, searching frantically for the 0.38 she kept there and thought she'd never need. She saw Jack, uzi levelled, glancing up and down an empty corridor. She saw the s-bots converging on him like spiders on a web-snared fly.

There was no selective intertalk in the rig's primitive intensor. No private channels. No way to poll Jack or even to page him, since he hadn't got a pager. She'd have to resort to the public-address system.

Donning the headset she shouted, for the whole of Platform Two to hear:

"Jack! Tvoul's making for the survival capsule in Number Three Leg…"

31   The fall of Titan

The striped shape advanced, arms outstretched in clear sign of peace. Jack's uzi sagged in his hands, but he made no gesture in response.

Suddenly behind him the double doors crashed open. Gabrielle, her face twisted in a scream, lunged at him and tried to wrest the uzi from his grip. Locked in an absurd dance, they staggered and galloped round each other.

"Mama-duck! He wants to kill you!"

The striped figure leapt into a corner, opened a hatch and began to lower itself through. With a sudden wrench, Jack detached the uzi from Gabrielle's grasp, the act of doing so hurling her to the floor. Swivelling on his heels Jack squeezed the trigger. The safety-catch bit. Swearing and slipping it off he sprayed a burst of fire at the trapdoor. Too late—the lid thumped shut. Heaving it open again—a fire-escape: it couldn't be secured—Jack clattered down the steel ladder after the ungainly fleeing shape. An ugly shape it looked, in its wasp-striped yellow and black.

At the bottom he glanced hurriedly about him to see which way his quarry had gone. Loud and clear, Shval's voice came over the public-address system.

"Jack! Tvoul's making for the survival capsule in Number 3 Leg. Don't let her reach it—or you'll never get her out before you're overpowered."

Jack started running. "Other way!" screamed Shval.

Turning to dash back the way he'd come, Jack caught sight of a yellow blur vanishing round the end of a short corridor. Speeding down the corridor, Jack turned the corner to see a striped torso scrabbling through a hatchway in the floor. Without taking aim, he fired. Simultaneously he thought he heard a man's voice cry out "Dad...!"

The silvery visor flew off in bits. Knowing all too well how much it took to kill a groubian, Jack didn't release the trigger until the firing stopped of its own accord.

His quarry arched its back, convulsed. Coloured body-fluids mixed and sprayed across the floor. Like a baby being born in reverse, the torso was engulfed by the hatchway. As Jack dashed forward, uselessly brandishing his spent weapon, there was nothing to be seen but visor fragments scattered round the hatchway's open throat.

Face-down to the floor, Jack crept forward until his head was over the blood-smeared hole. The blood was red—but the significance of that didn't strike him. He expected to be looking down into some sort of living-quarters, with the body of Tvoul crumpled on the floor directly below. But what he saw instead was a column of rungs fading into darkness. Rungs made of steel rods bent into D-shapes, welded to the wall of a giant cylindrical void over 30 ft across, still booming to the sound of gunfire. He couldn't see the bottom.

He was looking down into one of the four hollow legs of the rig. They stood in the methane ocean, which swelled, reared and dashed itself like a billion cobras against nine-inch walls of iron, in the everlasting fury of the Titan storm.

••••• ✴ ● ✴ •••••

Rolling to one side Jack saw Gabrielle half-crouching, gripping a 0.38 automatic in knuckle-whitened hands. Around them the s-bots dispatched by Sprenger to the scene stood motionless, tasers levelled.

He thrust aside the uzi. "You won't be needing that, bonny lass. My gun's empty. I'll come quietly."

Gabrielle slowly rose to her full height. *"Jack Williams,"* she rasped. *"What have you done?"*

Jack sat up. "I'll tell you what I've done. I've shot a groubian that's *eaten* my son! I've chased her all the way to this god-forsaken sea platform—and at last I've *got* her!"

He tried to scramble to his feet, but his heel slipped in blood and he fell back. To his surprise the s-bots made shift to help him up. He turned to face Gabrielle and saw her eyes full of hopeless pain.

"That wasn't a groubian, Jack. That *was* your son!"

Supported by two s-bots, Jack loured at her, head hunched into his shoulders. "Look here, flower—that was Tvoul. The famous *Tvoul Rainbow!* She's been going around calling herself 'Tvoul Williams', for God's sake."

Gabrielle, lips tightened in a bloodless line, shook her head in little jerks. "You don't understand a damn thing, do you?"

She seemed to relax and not relax, fastening the 0.38 safety-catch and putting it away. "Yes—Tvoul took the surname Williams when she married your Harry. But after edulating her in Brazil—*he* then took *her* name."

Clutching at the edge of a recess, Jack swung back against the wall.

"It was the custom among groubians," continued Gabrielle, "out of respect for the dead, for the edulator to adopt the persona of the edulee, pending parturition."

In a stunned whisper Jack said "Then where's me daughter-in-law?"

"Lying dead in the Amazon rainforest."

"...Where's me son?..."

"Lying in the sump at the bottom of Number Three Leg, where you've just dropped him."

•••••★●★•••••

Shval was now under siege in the guardroom. Using the public address system had attracted unwelcome attention. The two captured 0.38s were her only weapons, but she'd been using them to great effect, one in each hand like a Wild West gunslinger, in spite of her crushed finger. She had been glad to discover that they fired the ammunition in the uzi magazine Jack had left with her.

She had found a portable v-screen which Sprenger could have used as a roving command post. This meant she was no longer confined to the guardroom—provided of course she could escape from it. Going back into the side-office, she undid Sprenger's triton pistol in its calf holster and strapped it on her own calf. Returning to watch the screen, she waited for the next attempt to storm the guardroom door. Bodies lay strewn around, both outside and this side. She'd been hit herself, but it took more than a few rounds to kill a groubian.

She decided to risk the public address system again. "Jack—there are hibernators in the survival capsule. Get Tvoul into one and bring her to the flopper."

But by then Jack was descending into Number Three Leg.

•••••★●★•••••

Wrenching himself free of the s-bots, Jack started climbing into the hole, with every intention of making it to the bottom unaided. The s-bots grabbed him again before his shoulders had descended below deck level. One of them felt the metabolo in Jack's breast pocket and extracted it. Reaching across, Gabrielle seized it. As a nurse she knew just what it was and how to use it.

"Thanks, I'll take this. Now Jack: behave yourself—or I'll switch you off."

"Let me go!" Disregarding what she'd said, he tried to struggle free.

"Jack!" shouted Gabrielle in his ear. "Didn't you hear me? This metabolo I've got in my hand—it's all that's keeping you alive!"

"So you're gonna stop me going down to get *me own son?*"

"It's 700 ft to the bottom, if it's an inch. That's almost a thousand rungs. You'll slip and fall—and then you'll perish too."

"I don't care!"

"Look," she said in desperation, "there's tackle in the lockers. Why don't you abseil down?"

It was one single gleam of sense in the whole crazy nightmare. Going limp, Jack let the s-bots drag him out of the manhole.

••••• ★ ● ★ •••••

Presently Jack was back inside the hole, this time properly equipped. Reaching the survival capsule, he located hibernators inside and attached a line to one of them. The s-bots hauled it up.

With no place to go, evacuation of the rig figured nowhere in its emergency plan. Each of the four legs had survival capsules, with provisions to keep one person alive for three months, plus enough hibernators for the entire rig's complement divided between the four legs. These were deemed to be the strongest parts of the structure and would best withstand a fire or other catastrophe. There was no experience of the capsules' use, but they proffered some assurance, of a feeble sort, that living on Titan didn't place you altogether beyond the aid of distant worlds.

The capsule, bolted to the wall, was set to one side of the ladder. Jack had hoped to find Harry's body draped over it, but he was disappointed. The ladder went on past the capsule, down into the darkness. This was now where Jack had to go.

Descending in long hops, continuous thunder in his ears, Jack paid out the rope, yard upon yard of it. In the beam of the headlight they'd clamped to his helmet, Jack came at last in sight of the pool of thick black sludge which filled the bottom of the leg. Suspended somewhere in that pool was Harry's corpse.

Suddenly he became aware of a red glow. A vicious snarl made itself heard over the incessant booming. A blazing dot was floating down towards him, leaving a trail of white smoke that flashed in the beam of his headlight. A bloody-butcher had come to join him in his search. Memory struck a chill through him, like a spit of frozen steel. For nearly a minute he was unable to move.

But the CRW paid him not the slightest regard. It was doing the humanitarian job it was originally designed for: recovering bodies from inaccessible places. It hovered here and there, like a dragonfly above a glistening swamp. Unable to find Harry's body after thirty seconds its fuel ran out and it dropped in the sludge.

Jack tried shouting up to Gabrielle, but his voice was dispersed in its own echo. She must have lowered down a speaker however, because a moment later he heard a small clear voice next to his ear.

"The body is too far down for the CRW to sense it, Jack. Feel all around you near the ladder. If you can locate it and pull it up a few rungs, we'll send down another CRW to haul it up."

Step by step Jack worked his way down the slippery rungs of the welded ladder, giving himself time to sink in the sludge. Even with the knowledge that he had an SP unit and didn't need to draw breath, he couldn't forestall a sense of panic as treacly blackness closed over his helmet. Taking charge of himself, he stopped thrashing about and began purposefully to grope around him. Very soon his hand closed round a boiler-suited limb. Gripping it firmly he began to climb. If it had been easy to lower himself into the ooze, it was a heavy burden he found himself lifting out—dragging it, as it were, out of a bog.

There came the snarl of a second CRW, which chilled his chine no less than the first had done. There was a sharp crack in his face as it shot its talons into the corpse he was holding. Then the burden began to be drawn upwards, slithering out of his parental embrace like a baby dragged by forceps from the womb. Exhausted, he hung back limply against the rungs.

Jack came-to as the lifeline round his waist delivered an urgent tug. But he was now chilled through and disinclined to move. The lifeline tightened and its pull grew stronger until his feet forsook the rungs. Feebly trying to help himself along, whenever a hand or a foot chanced to touch the ladder, Jack was winched up and up... until he emerged through the hatch into the light.

Harry was lying on the deck beside him. The s-bots had hosed the sludge off him and cut away his striped boiler suit. The body was covered in plum-coloured lumps, each the size of a fist. Jack recalled his sight of Vermat's shattered physique, as she bared herself to Arne the masseur.

Gabrielle was running a stethophone over the corpse. As it came near each lump it emitted a succession of little ticks, like an old-time pocket watch. "The foetuses are still alive." An agonised smile of relief drew back her lips. "Get him into the hibernator," she commanded. "They'll stay alive until we get him back to civilization."

The lid shut down and a bubbling hiss announced the commencement of Harry's journey into eternity. Then the s-bots turned their attention to Jack, who knelt like a basalt angel in a forgotten graveyard. Almost tenderly they hosed him down with hot water, getting off the worst of the black sludge.

Suddenly the public address system came to life.

Kraken Attack! Kraken Attack! Kraken Attack!...

A pre-recorded voice cackled its frenetic message over and over. Lights flashed and sirens were roused to wail through miles of corridors. From all around there came the hiss of pneumatic doors, the clatter of boots on steel gratings and men's urgent voices, anticipating disaster.

·····✱●✱·····

The ornithopter had arrived at last. It was fluttering overhead, keeping its cockpit steady in the gale like a kestrel's eye. At any moment it would swoop down upon one of the three vacant orni-pads. It called for desperate measures. If Shval failed to stop it, Agent Zero would be at large on the rig, hidden in its maze of corridors.

High on the wall was a glowing orange box. Its glass cover depicted a nursery-book octopus, sporting a vampire-toothed sneer and curling the tips of its tentacles into precious little fists. Smashing the glass with her pistol butt, Shval pulled on the red handle.

Kraken Attack! Kraken Attack!...

The result was instantaneous. Everyone dropped what they were doing. Everyone with the exception of Jack and Gabrielle, standing over Harry's casket. They stayed their ground, frozen in anticipation, having a fair idea what Shval was up to.

But the rest of the rig didn't—and they didn't stop to ponder. Tugging on helmets and snapping visors shut, men poured out of the air-locks onto every deck of the rig, lining the railings like penguins on an ice floe watching for the sea-lion. Some climbed the ladder on the flare-off stack to get a better glimpse of the alleged attacker and a surer shot.

The rig had no permanently mounted weaponry. That would simply have offered a fixed target to a creature fabled to have a hundred eyes and thousands of suckers with razor rims, plus the malevolent wits to put them to optimum use. It was for precisely this eventuality that every person on Platform Two carried a triton pistol. Toting a couple of hundred of these, plus twice that number of eyes, humanity was now supposed to be in with a chance.

"Hold your fire until you see a clear target!" shouted the shift leader over a megaphone, hoping to conserve precious T_2O. But all in vain. Panic invested each plume of spray, whipped from the cusp of every wave, with the appearance of tentacles wriggling over the sea towards the rig. The howling darkness was soon splintered in searing flashes as toroids of thermonuclear plasma swept out recklessly over the surge.

Under cover of the general confusion, Shval too stepped out on deck. Stretching out her triton pistol in both hands, she took aim. In a single flash among several, the swooping ornithopter was momentarily emblazoned on the ochre tapestry of sky like a divine dove. Then the apparition of glory dissolved in blinding gledes, tumbling onto the rig in a rain of molten metal.

The guardroom roof caught fire.

•••••✸●✸•••••

Jack startled as the door of a nearby locker opened by itself. Out stepped a groubian figure clad in Zasta blue-and-white. "One of my ectoplasts," exclaimed Gabrielle.

"Agent Zero!" cried Jack in glad recognition. "How did _you_ get here?"

"Shval has just shot down my flopper under cover of a bogus kraken attack. But back on _Prometheus_, while we were still in the asteroid belt, I downloaded my intensions into every ectoplast destined for Platform Two. I can animate only one at a time, but I can choose which. If Shval blasts me again, I'll simply animate another."

Agent Zero turned to Gabrielle. "Now please, Gaby, where is Mama-duck? I'm dying to see him again."

"Tvoul, I'm sorry… so… very sorry." Gabrielle let her tearful gaze drop to the object at her feet, Tvoul following her eyes down.

"My love!" With a shriek Tvoul fell on her knees beside the hibernator. As she stared at Harry's frozen face behind the glass, her skin began to smoke in agonies of grey-and-purple. Jack fidgeted in shame as she lay silently clasping the casket.

Presently she raised herself on her arms. Her voice was icy calm. "_Dead or alive_, they said, Jack? How can I complain? It's only what we all agreed at TMG Headquarters."

Slowly she turned back to the casket. "And if it's any consolation, you've spared your son the agonies of parturition." Her gaze roved up and down the hibernator. "The Titan Curse. Something only Titans should ever have to endure…"

Then she could contain her anguish no longer. "But why do we have to endure your *bitterness?*" Tears started in her eyes—real tears—whether they were water-based or not. "I loved your Harry. And he loved me. What part of *love* do you not understand?" Her brimming eyes focussed burning-glasses on Jack's brow. "How else could he have done this thing for me? How else do you suppose… *we* could have done it for each other?"

She turned back to peer through the frosted glass. "Or can't your fleeting gaian mind grasp things like that? How could you look on Love itself… and see only *interspex?*"

She sank down again, crouched over the casket, as if to cradle Harry's head. "He didn't do it just for me, but for all humanity. And because I loved him and shared his dream… I gladly went along with it."

Smiling bleakly through her tears, she shook her head. "For as long as we've known about gaians, the secret has eluded us. But in the end it was all so simple. Don't be the edulator—*be the edulee!*"

Slowly Jack knelt down beside Tvoul to gaze at Harry's crystal face. As he did so, his fingers crept over her shoulder. "So Tvoul Rainbow endured edulation, death and dishonour, becoming class zero, for the greatest thing she could imagine. Did she ever think… did *you* ever think… that one day you'd wake up as the Unperson?"

"Even when I took on Shval's persona," she whispered, "deep down I knew it. What lies here before us is redemption for the groubian species. And, for humanity—the way to the stars." Then, shutting her eyes to squeeze out tears which plunged down her cheeks, she slid her fingers over his.

•••••✱●✱••••••

"Kraken Attack! Kraken Attack! Kraken Attack!…" The robot voice babbled its frantic warning, but on Level Five all was still. Nobody came. The crew were out on deck, battling the mythical Kraken. The s-bots lowered the hatch to Number Three Leg and sealed it. Now the threesome sat around the hatchway, waiting for the panic to subside and contemplating what to do next.

"One thing still puzzles me," said Jack. "How did my Harry manage to get here?"

"Harry took my name, *Tvoul*—as was the ancient custom—and embarked on the *Oberon*. You spotted him on board and made as if to speak to him, but failed to register who he really was. Nevertheless he made sure to keep out of your way for the rest of the trip. He had already run huge risks in tricking you out of the Gaiascope in the nick of time, before it was sent up in flames by Shval's Byzantine scheming."

"So it was Harry who lured me to the Moon Dog rendezvous?"

"Yes. He couldn't let his own father die. Otherwise he took great care to hide himself. As soon as *Oberon* reached Mars and reconciled with the Nix intensor, it registered Tvoul Williams as a new persona. But anyone polling the intensor would discover that Tvoul Williams was not on Mars—and never had been."

"That's what Sviatoslav kept telling me, but I thought I knew better. So he and Miro knew that Harry was alive—and Tvoul Rainbow dead?"

"Oh, no. Nobody on Mars could have known that. But MM knew, as I was amazed to learn today. Harry was careful not to make landfall on Mars, which would have spoilt everything. He transferred straight to the *Prometheus*, thus shaking off pursuit. MM would have checked him aboard as 'Tvoul Williams', but known he wasn't groubian. That's how it deduced that Tvoul Rainbow was dead."

Jack nodded.

"Miro assumed the same thing as you did, Jack—the same as everyone—that it was Harry who'd been edulated in Brazil, not me. Everyone was on the lookout for a groubian, not a gaian. It was the perfect disguise. And unwittingly Shval reinforced it by masquerading as me in order to get back to Mars. She too, for reasons of her own, was keen to cover Harry's tracks."

'Kraken Attack! Kraken Attack! Kraken Attack!...' The robot voice cackled on and on. But now a second robot voice began to accompany it in absurd counterpoint. *'Fire! Fire! Fire!...'*

Shval's living voice cut-in over the racket. "Jack. I can't get back into the guardroom—it's on fire! Bring Tvoul's hibernator to our flopper. Then let's get back to Mars."

Her voice began to rise in unmistakable panic. "I can't see you, Jack. Pick up any t-unit and *talk to me!"*

Tvoul leapt to her feet, fury scoring her skin with silver veins. "Yes," she hissed. "Let's do that. Let's get the hibernator to the flopper. But my zygocysts are not going to Mars. They're going back to Gaia." She placed her hand on Gabrielle's forearm. "Gaby—if you come through this alive, can I depend on you as planned?"

"Yes," said Gabrielle, wiping tears away. "You certainly can!"

"I won't be coming with you," said Tvoul. "I'll have to stay and take care of Shval. She won't let you get away with the body. She'll try to shoot you down like she did me."

She picked up Harry's triton pistol. "I have many scores to settle with my sister. Not the least—for trying to steal my babies." She then picked up the uzi which Jack had tossed aside, sliding out the empty magazine. Turning to Jack with a perceptible shudder she said "Have you any more ammunition for this awful thing?"

Sheepishly Jack bent down and slid out the remaining magazine from his shin pocket. He handed it to Tvoul, who expertly clipped it in place. This was the heroine of the Siege of the Nix, as Jack recalled. "Let's go." she said.

The s-bots picked up the casket by three of its lay-holds. Jack got a grip on the fourth. With Tvoul leading the way, machine-pistol at the ready, and Gabrielle following behind, swinging her 0.38 this way and that, they began to run for the ornithopter. As far as they knew, it was still there on the guardroom orni-pad. A better-armed and more determined funeral cortege had never paced the rig.

But they met no resistance—from Shval or anyone else. Everybody was on deck. Some were still firing plasma-rings at phantoms in the waves. Others, in increasing desperation, fought the guardroom fire.

As yet there was no sign of Shval. But there was every chance that once more she was listening-in—or watching them. She would certainly be watching the guard-room orni-pad, which held the one remaining flopper on Titan.

32   The grave of the All-Mother

The party stopped by a doorway. Gabrielle said "We're now one floor down from the orni-pad. Behind those doors there's a stairway which runs between decks." She turned to Tvoul. "What do we do now?"

Tvoul replied "As soon as we pass through those doors we're likely to run into Shval. Let me go first."

"Tvoul—if we do meet up with Shval," said Jack, "Can you be sure of killing her outright?"

"No—not even with this thing. You know how hard groubians are to kill. But it's a risk we've got to take."

"No it isn't!" cried Jack. "We can negotiate with her."

"Useless." Tvoul snapped back at him.

"Listen," said Jack. "This is my *triadnik* you're talking about. I happen to *command* her!"

Tvoul turned slowly round in wonderment to stare into Jack's face. "And who commands you?"

"Peter Zwillinge. Locked away in hibernation, on captain's orders."

"Jack," cried Tvoul. "What a Faustian pact you're caught up in…!" She hesitated, pondering. "But it might work. No matter how far a groubian falls, the last thing she lets go of is triada loyalty."

She tightened her grip on the uzi. "But she expects loyalty of you too, Jack. In return for her absolute obedience you've given your solemn vow to cherish her and defend her with your life."

Jack swallowed hard. "I'll have to tell her where we are."

"That's if she doesn't know already." Tvoul looked up and down the corridor. "Let me get out of sight. When you hear me shout *'down'*—hit the floor, all of you." She raised herself on her toes to look over his head. "S-bots included."

"Tvoul…"

"Yes, Jack?"

His voice tripped as he tried to speak. There were so many different things he wanted to implore her. To spare the triadnik he'd just betrayed? To be merciful to her? To have a milligram of pity? Would Tvoul take the slightest bit of notice?

"You *will* make bloody sure of her, won't you?"

Without answering, Tvoul slipped into a side-corridor and was gone.

Jack went to the t-unit mounted beside the door and picked up the handset. But when he tried to speak, he found he couldn't. Screwing up his eyes he feinted axe-blows with his open hand, as if that would help.

"Shval, petal..." he eventually managed to say. "Can you hear me?"

A pause...

"*Jack!* Where *are* you?" Shval's frantic voice came back over the public address.

"We're at stairway 22, level 5," said Jack, reading it off the plate above the door.

"What do you mean: *we?* Who's there with you?"

"Why—Gabrielle, of course. And three s-bots helping us carry the hibernator. They're okay—they're doing what we tell 'em."

There was a significant pause. "And who else?"

"Not a soul." It was the literal truth.

They waited in silence for Shval's response. Instinctively Gabrielle drew close to Jack and put her arm around his waist. The s-bots took up defensive positions in a triangle around them.

"So put away your weapons and come to your Jack, eh? Just to please me?"

Still there was no reply from Shval. To blunt the urge to panic, Jack started counting, silently mouthing the numbers. 1, 2, 3, 4, 5...

He got to 13 when everything happened at once.

With a spiteful hiss the pneumatic doors sprang apart. There just out of reach was Shval, half-crying, half-smiling. She held out empty hands towards Jack.

"Down!"

It was Tvoul's voice—from the stairwell behind Shval. Gabrielle and the s-bots dropped to the ground. But Jack stood staring, just as Judas must have stared at his erstwhile master. Lunging upwards like a tigress, Gabrielle clawed him to the floor.

The uzi blazed out. Stumbling to her knees in the bullet-storm, sepia spraying from her body, Shval turned and levelled her triton pistol. A ripping flash—and the uzi stopped, instantly vaporised along with its firer.

Shval fell face-down. Over her body freezing orange fog poured in through a huge gash in the outer wall. Jack's visor shot across his face. But Gabrielle was wearing no helmet. Clutching wildly at Jack, she convulsed in his arms, choking in the paraffin atmosphere.

Mercifully the safety systems detected a massive leak in the stairwell and the pneumatic doors slammed back shut—with Shval on the other side. One s-bot produced an emergency breathing mask, clapped it over Gabrielle's face and picked her up. The other two picked up the casket. Jack staggered along behind them as they hastened back the way they'd come, making for stairway 21 and the gangway outside.

Shval's voice came shrieking over the public address system. *"Jack, you double-crossing bastard. I'll kill you!"*

The s-bots raced up stairway 21 and struggled out through the airlock with the hibernator. Thirty yards away, on the other side of the hole, stood the ornithopter. Still intact on its pad, glimmering in the fire which flared behind the guardroom windows, it tempted them like bait on a mousetrap.

There was enough of the buckled gangway to clamber past the triton-blasted hole. The two s-bots carrying the casket put it down and covered Jack's and Gabrielle's passage, weapons at the ready. As Jack reached the ornithopter, he banged frantically on the door. Nothing happened. The s-bot carrying Gabrielle thrust past him and touched an unobtrusive panel. The airlock sprang open and Gabrielle was carried in. The other s-bots brought up the rear with Harry's casket and Jack stood aside to let them enter.

Before following them he turned and glanced back. As he did, a 0.38 slug ripped through his chest. Superox spurted out of him. Mixed with blood the oxidising spray ignited in the paraffin-laden atmosphere, transfixing him with a brilliant javelin of fire.

In the light of the blazing guardroom, Jack saw Shval crawling on the deck. She'd dragged herself through the yawning hole as the last s-bot had reached the ornithopter. The uzi had lacerated her body and the burred edges of the hole had opened up her dust suit, tearing back the flesh of her mantle in a great flap. Like a crushed slug, she'd left a grainy trail of guts, rapidly glazing over in the intense cold.

She came to a halt. Her lower half was now stuck fast to the steel deck. "Jack!" Her voice, like a panicking child, came squealing over the IR link. "Don't leave me. Not here—*not on Titan!*"

In the last extremity of despair, Shval fired again and again. This time the bullets came close to Jack's head, ricocheting off the ornithopter. He couldn't tear his gaze from her dreadful eyes as she kept on squeezing the trigger. It didn't occur to him to scramble through the airlock to safety.

Now Shval had fired her last shot. The automatic clicked uselessly once... twice. She relaxed her fingers, letting the gun drop onto the deck. Her open hand stretched out towards him, not to claw, but as if to caress.

Jack turned his back on her to climb inside, but stopped as the narrow flame reddened a heart-sized patch on the airlock. How could he forsake his triadnik, whom he'd vowed to cherish and defend with his life? Was she so hateful that she was only fit to be abandoned in her last despair?

Well—that made two of them.

Turning and reaching out one arm, Jack staggered back towards her. She shied away, hand raised to ward off the fiery javelin sprouting from his breast. Kneeling down, he let the flame punch through the deck. Steel turned white in a shower of sparks and bubbled up in droplets. He was a thermic lance. Turning slightly to keep the jet of oxygen well clear of her, he clasped Shval's outstretched hand...

* * * * * ★ ● ★ * * * * *

Regaining consciousness, Jack found himself inside the ornithopter.

An s-bot had emerged from the aircraft and paralysed the two of them with a taser shot. Then, spraying Jack with halon, it had quenched the flames. It had even tried to plug the foaming wounds, but that was beyond its competence. Beyond anyone's now, save the Galen.

"Let me go back to her." he screamed. "We can't leave her. She's going frantic out there!"

Gabrielle, recovered now, was sitting at the controls. She turned and glared at him. It was she who'd ordered the s-bot to bring him in.

"What am I supposed to do? Leave you out there to die—in the arms of that alien trash?" She wrenched herself round in the pilot seat and jabbed at the console.

Like an eagle rising from its eyrie, the ornithopter reared up on its legs, still clamped to the perch, gathering wingfuls of brown wind for take-off. Jack groaned and curled up in a foetal ball, his eyes shut tight. Blood mixed with superox sprayed through his fingers onto his visor.

Flapping vigorously, the ornithopter let go its perch. It fought to make headway against the gale, which strove to sweep them back onto the blazing roof. Still frozen in her mucus to the deck, Shval too was regaining consciousness. She drew Sprenger's TP from its calf holster and tried to level her wavering arm to turn this flopper also into glittering rain.

Suddenly the craft decided to go with the wind, not against it— skipping over the rig like a dry leaf. But as it did so, its right wing struck the central stack, bringing it crashing down in a blossom of fire. Spinning full-circle, the aircraft careered out of control. It bounced twice on the waves, each time managing to free itself from the engulfing spray with vigorous thrashes of its one good wing. Spiralling skywards, it was presently high over the rig. It couldn't have presented an easier target.

Struggling to hold her arm up steady, Shval suddenly gave up the effort. Her features soaked in agony and tears, she lay on the frozen steel, shaking her head from side to side.

Then something caused her to open her eyes.

Standing in the hole, flickering in the light of hopeless fires, a second ectoplast had come to life and stood eyeing her along a TP barrel. Tvoul Rainbow was about to waste her sister—who had herself wasted so many others.

Shval squeezed the trigger of her own TP. A figure-eight of infinite temperature ensnared the twins in a macro-p-orbital. Plasma resonance occurred as the fermions of diametrically opposed personas paired and became bosonic: a stationary state of dreadful synergy. A microsecond later there was mutual annihilation.

Inside the ornithopter, blinding light flooded the cabin. Gabrielle screamed and Jack tensed up, certain he was about to die.

······ ✶ ● ✶ ······

He was back on Wearmouth Bridge, standing in a shining mist before the Sunderland coat-of-arms:

NIL DESPERANDUM

Looking down he noticed, as if for the first time, the full inscription as it carried on beneath the shield:

AUSPICE DEO

There is nothing to despair about. Look to the Will of God.
Else what is the value of life, that we take such pains to hold on to it?
Nothing.

······ ✶ ● ✶ ······

Suddenly the light faded. They were still flying. Raising himself on his elbow, Jack gazed in awe out of the rear of the cockpit. A gigantic fireball, a sickly-green cauliflower of ash and flame, was ascending into the Titanic stratosphere in a writhing bubble. Underneath, feeding it a boiling column like the trunk of a shining tree, an even bigger ring of rolling spume tumbled outwards in a massive breaker. Expanding steadily from this abomination, as though it were a trick of the light, a perfect hemisphere inflated to engulf everything there was.

When the shock-wave struck, it all but hurled them into the sea. Fluttering its wings, the ornithopter righted itself and resumed its climb through the dust-laden atmosphere, high above the methane waves. When it began to flap against emptiness its rockets ignited, enabling it to climb higher still.

It was being drawn back to the black cone of *Prometheus*, drifting overhead with its crew of dead men. The double-doors of the docking bay lay open, as Agent Zero had left them. Like a swift returning to its nest, the ornithopter rose between them and clamped itself to its perch.

But Jack took no notice. The last of his superox had bubbled away in pink foam and his SP unit had shut down in damage-mode. Straightaway the s-bots put him in the casket brought for Tvoul.

•••••★●★•••••

Four figures floated out of the ornithopter into the darkness of the stricken *mir*. Gabrielle, in emergency oxygen mask, led the way, dragging Jack's casket with the help of an s-bot. The other two s-bots came behind with Harry. Soon they felt the pull of quasi-gravity and were able to walk upright.

On the control deck, Gabrielle stepped over bodies to reach the v-screen. MM appeared and acquainted her with the situation. She turned to stare at Jack's hibernator, slowly shaking her head.

"I'm sorry Jack, I shall have to resuscitate you. Or else we're going to circle this dead world forever."

The s-bots came back with Jack on a trolley, an oxygenation lead in his arm. He had fared no better in his second resuscitation than his first. Reverently they laid aside Captain Kahlil's body and propped Jack's comatose form in its place. Gabrielle cradled Jack's head whilst working the metabolo.

MM's mouth opened onto the void. *"Kaptén Dzhak Viliáms."*

Jack's eyelids sprang apart and he lurched forward, as if aroused out of a horrid dream. Gabrielle clung to him, looking in vain for a gleam of reason in his eyes.

"Koudá?" said MM.

Jack groaned, as if he'd been asked a question of such enormity that it would take mankind a thousand years to answer.

"Jack, bonny lad," murmured Gabrielle in his ear, "where're we gannin', like?"

Jack closed his eyes, like a man laying down a heavy burden. His trek from Earth had begun to the sound of Gabrielle's soft voice. Now it was ended. "Gan 'yem," he muttered—and never spoke again.

The coloured bars sank to nothing and a flashing skull appeared. The metabolo slipped unnoticed to the floor as Gabrielle began to weep on Jack's shoulder.

"Na Geia," MM confirmed—and its face faded to stars. Great smoky wisps of stars in countless numbers, streaming through space like pollen in a sunbeam. Each grain a mighty sun, waiting down the ages to be garlanded with worlds of ice and steel.

One blue dot among a wisp of stars grew to a crescent, frosted by swirls of cloud. The crescent grew until it filled the screen.

•••••✹●✹•••••

The stars no longer shine. The sky is bright. Clouds drift across in ever-changing shapes.

The clouds are clearing from the sky. Beneath a few remaining wisps of white there stands a crenellated tower. At its foot, eight boys and one girl kneel around a well-kept grave.

The smallest of them, Anitra, solemnly leans forward and places a wreath at the gravestone's foot. A new inscription has been added. Now it reads:

> *Hilda Margaret Williams*
> *Born 16/4/1907, died 13/6/1974*
> *Beloved wife of Jack Williams*
> *Died of a broken heart.*
> *And here too lies her heartbreak's cause*
> *Tvoul Williams, her bonny bairn Harry*
> *And her dear husband Jack*
> *At peace now in eternity's embrace.*

For eternity is here. It is now. Let a thousand years pass—a million years—and people will still be making the pilgrimage from all over the galaxy to the traditional site of the tomb, in what is widely held to be ancient Esh Winning, on one of the better candidates for being Gaia of the fairytales. They will be drawn to this hallowed spot by an enduring myth: to pay homage to Gilda, the All-Mother.

•••••✹●✹•••••

Anitra glances either side at her brothers. Solemnity crumbles into giggles. Children they are still, for one last sunny day. Their footprints still wander through Wear Valley. Tomorrow they are eighteen, every one, for they share the same birthday: Midsummer's Day. Tomorrow they will make plans to leave Esh Winning, Durham, England, Europe, Gaia, System Sol... for worlds more distant still.

Grey ripples course across their faces, tumbling in their eyes, displacing pastel colours on their ever-changing skins. Colours of pregnant fantasies they couldn't hide to save their everlasting lives. For these are the stellans: the star-children. Together with gaians and groubians they comprise the three species of humanity.

They scramble to their feet, shouting and laughing, as they play catch-as-catch-can all the way back to their rainbow-coloured bus. There, sprawled across both seats behind the driver, is Uncle Peter: an ugly great lovable octopus of a man, who has lived with them for as long as they can remember. And Gabrielle, her mortal skin now putty-grey with cancer, sits in maternal patience at the wheel.

As each child passes them both, they are brushed by hands that turn rose-pink with love. And as the children crowd into their seats and look out through the windows, they lift their eyes to the sky, letting its azure hue flow down their cheeks. For they know that, however far they roam the galaxy, their beautiful round sapphire eyes will always reflect the memory of Gaia.

For on Gaia the sky is blue.

THE END

Appendix A. Glossary

All entries are M2 words, including loan-words from M1 and Selensk.
Starred entries, eg ***Cydonia**, are authentic physical or astronomical terms.
Words in italics refer to another entry in this glossary, e.g. *world*.

Adin Beam, Adin Satellite. A beam of protons (ionised hydrogen) collected from the solar wind by means of a Fresnel lens of concentric superconducting rings placed at the L4 and L5 libration points of the Earth-Moon system. These focus the beam onto a series of orbiting collimators as they come past. The collimator, or *Adin satellite*, directs it to a precise surface target.

Adin's Process. Chemical process of making water on the Moon by directing an *Adin Beam* onto the surface to react with aluminium and silicon oxides in moon rock.

Agent. A robot *persona* taking the form of an *ectoplast*, or else simply an animated image on a screen. Also the official title of a *z-nik*—a police officer of *Zasta*. (M1: *agént*).

Areopagus. (Gk: = "Rock-of-Mars".) Massive rock in the centre of Nix City; also the park cultivated around it.

*Bloody-butcher. A terrestrial trout-fishing fly, of a blood-red colour. See: *CRW*.

*Bose-Einstein [statistics], [-condensate]. Statistical-mechanics laws governing particles having no separate identity. Obeyed at the sub-atomic scale by photons. *Bose-Einstein* entities cannot be distinguished; if assembled or reckoned together they form a *Bose-Einstein condensate*. See *Fermi-Dirac statistics*.

Chimorg. A genetically engineered organism incorporating human genes, prohibited by the *transgenic laws*. See: *Human*.

Circadian. A day in the waking life of the *denizens* of a given *world*. On Earth the *circadian* is identical to the Terrestrial *sol*: 24 h. On Selene the *circadian* is 25 h but may include *forlorn tid*. On *Oberon* too the *circadian* is 25 h, but without the *intercalary* period imposed by *seltid*. On Mars the *circadian* is either 24 h or 25 h to keep up with the Martian *sol*.

CRW. Corporal Retrieval Winch. A device for retrieving bodies from inaccessible places, also employed by *Zasta* for stopping fugitives. Essentially a remotely-controlled buzz-bomb shooting talons into the body, tethered by a strong filament to an electrical winch. Colloquially called a *bloody-butcher*.

*Cydonia. Region on Mars, famed for its spectacular natural features: pentagonal pyramids and the notorious "Mars Face".

Dag[er]. The *seltid* "day", or *circadian*, of 25 h duration. See *Uge*.

Denizen. A legally-recognised permanent resident of a *world*. C/f "citizen".

Doróga. A north-south thoroughfare in Nix City. (M1: *doróga* = road.) See: *oúlitza*.

Ectoplasm, Ectoplast. Electrostatically-configurable paste of nano-particles. Animated doll consisting of a colour-changing plastic membrane filled with this material, capable of realistic appearance, movement and feel.

Edulation. Groubian sexual intercourse, entailing consumption by the edulator of the edulee's vitals. Fertile only between an edulator and an edulee of the opposite sex.

Elstat. An electrostatic grenade. Essentially a 100 microfarad capacitor charged to 100,000 volts (the energy-equivalent of approximately 1lb of TNT). Kills everyone in a room without significant damage to property.

Fall of Titan. Catastrophe, of undetermined nature, which wiped out the *groubians* on Titan some 50,000 years ago.

*Fermi-Dirac statistics. Statistical-mechanics laws governing particles having identity, which prevents them occupying the same spatio-temporal position and momentum (which in Quantum Theory would make them indistinguishable). Obeyed on the sub-atomic scale by protons, neutrons and electrons, but not photons. See *Bose-Einstein statistics*.

Flopper. See *Ornithopter*.

Forlorn tid. A (normally) 2-hour intercalary period inserted between lørdag and søndag (see: *Uge*), during which time the clocks stop. The period is longer for the first søndag of the *månad* (the average being 2 h 44 m to synchronise *seltid* with the synodic lunar month). (Selensk: *forloren* = lost + *tid* = time.) See *Seltid, Månad*.

Four Worlds, the ~. The signatories of the *Treaty of Moscow*, viz *Gaia, Selene, Mars* and *Oberon*. See also: *inner planets*.

Gaia, Zemlia. Planet Earth, both names being chiefly used by non-Terrestrials, *Zemlia* avoiding the mystical overtones of *Gaia*. (M1: *Gáia, Zémlia* = the planet Earth.)

Gaian. An ape of the species *Homo sapiens*. NB: never used for someone from the planet *Gaia*; *zemlian* or *terrestrial* being employed instead.

Gaiascope, the ~. Huge leisure complex in the centre of Jordvik, built around an Earth-viewing observatory, the "Camera". (Selensk: *Gaiaskop[et]*.)

Groubian. A cuttle of the species *Sepia sapiens martialis*, legally recognised as *human* by the Treaty of Nix. (M1: *groubián* = tramp [obsolete], groubian.)

*H₂-hybrid. A road vehicle with electric transmission and storage batteries charged by an on-board hydrogen-powered internal combustion engine.

Holoface. Holographic face. A digitally-generated mask, often fancifully chosen, to hide one's true face or expression.

Hopper. A light rocket-powered vehicle used on the Moon and other planets lacking an atmosphere to sustain aerodynamic lift.

Hugglephone. Communication device consisting essentially of the upper half of an *ectoplast*, taking on the appearance and feel of the communicant and transmitting back sensations of touch.

Human. Pertaining to those sentient beings to which the *Strana of Olympia* has accorded human rights. Includes all *gaians* and *groubians*, but excludes robots and *chimorgs*.

Inner Planets, the ~. Strictly Mercury, Venus, Earth and Mars, but used legally to mean all *human* settlements from Mars inwards towards the Sun.

Intensions. Numerical parameters of the *intensor* relating to a given individual. Generalises the terrestrial notions of character, personality, integrity and social status.

Intensor. A spatio-temporal field defining a covariant tensor of rank 2, conveying information via facial sensations about a nearby person. Mediates all transactions between citizens, taking the place of money, credit, credentials, personal identification and all other forms of advertisement. See *intensions, persona*.

*Intercalary. A bridging time-interval required to resynchronise a given time-standard with some astronomically-defined event, e.g. February 29, UT, which is required every four years to resynchronise the solar year.

Interspex. Interspecific (inter-species) sex. M1 and M2 word, technically covering all forms of bestiality, but used mainly and pejoratively of non-edulatory gaian/groubian sexual intercourse.

Intertalk. An IR or RF speech-channel for the Martian helmet. Supports short-range conversation even in an airless environment.

Klarside. (Pronounced 'KLAR-seel-er', with guttural 'r' and soft 'd'.) The side of the Moon which always faces towards the Earth. (Selensk: *klar* = bright + *side* = side.) See: *Mørkside*.

*Lunar. Pertaining to the Moon as a celestial body. See: *Selenean*.

M1. Russian; the first of the two official languages of the Strana of Olympia. The main gaian language (often the only one) learned by groubians. (M1: *Mársnii Odín* = Martian One.)

M2. English; the second of the two official languages of the *Strana of Olympia*. Characterises the underclass.

Månad. The Selenean "month" synchronised with the synodic lunar month (the average moon-phase cycle), which is 708.73416 h. The *månad* is divided into 4 *uger* ("weeks") of 7 *dager* ("days") of 25 h, giving 700 h. The remaining synodic 8.73416 h are divided into 4 *intercalary* periods (*forlorn tid*) inserted between lørdag and søndag. Three of these intercalaries are 2-hour ones, the fourth (commencing the *månad*) is 2.73416 h.

Månehundtorv[et]. Main city-square of Jordvik, situated just north of the *Gaiascope.* (Selensk: *Månehund* = the Moon-Dog + *torv* = square, plaza + *[et]* = the neuter definite article.)

Marscar. A self-steering voice-directed vehicle lacking wheels, designed for use on Martian roads, which are little more than channels of dust.

Marsgrav. The larger of the two pods of *Oberon*, maintained at Mars gravity by the vessel's off-centre rotation, the pod preferred by *Martians*. (M1: *mársgrav* from: *Mársnaia gravitátzionnaia sredá* = Martian gravitational environment.)

Marsvrem, MV. Official time/calendar on the planet Mars, defined on the meridian passing through the *Areopagus*. *Marsvrem* and *zemvrem* (=UT) both have hours, minutes and seconds of the same duration, however the Martian *sol* (24.6598 h) does not contain a whole number of hours. But the MV *circadian* does, an *intercalary* "twenty-fifth hour" being periodically inserted. The Martian solar year is 668.6 sols, but the MV calendar year is roughly one-half as long, i.e. 336 circadians (*not* sols). This gives 12 months of 28 circadians each, the Terrestrial names of weekdays and months being used. Every fourth year is a "leap year" in which 7 circadians are dropped from the end of December. NB: because the calendar year, whether "leap" or not, contains a whole number of weeks, New Year's Day on Mars always falls on Sunday, as does the first circadian of every month. (M1: *mársvrem* from: *Mársnoe vrémia* = Martian time.)

Mars. *World* or *mir* established on the planet Mars. Occasionally: the planet itself.

Martian. Term referring both to the planet itself and to its *denizens*. See: *World*.

Metabolo. A wireless control unit for a human patient fitted with metabolic control.

Mir. M1 loan-word equivalent to *world*. Used especially to refer to a *world* as a legal entity, e.g. the Titanian *mir*.

Mørkside. (Pronounced 'MURK-seel-er', with guttural 'r' and soft 'd') The far side of the Moon, never visible from Earth. (Selensk: *mørk* = dark + *side* = side.) See: *Klarside*.

Nix, The ~. Caldera of Olympus Mons, historically called *Nyx Olympica* by Terrestrial astronomers.

Oberon. *World* or *mir* established on the space-going vessel *SV Oberon*.

Olvoi. Volunteer defence force of the Strana of Olympia. (M1: *Olímpiskaia Vóiska* = Olympian Force.)

Olympia, Strana of ~. Administrative region (*strana*) surrounding Olympus Mons on Mars. Capital: Nix City.

*Ornithopter. (Also *flopper*). An aircraft with moveable wings emulating the flight of a bird.

Oúlitza. An east-west thoroughfare in Nix City. (M1: *oúlitza* = street.) See: *doróga*.

Persona. Total information (*intensions*) about a given person, as registered by the *intensor*. Considered to embrace all aspects of personal information and identity. An intelligent machine possesses a *persona*, but legally this must be of a reduced class (and neuter gender) incapable of being mistaken for a human being.

Rumhavn[en]. (Pronounced 'ROOM-how-n', with guttural 'r') Used by itself to refer to Lipsky Rumhavn, the spaceport of Lunaborg serving all of Selene. (Selensk: *rumhavn*, from: *rum* = space + *havn* = port + *[en]* = the common definite article.)

Selene, Sel-. *World* or *mir* established on the Moon; *sel-* being a prefix designating that world, eg *seltid, selkroner*.

Selenean. Term referring to the *denizens* of *Selene*. See: *World*.

Selensk. Official language of Selene. A dialect of Danish.

Selkrone[r]. (Pronounced 'SEL-krooner', with guttural 'r'). The Selenean Crown, the official currency of Selene. (Selensk: *sel-* + *krone* = crown. Plural: *selkroner*.)

Selstyrke. (Pronounced 'SELST-you-r-ger', with guttural 'r'). The Selenean militia, combining the functions of police and defence force. (Selensk: *selstyrke* = moonforce, from: *sel-* + *styrke* = armed-force.)

Seltid. (Pronounced 'SEL-teel', with soft 'd'.). Selenean time-standard based on a lunar month (*månad*) of 28 25-hour *circadians* (*dager*) commencing at sunrise on the zero meridian, which passes through Jordvik. This coincides with the Moon's first-quarter as seen from Earth. Four intercalary periods (*forlorn tid*) totalling 8 h 44 min averaged over time are needed to synchronise the *månad* with sunrise. (Selensk: *seltid* = moon-time, from: *sel-* + *tid* = time.) See: *Zemvrem, Marsvrem, Forlorn tid*.

*Sol. Solar "day" on a given planet, especially Mars, the interval between successive sunrises. The duration of the Martian *sol* is 24 h 39 min 35 s. See: *Marsvrem*.

Spatio-color. Groubian skin-language, a code of communication based on evolving patterns of colour. (Latin: *spatio-color* = area-colour.)

SP unit. *Superox* perfuser, an internal heart-lung device occupying most of the thorax.

Strana. An autonomous region of Mars, the most important being the Strana of Olympia. Others include Cydonia and Valles. (M1: *straná* = land, country.)

Superox. Trade-name of nearly pure hydrogen peroxide, H_2O_2, used in an *SP unit*.

System Sol. The solar system, as a place-name.

*Taser. Stun-gun. A hand-held weapon employing a high-voltage, low current electrical discharge to stun the victim.

Terrestrial. Term referring to the *denizens* of Earth. See: *World, Zemlian*.

Titan. Largest moon of the planet Saturn. Also, a groubian former inhabitant of Titan. Used pejoratively of any groubian, even those born on Mars.

Titan Kiss. Pejorative colloquialism for *edulation*.

Titan Two-step. Pejorative colloquialism for *interspex*.

Titanic, Titanian. Terms referring to the body itself and to its *denizens* respectively. See: *World*.

Transgenic Laws. Laws of the Strana of Olympia forbidding the creation of new *chimorgs* and granting existing ones restricted human rights.

Treaty of Moscow. Treaty governing the rights and duties of inter-world travellers, signed in 1872 by the *Four Worlds: Gaia, Selene, Mars* and *Oberon*. Subsequently Gaia's status as a properly constituted *mir* was withdrawn until such a time as it could furnish a plenipotentiary representative to the Council of the Inner Planets. Meanwhile any terrestrial government wishing to benefit from its terms are bound by the treaty to conceal the existence of extra-terrestrial colonies from its populace.

*Triton. A subatomic particle consisting of one proton and two neutrons bound together; the nucleus of tritium, the ^{3}H-isotope of hydrogen.

Triton pistol. A hand-held weapon firing a thermonuclear plasma toroid fuelled by *tritons* supplied as tritium oxide (superheavy water, or T_2O).

Uge[r]. The *seltid* "week" consisting of 7 *dager*, named søndag, gaidag, tisdag, onsdag, torsdag, fredag and lørdag. English-speakers on the Moon use these names rather than Sunday, Monday, etc, to avoid confusion with UT days (d), which are of 24 h duration, not the 25 h of a normal *dag*.

*Universal Time, UT. Intermondial time-standard (Z) based on the Earth's rotation, superseding Greenwich Mean Time (GMT). See: *Zemvrem*.

Valles. Town and administrative region (*strana*) including most of Valles Marineris, the conspicuous canyon complex on Mars.

Vratch, the~. Olympian medical police, providing a free compulsory public health service. Organised and armed like *Zasta*. (M1: *vratch* = medic.)

Vratchnik/Vratchka. Male/female medic, paramedic or nurse employed by the *Vratch*.

Voronka [Cosmodrome]. Spaceport serving Nix City. (M1: V*orónka* = The [Blast-]Crater.)

World. Human population of a given celestial body or space platform. Always autonomous, bound only by treaties with other worlds and having its own clock and calendar. The inhabitants of a *world* are called its *denizens*.

Zasta. Olympian Information Police, charged with guarding the integrity of the *intensor*, which extends to general policing duties. Unlike *Selstyrke* on the Moon, *Zasta* does not have responsibility for defence, this being the mission of *Olvoi*. (M1: *zastavlénie* = enforcement.)

Zastavlennik, z-nik. *Zasta* agent.

Zemlia, Zemlian. Terms referring to Planet Earth and to its *denizens*. See: *Gaia, Gaian, Terrestrial*.

Zemgrav. Smaller of the two pods of *Oberon*, kept at Earth gravity (*g*) by the vessel's off-centre rotation. The preferred pod for *Terrestrials*. (M1: *zémgrav*, from: *Zémnaia gravitátzionnaia sredá* = Earth gravity environment.)

Zemvrem. Martian (M1 and M2) name for Universal Time (UT). (M1: *zémvrem* from: *zémnoe vrémia* = terrestrial time.) See: *Marsvrem, UT*.

Zygocyst. *Groubian* foetal sac forming in the parental tissues as the result of *edulation*.

Zygogeny. Mass-event among groubians to conceive progeny during which *edulation* was formally undertaken. The Last, or Titanic *zygogeny*, occasioned by the *Fall of Titan*, took place on Mars 50,000 years ago.

Appendix B. Selene

From: Welcome To Selene! (Commune of Jordvik, 1975)…

If you are new to Selene you may appreciate a few facts. Formerly a
Danish protectorate, Selene became independent at the same time as
Greenland in 1941. It is a sovereign state with its own language, Selensk,
resembling an archaic Danish dialect), its own laws and traditions (*Sellov*),
calendar (*seltid:* "moontime"), militia (*Selstyrke:* "moonforce") and currency (*selkrone:* the Selenean crown). However all major Terrestrial
currencies are accepted in hotels and public facilities, plus of course the
Martian *econinst.*

The chief cities are Lunaborg (pop. 1.3 Million) and Jordvik (pop.
80,000), situated diametrically on the lunar equator. Several other smaller
settlements, mostly of a specialist nature such as farms, scientific stations,
religious foundations and penal establishments, are scattered over the
lunar globe.

Visitors often express surprise that a small country like Denmark was
ever given charge of the Moon. There were several reasons for this.
Being small and with no declared enemies, Denmark was universally
trusted to administer the lunar colonies impartially. Historically speaking
it was well suited to the task. In the 17th century it guaranteed one of the
most important Hanseatic trade routes: the Øresund, the narrow water-
way between Scania and Zealand. Today it fulfils a similar function
between Gaia and Mars.

Being itself spread over several islands, Denmark had ample
experience of administering a scattered territory linked by numerous
bridges and ferries. The historical administration of Nunavut (formerly
Greenland) and Norway gave it unsurpassed experience of controlling
and developing vast tracts of mountainous terrain. Many Seleneans are
of Inuit (Greenlander) descent, which they proudly claim suits them to a
cold hostile environment having long spells of darkness.

But the fabled harshness of the Moon is a thing of the past.
Lunaborg and Jordvik are cities with every modern amenity and know
how to cater for visitors. Seleneans are warm and friendly, noted for
their hospitality and *hygge*—an untranslatable word with overtones of
cosiness and companionship.

Appendix C. Groubians

From Areopedia (main entry): Groubian Species…

Groubian (*Sepia sapiens martialis*): A cephalopod of the genus *Sepia*, phylum *Mollusca*, closely related to terrestrial cuttles. Of the once considerable colony on Mars, scarcely 5,000 groubians remain alive. They are mostly to be found in Nix City, in former times their biggest settlement. By the terms of the Treaty of Nix, which concluded the Second Olympian War, all groubians were extended full human rights by the victorious coalition and are today recognised as human under Olympian law. Although the original sense of *groubián* in M1 (the first of the two official languages of Olympia) to mean 'filthy' has dropped out of use, opprobrium continues to surround the word *interspex*: a contraction of "inter-species sex".

In the absence of males, the groubian species is technically extinct; a living fossil. No new individuals can be conceived; and in view of numerous contraindications to cloning, the groubian population can only diminish. This state of affairs has endured for a remarkably long time. It may explain why groubians attempted to mate with the first settlers on Mars, the declared cause of the First Olympian War. Ever since, so-called groubian weddings have been outlawed on Mars and prosecuted as fifth-rank murder.

In spite of their comprising a miniscule proportion of the population of Mars (currently less than 5,000 individuals), groubians are immensely influential, pervading all walks of life. The very foundations of Martian society are architected along groubian lines, which makes living on Mars an altogether different experience from anything a Terrestrial can imagine.

History. Contrary to popular belief, groubians as a distinct species did not originate on Mars, but on Saturn's largest moon, Titan. The Chicxulub Event on Gaia (circa 65,000,000 BCE) which was violent enough to extinguish the dinosaurs, along with 95% of all terrestrial species, ejected an estimated 3,000 cubic miles of biologically potent material into space, wholly dispersed in the zodiacal plane. This material, deriving from surface rock and shallow coral seas, was rich in spores, seeds and eggs preserved by flash-freezing on being flung out into space. It inoculated all the bodies of the solar system, but only on Titan is it known to have given rise to a colony of life-forms persisting for more than a million years.

In the nurturing environment which Titan then afforded, the Chicxulub detritus quickly gave rise to an extensive biosphere, ranging from the most primitive life-forms to the most advanced. This is not to assert that conditions on Titan remotely resembled those on Gaia, then or now. There is no hope of reconstructing them: our only source for what they must have been like is the Book of Titan, a perplexing spatio-color document defying translation and said to be truly comprehensible only by groubians.

Approximately 50,000 years ago, a cataclysm known as the Fall of Titan (which may or may not have been natural) sterilised that world, giving rise to the hostile environment in evidence today. The Titanic civilisation was extirpated, leaving only the tiny colony on Mars.

Some groubians question that Titan was altogether sterilised, arguing for the persistence to this day of a massive and dangerous life form: the Titan Kraken (another cephalopod) able to endure the low surface temperatures, at which methane liquefies.

No substantial evidence for the existence of the Kraken has been forthcoming; in its absence these conjectures can be dismissed as furthering a politico-religious agenda. For groubians, Titan is a world under a holy ban. Nothing can justify people visiting it ever again.

Anatomy. Groubians resemble gaians in physique, but in the absence of familial relationship this must be put down to convergent evolution. It has been suggested that the adoption of humanoid appearance is both conscious and deliberate on the part of groubians, to reinforce their claim to human status. Be that as it may, no groubian has reliably been observed in anything other than humanoid form.

Lacking calcified bones (the sole calcareous tissue being two dorsal plates of cuttle-bone; the vestigial molluscan shell, each situated roughly where the scapula occurs in gaians), groubians retain their humanoid shape by tough ligaments resembling bones when palpated. The arrangement of their internal organs bears no relationship whatever to mammalian anatomy.

The brain is notably absent as a recognisable organ; its function being subsumed by a network of ganglia distributed throughout the body. Those mental functions which are thought to be the provenance of the cerebral cortex in gaians are taken over by the skin, an organ rich in nervous tissue; and one responsible for the groubians' most spectacular faculty: the ability to change colour instantaneously at will.

As in terrestrial cephalopods, colour changing is performed by pigmented cells called chromatophores, which expand on receiving signals along afferent nerve fibres, thus displaying their characteristic colour in the semi-transparent skin. In the absence of nervous activity the chromatophores contract altogether, conferring a milky white appearance on dead or comatose individuals.

Groubian chromatophores divide into six categories matched by corresponding types of retinal cell: red, yellow, green, blue, violet and ultraviolet, each with different neurological properties. This underlies their role in signalling the emotional state of the organism. Groubians maintain that all aspects of their mental life, including superior activity analogous to poetry or music, are displayed openly on their skins. However as a rule the patterns observed are ones which only another groubian can correctly interpret.

Reproduction. Terrestrial cephalopods mate in a way surprisingly reminiscent of mammals, the male employing an adapted tentacle to penetrate and impregnate the female, which then goes and finds some rocky fissure in which to give birth to a batch of infants, each a tiny copy of the adult. The mother stays with the infants to protect them until she dies, which is not long after giving birth. Her total lifespan has then been little more than a terrestrial year. Females which do not mate may live longer.

From earliest times the sepias on Titan adopted a social organisation resembling communal wasps. Early on they abandoned their ancestral mode of reproduction as a by-product of prolonging their lives indefinitely, some say as a result of conscious intervention by the species in its own genome. Quite possibly however it was a chance mutation, which would have conferred superior status on the individual thus immortalised. Strangely though, for a communal species, the adaptation became extended to all individuals, the expected short-lived slave-class either dying out or never arising in the first place.

Sexual intercourse became infrequent, and was never spontaneous. For reasons to become clear, it was always pursued as an extreme expedient, in obedience to dire social imperatives. It became adapted to the restriction of the species, as well as its reproduction. It generally took place in a mass-event called a zygogeny.

Courtship between two individuals took place over a period of days, a process known as edulation. During this deeply invasive method of intercourse, the edulator would consume the internal organs of the edulee, who died in the act of coitus.

Gametes from the edulee's gonads, provided he was male, spread through the entire body of the edulator, fusing with cells at random.

About 10 to 100 viable foetuses resulted, each feeding off the flesh of the parent, prompting womb-like structures called zygocysts to emerge throughout the body. The duration of pregnancy was anything from 1 to 5 Martian years (2 to 9 terrestrial years), governed by the totality of live foetuses. Parturition was simultaneous and invariably fatal, due to shock both nervous and anaphylactic, plus the rupturing of vital organs, the skin in particular. The offspring were brought up by the whole community.

The Age of a Groubian. Almost all groubians alive today were conceived during the Last (or Titanic) Zygogeny, prompted when the colony on Mars received news of the Fall of Titan. At that time females already significantly outnumbered males. No male groubians survived; this being intentional. However the failure, due possibly to a sex-linked retrovirus, of any male progeny to come to term was unintended and unforeseen. It confronted the colony with the fact that the zygogeny, in spite of yielding a host of new individuals, had failed in its purpose. As a species, groubians had become extinct.

Belying their resemblance to gaian women in their twenties, it follows that every living groubian is of the same advanced age. Yet no groubian has ever volunteered a coherent account of her life further back than six or seven years. In spite of conferring impressive powers of medium-term memory, the groubian genome contains no mechanism capable of laying down long-term memories commensurate with its unnaturally extended lifespan. On the other hand a memory horizon is a plausible defence mechanism in a long-lived sentient organism, permitting it to endure the endless accumulation of painful experiences without being driven to despair and suicide. Groubians rely on spatio-color documents like the Book of Titan to give a sense of continuity, not to say meaning and purpose, to their literally interminable lives.

Appendix D. The Olympian languages, M1 & M2

M1 and M2 (*Mársnii-Odín i Mársnii-Dvè*) are the official languages of the Strana of Olympia. M2 is a form of English, being characteristic of the underclass. It follows British spelling, with numerous M1 loan-words.

M1, the primary language, is descended from the Ukrainian and Russian of gaian immigrants from the Varangian *Rus* onwards, who reached Mars with the aid of groubian adventurers. It is written here using the Roman alphabet augmented with accented vowels: á é è ë í ó ú, each marking the syllable on which stress falls. All M1 quotations are italicised, although loan-words in M2 and English like 'Strana' or 'Vratch' are not. It follows the *pronunciation* of present-day Russian, not its transliteration. For example the M1 blessing: *fsevó xoróshevo* (=all the best) becomes in Russian: **всего хорошего** – which conventionally transliterates as: **vsego choroshego**. This is utterly useless as a guide to pronunciation for non Russian-speakers.

English-speakers however can achieve a more-or-less accurate pronunciation of M1 by following these rules.

Vowels need paying careful attention:

- M1 words are stressed on precisely one of their syllables, though which syllable can be hard to guess. So the stress is shown by an accented vowel, e.g. *evó* (=his), pronounced 'yeh-VOH', *eë* (=her), pronounced 'yeh-YOH'. Conversely an accented vowel is always stressed. **Example:** *Nedélia Slëz* (=Week of-Tears) is pronounced 'nyeh-DYEH-liah SLIOZ'.

- Unaccented *e* is always pronounced 'yeh'. The preceding 'y-' sound is inaudible after sibilants, eg *tózhe*, pronounced "TOH-zheh". Whenever the vowel-sound 'eh' is required, it is written *è*, e.g. *ètot* (=this), pronounced 'EH-tot'. The sound of *è* is as in 'there', not 'rate'.

- Vowel-pairs in M1 should be pronounced exactly as they are spelled, viz as two syllables. Thus *mársnoe* (=Martian [N]) is pronounced 'MARSS-noh-yeh', not 'MARZ-noh'.

- Exceptions to this rule are: *ia, io, iu, ou* and *ii*. The first three: *ia, io, iu,* are hard for an English speaker to copy, since the leading *i* is absorbed into the preceding consonant, softening it. Thus the first syllable of *liubóvka* (=lover [F]) is pronounced approximately like the '-lue' in 'value'. **Note:** where *l* is *not* followed by one of these vowel-pairs, as in *málaia* (=little [F]), it is pronounced with a distinctly hollow sound, as in "wall".

- The vowel-pair *ou* (as in the M1 name *Tvoul*) is not a dipthong but a pure vowel sound, rhyming with 'cool', not 'out'.
- The vowel-pair *ii* is a long 'ee'-sound as in 'fee', but usually pronounced with a hollow throat as if saying 'oo'. Thus, to English ears, *Pérvii* sounds more like 'PYER-vuih' than 'PYER-vee'. The single *i* in *ti* (=thou) is also pronounced the same way.
- Apostrophe: ['] serves as the 'soft sign' (M1: *miáxkii znak*) – a scarcely audible 'y'-sound, rarely occurring anywhere but the end of a word. Thus in *znát'* (=to know), *-t'* resembles the first 't' in 'initiation' (*-t'* forms the infinitive of verbs in M1). Similarly in *krov'* (=blood), *-v'* resembles the 'v' in "view", or sometimes the 'f' in "few" (omitting the following 'i').

Consonants are pronounced as in English, with these exceptions:
- The consonant *x* is pronounced gutturally: '<u>H</u>' like the 'ch' in Scottish 'loch'. Example: *ti xótchesh* (=you want) is pronounced 'tuih <u>H</u>AW-tchesh'. (NB: *ti* being always used for the singular of 'you' and *vi* for the plural, the "polite" form *vi* of the singular being obsolete.)
- The consonant *r* is always trilled (briefly but sharply), never rolled as in Selensk.
- The consonant *s* is always unvoiced, as in 'mass', never as in 'toes'. Thus *Mars* is pronounced 'mar-ss', not 'marz'.
- The English letter 'j' is replaced by *dzh* in loan-words from English and M2, viz. names like *Dzhein* (=Jane), *Rodzher* (=Roger) and of course *Dzhak* (=Jack).
- The sounds of the English letters 'h', 'w' and 'th' do not exist in M1. In English and M2 loan-words, which are not names of people, 'h' is replaced by *x*, e.g. *xelló* (=hello), but in names of people, 'h' is replaced by *g*, e.g. 'Hilda' becomes *Gílda*. The sound 'w' is replaced by *v*, e.g. 'Williams' becomes *Viliáms* ('s' as in 'mass', not 'maze'), and 'Aurora' becomes *Avróra*. Likewise the sound 'th' is replaced by *f*, e.g. *Feodor, Kennef*.

Appendix E. The Battle of Mars

In Chapter 8, Kitty prepares a talk on the Second Groubian War, quoting from a poem entitled: *The Battle Of Mars*. The full text of the poem is given below:

Old men reminisce on their campaigns and wars…
But no one remembers the Battle of Mars.

Of crucial importance in ruling the sky;
Mankind went to live there, and men went to die…
They died in their thousands, so we sent thousands more,
To stain Rugged Red ever redder with gore.

Old men scribble reams on their campaigns and wars…
But no one spills ink on the Battle of Mars.

Formidable castle commanding the plain;
The Nix was assaulted again and again.
Through dust and through craters the mars-rovers roamed,
Spilling blood on the soil which bubbled and foamed.

From their campaigns and wars, old men show their scars…
But no one trades wounds from the Battle of Mars.

While on Earth, loved ones prayed as they gazed out in space:
Oh! Bring the boys home from that terrible place!
But for all that she wept and implored for his life;
Not a soldier came back to the arms of his wife.

Let them sing their vain songs about victories in wars…
There are no tunes of glory from the Battle of Mars.

And when weapons fell silent and death lay around,
From Victory's trumpet came forth not a sound.
There's none can recall how the battle got started;
For victor and vanquished alike have departed.

Let generals proclaim that there's honour in wars…
But there's nothing but shame from the Battle of Mars.

We pick up the pieces to this very day.
The war's not been fought that blows problem away.
But, with every fresh battle, new issues unfold;
To stand alongside and tower over the old.

Let us never forget, as we sail for the stars,
That the voyage began with the battle for Mars.